TAKEN BY STORM

What Reviewers Say About Kim Baldwin's Books

"[Kim] Baldwin and [Xenia] Alexiou have written a barn burner of a thriller. The reader is taken in from the first page to the last. The tension is maintained throughout [*Dying to Live*] with rare exception. Baldwin and Alexiou are defining the genre of romantic suspense within the lesbian genre with this series."—*Lambdaliterary.org*

"Totally tense from nearly word one. [*The Gemini Deception*] has a good deal of twists and turns and one of the scariest villains I have ever come across. Hang on to your seat; it is not only going to be a totally bumpy ride, but the wildest and most engaging thriller I have ever read."—*Rainbow Book Reviews*

"With vivid scenes, sexual tension, and gorgeous word pictures, [*Breaking the Ice*] is a book that will glue you to your chair until the last page is turned."—*Just About Write*

"*Missing Lynx* puts the thrill in thriller. A dark, edgy, often grisly tale, *Missing Lynx* has the grit and pacing of a Bourne saga, but with highly engaging and thoroughly challenging female characters. Not for the faint hearted."—*Lambdaliterary.org*

"It has been a honey of a ride going from book one to book six [in the *Elite Operatives Series*]. The elaborately intricate, tense storylines, the extraordinary primary characters with their heart wrenching yet elevating love connections, and the pulsating multiple cliffhangers combine to produce a top of the line reading experience. Please, someone make a movie out of one or all of these books!"—*Rainbow Book Reviews*

"Fast paced, with dazzling scenes that stir the heart of armchair travelers, *Thief of Always* grabs the reader on the first page and never lets go. [Kim] Baldwin and [Xenia] Alexiou are skilled at fleshing out their characters and in describing the settings…a rich, wonderful read that leaves the reader anxiously awaiting the next book in the series."—*Just About Write*

"With each new book, Kim Baldwin improves her craft and her storytelling. *Flight Risk*…has heated action and vibrant depictions that make the reader feel as though she was right in the middle of

the story. ...Fast moving with crisp dialogue, and effective use of the characters' thoughts and emotions...this reviewer could not put the book down. Baldwin outdid herself with *Flight Risk*. ...Her best storytelling to date. I highly recommend this thrilling story."
—*Independent Gay Writer*

"A hallmark of great writing is consummate characterization, and *Whitewater Rendezvous* does not disappoint...Captures the reader from the very first page...totally immerses and envelopes the reader in the Arctic experience. Superior chapter endings, stylishly and tightly written sentences, precise pacing, and exquisite narrative all coalesce to produce a novel of first-rate quality, both in concept and expression."—*Midwest Book Review*

"Unexpected twists and turns, deadly action, complex characters and multiple subplots converge to make [*Lethal Affairs*] a gripping page turner."—*Curve Magazine*

"Nature's fury has nothing on the fire of desire and passion that burns in Kim Baldwin's *Force of Nature*! Filled with passion, plenty of laughs, and 'yeah, I know how that feels...' moments, *Force of Nature* is a book you simply can't put down. All we have to say is, where's the sequel?!"—*Outlookpress.com*

"'A riveting novel of suspense' seems to be a very overworked phrase. However, it is extremely apt when discussing...*Hunter's Pursuit*. Look for this excellent novel."—*Mega-Scene Magazine*

"[*Hunter's Pursuit*]...a fierce first novel, an action-packed thriller pitting deadly professional killers against each other. Baldwin's fast-paced plot comes...leavened, as every intelligent adventure novel's excesses ought to be, with some lovin'." Richard Labonté, *Bookmarks*

"In a change of pace from her previous novels of suspense, Kim Baldwin has given her fans an intelligent romance, filled with delightful peeks at the lives of the rich and famous...the reader journeys into some of the hot dance clubs in Paris and Rome, and gets a front row seat to some very powerful sex scenes. Baldwin definitely proves that lust has gotten a bad rap. *Focus of Desire* is a great read, with humor, strong dialogue and heat."—*Just About Write*

Visit us at www.boldstrokesbooks.com

By the Author

Hunter's Pursuit

Force of Nature

Whitewater Rendezvous

Flight Risk

Focus of Desire

Breaking the Ice

High Impact

Taken by Storm

The Elite Operatives Series with Xenia Alexiou

Lethal Affairs

Thief of Always

Missing Lynx

Dying to Live

Demons are Forever

The Gemini Deception

One Last Thing (January 2015)

TAKEN BY STORM

by

Kim Baldwin

2014

TAKEN BY STORM

ISBN 13: 978-1-62639-189-5

THIS TRADE PAPERBACK ORIGINAL IS PUBLISHED BY
BOLD STROKES BOOKS, INC.
P.O. BOX 249
VALLEY FALLS, NY 12185

FIRST EDITION: SEPTEMBER 2014

CREDITS
EDITOR: SHELLEY THRASHER
PRODUCTION DESIGN: SUSAN RAMUNDO
COVER DESIGN BY SHERI (GRAPHICARTIST2020@HOTMAIL.COM)

Acknowledgments

In considering the dedication for *Taken by Storm*, the choice was easy. A few days after I completed this manuscript, I flew to Greece to finish the final chapters of *One Last Thing*, the last book in the Elite Operatives Series, with Xenia Alexiou. Writing with Xenia, and helping to bring her amazing stories to readers, has been a joy beyond measure: full of laughs, always inspiring, and involving many wonderful, memorable trips to Europe. But most importantly, our long collaboration has resulted in a deep and enduring friendship that I will always treasure.

My appreciation also, as always, to all the women at Bold Strokes Books who contribute so much to making my books the best they can be. Radclyffe, for her leadership and vision. Editor Shelley Thrasher, who challenges me to always improve my craft and catches me when I fall short. Graphic artist Sheri, for another amazing cover. Connie Ward, BSB Publicist and first-reader extraordinaire, and all of the other support staff who work behind the scenes to make each BSB book an exceptional read.

I'd also like to thank my dear friend Jenny Harmon for your invaluable feedback and insights. Jenny, you help keep me on track and motivated during the writing of each manuscript more than you'll ever know.

And I am blessed to have a circle of friends who provide unending support. A special thanks to Marty, my closest family for more than 40 years, who takes such great care of my cabin and cats during my frequent and lengthy trips abroad. Thank you, too, to my brother Tom, always willing to chauffer me to the airport.

Finally, to all the readers who encourage me by buying my books, showing up for my personal appearances, and for taking the time to e-mail me. Thank you so much.

Dedication

For Xenia

Never a dull moment
Thank God my weirdness amuses you

CHAPTER ONE

Sultan, Washington
September

"Ooooh. Nice. Travel guides." Steffi Graham kept her voice low out of habit, though they were in the back office of the Sultan Public Library at the moment and out of view of patrons. New guidebooks for Europe and Alaska beckoned her through the shrink-wrap of the box she'd just opened. Once she'd sliced through the sheer plastic with her box cutter, she emptied the contents onto the table one book at a time with an excited near-reverence, running her hands over the glossy jackets, pausing now and then to thumb through photos of exotic destinations.

She sorted them as she went: the travel guides together, biographies, true crime, and cookbooks. Since UPS had delivered three big boxes in all, Steffi knew they wouldn't have time to process everything today, so she set aside a handful of titles to take home tonight. She loved that perk of her job—to get first crack at the latest releases, when they were fresh from the printers and still pristine. And certainly it helped her readily call up the right books and authors when patrons asked for recommendations.

"When are you going to stop compiling dream destinations and actually book a ticket somewhere?" Kris Colson opened the second box and started stacking new fiction, mystery, and science fiction titles into their own piles.

"I don't know," Steffi replied as she leafed through the latest *Frommer's Greece*. "I've got plenty of vacation time, and my getaway fund has enough now for a couple weeks most anywhere. I just can't decide where to go." Photos of white sand beaches and azure water, colorful tavernas and ancient ruins enticed her to set the book atop her growing take-home stack. "And frankly, I'd kind of rather go *with* someone than by myself. But purely platonic."

"Still?" Kris asked.

"And for the foreseeable future. I don't want to keep making the same mistakes. I swear, I'm not going to let my libido rule me the next time I meet someone special. Look where that's gotten me, especially the last time. If it weren't for she-who-must-not-be-named, I'd have been able to take a vacation long ago."

"You know what's best for you." Kris unpacked the third box and started sorting through new large-print, young-adult, and children's books. "Hey, if you're serious about looking for someone to travel with, you could put a notice up on the club's bulletin board."

"Maybe." She hadn't really considered using the resources of their climbing club to find a vacation partner, though she had to admit she liked everyone she'd met there and done day excursions with. "I'd have to know somebody pretty well to room with them, though."

Kris snorted in amusement. "You? Really? Why, are you some kind of control freak or something?"

Steffi shot her a warning look. "Okay, so I like things a certain way. But I'm not about to be saddled with someone like...well, like the Hummer, or OhMyGodGirl, on a long trip. Can you imagine?"

The mere prospect made them both snicker. They had nicknames for a lot of the library's more eccentric patrons, and the aforementioned were two of their favorite regulars. The Hummer was a sixty-something woman who came in every other week to get biographies of dead Hollywood celebrities, all the while humming show tunes under her breath. She'd serenaded them that very morning with "I Could Have Danced All Night" as she checked out tomes about Lucille Ball, Patrick Swayze, and Katharine Hepburn.

OhMyGodGirl was a young twentyish blonde who stopped by often to rent movies. She was forever in a panic about losing one thing or another, and always reacted with the same predictable cadence. "OhMyGod OhMyGod OhMyGod OhMyGod Haveyouseenmygloves?" had been the most recent version. Most of the so-called lost items would inevitably turn up later in her purse, car, or home.

Between the two of them, Steffi and Kris had the lowdown on most of the people in town and their eccentricities. Many small rural libraries served as their area's main social gathering place and citizen resource, and that was especially true in Sultan, a three-square-mile everybody-knows-everybody community situated in the foothills of the Cascade Mountains. Since the library was located right on Main Street in the first floor of the Community Center, many of the town's forty-six hundred residents would drop in for one reason or another.

In addition to their routine duties assisting people in finding books, the librarians helped locals find jobs and homes, file for divorce, update their resumes, narrow down nursing-care facilities for their parents, discover cancer therapies, and more. Steffi sometimes wondered whether she didn't know more secrets about a lot of them than their own families did, and Kris was even more privy to the local gossip.

Steffi had been there seven years, since graduating with her Master of Library Science and Information degree from the University of Washington. She'd loved books her whole life and had never wanted to do anything else. In addition to being able to surround herself with her literary friends and their adventures, she got to help others discover the joy of reading.

And her near-compulsive need for order and organization also meshed perfectly with her chosen profession. She enjoyed such mundane tasks as alphabetizing the *New Fiction* rack, putting series books in order, or grouping cookbooks by cuisine. And she loved coming up with ideas for their monthly "theme" display; recent examples had included *Nautical Narratives*, *Beastly Bestsellers*, and *The Book is Better than the Movie*.

Kris had joined the staff two years before Steffi, but though they were close to the same age, it had taken a while for them to warm up to each other because of their very different ways of approaching their jobs.

Steffi had chosen her career in part because she was happiest in a quiet, well-ordered environment. Though shy by nature, she was at ease behind the front desk, greeting patrons and offering assistance as they entered, and checking them out once they'd selected their books. But she kept things professional and did nothing to encourage any particularly chatty patrons to expound on their lives at length, much as some of them obviously wanted to. Libraries were, after all, places of study and contemplation, so while she did all she could to assist people, she also placed a high priority on keeping the ambient noise level to a minimum.

Kris, on the other hand, was an extrovert who took serving the public to a whole new level when she was behind the desk, chatting up nearly every patron who came in, often at length and with particular attention to the troubled and isolated. She inquired about their health, their kids, cats, dogs, and whatever else she could remember about their lives. And she listened to them in times of trial, doling out soothing embraces and comforting words like candy at Halloween.

Steffi could certainly appreciate the human value of Kris's kinder, personal approach; in fact, she often admired the selfless and patient way Kris could allow someone to drone on and on about something in a purge of pent-up frustration or loneliness. But in her view, the library was simply not the proper venue for protracted discussions. And sometimes, Kris got so caught up playing social worker that her duties suffered: the return cart overflowed or the checkout line stretched to the point of grumbling complaint, and Steffi had to fill the void.

Initially, Steffi bit her tongue in annoyance every time Kris engaged ad nauseam with a patron about their recent knee surgery, the size of this season's tomatoes, or what part of their car needed fixing. She didn't want to make waves at work, and the library director was pretty relaxed herself about the level of noise she would tolerate, so Steffi wasn't certain she'd be sympathetic.

Her attitude toward Kris thawed about a month into their polite-but-distant relationship as coworkers, when they interacted for the first time outside the library. The occasion was the annual All-You-Can-Eat Spaghetti Supper at the local senior center, a benefit whose proceeds helped finance a Meals on Wheels program for the elderly.

Staffers from the library and town hall traditionally volunteered to act as servers for the buffet-style meal, and Steffi and Kris were assigned to work the dessert table.

During the first half hour, they were too busy cutting donated baked goods into individual portions and setting them out on paper plates for anything but small talk. They finished filling their table with neat rows of cake and pie slices just as the doors opened to admit hungry locals.

Steffi recognized the first family coming through the food line as library regulars. Kris warmly greeted every one of them by name and asked how the kids had liked their first trip to Disneyland.

That she knew so much about them wasn't a big surprise, since Kris had been in town longer. But Steffi was impressed when the trend continued throughout the next two hours as people streamed by. Kris seemed to know most everyone, and everyone knew *her,* and all of them, from the little kids to the grandmas to the tough-as-nails truckers, greeted Kris as warmly as a long-lost family member. Several came around the table to hug her. Everyone obviously regarded her highly because of the interest she'd taken in their lives, which made Steffi feel a bit ashamed of how petty and distant she'd been acting at work.

After her attitude adjustment, she started asking Kris to join her for lunch whenever they worked together, and they quickly became close friends. They found they had much more in common than they imagined.

Once the new books were all unpacked, Kris began putting Mylar covers onto the new fiction hardbacks, while Steffi barcoded the new paperbacks and entered them into the card catalogue. When a quiet buzzing alerted Kris to an incoming text, she stopped what she was doing and reached for her cell. Frowning, she muttered *shit* under her breath as she typed a reply.

"What's wrong?" Steffi asked.

Kris typed a few more keystrokes before she put the phone back in her pocket. "Nothing serious. Fin and I were going to climb tomorrow, but she's got to work."

"Ooo! Ooo! Pick me! Pick me!" Steffi raised her hand excitedly. "I know it's not quite as much fun for you, but—"

Kris laughed. "I'll survive, as long as you bring lunch." She resumed processing books. "Pick you up at seven. And don't forget dessert."

❖

Peshastin Pinnacles State Park, Washington
Next day

Steffi was so anxious for a day in the mountains she was ready to go long before Kris's bright-yellow Jeep pulled up in front of her apartment. She hadn't been out climbing in more than a month, though she'd kept in fair shape through her twice-a-week workouts on the wall at the gym. If she hadn't, she wouldn't have volunteered to accompany Kris, a much superior climber. "So, where are we headed?" Steffi inquired as she opened the back door to toss her pack and gear inside.

"Do you care?" Kris asked. "And you know better than to talk to me this early without an offering from the caffeine gods."

Steffi got into the passenger seat and pulled a thermos out of her coat. "No, I don't. And yes, I do. Double-shot latte." Their destination, she quickly deduced, was Peshastin Pinnacles State Park, on the other side of the Cascades. The thirty-four-acre desert park contained a grouping of sandstone slabs and pinnacles that rose two hundred feet into the air and was a mecca for area enthusiasts.

Both of them had been there many times, usually with their climbing club, and knew the area well. Kris figured that getting an early start would help ensure they'd beat the Saturday rush and not be hampered by other climbers. "I'll let you pick the challenge," Kris said as they pulled into the parking lot. "What are you comfortable with?"

"How about Dinosaur? I haven't done that since the club outing." The tallest and most massive crag at the Pinnacles, the Dinosaur Tower offered eight different routes up. From the top, they'd have a spectacular view of the sprawling orchards of the Wenatchee Valley and the Enchantment mountains beyond.

"Excellent. Beautiful day, huh?"

They donned their packs and hiked the half mile to the base of the Tower. Steffi's favorite way up was the Potholes, a route that had fixed bolts on much of the route. She knew Kris preferred the more difficult Primates ascent farther west, which was out of her comfort zone, but they could see a trio of climbers already heading up that way so she was spared having to plea for the easier route. Kris never liked to be limited by the speed of others, and the risk of rock falls decreased if no one was above them.

As they geared up for the ascent, they didn't discuss who would go first. Kris had several more years' experience and routinely led, or alternated lead, on club-sponsored trips. She loved the adrenaline rush of free climbing and had successfully soloed a number of challenging peaks without using ropes, anchors, and other aids. Mary "Fin" Fincannon, her lover and another member of the club, was equally skilled and just as much of a risk taker.

Steffi was content to follow. And though she'd grown confident in her abilities, she was prudent and insisted on using every safety precaution possible. So when it was just she and Kris, they always roped up and used bolts.

Kris stepped into her harness. "You know, I've been thinking about your trip-partner dilemma thing."

"And? Did you think of somebody?"

Kris grinned as she put on her helmet and looked up at the sandstone cliff. "I have a solution I think you'll like. I'll tell you at the top. Ready?"

"You're so obnoxious. Making me wait." Steffi attached her belay device to the one-hundred-fifty-foot rope that connected them. "Then get going, Flash. I'm right behind you."

A couple of hours later, they were three-quarters of the way up the sandstone tower. Kris had made the last pitch look ridiculously easy, scampering up the vertical rock face like a monkey on steroids. Steffi was taking twice as long and had to pause midway to catch her breath. Though Kris's greater experience and fearlessness certainly played a role in the speed of their individual progress, height was also a factor. At five-foot-eight, Kris had a four-inch advantage and could utilize holds Steffi simply couldn't reach.

After securing her harness to one of the fixed anchors, Steffi studied the next portion of the climb as her breathing calmed.

The highest part of the Potholes route always tested the limits of her upper-body strength. As she gazed upward, assessing the crooks and crevices of the next several yards, she flexed the fingers of one hand, then the other, and rolled her neck to relax the building ache between her shoulder blades.

"I want lunch," Kris called down from the narrow ledge above, where she was waiting on belay. She sounded close but was still out of Steffi's line of sight.

"And I want to know who I may be traveling with," Steffi hollered back.

Kris laughed. "Here's a hint. *Her peculiarities must not be punished.*"

Though Steffi remembered hearing those words recently, she couldn't recall the source. The quote had been among a half dozen or so that Kris had read aloud the day before, as she skimmed one of the new books. A book about…She wracked her brain.

Great Quotes From Classic Children's Books. That was it. And the book was? *Of course. Heidi.*

"Switzerland?" she shouted.

"Give that girl a gold star," Kris said. "Now, move your ass."

"Climbing," she announced, signaling to Kris she was on the move again and to keep the rope taut. The brief pause had reinvigorated her and she made steady progress, reaching Kris a short time later.

The sky was so clear and blue that the view was particularly awesome; she could see even farther than the last time they'd been up here.

"Not too shabby." Kris glanced at her watch as Steffi shrugged off her pack and settled next to her, clipping to the anchor between them. "When we did this route last summer, I know it took you at least thirty minutes longer to get this far."

"Who'd have thought, huh?" Steffi took a long drink from her water bottle. She was pleased she'd shaved a full half hour off her previous Potholes time. Though she still had a long way to go to match Kris's accomplishments and natural talent, the progress she'd made in just two years or so of climbing was immensely satisfying.

Kris smiled. "You should be very proud of how far you've come." She tore her gaze away from the spectacular view and looked at Steffi. "In fact, that's the answer to your dilemma. I think you've got the skills to do the club's big trip next year. Fin and I are going."

Cascade Climbers, the local climbing club they belonged to, organized several group outings a year. Most of the trips were within an easy drive of Seattle, but once a year, it planned a major adventure somewhere more exotic. The year before, members had done Patagonia. Kris and Fin had skipped it because of the expense involved, and Steffi was too inexperienced for the destination.

Besides, she'd wanted to go somewhere in Europe when she finally went abroad for the first time, and the Alps were high on her wish list. "So, Switzerland, huh?"

"Yup. Gary called me with the news last night. It'll be in the next newsletter." Kris was close to the current president of Cascade Climbers and always had the inside scoop about club gossip.

"When is it? For how long? I want details."

"Nothing more until I get fed." Kris unbuttoned a pocket on her cargo jeans, withdrew her Swiss Army knife, and opened the fork. "And it better be something besides PB and J."

Steffi rummaged through her pack for the Tupperware bowl she'd packed last night's leftovers in. Before she opened it, she glared at Kris with mock seriousness. "This is to *share*. You hear that? This was the only thing I had to pack our lunch in, emphasis on *our*."

"Yeah, yeah. Share, share. All good." Kris put her face closer to the plastic, trying to see what was inside. "Is that what I think it is?"

Steffi slipped off the lid and handed the bowl to Kris.

"Yay! Your pasta salad!" Kris dug in and ate four big forkfuls before speaking again. "This shit is so killer."

"Take a breath." Steffi stabbed a couple of big forkfuls herself while she still could. She had to admit it was a particularly tasty batch of her BLT pasta, made with garlic aioli, spinach, cherry tomatoes, pine nuts, pancetta, and penne. Kris often requested it when Steffi invited her for dinner because she loved it hot or cold and she always got sent home with leftovers.

They devoured the pasta within a few minutes. Kris scraped the bottom of the bowl and handed it back. "Yum, as usual. What else ya got?"

Steffi stuck the bowl back in her pack and withdrew a large Ziploc containing four brownies, but kept them out of Kris's reach. "Spill. Details, please."

"Ten days to two weeks, sometime in February. Dates aren't firm yet." Kris held out her hand.

Steffi placed one of the brownies into her palm, and once she'd scarfed down half of it, Kris continued.

"The club is working out a deal with this outfitter who can get us great discounts. It should be pretty reasonable, from what Gary says, especially since it's the off-season there. You could either pay a little more for private accommodations, or share with somebody, but at least it'll be somebody you know. And that's basically just sleeping, anyway. You can hang with Fin and me most of time during the day." Kris finished the brownie and beckoned for another. "What do you say?"

"Very tempting," Steffi replied as she handed the brownie over and took one for herself. "But where the hell would we be climbing in February?"

"An ice wall near St. Moritz, primarily. And I know what you're going to say," Kris added before Steffi could speak. "Yes, you don't have nearly enough experience on ice—"

"Enough? Try virtually none. One time, up a twenty-foot frozen waterfall. And that was months ago."

"I was going to say there's plenty of time for you to get up to speed between now and then. There's Skookum Falls. Dragontail. Or, Fin and I can take you up to B.C. for a weekend or two if there's not much ice locally. Over there, you'll be climbing with us, and there are routes for all levels of experience. I'll watch out for you."

"You really think I'll have time to get ready?"

"Absolutely."

Steffi pictured herself climbing in the Alps and sipping cocoa by the fire in some posh St. Moritz hotel. "Would we get time to sightsee as well?"

"That's the beauty of this outfitter. We all arrange our own itinerary. The company just helps facilitate transportation, hotels, guides, whatever else you need. You can spend three days climbing and seven shopping, or vice versa. Five days in Switzerland and five in Italy, if that's what you want. At any rate, you're priced accordingly. We'll fly there and back as a group and have a few arranged excursions, but most of the time you can be on your own and make plans as you like." She ate a couple more bites of brownie. "And we all know how you like to make plans."

"Funny how cocky you get once you have a full tummy." The realization that her first trip abroad was finally taking shape, and that it was just a few short months away, made Steffi's heart beat faster. Seeing Switzerland and Italy with good friends, and combining wild adventure with urban exploration in the same trip? How could she say no? She gazed out from their high perch and imagined herself half a world away. "Hard to resist."

"Not hard." Kris grinned. "Impossible. I see that little twinkle in your eye. You've already decided to go."

CHAPTER TWO

New York
February

Hudson Mead opened the door to the bedroom and shivered as the steamed cocoon of the bath evaporated around her. Halfway to the closet, she jumped, startled, when a sudden cacophony of soft thuds pummeled the windows. The storm outside raged on, a stiff gale driving huge heavy clumps of snow into her building. Not quite the Polar Vortex that had struck the East Coast this time last year, but it certainly could delay her getting to tonight's event.

And it could screw up her flight afterward, which would be a real tragedy.

Except for that, she loved seeing so much snow. While most of her fellow New Yorkers were daydreaming about a holiday on some sunny beach, she planned to spend every spare minute of her vacation immersed in the white stuff. If she wasn't so damn worried about the global warming that was a certain contributor, she'd be thoroughly embracing the Great Global Winter of '14, as some in the media had come to call it, because it should make for an awesome ski trip.

Hudson went to the window to assess the traffic conditions four floors below, but the dominant feature of her view—the vast whitescape of Central Park—won out for her attention.

Wet snow clung tenaciously to the trees, spreading thickly from the windward side around the branches and trunks and piling up fast, testing the weight of dead limbs too high to trim. The boughs of the spruces and their kindred evergreens were already well bent to submission, their silhouettes trimmed to half-closed umbrellas.

When she arrived home from the airport that morning, the park had been full of children taking advantage of their snow day, building snowmen and snow angels and pulling each other on sleds. But twilight and the worsening storm had sent all but the hardiest pedestrians indoors. A few had gathered at the edge of the park, and Hudson grabbed her binoculars to get a closer look.

Someone had spent long hours constructing a quartet of snow figures in the open space just across from her building, the famed Dakota apartment complex. These were not the typical three-tier snowmen with carrot noses and coal eyes, but true sculptures. And next to the curious passersby who paused to admire them, each animal was roughly the size of a minivan.

A tiger, chimpanzee, elephant, and giant panda. All endangered species. The display was a subtle but moving political statement by the artist, however transitory, and Hudson admired any effort to increase awareness of an issue of global importance.

The door chime shook her from her reverie. "Come on in, Bruce."

"Hey, girl," Bruce Fowler called out from the living room. One of Manhattan's most successful realtors, Bruce lived just below Hudson in an apartment with twice her square footage. He was a close friend who kept an eye on her place during her frequent overseas assignments. "Sorry I got delayed. Late showing in the village. I must say, honey, I'm not crazy about this ships-passing-in-the-night thing we've got going. I hate only getting an hour or two with you every couple of weeks."

"Me, too, Bruce. I'd hoped to have at least a day or two home before my vacation, but the flights getting back here were insane." She threw on a robe and walked into the living room. "Everything goes through Europe, and they're getting worse weather than we are. Or better, depending on your plans for the next two weeks." As Bruce embraced her warmly she imagined slicing through the deep powder of the Swiss Alps. He was still in his standard work apparel: tailored navy Armani suit, white shirt, burgundy silk tie. "I promise I'll make it up to you."

"I'm going to hold you to it." He pulled back and glanced at his Rolex, then eyed her robe disapprovingly. "Didn't you tell me Joe was picking you up at six?"

Hudson glanced at the wall clock. She had exactly seven minutes to finish getting ready. "Shit fuck." She hurried back to her bedroom as Bruce laughed.

The few hours home had flown by, mostly occupied by unpacking and repacking and doing multiple loads of laundry. She was out of clean underwear completely, and she wasn't going anywhere without her favorite jeans and lucky shirts, so rank from sweat, dust, and campfire smoke they'd required Ziploc quarantine on the way home.

She often wished she could cleanse her mind of the fallout from the job as easily as she purged her clothes of it. She'd just returned from South Sudan, where she'd reported on the shocking proliferation of forced marriages involving girls as young as twelve. One of the girls she'd met, a rail-thin fourteen-year-old with fawn eyes and a perpetual fearful expression, bore numerous whip scars all over her body. Through an interpreter, Hudson learned that the girl's sixty-four-year-old husband regularly beat her with a bamboo cane, not an uncommon practice in that part of the world.

The despicable cruelty she'd witnessed had begun to haunt her, chipping away at her faith in human nature, eroding some of the passion she'd always held for journalism. *Great night to be reconsidering your occupation.* "Talk to me," she called out to Bruce. "What's up with you?"

"Nothing too headline-worthy," he replied. "Got a new commercial listing off Times Square, and three new high-end apartments. Oh, and Andy and I split up."

Still half-naked, Hudson stuck her head out of the door and frowned at him. He was sitting on the couch, staring off into space. "In journalism, that's called burying the lead. What happened?"

Bruce shrugged without looking at her. "Apparently he's not ready to commit, or at least not to me." Though his tone was matter-of-fact, she could see the pain on his face. He'd been seeing the Wall Street trader exclusively for more than six months, and the last time she'd been home he'd declared that Andy was "the one."

"And you know this…how?"

A rosy blush colored his cheeks and neck as he leaned back and let out a heavy sigh. "I proposed."

"And what did he say?"

"He said…" Bruce finally met her eyes, "that I'm a terrific guy, but he's not ready to settle down…it's him, not me…he doesn't want to hurt me…blah blah blah."

"I'm sorry, Bruce."

"Yeah, well. What are you gonna do? It is what it is." He looked at her seriously. "I can almost empathize with your swearing off getting seriously involved again. I'm tired of getting my heart broken."

"Preaching to the choir. Once was more than enough for me. With all the traveling I do, I'm just not relationship material. But I really am sorry about Andy. You deserve better."

Bruce smiled halfheartedly. "Speaking of deserving, tonight's supposed to be about you." He glanced at his watch again. "You better get moving. Your ride will be here any minute."

She took his advice and returned to her closet. "When I get back," she called out, "we're going to have a proper dinner-and-movie night. I'll even let you pick, as long as we don't have to sit through *Magic Mike* again."

"You're on. Anything special you need done while you're gone this time?"

"Just the usual," she replied as she slipped on a pair of black Anne Klein pumps with two-inch heels. "Water the plants, get the mail. Oh, and would you mind picking me up some coffee next time you're at the grocery? I'm out. You know what I like."

"No problem. Anything else?"

"That should do it. Thanks."

Bruce's eyes widened in appreciation when she emerged from her bedroom in her feminized, tailored black tux and royal-blue silk blouse. "Don't you look fabulous." He grinned. "Told you that suit was made for you."

On and off the job, Hudson rarely wore anything but well-used brown leather hiking boots and jeans, paired with whatever top was suitable for the climate. It was her ensemble of choice since her youth as a tomboy surrounded by brothers and another perk of being a print reporter. She didn't mind having to dress up during those rare occasions that required heels and makeup, but she was so clueless about current fashion trends that Bruce always went shopping with her when she had to buy clothes. He'd insisted that she buy the tux during a Fifth Avenue excursion six months earlier, and she had to admit it was not only flattering but surprisingly comfortable. "Yeah, yeah. What would I ever do without—"

The sudden blare of the front-door buzzer interrupted them. She went to the intercom. "Marco."

"Polo. I'm in a loading zone."

"Be right down."

Bruce got her long wool coat from the front closet and held it up for her to slip into. "Have a blast tonight. I'm so proud of you."

"Thanks. Sorry we didn't get more time to visit." She grabbed her backpack and slung it over one shoulder. The carry-on contained her travel documents, iPad, a change of clothes, and other necessities. The rest of her luggage and ski gear had been picked up by a courier and was already at the airport.

Bruce started turning off lights. "Hey, I thought of a way you can make it up to me…and help me get over my broken heart."

"Name it." They left the apartment and headed to the elevator.

"This thing tonight. It's all journalists, right?" He punched the DOWN button.

"Mostly. So?"

"If you see Anderson Cooper, give him my number, huh?"

She laughed. Bruce had made no secret of his crush on the CNN newscaster. "He's got a partner, Bruce. You can dream on, but it ain't gonna happen."

He sighed dramatically as the doors slid open and they stepped inside. Bruce hit the 3 and G buttons.

"Seriously, though." She draped one arm over his shoulder. "I'm sorry about Andy. If you need to rant, you have my number. Use it."

"Thanks, hon." He embraced her in a bear hug. "I may take you up on it." When the elevator stopped at his floor, he pulled back and grinned at her. "And I promise, this time I'll keep the time change in mind."

She laughed and let him go.

"See you when you get back," he said. "Safe travels, and keep in touch."

"Will do."

When Hudson pushed open the door to the street, a blast of frigid wind hit her full-on, blowing open her still-unbuttoned coat and insinuating itself deep into her bones. Shivering, she pulled the garment closed and hurried toward the black SUV at the curb.

Her long-time photographer, Joe Parker, was waiting behind the wheel. He pulled away from the curb as soon as she got in, and she immediately stuck her hands in front of the warm air vents. "Brutal wind, huh?" he asked. "But the snow seems to be keeping a lot of people off the roads. We should get there okay."

"Between the weather and all the schmoozing going on, it'll never start on time, anyway. Who are we sitting with, do you know?"

"No idea," he replied. "Maybe another of the honorees and their entourage?"

"Entourage?" She laughed. "Are you *my* entourage?"

"Entourage, minion, lackey." He grinned. "Tonight, it's all good."

She reached over and ruffled his hair. "Get your gear off to the airport okay?"

"Yup. Right before I left."

"So…we duck out as soon as I'm done and hope I'm the first on the program." She tossed her backpack into the rear seat beside Joe's brown leather duffel. "You know, you should call the valet service as soon as it's my turn, because I won't talk long. That'll save us a few minutes."

"Flights are likely to be delayed, anyway," he said. "I'm sure we'll be fine."

They were nearly there when her cell chimed with a text message from her eldest brother.

Thinking of you tonight and wish I could be there. So proud of you, Sis, and I bet they are, too. Please reconsider my invitation. "They" referred to their parents, and the invitation was to a surprise party he was throwing for their father's eightieth birthday next month. Ever the optimist, she thought. Even though so much time had passed, she might not even recognize her parents if she walked by them on the street.

She messaged him back: *You're here in spirit, I know. Miss you, Bro.*

Joe pulled up in front of the Waldorf Astoria, and a valet came around to take the keys.

"Thanks again for agreeing to come as my plus-one," Hudson said as they headed inside.

"Of course. I'm honored. Where else would I be?" He grinned at her, but he had that same glint of mischief in his eyes that he did when he was about to prank her. They had a running competition of sorts in that regard, and she could sense when he was about to strike.

"I know that look. What are you up to?"

"Don't know what you're talking about. Would I dare risk your wrath as we're about to embark on our vacation?" He raised his hands innocently in surrender, but the glint remained unchecked. "Come on, we'd better hustle."

They checked their coats outside the entrance to the ballroom, near where a backdrop had been set up for press and tabloid photographers to take shots of arriving celebrities. Rachel Maddow and Barbara Walters were just making their way inside, so the photographers turned in their direction, anxious for the next subject.

"Don't you two clean up nice," the nearest one, a slight guy in his fifties, said as they approached. He snapped a couple of pictures, then put down his camera and hugged them both. "Congrats, Hudson. Way to represent." Another long-time veteran of the Associated Press, who had worked with Hudson on a few occasions before Joe became her regular photographer.

"Thanks. Great to see you."

Through the open double doors behind them, the ballroom lights dimmed.

"We'd better get in there," Joe said. "Looks like they're about to start."

They found two seats reserved for them at a table in front. Hudson was surprised to see her boss Bob Furness there, since he rarely attended any kind of social function, business-related or otherwise. He was a diminutive man with a big heart, and she respected him more than any other of her AP superiors. He'd become almost a father figure, in fact, since her own parents had written her out of their lives. He stood as they approached.

"What the heck are you doing here?" she asked as he pulled her into a hug.

"Free drinks?" he answered, then let her go and grinned at her. "This is a big honor for you. I wouldn't have missed it."

"I'm touched. I know it normally takes a grenade to get you out of your La-Z-Boy at night."

Bob laughed. "Got that right. So, is my dynamic duo all packed and ready for their big ski trip?"

"Yeah. We're ducking out right after I'm up," Hudson replied.

"And don't you *dare* call us," Joe said.

"Not unless it's a really, really big—" Joe muffled her with a hand over her mouth. She didn't blame him. More than a couple of their vacations had been cut short when a major news story broke in their vicinity.

Bob chuckled and held up his hands in surrender. "Joe, it's her you have to talk to, not me. She can always say no."

"Yeah, like that's gonna happen." Joe rolled his eyes.

The room fell silent as the event's host, Lesley Stahl, took the stage and headed toward the podium.

While Bob and Hudson took their seats, Joe put his hand on her shoulder and leaned down to whisper in her ear. "Be right back."

Before she could ask what was up, Stahl began speaking.

"The International Women's Media Foundation established the Courage in Journalism Award to recognize newswomen who bravely pursue their profession despite difficult or dangerous circumstances," Stahl said. "Many of the seventy-five previous recipients have been imprisoned, beaten, subjected to governmental intimidation, and even targeted for assassination, but they refuse to be cowed from covering the stories that others don't dare pursue."

After the opening remarks, Ann Curry took the podium to present the first award. The recipient was Khadija Ismayilova, a radio reporter from Azerbaijan, who spoke for twenty minutes and finished to a rousing round of applause.

As Stahl returned to the podium for the next presentation, Hudson peered around the darkened ballroom, looking for Joe. She thought he'd just been headed to the men's room, or maybe he'd seen someone in the crowd he wanted to say hello to. But she didn't see him anywhere, and he'd been gone too long for a simple pit stop.

"Our next recipient's byline," Stahl said, "has been at the top of some of the most important stories of the past quarter century." She looked directly at Hudson and smiled. "To introduce her, there is no one better than the man who has, for most of that time, witnessed and chronicled her courage under fire. Please join me in welcoming Associated Press photographer Joe Parker."

Joe? Joe was presenting her award? Hudson stared at him incredulously as he re-entered the ballroom from a side door and made his way to the podium, looking as nervous as he'd been when they were pinned down by insurgent fire in Afghanistan. He absolutely loathed speaking in public, so the fact that he'd agreed to this spoke volumes about the depth of their friendship.

He was carrying her award, a glass bird with outstretched wings. As he set it on the podium, he noisily cleared his throat. "I first met Hudson Mead in 1995 when we were paired up to cover the meningitis outbreak in Nigeria," Joe said. "More than a hundred thousand people were infected, and more than ten thousand were dead. To be honest, I wasn't crazy about the assignment, for obvious reasons, and I wanted to get in and out of there as quickly as possible. But that's never the way Hudson works."

The spotlight on the podium dimmed, and a massive projection screen descended from the ceiling behind Joe.

"I can attest that she'll go anywhere, anytime, without reservation," he continued, "if there is a need to bring attention to a serious issue that is being under-reported. Particularly if the situation involves women and children, and abuses of basic human rights."

Photos began appearing in a slideshow behind him. Hudson recognized them as the images Joe had taken to accompany her stories. Starving children in Ethiopia. Ebola-infected patients in an overcrowded hospital ward in Zaire. Families cowering in their homes during the siege of Sarajevo. Mass graves in Rwanda. Armed thugs using children as human shields in Syria.

"Some of you may have noticed that Hudson has never appeared in any of the photos tagged with her stories. That's a hard-and-fast rule for her. It's always and only about the subjects of her stories. But that doesn't mean I haven't taken a few pictures of her during our many years of working together. And I thought, as I prepared for this evening, that they'd do a pretty good job of illustrating her fearless reporting. As well as her selflessness."

As Joe's previously published photographs gave way to candid shots of Hudson in the field, he added, "She's never seen these, by the way. Hudson, I hope you don't mind."

The first photo showed a much-younger Hudson standing face-to-face with an obviously irate Russian soldier in war-torn Chechnya. Her face was calmly impassive, despite his fury and the fact he was pointing his AK-47 in her direction.

In the next, she was hunched down behind a Humvee in Afghanistan, dressed in camo body armor and a helmet. The U.S. convoy they'd been riding with had just been ambushed. The soldiers around her were firing back, and dark smoke rose from somewhere in the distance.

The third photo, badly framed, showed her surrounded by a mob of men in Tripoli, who were shouting at her and reaching for her clothes. Hudson remembered the incident vividly. She'd been groped repeatedly and had lost her jacket before Joe, their interpreter, and two strangers managed to extricate her to safety.

In the next picture, she was one of thirty-or-so volunteers searching for survivors among the debris of the Haitian earthquake. Then she was assisting Red Cross workers in the distribution of food and water to starving villagers in Burkina Faso.

The helpless frustration Hudson so often felt in such situations burned anew as memories of those events came roaring back into her consciousness, marring her enjoyment of the otherwise humbling and satisfying tribute. No matter what she did, the desperate situations of the people she interviewed rarely improved much.

"I'm grateful for this opportunity to pay tribute to a woman I've come to greatly admire and respect. Even if I do think she's a bit too impulsive at times," Joe said, over a photo of Hudson wincing as an army medic dressed shrapnel wounds in her arm. "Because she's changed the lives of so many who cannot speak up for themselves."

The final slide showed Hudson surrounded by street children in a Cairo slum. Her well-used backpack was open, and she was distributing the contents to their eager outstretched hands. Several kids gleefully ripped into snacks—potato chips, candy bars, gum, a bottle of soda. Others held aloft her simple travel possessions as though they were precious treasure: a ball cap, a jackknife, a travel mug, a T-shirt, a deck of cards.

"It is my great pleasure," Joe said as the spotlight came back on and the projection screen retracted, "to introduce my dear friend, Hudson Mead." He grinned at her as applause filled the ballroom.

She got up and headed to the podium. As Joe hugged her, she whispered, "Well played. You're usually such a shit at keeping secrets."

He laughed as he handed her the award, then stepped back as she faced the gathering.

Several seconds passed as she waited for the applause to diminish. "Thank you, ladies and gentlemen, friends and colleagues. When I started with the Associated Press twenty-five years ago as an intern, female war correspondents were a novelty. Most of our male bosses thought us ill equipped to cope with the dangers of reporting from hostile areas, and it's certainly been proved since then that in many regions of the world, women in the field are at much greater risk of sexual violence and other abuses than their male counterparts." Hudson set down the award and gripped the podium.

"But the atrocities that have been inflicted against our sister journalists haven't deterred them from their duty," she said. "Nor has it discouraged young women from pursuing this noble profession. In the past decade, some seventy percent of the nation's journalism and mass-communications graduates have been female."

Hudson paused as applause resonated through the ballroom.

"The result of this greater parity on the front lines? In recent years, there's been an increased awareness of the human cost of such conflicts, because women often report war differently than men. We are, in general, less preoccupied by statistics, strategies, and high-tech weaponry...and more focused on the impact on the innocent—particularly women and children who've been kidnapped, orphaned, tortured, maimed, sexually abused, or forced from their homes."

More applause.

"I'm deeply appreciative to the International Women's Media Foundation for this honor, and humbled to be in such esteemed company." She held up the award as cameras flashed around the room. "Now, if you'll excuse me, I have a bone to pick with my faithful photographer here."

More laughter and applause followed them as she took Joe's arm and they exited by a side door.

As soon as they were alone in the hallway, Joe put his hands up as shields, clearly expecting one of her usual punches. She'd routinely give him a solid whack on his shoulder whenever she was either really angry or really excited, and she had justification for both emotions at the moment.

"None of the photos of you were bad," he said before she had a chance to move or speak. "None sleeping with your mouth open, or anything. And believe me, I have lots—"

"Relax. I just said that so we could duck out of there and make our flight." She started toward the coat check but remembered the award in her hand. "Shit. I didn't think about what I'm going to do with this. Can't very well take it with us, and we don't have time to drop it off at the apartment."

"I bet Bob would be happy to babysit."

"Brilliant. Get our coats and I'll meet you at the door." She ducked back inside to unload the award, and ten minutes later, they were in the SUV headed to JFK International.

Joe glanced at the dashboard clock. "Going to be cutting it very close, as usual. Don't you ever do anything the easy way?"

CHAPTER THREE

New York
JFK International Airport

"What a zoo. At least we don't have to deal with that." Hudson and Joe jogged past the long line of travelers waiting to go through security and queued up behind two other first-class passengers in the Delta Sky Priority lane. As Diamond Medallion members, they'd be expedited through the checkpoint, but with only twenty minutes left before their scheduled departure and their gate on the far end of the terminal, Hudson wasn't optimistic they'd make it.

They ran the length of the concourse, arriving out of breath to find the gate area still crowded with passengers. Before they'd had a chance to approach the counter, the Delta agent was reaching for the intercom. "Ladies and gentlemen, we apologize again for the delay and thank you for your patience. We'll begin boarding momentarily with our first-class, business, and Delta SkyMiles members, and then economy by the zone indicated on your boarding pass. Since many of you have tight connections once we land, we ask everyone to please find your seat and get settled quickly so we're able to get off as close to schedule as possible."

"I'm going to change." Joe scanned the area for the nearest men's room. "See you onboard."

"Later." Hudson considered doing the same until she spotted a news-and-snack concession not far down the concourse. As she hurried toward it, she heard another announcement that boarding had begun, so she didn't dare linger long. Finding the reading material she wanted took a couple minutes. *Time* and *Newsweek* were both prominently displayed by the cash register, but *Powder*, which had a feature on the Euro X Games, was harder to find on the massive wall of special-interest magazines.

As she waited to pay, she perused the selection of snacks and candy that surrounded the cashier's station, grinning broadly when she spotted a row of Snickers Peanut Butter Bars. She and Joe both loved them as a quick energy lift when skiing, and she'd never seen them sold abroad, so she stepped out of line to get some.

But just as she was about to reach for the candy, a young woman overloaded with a heavy backpack and tote bag swooped in and scooped up the whole lot.

"If you take them all," Hudson said benignly from behind her, "I'll have to have you killed."

The woman pivoted to face her with a shocked expression, clutching the half dozen or so candy bars to her chest. "Excuse me?" She was cute, blond, and young, probably in her late twenties.

"You heard me. Are you tired of breathing?" Hudson tried desperately to maintain a straight face, none too successfully. "Put some back, walk away, and no one gets hurt."

The blonde's expression softened from alarm to bemusement, and she smiled. A very nice smile, Hudson thought.

"You said *have* me killed," the stranger replied. "But I don't see anybody here but you." She looked Hudson up and down. "And while you do have an advantage in height, weight, and snappy dressing, I can run *really* fast."

Hudson laughed. "Oh, yeah? Even when you're decked out like a pack mule?"

"I wouldn't bet against me when these are at stake." The blonde held the candy bars even more possessively against her parka.

Feisty. She liked that. And from the available visual clues—brand-new backpack and coat, pristine passport peeking out of her pocket—Hudson guessed that the woman was likely embarking on some grand adventure and probably didn't travel abroad too often. That would account for her buoyant demeanor, when most everyone around them wore the weary, harried expressions of the frequent flier.

She was also an environmentalist, according to the Greenpeace logo on her tote bag. Single—no wedding ring. And middle class, from the quality of her clothes and shoes.

She'd have liked to have had another minute or two to trade quips with the cute blonde, but when she heard the final boarding call for her flight over the intercom, Hudson realized she needed to resolve the situation quickly, one way or another. "Why don't we just cut the crap and get down to business? What're they worth to you?" Hudson pulled a crisp twenty-dollar bill from her wallet and held it up.

"Sorry. I'm not the type who can be bribed," the blonde responded.

Nice try. Everyone has a price. "No?" Hudson added a second twenty to the first. "How about for just half of them?"

"No, I'd hang on to your money, if I were you." The stranger shook her head. "Sounds like you're due for a hearing aid." She turned toward the cashier. "Sorry. Gotta run. My plane's boarding."

As much as Hudson wanted to come out on top in this battle of wills, she didn't have time to dicker further. She got in line behind the blonde to pay for her magazines.

The stranger didn't immediately leave, however, once she was done with her transaction. She stood off to the side until Hudson had paid as well.

"A word of advice?" The blonde said.

"Okay."

"Kill 'em with kindness." The stranger pulled three of the candy bars out of her bag and handed them to Hudson. "Makes a better impression than threats and bribery, don't you think?" As she hurried off with a satisfied grin, she added, "Have a nice trip."

Hudson was so dumbfounded she stared down at the candy for several seconds before rushing off to catch her flight. The gate area was already empty except for a few standby travelers clustered around the agent, so she went straight onto the plane.

Joe was sipping a beer in first class. He'd changed from his suit into jeans and a wool sweater. "There you are. I was getting worried."

Hudson's seat was directly across the aisle.

"May I take your coat and help you with your bag?" the flight attendant asked. "We're about ready to depart."

"Sure. Thanks." As the steward dealt with her luggage, Hudson glanced back down the long aisle toward economy, just in time to see the blonde wrestle her backpack into the overhead storage compartment.

"What's up?" Joe asked, turning in his seat to see what Hudson was staring at.

"Nothing. Just an interesting face."

Once they were airborne and the seat-belt sign had been turned off, Hudson changed clothes in the cramped, first-class restroom and, at long last, finally began to feel as though she was on vacation.

"Excited?" she asked Joe.

"Sure. Can't wait. Monster year for snow everywhere." Joe had been her extreme-ski buddy for more than ten years, though her friend and cameraman much longer. They were advanced skiers, not quite in the expert category. "You know, I chatted with some people while we were waiting to board. Lot of others booked with the same outfitter, though they have different types of trips and final destinations. They must have chartered a good portion of this flight."

"That so?" She wondered briefly whether the blonde was also an adventure traveler and, if so, where she might be headed. But her own vacation plans, too long denied, soon took precedence. As she drifted off to sleep after dinner, she imagined carving through pristine snow on some distant mountain peak, the disturbing images from her job distant memories, at least for a while.

Joe and most of the other passengers were still sleeping when she awoke much later, and breakfast service was still an hour or more away. She unbuckled her seat belt and put her shoes back on. A veteran long-distance flier, she knew the value of occasionally getting up to stretch her legs, and it was a good excuse to check out the blonde from the airport a little closer.

❖

Steffi flipped through the selection of onboard movies as Kris snoozed beside her, and Fin as well, farther down the center row. Around them, other members of their climbing club were also dozing, but she was far too excited to sleep, though she knew she'd be dragging when they landed in Europe in another few hours. Detouring to the snack place for Kris's favorite candy had nearly made her miss her flight. She was still astounded by the speed with which they managed to get some three hundred passengers aboard the jumbo jet.

She smiled, recalling her encounter with the woman in the airport. Steffi wondered who she was. A celebrity of some kind, perhaps, judging from her model-worthy face and figure, and that classy woman's tux. She was probably headed overseas as well right now, since all the gates around the newsstand were for international destinations. But that didn't make sense. If she were headed for some big event in Europe or Asia, that tux would be a mass of wrinkles by the time she arrived.

Pushing the puzzle out of her mind, Steffi dug her itinerary out of her tote bag and checked it over, though she'd already memorized most of it. They'd have a nearly two-hour layover in Rome before their flight to Zurich, where they were booked at a three-star hotel. She figured that by the time they checked in and dropped their bags, it'd be mid-afternoon. Not much time to sightsee, since they'd be off again early the next morning, so she had a priority list of local attractions she wanted to hit.

She was determined to make the most of every single moment during her first trip abroad, to fully immerse herself in the local architecture, cuisine, and history as much as their schedule allowed. After copious hours on the Internet researching possibilities, she'd come armed with a thick stack of printouts.

After checking in with their outfitter, she, Kris, and Fin would head to Old Town, with its narrow cobblestone streets and quaint shops, to grab a bite to eat, take some pictures, and wrangle a few souvenirs. The Swiss National Museum, housed in an ancient castle, was also a must-see, and two massive churches as well: St. Peter's Cathedral and the Church of Our Lady, which had stained-glass windows by Marc Chagall.

Steffi also compiled a list of nightlife possibilities, though they were mostly for Kris and Fin. Though the three of them planned to hang out together, Steffi knew she'd be turning in much earlier than her friends. They had to be at the Zurich train station by seven the next morning, and no way would she be anything but absolutely wide-awake for that part of the trip. They would be traveling on one of the most scenic train routes in the world, and she didn't want to miss one minute of the experience.

Steffi studied the photos she'd printed off the web. The highest mountain railway in the Alps, the Bernina Express carried passengers from Chur, Switzerland to Tirano, a village just over the Italian border, passing glaciers and lakes and spectacular mountain peaks along the way. Adding to the stunning natural phenomena were the man-made ones. During its four-and-a-half-hour journey south, the train passed through fifty-five tunnels and over nearly two hundred bridges that looped and snaked through the unforgiving terrain. The Bernina Railway was also one of the steepest in the world, with inclines of up to seven percent.

Kris yawned loudly and straightened in her seat, groggily rubbing her eyes. "What time is it?" she asked as she flicked on her overhead light. "Tell me I didn't miss breakfast."

Steffi glanced at her watch. "It's only four thirty. Another three hours or so until we land, so I bet we don't get food for a while." The interior of the plane was still dark and most of the passengers dozed. She hadn't seen a flight attendant pass by in a long time; they were clustered in the back of the plane, probably taking a break or catching a nap.

"I'm starving."

"Of course you are, goofball. You only had dinner four hours ago."

"You can't call that a meal. For a kid, maybe, but not for somebody with my freakish metabolism."

"How you manage to eat what you do and not gain weight is one of life's eternal mysteries," Steffi replied. "Fortunately for you, I anticipated this and have a little surprise to tide you over." She dug into her tote bag for one of the Snickers Peanut Butter Bars. They were candy crack to Kris. "Here you go."

"You didn't!" Kris snatched it from her hand and tore open the wrapper. "Fin tried to score some of these for me at the grocery, but they were out." She held up one of the chunky, chocolate-covered squares. "Oh, yeah. Come to Momma."

"Make it last," Steffi advised her as Kris bit the first square in half. "I was only able to get a couple more for the whole trip."

Kris would normally have polished off the twin confections straightaway, but this advisory immediately had the desired effect. She slowed her chew rate considerably to relish the precious final bites. "Yummm," she said, smiling broadly at Steffi with chocolate-covered teeth.

They both laughed.

Kris took another bite and, as she chewed, moaned softly with pleasure. "Ecstasy in chocolate. I owe you big-time. Whatever you want, it's yours."

"Those are great, aren't they?" a female voice chimed in from the aisle.

Steffi looked up and directly into the tantalizing, dark-brown eyes of the woman from the airport. She'd changed into jeans and a turtleneck, which somewhat answered the wrinkled-tux question. But before Steffi could come up with something witty to say, Kris chimed in.

"Oh, yeah. Very hard to find, though."

"Don't I know it," the stranger answered, a grin tugging at the corner of her mouth.

"As you can see, I'm already down one," Steffi said. "Did you come to bully me into relinquishing the others?"

The stranger laughed and held up her hands in surrender. "Oh, no. I've learned my lesson."

"You two know each other?" Kris asked.

"We've...crossed paths," Steffi replied.

"Crossed swords is more like it." The stranger smiled. "But in a delightfully unexpected way. Thanks for the candy. And the advice."

"Don't mention it."

The interior lights of the plane flicked on, startling them all, and a young male voice rang out over the intercom. "Ladies and gentlemen, we're about to begin serving breakfast. Please take your seats and keep the aisles clear."

"Well, I better run. Thanks again." The stranger turned and headed toward the front of the plane. She disappeared through the partition leading toward the first-class cabin.

"What was all that about?" Kris fished the second candy square from its wrapper and bit it in half.

"We met at the concession stand. She's about as addicted to those things as you are, I think, and begged me for some when I cleared out their stash."

Kris stopped chewing. "You had more of these and you gave them away? I don't think I could be that generous." She grinned. "Even for someone as cute as she is."

"Oh, hell, it wasn't like that. I mean, we weren't flirting with each other or anything. I did it as a random-act-of-kindness thing."

"Which I applaud, except where these are concerned. No one can truly appreciate the magnificence of this splendid concoction like I do. I'm under its spell."

"You do realize we're about to land in a country known for its chocolate, right?"

"And I plan to sample every bit of it I can, but that doesn't mean it'll be easy to displace these as my number-one favorite." Kris popped the last morsel into her mouth and relaxed against the seat, chewing slowly, eyes closed. "And, for the record, she *was* kind of into you."

Steffi was inexplicably pleased by Kris's assessment, though she doubted it had any real merit. And not that it mattered. She'd given up on romantic entanglements for the foreseeable future, and since first class would disembark long before the climbing club did, she'd likely never see the woman again, anyway.

❖

Hudson hadn't immediately recognized the blonde as she came up the aisle, though she was one of the few with her overhead light on. Without her heavy coat and backpack, the woman looked more diminutive than she had in the airport, though fit and comfortably fashionable. Her tailored navy V-neck shell and matching cardigan looked to be a size six or so, worn over khakis. Minimal jewelry—a couple of silver bracelets and small, silver loop pierced earrings Hudson hadn't noticed in the store. She was struck again by the tangible glow of excitement about the woman, no doubt fueled by the numerous color printouts and travel materials in her lap. Her obvious zest for life was compelling. And now Hudson was also curious about the stranger's sexuality.

The blonde's traveling companion was almost certainly lesbian; her short spiky hair and black cargo pants had Hudson's gaydar pinging off the charts. And the snippet of conversation she'd overheard—*"Ecstasy in chocolate. I owe you big-time. Whatever you want, it's yours"*—was said so provocatively it suggested an intimacy between the two women. But the blonde was tough to read, and the body language between the two didn't support her theory that they were lovers.

Hudson's favorite pastime was people watching. She used their clothing choices, body language, and other clues to assess where they were from, what they did for a living, even what their secrets might be, and she was very good at it. In airports, on trains, in cafes, both at home and abroad, she occupied her idle moments scanning the crowd for an interesting face or group. Sometimes she'd engage them, sometimes not. Her ability to draw out chance-encounter strangers who caught her eye had led to some of her most important and satisfying reports for the AP.

But most of the time, the game served only to satisfy her insatiable curiosity about people. She cared how they lived, what they believed, how their early lives had shaped them, what their dreams were. Some of the stories she'd heard were too private or painful to ever share publicly. She often felt on those occasions she'd filled a need—both in herself and in her subject—simply by listening.

Joe said that she sometimes looked like a lioness on the prowl, assessing her potential prey from a distance, then moving in with an ever-adaptable approach: charm, cajolery, empathy, humor, challenge. Whatever it took. Most people, she'd found, once they got past an initial wariness of being the object of some con or pitch, were happy to tell their stories, pleased to be singled out.

She was a bit sad she hadn't time to get the blonde's story, but someone else would capture her attention in no time.

Chapter Four

Zurich, Switzerland

As soon as they got off the plane, Hudson and Joe headed straight to the passport-control checkpoint. Their first-class status put them in line ahead of their nearly three hundred fellow passengers so they had only a five-minute wait, and by the time they arrived at baggage claim, their priority-tagged bags were on the belt.

"Where do we catch the tram? Do you remember?" Hudson asked Joe as they claimed their wheeled duffels. They'd been here a few months ago on a story, but they'd been in so many airports in the interim she'd forgotten the layout.

"It's underneath the main passenger terminal." He led the way and they were soon aboard the number ten headed toward the center of the city, eight miles south. The trams ran so frequently they had ample empty seats around them to stow their gear in.

"Where are we staying?" Hudson asked. "What stop are we looking for?"

Joe pulled out their itinerary. He always handled their work travel arrangements because she hated having to deal with such logistics. Getting into some of the remote areas they needed to for stories was often problematic and time-consuming, and she just didn't have the patience for it. Joe had booked their vacation as well, a relative cakewalk by comparison because their adventure outfitter had taken care of most of the details.

EurAdventures was globally known as a leader in offering customized trips for extreme-adventure enthusiasts: rock, ice, and mountain climbers, skiers and snowboarders, glacier-trekkers, snowshoers, and more. You gave them your time frame, interests, and what you were willing to spend, and they booked your whole itinerary. Though a multitude of companies offered similar travel help, EA had risen above its competitors by utilizing charter flights and bulk deals whenever possible to save clients money, by engaging only experienced guides, and by maintaining extremely high standards for safety and cleanliness in the accommodations booked.

Hudson and Joe had chosen to go with the EA's standard package, which would guarantee a nice, clean room in a three-star hotel. While they loved being able to fly first class with all the frequent-flier miles they'd accrued from work, neither felt the need to spend their own hard-earned money on deluxe accommodations. Their upgrade from the economy package was worth the extra dollars to both, however, because the lowest-cost option didn't allow them to have separate rooms.

"We're at the Coronado. Look for the Milchbuck stop. The hotel's very close to the main train station and right across the street from the EA office where we check in."

"Great. Let's get that out of the way as soon as we drop our bags so we don't have to do it in the morning. Isn't our train to St. Moritz at some cruelly early hour?"

Joe shuffled papers, looking for the right one. "Yeah. Seven. But we're not getting off there, by the way."

"Say what?" She and Joe had decided together to make St. Moritz—the birthplace of winter tourism in the Alps—their first ski destination. The four major resorts in the area offered more than two hundred miles of groomed slopes, most of them for intermediate-level skiers, so it was a good place to refresh their skills. It also had heli-skiing options they planned to take advantage of. Both she and Joe most enjoyed the kind of extreme skiing where they were alone, at high altitude, breaking pristine new powder, and challenging the limits of their capabilities.

They were to spend the second week of their trip in Verbier, Switzerland, one hundred and thirty miles to the west. One of the world's foremost destinations for extreme skiers, Verbier offered some of the deepest snow and steepest off-piste skiing in the Alps.

"We'll still be in St. Moritz by suppertime," Joe explained. "But you're going to indulge me in this. When I was talking with the outfitter, they highly recommended we don't miss the full Bernina Express experience. The route's apparently got some really spectacular views between St. Moritz and the Italian border, where the train goes over a bunch of looping, winding bridges and through tunnels. With all this snow? Massive photo ops I can't pass up. We just go a few extra stops and then turn around and come back. We'll still be skiing by tonight."

"Fine by me. But if we're going to be on the train most of the day, we'd better make sure to pack some food. You never know what you're going to get onboard."

"Yeah, good point. We can swing by a grocery or something while we're out and about." Joe shuffled through some more papers. "Going beyond St. Moritz also takes us past the Morteratsch station, where we may be able to scope out the glacier."

"That's the one with the ski run, right?"

"Yeah. Takes something like forty-five minutes to ski the whole thing. Should be spectacular. Crevasses all around, amazing views all the way."

"Sounds like you've got every detail covered. This is going to be such an awesome trip, Joe. I so need this."

"You and me both," Joe replied as their stop was announced over the tram's intercom. They collected their bags and headed toward the nearest exit.

"By the way, I also printed out a list of clubs for tonight," Joe said as they waited. "One for you and a couple for me. Let's get this party started."

They dropped their bags at the hotel, freshened up, and headed directly for the EA offices to check in with their outfitter and get their bag of rented ski gear. The reception area was full of other adventure travelers. Hudson heard snippets of Italian, French, German, and Japanese, as well as English, and an Eastern-European dialect she didn't recognize. They got in line behind a fortyish platinum blonde with long, wavy hair, who was wrestling with the zipper on her duffel bag.

"Can I help?" Joe offered.

She turned and straightened, her face a study in frustration. She was petite, attractive, and endowed with an impressively hourglass figure. "It may take a grenade to get this open, but I'd appreciate the effort." She stuck out her hand in Joe's direction. "Anna."

He shook it. "I'm Joe. This is Hudson." He bent to give the zipper a look.

"Where you from?" Hudson asked.

"Boston. You?"

"New York," Hudson answered.

Anna's expression brightened. "I thought you two looked familiar. Weren't you on the plane from JFK this morning?"

"Yeah. Small world."

"Not so much," Anna replied, as Joe continued working on the zipper. "I think half the plane was EA people."

Hudson tilted her head in the direction of the check-in desk. "Where are you headed? You here for skiing?"

"No way. I'm such a klutz I'd break my leg in the first five minutes." Anna laughed. "I'm just here to get as far away from my kids as possible. Twin boys, in their fearsome fourteens."

Hudson and Joe laughed, too. "That bad?" Joe asked.

"Since their hormones started kicking in, they're exhausting. So once a year, their father gets to deal with them while I get some precious alone time." She held up the camera around her neck, an expensive Canon SLR with a telephoto lens. "Kind of a photography nut, though it hasn't gone anywhere, yet. Last year, I did the Great Wall of China."

"So, what's your plan here?" Hudson asked.

"I'm taking the Bernina Express tomorrow and the Glacier Express the day after that." Anna pulled a slip of paper from the back pocket of her jeans. "Then I've got a helicopter sightseeing trip booked where you land on a glacier and have a picnic lunch. End of the week, I head to Italy. I've always wanted to see Venice."

"Sounds great. We'll be on the Bernina train, too, tomorrow," Hudson said. "If you're alone and want some company, come find us."

Anna smiled. "Hey, I'll do that."

Just then, Joe finally got the stubborn zipper to work. "You're back in business."

"You rock, Joe. I was ready to slash it open." She stooped to fish her passport out of the duffel as the line inched forward. "I have an extremely low threshold for bullshit aggravation."

Joe chuckled. "You and Hudson both."

They chatted some more as they waited in line, Hudson and Joe thoroughly engaged by Anna's sharp wit and unapologetic candor. Especially entertaining was her description of her plumber husband of eighteen years. "He snores like a damn jet engine—I mean, that man has a serious set of lungs on him—but that's about my only complaint. He helps out with the chores with minimal prodding, and he always gives in to my whims, whatever they might be."

"Whims? Like what?" Joe asked.

"Well, like...say I have a craving for ice cream," Anna replied. "He'll run down to the 7-Eleven, even if it's two a.m." She waggled her eyebrows provocatively. "And of course, there are certain dress-up occasions I've suggested that might give other men pause." When confusion clouded Joe's face, she explained, "Batman and Batgirl? Wolf and Little Red Riding Hood? Gladiator and Roman slave?"

As Joe's face flushed red, Anna turned to Hudson with a mischievous grin. "I take it you two aren't really into role-playing."

Hudson laughed at the mental image of Joe in a gladiator suit. "We aren't a couple. Just very good friends, and we work together."

"Pity," Anna said. "You make a striking pair. What do you do?"

"I'm a reporter and Joe's a photographer. We work for the Associated Press."

Anna's eyes widened. "That so?" She gave Joe her full attention. "I'm definitely going to come find you on the train tomorrow, then. Maybe you'll give me some tips?"

"Only if you continue to entertain us," Joe replied.

"That's easy. I haven't even started in on the twins." It was Anna's turn next at the check-in counter, so she readied her passport and itinerary. "Remind me to tell you about the time they washed the car when they were six."

"Don't stop now," Hudson said.

"A garden hose on the inside and steel-wool dish scrubbers on the exterior," Anna explained, giving them both her best "you're in such deep shit now" look as they roared with laughter. "Fortunately, it was my husband's car, not mine, or they'd still be locked in their room."

As she stepped up to talk to the clerk at the check-in counter, Joe turned to Hudson with a grin. "She's a pistol."

"Yeah. Don't you just love her?"

❖

"I know you've got every single second planned," Kris said as she, Fin, and Steffi headed out of the hotel after dropping their bags. "Can I beg a stop for lunch somewhere before we start your OCD itinerary?"

"Really? You're hungry?" Fin rolled her eyes.

"A mini banana and yogurt do not qualify as breakfast."

"I was going to have us check in over there first." Steffi pointed toward the EurAdventures office across the street as a large group of Japanese tourists went inside. "But we can head to Old Town—it's not far—and come back later. They may be less crowded then."

"Sounds like a plan," Fin said. "Lead the way."

Like the rest of Europe, central Zurich had been struggling all winter with a record amount of snow, but the sun was out today, the cobblestone streets were clear, and shops in the historic district were operating normally. They grabbed sandwiches from a take-out place and ate as they walked, Steffi providing commentary on some of the attractions she'd researched.

"That's the biggest clock face in Europe," she said much later as they gazed up at the tower of St. Peter's from a bench outside. "It's thirty feet in diameter."

"I swear, you're like some weird savant with all the shit you can remember." Fin took a hefty swig from her water bottle.

"It's selective memory. I can name the latest release of most every top author in the country off the top of my head, and I've looked at so many travel websites and guidebooks I've got our itinerary down pat." She chuckled. "But useful stuff like passwords and grocery lists and people's birthdays? I know I've missed Kris's at least once."

"I'd forgotten that. No pun intended." Kris took another drink of water. "So, what's next on the agenda?"

Steffi got to her feet, and Fin and Kris followed suit. "You know, you're both being incredibly sweet to let me drag you around like this.

I know it's not your thing to spend the day looking at churches and historic sites."

"No lie I'm here for the climbing. But this has been okay," Fin said.

"Yeah." Kris chimed in. "You're such a kid at Christmas right now, it's all good."

"One more church, a walk by the river." Steffi read from the rest of the afternoon's itinerary. "With a stop back at the outfitters and a detour to find watches." They were all looking to score some Swiss watches as souvenirs, and they had the best chance for a good selection in Zurich.

They set off for the nearest tram stop, but Kris pulled up short when her cell phone chimed. "Hang on a sec. I just got a text." She checked the message and grinned. "It's from Nick," she said. "Everybody's going to meet up for dinner, drinks, and dancing later. They want us to join 'em. You game?"

"I am *so* there," Fin replied.

"You two go ahead." While Steffi enjoyed spending time with the other climbers, she knew they'd be partying hard late into the night. "We're here such a short time, I'd rather see some more of the city. And I don't want to be sleep deprived and hungover for the train ride tomorrow."

"That's okay. We'll stick with you." Kris shoved her cell back in her pocket, but disappointment was evident on her face.

"Look, I know you both want to go," Steffi said. "And it's cool with me. Really."

"We don't want to leave you alone," Fin added. "What fun is that?"

"I'm sure I can find plenty to keep me occupied. Look, we'll finish our afternoon of sightseeing and check in with EA, and then you guys can meet up with the others and I'll go exploring on my own a while, close to the hotel."

"You sure?" Fin asked.

"Absolutely. Text him back."

"Okay." Kris got her cell phone out and started typing. "But I'm still hoping you'll change your mind and come find us. I'll leave you the address."

Chapter Five

Zurich
Later that evening

Hudson headed away from the hotel at a leisurely pace, pausing to window-shop, admire an architectural detail, or study an interesting face. While she and Joe both relished finally getting some quality leisure time after three months on the road, they were at odds on how to spend their first night in Switzerland. After a quick nap and shower, Joe headed off for a tour of the local bars and clubs in search of fun. She certainly could empathize with his acute level of sexual frustration, but while he was content to resolve his with some stranger in a crowd, she usually preferred to get over hers with other distractions. And being in an unfamiliar city never failed in that regard.

She'd flown through Zurich more times than she could count and had stayed there a few times for work, but had never had the time before to explore its attractions. Museums, monuments, and other typical tourist draws held little appeal. When she hit a new place, she usually sought out the best local cuisine, offbeat events, and anything with an adrenaline rush. An online search had turned up nothing on the city's calendar that interested her, and she'd get plenty of excitement on the slopes in a day or two, so right now, her stomach ruled. Something substantial, like ribs and fries maybe. Ethnic was all good, too.

An Argentine steak restaurant two doors down from the hotel had been a contender, but the lack of patrons at this prime dinner hour of eight p.m. propelled her onward. The next block held a Spanish tapas place, another favorite cuisine, so she hurried toward it. A menu posted by the door looked promising, and the big windows that dominated the Taverna Catalana allowed her to see that the place was packed with diners.

Including one she recognized. The intriguing blonde from the plane. And she was sitting alone.

Decision made, Hudson entered the restaurant and found a sign in four languages directing patrons to seat themselves at any of the white-linen-topped tables. She headed toward the blonde, after visually confirming that her table was set for only one. "Mind some company, if I promise no death threats? No fun to eat alone."

Startled, the woman nearly dropped the menu she was holding. But when she looked up to see who'd addressed her, her expression changed from surprise to one of shy delight. "It's you! I mean…" She laughed at herself, and her smile widened. "Sure. Please." She gestured toward the empty chair opposite hers, and Hudson took it.

"Thanks.

"Three chance meetings in a row?" the stranger said. "Not that I'm complaining, but it's beginning to feel as though you're stalking me."

Hudson grinned and offered her hand. "You got me. I'm Hudson. Just so you know what name to write at the top of the restraining order." Humor and charm were the primary tools she used to break the ice with someone new. When budding journalists asked for her advice about conducting impromptu interviews, she told them: *Treat them with respect, and make them laugh, if you can.* The combo quickly put most strangers at ease and got them to open up.

The blonde laughed. "Steffi," she offered as they shook. "Good to actually meet you."

"Same here." Hudson was impressed by the woman's unusually strong grip. "Where you from?"

"Sultan, Washington. Not far from Seattle. You?"

"New York." Before Hudson could say more, a harried waiter dressed in black appeared at her elbow.

"Will you be having dinner, ma'am?" he asked.

"Yes."

"Very good. I'll be back with a menu and silverware. May I bring you something to drink?"

Hudson spotted a well-stocked bar against one of the wood-paneled walls. "Amaretto. Rocks."

"Right away."

"You really do have a sweet tooth, don't you?" Steffi asked.

"I burn a lot of calories." Hudson shrugged out of her coat and put it on the back of her chair.

"It shows. Wish I had that problem." Steffi sipped her white wine.

As an adult, Hudson was indeed grateful she could pretty much eat whatever she wanted and not gain weight. But before she'd hit puberty, her naturally lean frame had given rise to some not-so-kind nicknames. "I apologize in advance for how much I'm going to eat, but I'm really starving."

The waiter returned with her drink, place setting, and menu. The list of tapas was extensive, the possibilities described in both German and English.

"Maybe you can help me figure out what to try." Steffi studied her menu. "I've never heard of most of these dishes."

"You've had tapas before, though, right?"

"I don't think so."

"Tapas are 'little plates.' Sort of sample-sized. So you can try a lot of things between two people. I say we start with eight or so." Hudson considered the choices. "I'll be happy to do the ordering, if you want."

"I'm game."

"Anything you particularly like or don't like? Any allergies?"

"Well, I generally eat really healthy," Steffi replied. "But I am on vacation, so I'll allow myself a few extra calories. I like fish and seafood a lot. Most any kind. "

"That helps." She picked a few of her favorite seafood dishes. "Grilled sardines, then. And sun-dried, marinated octopus, scallops au gratin, prawns with Romesco sauce. You like spicy food?" She looked up to see Steffi nod. "Good. We'll do the chicken chorizo skewers, too, then. They come with a hot-chili glaze. And…let's see. Fried potatoes with aioli, ham croquettes, zucchini fritters." Hudson set down the menu. "Probably good to start. With a big basket of bread. Unless you see something I missed you want to try?"

"No, those all sound great."

As the waiter came to take their order, a table in front of the window opened up.

"We're moving over there," Hudson told him with her biggest smile as she got to her feet. "Better view," she told Steffi as she grabbed her amaretto. "Do you mind?"

"I'm with you. Lead on."

They settled in to their new table and Hudson gave the waiter their order.

"I'm so glad you moved us." Steffi smiled as she took in the view. Despite the chilly weather, the Old Town district, with its cozy old-world ambience and numerous restaurants, clubs, and hotels, was busy with pedestrians.

"People watching is kind of a hobby," Hudson said.

"Really? Me, too. I know it probably sounds strange, but sometimes I make up stories about the people I see."

"Do you? Hit me with one."

"Before you came in, I was working on those two." Steffi glanced over at a table by the bar, where a couple in their fifties laughed over coffee. As they watched, the man offered the woman a bite of cake off his fork, and she ate it in a way that was playfully flirtatious. "They have three kids and the last one just moved out, so they're celebrating with their first real vacation alone in years. Kind of a second honeymoon."

When she turned her attention from the couple in question back to her dinner companion, Hudson was struck again by the almost infectious joy that seemed a permanent fixture on Steffi's face. Her hazel eyes were warm and expectant, and she smiled at the slightest provocation, clearly enjoying every second of her time away from home. For Hudson, the upbeat company was a welcome change after too long covering war zones and natural disasters. "Are all your made-up stories so romantic?"

"Pretty much, I guess. I like happy endings."

"When I study people, I try to ascertain their reality," Hudson said. "From their clothes, body language, belongings. Whatever clues I can get."

"Oh, yeah? What's your take on my happy parents?"

Hudson studied the couple again and watched them interact for a minute or two. "They're not married. In fact, they haven't known each other very long. Typical second- or third-date behavior. She's got on too much makeup and keeps toying with her hair. Prolonged eye contact with the guy makes her a little embarrassed and shy, but she's loving the attention. She's been married before, but not for a while, judging from the slight indentation on her ring finger."

"Wow. That's pretty good. You sure see a lot more than I do. And the man?" Steffi asked.

"Now, though he *is* wearing a wedding ring, I'm guessing his wife died," Hudson replied. "He'd likely have taken the ring off after a divorce, but not if he's a widower."

"How do you know he's not married now and cheating on his wife?" Steffi asked.

"Possible. But unlikely with that unibrow he's got going on and botch job of a haircut. What wife would let that go? And that suit-shirt-tie combination. Really? Is he color-blind? He's got desperate bachelor written all over him. At their age, a good guess would be that they met through an online dating site or mutual friends. Or, could be they work together."

"Impressive. If true, of course." Steffi waggled her eyebrows skeptically.

Hudson laughed. "Want me to go ask them?"

Steffi looked aghast at the suggestion. "You're not serious."

"Why not?" She smiled. "I'm not shy about talking to people."

The waiter materialized with a tray of tapas and set them on their table. "Ladies, let me know if you need anything else."

"Thank you. Looks wonderful." Steffi sampled a grilled sardine and moaned in satisfaction. "I've died and gone to heaven. Now, back to your sizing-up-someone-from-a-distance abilities. What can you tell about *me*?"

Hudson dipped a zucchini fritter in aioli. "It's your first time in Europe, and you've wanted to come here for a long time." She took a bite of the fritter and chewed. "You spent today visiting churches and museums, and pretty soon you're going to be doing some kind of winter sport. I'd guess snowboarding."

Steffi's eyebrows peaked in surprise. "Pretty good. The snow-boarding part is wrong. Never been. But the rest, and the winter-sport part, is right."

"I'd also venture a guess that you have a very tidy home, and you're following a pretty detailed itinerary for this vacation."

"True enough," Steffi said. "Tell me how you do it."

"Not that difficult. You had a lap full of brochures and maps on the plane and were too excited to sleep. Your stuff looks brand-new. And you have this kind of…wide-eyed hyper-awareness common to people in an unfamiliar environment. The bit about your home and itinerary? Well, you just strike me as a meticulous person. One who likes order and control. Your hair and makeup are flawless, and your clothes are stylish: neatly pressed blouse, crease in your slacks. And as soon as you sat down here, you unconsciously straightened your silverware."

Steffi blushed. "Pretty observant."

"I'd say so." Hudson sipped her drink.

"But how did you know how I spent my day?"

"The typical first-time tourist starts their vacation by seeing the A-list sights. Guidebooks are big on churches and museums."

"I'll give you that. But it doesn't explain the winter-sport thing." Steffi nibbled on a piece of octopus.

"Easy. EurAdventures chartered much of our flight. You look pretty athletic, and because we're running into each other again just a couple of blocks from the EA office, I'm guessing you're one of them."

"Since you know all that, you must have booked a trip with them, too."

Hudson nodded. "I'm going skiing. Up around St. Moritz, mostly. You?"

"Ice climbing. I'll be in the same area. There's a big ice wall at Diavolezza."

"Ice climbing, huh? That's pretty hard-core." Hudson was always glad to see women tackling, and excelling at, any extreme sport long dominated by men.

Steffi speared another sardine with her fork. "I am a little nervous about it. I've rock-climbed a lot, but I've been on ice only a few times."

"So, your candy-loving friend on the plane…she a climber, too?" Hudson asked.

Steffi grinned. "Yeah. In fact, she got me into it."

"Where's she now?"

"At a club with some other people from our climbing group."

"Loud music and crowds aren't your thing?" Hudson asked.

"Clubs are okay, but I can do that back home. I'd rather try some new food…which, by the way, is all amazing…" Steffi popped a plump scallop into her mouth and chewed. "After, I thought I'd wander around a little. Take some pictures."

"What do you do, back in…Sultan, was it?"

Steffi nodded. "I'm a librarian."

"That may explain why you like happy endings." Hudson flagged down the waiter and ordered another round of drinks. She was enjoying their conversation and wanted to linger a while, though they were rapidly tearing through their tapas. "Who's your favorite author?"

"Too tough to choose just one. I like Nora Roberts a lot, and Karen Rose. Janet Evanovich. Allison Brennan. Daniel Silva. David Sedaris, though he's not a novelist. I really could name twenty others, probably. At least."

"How many books do you read in a week?"

"Probably six or seven. I don't watch a lot of TV. Do you read?"

"Not nearly as much as I'd like," Hudson replied. "Not enough time."

"What do you do?"

"I work for the Associated Press, so I'm on the road a lot."

"Are you a reporter?"

"Yup."

"How cool! That's got to be exciting. Do you get to go overseas?"

Hudson nodded. "That's the rule, rather than the exception."

Steffi leaned in closer, obviously enthralled by the revelation. "How many countries have you been to? And what are some of your favorites?"

"How many precisely, I have no idea. More than a hundred, for sure." She looked out the window as a group of tourists passed by and saw that it had started to snow. "As to favorites…where to start?

Alaska and the Himalayas are both extraordinary. And Greece. Fiji. Thailand. New Zealand."

"Your passport sure gets a workout."

Hudson laughed. "Yeah. I usually have to get a new one before the old expires, even when I get the extra pages added."

"I hope I can get to just a fraction of where you've been. I'd love to travel. What kind of stories do you cover?"

"You name it, I've probably been there, done that. Katrina, Syria, Iraq, Afghanistan. Haiti."

"Dangerous places. Don't you ever get scared?" Steffi, Hudson noticed, was so engrossed in hearing about her work that she'd stopped eating.

"Sometimes. Mob and battle situations can go wrong real fast."

"I can't imagine what you must have witnessed." Steffi shook her head in wonder. "Sounds like you've been a reporter a long time."

"Twenty-five years." Hudson smiled at Steffi's shocked expression. "I started with AP when I was ten."

Steffi blushed. "Sorry, I didn't mean…"

"It's all right. I take your disbelief as a compliment."

"You know, I thought you were some kind of celebrity. The tux, I mean."

"I'd come straight from an event and didn't have time to change, that's all. I'm no celebrity. Just doing a job, like anybody else."

"I doubt that's true since most of the places you named were war zones. Got some interesting battlefield stories, I bet." Steffi pushed her plate away with a sigh. "Care to share?"

"Enough about me. I'm more interested in your story." Hudson was happy to polish off the rest of what was left of their tapas, though she was getting full, too.

"*My* story? I don't have a story."

"Everyone has a story."

"Well, maybe so. But not everyone has an *interesting* story. Let's put it that way. Mine would fit on the back of a cereal box and put you to sleep while you're reading it."

"I doubt that."

"Then you're not as good at figuring out people as you say. Believe me, I live a pretty routine, ordinary life."

"No near-death experiences? Memorable achievements? Heart-wrenching obstacles you've had to overcome?"

Steffi smiled and shook her head. "Sorry to disappoint you."

"I'm not disappointed," Hudson said. "Just a little puzzled. You know, in twenty-five years of asking people 'What's your story?' I think I've had only a couple of people besides you say they don't have one."

"Because you're interviewing world leaders and people who have just been through a hurricane or something. That makes perfect sense."

"In those cases, sure. But I've asked that question of a lot of... in your words, people who live routine, ordinary lives. And usually, even *they* have had *something* happen in their life they want to talk about. A moment of heroism. Their kids. Something or someone that shaped them, or challenged them. A fear they've overcome. A cause they fight for. A regret that haunts them."

"None of the above." Steffi shrugged. "Maybe my story just isn't written yet."

"Perhaps," Hudson replied. More likely, she thought, Steffi's story was one she wasn't ready to share with a stranger. *Pity.* Something about her piqued Hudson's interest, and in a way that was more personal than professional.

Chapter Six

S teffi tried not to squirm. Just routine dinner conversation, no doubt, for the woman sitting across from her, but she wasn't used to being asked such personal questions. And as much as she was enjoying Hudson's company, the reporter had an intensity about her that was as unsettling as it was fascinating.

"If you're so keen on travel and you've wanted to come to Europe for a long time, why haven't you before now?" Hudson asked.

"Lot of reasons. Mostly financial. As much as I love my job, librarians don't make much, so I couldn't save a lot until I started buying and selling rare first editions on the side, online."

"You really are all about books, aren't you?"

"Never wanted to do anything else. You?"

"Same. I was a very curious and inquisitive kid. Used to spy on the neighbors with binoculars," Hudson replied. "And I was always taking things apart to see how they worked. The toaster, the telephone."

Steffi laughed. "Your parents must have loved that."

"How about an espresso and dessert?" Hudson asked. "Or do you have to be somewhere?"

Steffi noticed the subtle but effective change of subject, as well as Hudson's visible discomfort at the mention of her parents. She'd inadvertently touched a nerve, apparently, one that had triggered an abrupt end to their relaxed banter. "Coffee, yes. I'm too full for anything else." She checked her watch and was surprised to see it was already well past nine.

"Great." Hudson flagged down the waiter. "Espresso for me, and…" she looked over at Steffi.

"A decaf regular coffee. Black, please."

"Would either of you care for dessert?" the man asked.

Steffi shook her head. "None for me, thank you."

"Got something chocolate?" Hudson asked.

"Of course, ma'am. May I suggest our layered mousse cake with dark-chocolate ganache? It's very popular."

"Sold."

"You must have met a lot of famous people in your job," Steffi said as the waiter departed.

"A few."

"Anybody surprise you? I mean, that they turned out to be really different in person than you imagined they would be?"

Hudson took several seconds to consider the question before she answered. "It happens, sure. Celebrities who are really shy in person. A politician who actually tells you the truth."

Steffi laughed. "Jaded, much?"

Hudson smiled. "Comes with the territory. Hard to cover politics and still be naïve about the way things really work. Once in a while you get a good one, though. I like Hillary."

"Me, too. I hope she's our next president."

The waiter returned with their coffees and Hudson's dessert, a massive slice of cake with alternating layers of light-chocolate mousse and creamy, dark ganache.

"Look at this. Can't possibly eat it all by myself. Will you share it with me?" Hudson smiled encouragingly as she picked up her fork.

"Very tempting, but no thank you." She'd worked so hard to get in shape she normally had no problem passing on sweets, but today had been one test of willpower after another. Kris had insisted they stop at two chocolatiers and a patisserie during their sightseeing, and the temptation of all those pastries and tarts had been excruciating. Now this.

Hudson took her first bite and sighed with contentment. "France has the best pastries, but the Swiss sure know their chocolate," she said, before going for another fork full. "Still time to change your mind. You're missing out."

"I'd be having a tougher time resisting if I wasn't so full." Steffi forced her gaze away from the cake to the view outside. The snow was really coming down now, whipped sideways by a gusty wind. Pedestrian traffic had slowed considerably in the worsening conditions. "Can you believe how bad winter has been everywhere this year? I hope this stops by tomorrow."

Hudson pulled out her cell and typed in a few strokes. "It's supposed to. The forecast calls for clear and sunny, at least until late afternoon." She set the phone on the table and resumed eating.

"Awesome. We're taking the train tomorrow that goes through the Alps to Italy, and it's supposed to have this incredible scenery."

"The Bernina Express?" Hudson asked. "We're on that, too."

"Leaving at seven a.m.?"

Hudson nodded. "Looks like we may be running into each other yet again. Where you sitting?"

"Hang on." Steffi dug into her bag for their tickets. "I'm in one of the second-class panorama cars. Seat 32A. I think they put our whole club together."

"Joe and I are in the panorama cars, too. First class. I'll have to come find you, say hello."

"I hope you do. I've enjoyed our chats." Heat rose to Steffi's cheeks. She always resented her inability to hide how easily she could be embarrassed. "I have to admit, though, I can't imagine why, with all you've seen and done, you singled *me* out to have dinner with."

Hudson smiled. "I just saw you through the window as I was shopping for a restaurant and thought I'd probably have more fun eating with you than alone. And I was right, so don't sell yourself short." As she took another bite of cake, Hudson's cell rang. She grabbed it off the table before it could ring a second time and checked the display. "Sorry," she said to Steffi before taking the call. "Hey."

Hudson listened for several seconds and laughed. "Okay. Okay. I will. I promise." She looked at Steffi apologetically as she listened again, then said, "Ten minutes. Maybe fifteen." She disconnected and signaled the waiter for their bill. "Sorry, but I have to leave."

"Oh, of course. Thanks again for joining me. Hope we run into each other tomorrow."

"Me, too." Hudson got to her feet and started putting on her coat when she saw the waiter heading their way.

Steffi dug around in her bag for her wallet, but by the time she had it out and looked up, the waiter was already heading away again, with a hundred Euro note in his hand.

"Dinner's on me," Hudson said.

"That's very sweet, but you really shouldn't—"

"You can buy me a cocoa on the train. Great meeting you, Steffi." She held out her hand.

Steffi got to her feet as they shook. "You, too, Hudson."

She sat back down to finish her coffee as Hudson hurried out of the restaurant. *Such an interesting woman. Beautiful, brainy, and brave.* What kind of courage must it take, she wondered, to spend your life going into war zones? And what toll on the psyche, to witness firsthand the horrible things Hudson must have seen in places like Syria, Haiti, and Iraq. Human cruelty, mass devastation, endless suffering.

Though she knew little about the news business, she was certainly aware that the broadcast networks and most mainstream media censored material that was too graphic or gruesome. The short glimpses that Steffi saw on her TV every night of such stories were heartbreaking. How much worse it must be for Hudson, living with the reality, she couldn't imagine.

By the time she departed the restaurant, it was nearly ten. The heavy snow had driven most tourists off the streets and into restaurants, cafés, and bars, but a few hardy souls were still out and about. Steffi bundled up and took a roundabout way back to the hotel to extend her first night abroad. As she ambled along, she marveled anew at how wonderfully *different* everything was. The narrow and winding cobblestone streets and the medieval buildings and churches made her feel as though she'd stepped back in time to the Renaissance. She took a few night photos, mostly of the illuminated landmarks and boats along the Limmat River, which separated the two halves of Old Town.

Though she was starting to feel a pretty serious case of jetlag by the time she returned to her room, Steffi was determined to stay up a little while longer. No telling when they might have Wi-Fi again.

After changing into her pjs, she climbed into bed with her iPad and went online. The keywords *Hudson Associated Press* yielded hundreds of thousands of hits, the first of which was an impressive official biography on the AP website.

Her full name was Hudson Mead, and she was chief foreign correspondent for the AP. The portrait photograph was a bit dated, as it depicted Hudson with hair to her shoulders instead of the short, layered cut she had now, but she had the same earnest intensity in her dark eyes.

Beneath the photo were Hudson's achievements, a lengthy list of honors and awards that included a Pulitzer for her reporting on the Rwandan genocide. A brief bio informed readers that Hudson had started with the AP as an intern while still in college and was hired full-time upon graduation. She'd been assigned to cover international news, her true passion, after a brief stint on the political beat.

The next hit on Google was a Wikipedia entry for the reporter that chronicled many of the important stories she'd covered and contained more personal information.

Hudson Mead was born in Chicago on January 29, 1969, which meant she'd just turned forty-five. Steffi found that difficult to believe, given Hudson's nearly flawless complexion; she would have guessed she was ten years younger.

The discrepancy made her briefly wonder whether Hudson might've had some work done. Botox or something, at least. It certainly was possible, given that she was in the public eye. But there were no visible scars or the scary-bad lip jobs a lot of older Hollywood celebrities were sporting, and Hudson didn't appear the type at all. She seemed grounded and genuine, the kind of person who looked you right in the eyes when she talked to you.

And she really *listened*, in a way few people did. Didn't matter whether she was talking to some world leader or a small-town librarian.

Reading Hudson's bio made Steffi a little ashamed she hadn't known of her before. She surfed the news online every morning over coffee. Surely she'd read some of Hudson's stuff, but she rarely if ever noticed the name on the byline. She'd start paying closer attention.

She typed Hudson's name into the Google News search field, expecting to come up with some of her stories. But the most recent entry wasn't *by* Hudson; it was *about* her. The *Huffington Post* article, filed less than twenty-four hours ago, was about the Courage in Journalism Awards ceremony in New York, presented by the International Women's Media Foundation. Hudson had been one of the recipients. Steffi scrolled down for photos, and there she was, onstage, holding up her award. In her tux. Another shot showed her on a red carpet with a man identified as her long-time photographer, Joe Parker.

Quite an accomplished woman. She felt honored to have shared a meal with her. *Hudson Mead bought me dinner!* It would make for a good story back at the library. And with any luck, she might run into her again in not too many hours.

On the Bernina Express! As excited as she was about the long-awaited sightseeing trip, she knew she'd better get some sleep or she'd be dragging tomorrow.

CHAPTER SEVEN

Next morning

Hudson poured herself a mug of coffee and carried it to the window. Her room at the Coronado overlooked the Irchel University Park, a massive urban oasis whose trees, man-made lake, and grassy meadows no doubt drew big crowds during the warmer months. But two hours before dawn on this chilly February morning, the only pedestrians in sight were two tourists with backpacks and a lone dog walker.

After meeting Joe for a quick drink after dinner, she'd returned to her room and drifted off almost immediately, but six hours wasn't enough to catch up on her accumulated sleep deprivation. A long, warm shower helped revive her, but she was still happy they would be sightseeing, not skiing, today. She wanted to be fully rested and alert when they tackled the big mountains near St. Moritz.

She dressed and packed and found Joe already waiting for her in the lobby when she went down to check out a half hour later. He was slumped back on a massive leather chair, eyes closed, his duffel bag an impromptu ottoman.

Hudson could tell from his slow, deep breathing that he was sound asleep. The opportunity to prank him was impossible to resist.

She pulled a bright-red lipstick out of her bag and generously painted his lips before she shook his shoulder to wake him. "Get any sleep at all?" she asked.

"Couple of hours," he replied groggily, then smiled. "Remember the redhead?"

"Niiiice," she replied. They had similar tastes in women, and if she'd been in the mood to pick up some company last night, she might have vied for the same one Joe ended up with. "You ready to head to the station?"

The train depot wasn't far, but since they had both their regular luggage and their EA-supplied ski-equipment bags, they opted to cab it there. If the driver noticed Joe's lipstick in the predawn darkness, he didn't remark on it. They were halfway to their destination when they passed a group of tourists, most with backpacks and EA gear bags. Hudson recognized Steffi among them, walking alongside the woman who'd been with her on the plane.

She and Joe ran into another familiar face once they got inside the station—Anna, the funny platinum blonde they'd met in the EA line.

"Hey, guys!" Anna hailed them from a bench halfway down the platform and they went to join her. The train to Chur, where they would transfer to the Bernina Express, was due to arrive in ten minutes.

When they got closer, Anna smirked at Joe. "Well, don't you look lovely this morning?"

He didn't catch on. "Where'd you get that?" Joe pointed to the large paper cup in Anna's hand.

"A little coffee stand that way." She pointed toward the end of the terminal.

"You want your usual?" he asked Hudson.

"Sure. Thanks, Joe."

As he headed away, stifling a yawn, Anna said, "Your work, I take it?"

Hudson nodded gleefully.

"You and my evil twins are kindred spirits. Can't tell you how many times my husband's gotten up from a nap looking like the love child of Bozo and RuPaul. Once I sent him down to the corner grocery like that. Served him right 'cause he was supposed to be watching 'em."

Hudson laughed. "Joe should know better than to doze off around me. Want to make a wager on when he clues in?"

"Nah. I don't dare piss him off. I want some photography tips."

"I'd at least wait until the sun comes up and he's more coherent," Hudson said. "You're not going to see much scenery in this light, anyway."

"That's okay. I'll wait 'til we get on the panorama cars." Anna glanced at her ticket. "We don't have reserved seats on this first train. Mind if I sit with you two?"

"Please do," Hudson replied. "Here he comes. Apparently no one's told him, yet."

Joe returned with a cup of coffee in each hand and a small paper bag tucked under one arm. He handed one of the coffees to Hudson and sat between her and Anna. "Got some croissants," he said as he opened the bag and held it out toward Anna. "Care for one? Fresh-baked. Still warm."

"Thanks. Don't mind if I do." She plucked one out and winked at Hudson while he wasn't looking. "You know, Joe, you'd be a bitchin' Martha Stewart."

"I think I'll keep my day job," he replied benignly as he offered the bag to Hudson and then claimed the third croissant for himself.

He'd scarfed half of it down before he took his first sip of coffee and saw the stain he'd left behind on the rim of his cup. "What the fuck?" When he ran the back of his hand across his mouth and came away with a wide gash of red pigment, he turned and glared menacingly at Hudson. "*So* wrong."

Anna and she roared with laughter as he darted off toward the nearest restroom.

"You two do this sort of thing a lot, I gather?" Anna asked.

"Constantly. This is payback for a very realistic rubber snake in my sleeping bag." Hudson sipped her coffee.

"What's been the best prank of all so far?"

Hudson had to think about that a minute or two. "The last vacation we took together, we had adjoining rooms. He comes in late, with a girl, and, you know…they've been drinking and are all over each other the minute they hit the door. Never noticed I'd loaded up his bed with glitter." As Anna laughed, she added, "Let's just say it got into some pretty inconvenient places."

Anna roared harder, and Hudson joined in.

"What's his best one on you?" Anna asked.

"He pulled the old shoe-black-on-the-binoculars trick on me when we were in Iraq. I went around looking like a raccoon for six or seven hours, none the wiser. Several of the soldiers we were embedded with had their pictures taken with me, so that prank went viral pretty fast."

"I should be taking notes," Anna said. "For the next time the boys decide to try to pull something on me. Serve 'em right, the little monsters."

As Joe rejoined them with a freshly scrubbed face, Hudson spotted Steffi and her friends coming out of the station. She waved, and Steffi waved back.

"Who's that?" Joe asked.

"Her name's Steffi. She's here with an ice-climbing group from Washington state. We had dinner together."

Joe watched the group head in their direction. "Oh? Did you now? You didn't mention that last night."

Hudson caught the tone and quickly shot down the inference. "Two American women in the same restaurant who didn't want to eat alone. Nothing more. Get your head out of the gutter."

"She's cute, though, don't you think?" He lowered his voice as the group got closer.

When Hudson didn't answer, Anna piped up. "Yeah, she's definitely cute. Super cute. She your type, Hudson?"

"Stop it, both of you," she muttered under her breath.

"Nice to see you again," Steffi called out when she got within earshot.

"You, too." Hudson stood. "Steffi, this is my friend Joe…and that's Anna. She's from Boston."

"Nice to meet you both." Steffi turned toward her climbing-club friends, all of whom had backpacks and heavy gear bags. "Guys, this is Hudson Mead."

Before she could make further introductions, their train pulled into the station. Hudson tossed her half-empty coffee into the nearest trash bin, and Joe followed suit.

"Let's all sit together," Anna suggested, and the rest were quick to agree. They moved toward the nearest car as the doors opened but had to queue up because they all had luggage and were gaining access from a single steel stairway.

Hudson set down her ski gear and caught Steffi's arm as they waited. "You know, I don't remember telling you my last name."

Steffi blushed. "I…uh…" She looked down at her feet. "Okay, I looked you up last night online. I admit it. But, in my defense, I'm a librarian. That's what I do."

Hudson smiled. "I don't mind. I'm the curious type, too, remember? But that puts me at a distinct disadvantage."

"Ma'am?"

Hudson turned toward the voice and found a tall, stocky guy with a crew cut watching her from a couple of feet away. He was probably closing in on fifty and was dressed in new blue jeans, flannel shirt and sweater, and the kind of insulated Carhartt barn coat that farmers and ranchers wear. His beige cowboy hat had bent-up sides and was molded to his head as though he'd worn it for years. He had the kindest eyes she'd ever seen.

"Sorry to interrupt, but I'd be pleased to help you with those bags," he said softly in a thick Southern drawl as he grinned at her. "I don't have any luggage myself."

"That's very kind of you. I'd love some help with my ski stuff. That duffle, there." Though it was nice to have an extra hand with all this luggage, Hudson accepted the offer primarily because she wanted to spend a few more minutes with him. She sensed something about him; she didn't know what. He seemed oddly out of place, especially since he seemed to be alone. "I'm Hudson." She held out her hand. "Thank you, Mister…?"

He politely took off his hat before extending his hand. "Clay. Just call me Clay."

"Where you from, Clay?"

"Knifley, Kentucky. You probably never heard of it."

"Knifley? No, I don't think so."

"Less than eight hundred people," he said. "Small, but close-knit, you know?"

"I live in a place like that," Steffi said. "Hi, Clay. I'm Steffi."

"Pleasure," he said, and shook her hand, too.

"You traveling all by yourself?" Hudson asked.

He nodded.

"Then come sit with us."

"I'd like that. Never expected I'd miss hearing English so much. Don't understand a dang thing anybody's sayin'."

Soon it was their turn to board. Steffi went up first, pausing to stick her backpack beside those of her friends, in one of the large luggage racks at the end of the car. Hudson found room for her rolling duffel and directed Clay where to put her ski gear. Then they all made their way toward their growing and eclectic group of Americans. The only other passengers in the car on this frigid early morning run were two Italian couples in ski gear, no doubt bound for St. Moritz, and an elderly woman with two small children.

The train was a modern local, all shiny steel and polished glass, with large, comfy seats that reclined, two on each side of the aisle. Joe had already claimed a window seat, so Hudson took the one beside him. Steffi went a few rows farther forward to join the rest of her climbing club. Anna was with them as well, chatting excitedly with one of the couples.

Clay, though, wasn't ready to park it just yet. He ambled slowly up and down the aisle, studying every aspect of the interior of the train. Hudson watched him smooth his hand over the upper handrail as lovingly as though he was stroking his favorite dog. Only when the train started moving did he finally claim the seat across the aisle from her.

"Wake me when we get to Chur." Joe reclined his seat and slumped back against the window. "And no funny business with the lipstick," he added before closing his eyes.

"Lipstick?" Clay asked.

"Don't ask," Hudson replied with a grin. "So, Clay, tell me… what do you do?"

"Farmer," he replied. "Mostly wheat and corn. I raise some pigs, too, but just for the family and a few neighbors."

"Tell me about your family. Got any kids?"

Clay smiled, but Hudson could see him tearing up a little at the mention of them. "Two boys and a girl," he replied. He reached into his back pocket for his wallet and withdrew a photo that he handed to her. The edges were worn, as though he'd carried it around a long time.

Hudson studied the family photo, evidently taken at a backyard barbecue. Clay's kids, all in their teens, were clustered around a picnic table loaded with ribs and corn on the cob, grinning at the camera with sauce-smeared faces. The woman in the picture wore a faded sundress from the eighties, and the modest house behind them needed a new coat of paint. The family obviously was just scraping by, and Hudson wondered how Clay could afford a trip to Europe. "Your wife's a very pretty woman."

"Ain't she, though? Still don't know what she ever saw in me, but I'm glad for whatever it was."

"How long have you two been married?"

"Twenty-two years next month." He choked up when he said this, and a tear escaped the corner of his eye. He swiped it away with the back of his hand.

"Why aren't they with you, Clay? Why are you here by yourself?"

The question eroded the big man's tenuous composure. Two more tears streamed down his face as he swallowed hard and squeezed his hands together. "I been wanting to come here a long time. Never thought it'd happen in a million years, though. Couldn't afford it. Can't even afford to send my kids to college." He took the picture back from her and stared down at his family. "I got sick a couple months back," he continued in a low voice. "And while I was in the hospital, a bunch of people from town got together and threw a couple big fund-raisers. Spaghetti dinners, you know?"

Hudson nodded encouragingly but said nothing.

"After the medical bills, they used the rest to buy my plane and train tickets, and to pay for the hotel. 'Bout everybody in the county pitched in, much as they could." He shook his head in wonder. "I got great friends. But there was only enough for me to come, and Sarah—that's my wife—she pretty much insisted I do it. She always gets her way."

"What made you sick, Clay?" she asked, though she was pretty sure she could make a good guess. Something lethal, imminent, and irreversible.

"Brain tumor." He sighed heavily. "Nothing they can do."

"I'm so sorry, Clay."

He swiped again at his tear-streaked face. "Yeah, well, them doctors don't know everything. My people are prayin' up a storm."

"Have you talked to your family since you got here?" she asked. From the sound of it, Clay was pinching every dime of that donated money, so she doubted he'd sprung for the cost of a pricey international call from the hotel. And he definitely wasn't the type of guy to have his own cell phone.

Clay shook his head. "Sarah told me not to. So I'd have enough for food and all."

Hudson checked her watch and calculated the time difference. "It's after midnight there," she told him as she pulled out her cell. "Think she'd mind getting a call this late to hear you made it all right?"

"That's very kind, but I couldn't ask—"

"Don't give it a second thought. I bet she's worried about you." Hudson typed in O11, the international code from Europe to the U.S. "What's the number?"

As he gave it to her, his face brightened with the anticipation of reconnecting with his family. "Bless you, Hudson. I'll be lickety-split quick," he promised her.

"Don't you dare." She handed the phone to him as soon as she heard ringing on the other end. "Take your time. I mean it."

"Sweetheart? It's me." Clay's voice took on an almost boyish wonder. "I'm here. I'm really here."

She got up from her seat and moved forward to give him some privacy. Joe was out cold, and he was such a deep sleeper that nothing short of alarm bells or a physical shaking would wake him.

Chapter Eight

Hudson found Anna regaling the climbing club with stories about her family, to much amusement.

"They're in their pyro phase right now," Anna told the group. "What is it about teenage boys and their fascination with fireworks? They blew up all my Tupperware and put dents in half my pots and pans in one afternoon."

Everyone laughed, but the story struck a special chord with one of the men. "I set fire to the garage when I was ten, napalming my little army men with globs of rubber cement. Singed off my eyebrows in the process, too. Took them forever to grow back."

"My parents would say girls aren't any easier," remarked the butchy woman who'd been sitting with Steffi on the plane. "I was climbing trees and falling out of them every chance I got. We had to go to the E.R. so much they knew me there by name."

"Kind of glad you never told me that when we started climbing, since I'm always tied to you," Steffi remarked, which made the whole group laugh harder.

"Look, the sun's coming up," someone said, and indeed they could finally begin to make out some of the terrain they were passing: the pinpricks of lights from sleepy villages, frozen lakes, vast stretches of white that might be farms or pastures. Up ahead, the mighty Alps dominated the skyline.

Clay came up behind Hudson and handed her back her phone. "Sarah said to say thanks. Mighty nice of you."

"You're very welcome." She turned back toward the group. "Has everybody met Clay? He's from Kentucky." Quick introductions were made and greetings exchanged.

"What brought you to Switzerland, Clay? You a skier?" Anna asked.

"Not hardly." Grinning, he pulled a thick stack of photographs from his jacket pocket and handed a few to each person. "This is why I'm here." He didn't say anything more for several seconds, so that everyone could make sense of what they were seeing.

Hudson looked down at the four he'd given her. One was a close-up of a red train with panorama windows, against a snowy backdrop. Bernina Express was written on the side, and for an instant she thought it was the train they'd soon be on. No, something was off. She wasn't sure what.

She flipped to the second photo, which showed the train and a corkscrew section of tracks from a greater distance, and it was then she could tell it wasn't the real thing, but an extremely realistic model-train setup. The third shot showed a much-younger Clay hunched over a long worktable. He was painting a section of the Alps that appeared to be maybe four feet high. What he'd already finished looked amazingly like the landscape dominating the view outside their train, while the unfinished portion was bare white. Clearly, the man had some chops as an artist.

The final photo, a wide shot of what she presumed was Clay's basement, did a capable job of showing the scope of his railroad obsession. He'd meticulously re-created what looked to be nearly the whole Bernina Railway from Chur to Italy in winter, complete with frozen lakes, little train stations, and, most impressively, all the amazing bridges and tunnels the route was known for.

Hudson had never seen anything like it. It must have taken him years to complete.

"Amazing," one of the climbers remarked.

"You did all this?" another asked.

"Every bit. I've always been a nut about trains," Clay replied as people began exchanging their photos to get different views and close-ups of his incredible attention to detail. "House I grew up in was next to some tracks, and I'd run home from school to watch the big freight train that came through at 4:10."

"How long did this take you to make?" Hudson asked.

"Twelve years, two months," Clay said. "Before this one, I did the Amtrak Empire Builder, which goes through the Rocky Mountains. It was the first train to get a Superliner. You know, them big double-decker passenger cars? Anyway, I caught a TV special on the Bernina Express and just had to do it next."

"I thought the Bernina Express was all red," Steffi said. "Your front half looks like a regular passenger train."

"It's all red in summer," Clay explained. "In the winter, they have fewer tourists, so they haul a handful of panorama cars behind a regular local."

"How many times have you ridden it so far?" one of the climbers asked.

"Never," Clay replied. "This'll be my first time."

"First time?" Steffi repeated the words incredulously. "I can't believe you built this without actually coming here first."

"I probably read everything ever written about it. Sent away for some of it, and my son took me to the library so I could print pictures and watch videos on the Internet. There are lots of 'em," he said. "But it's sure not going to be anything like riding the real thing, let me tell you. It's a dream come true."

Hudson was standing slightly behind Clay in the aisle. She reached up and squeezed his shoulder. "Lucky us to get to be with you. You can tell us about things along the way."

"Yeah, we all need to get on the same car," Steffi said.

"We have assigned seats on that one, don't we?" Anna started to reach for her ticket.

"Yup. We do," Clay replied. "Anyone sitting around 56D in second class?"

"Shouldn't matter this time of year if we change," Hudson said. "I bet there'll be a lot of empty seats in the panorama cars, especially after Saint Moritz."

"We certainly can't break the group up now," Anna said.

"Where y'all from?" Clay asked. "And what do you do, if'n you don't mind me asking?"

"How about if everybody tells us a little bit about themself," Hudson suggested.

And so they all went around and volunteered a few tidbits to get better acquainted. Hudson always found it interesting what information people pushed to the forefront when they were asked about themselves; it often spoke of their priorities or gave a glimpse of their dreams.

The first of the climbers to speak was Nick, a tall, lanky guy with a meticulously groomed stubble of beard and close-cropped hair. He told them he was thirty-two years old and single, and had lived in Seattle all his life. Hudson strongly suspected he was also gay, but that fact wasn't among the information he cared to share.

Gary, the club president, was a balding bartender with multiple tattoos and round, wire-rimmed glasses that magnified his pale-blue eyes.

The lone married couple in the group, Patti and Curt, had met through an online dating site. Though together for two years, they'd never really taken a honeymoon, so Curt had surprised his much-younger wife with this trip and booked them into luxury accommodations at every destination.

Mary "Fin" Fincannon was a UPS driver who volunteered that she was big into martial arts. Nick chimed in to say she had black belts in both karate and judo and was not to be messed with, a revelation that drew knowing nods from the rest of the climbers and a smirk of satisfaction from Fin.

Kris and Steffi came next and talked about their jobs at the Sultan Public Library. Though neither volunteered any personal information, Hudson was able to satisfy her curiosity about their relationship. She surmised from their body language and other clues that they were close friends, but not lovers; it was Kris and Fin who were giving each other the knowing looks and glances that bespoke the intimacy of a couple long together.

Anna followed, with a few more tidbits about her family, and then Clay was up to tell his story. He shared nothing about his diagnosis, or the way all his friends had chipped in to send him on this trip. He talked only about his kids, and wife, and the farm that had been passed down to him by his father.

Finally, it was Hudson's turn.

"I'm a reporter and live in New York. My hungover friend and photographer back there is Joe," she said. "We're here to do some skiing."

"She's being modest," Steffi cut in. "Hudson works for the Associated Press and has a Pulitzer Prize, among a bunch of other awards. And she's covered about every major news story you can think of. Wars, hurricanes, political upheavals."

"We got a real live celebrity in the house, huh?" Gary asked, peering at her owl-like through his thick lenses. "That sounds like a cool job."

"Most of the time," Hudson replied. "It's tough, though, to see people in danger or suffering and not be able to do anything much about it other than tell their story."

"Your calling attention to their problems is something, isn't it?" Steffi asked.

"Once in a blue moon it helps bring about change, like an outpouring of donations to hurricane victims. But in places like Syria? North Korea? Much of Africa?" Hudson shook her head. "There's very little any one individual can do to change things there."

"Aren't you ever afraid?" Patti asked. "I read all the time about journalists getting killed in places like Syria. Or they're kidnapped, or locked up, or God knows what."

"Fear is good. It keeps you alert and focused. It's all about the way you manage that fear."

"Well, props to you." Nick absently stroked his stubble of beard. "They couldn't pay me enough to do what you do."

A prerecorded voice boomed over the intercom, speaking in German, then Italian, and finally came the English version. The train was coming in to Chur, so everyone started gathering up their gear. Hudson went to wake Joe.

They kept together as they got off the local express and found the platform for the Bernina Express. The train was already there, but not due to leave for fifteen minutes, so several people darted into the terminal for drinks and snacks to go. Since she and Joe had picked up some groceries the day before, they went right onto the train to find their seats. The only other people in their first-class panorama car were an elderly Japanese couple seated several rows away.

Clay tagged along to help with their gear. "I should go find my seat," he said once they had everything stowed in the luggage compartment at the end of the car. "Do you think it's okay, though, if I take a good look around first class before I do? Sure is fancy. Even more than the pictures."

"Of course. In fact, you can come sit here in my seat for a while once we get going, if you like."

"Or mine," Joe added. "I'll be taking pictures most of the time and won't even be here. These windows don't open."

"Very kind of you both." Clay meandered up the aisle, taking in the wide, plush leather chairs with footrests, sleek pop-up tables, power outlets, and charcoal-gray carpeting. The most jaw-dropping feature were the enormous panoramic windows that curved upward into the ceiling, creating a glass cocoon that allowed for nearly unrestricted views of the landscape and sky.

As he passed by to exit the car, Hudson told Clay, "We'll come find you once we get under way. I'm sure we can all sit together for most of the trip. Doesn't seem to be a lot of people on the platform. At least not for these cars."

Hudson could see a few dozen people getting onto the regular passenger cars in the front of the train, but only a handful had apparently opted for the extra expense of the panoramic view. They might gain a few more people in St. Moritz and other smaller stations along the route, but that should still leave ample empty seats.

She saw the climbing club come out of the terminal, walking slowly because of their heavy packs and the bags in their hands. Anna was with them.

Not far behind them all were four kids: a young girl of about sixteen and three boys, probably between ten and twelve. She recognized them by their distinctive clothes, features, and other clues. Romanies. Gypsies.

Millions of them, displaced from their homelands, had settled throughout Europe and beyond, mostly in urban areas. Long persecuted and ostracized because of their cultural differences, some kept to their traditionally nomadic lifestyle, going from crude encampment to crude encampment. Others assimilated into their host countries, often in low-paying seasonal jobs because they lacked the proper identification papers. But there was also a criminal element among the Romanies: organized gangs, often made up primarily of women and children, adept at thievery and cons of all descriptions. Their primary targets were distracted tourists, and they did most of their work at crowded landmarks and on buses, subways, and trains.

"Joe, take a look," she said. He'd been with her when she'd done stories on them in the past, and both had thwarted several attempts to pick their pockets while on assignment.

"Oh, that's not good," he said as he studied the scene unfolding out their window. "Over there." He pointed at a man on a bench pretending to read a newspaper but surreptitiously watching the goings-on as well. Another Romany, likely the mastermind of the group.

"Keep an eye on our stuff," she told him as she got up and headed quickly toward the doors.

Chapter Nine

Steffi was chatting with Anna about their vacation itineraries when a flash of movement out of the corner of her eye made her look toward the train, just in time to see Hudson emerge from one of the panorama cars. She had a stern, almost angry expression, and she was on a near dead run toward Gary, who was busily chatting up an attractive young girl, who seemed to be admiring his tattoos.

Before Steffi had time to register what was happening, Hudson had swooped past Gary to roughly grab a young boy by the back of his coat. Two other boys standing near them scattered, quickly disappearing into the crowd.

"Give it back," Hudson warned the child with menace in her voice, "and no *polizia*." She held out her free hand and gestured impatiently.

Steffi saw her glance toward a man sitting on a bench nearby who was watching them all. He gave a very slight nod before he got up and headed into the terminal.

The boy relinquished something and scurried away when Hudson let him go.

"Hey! That's mine!" Gary said when he spotted the thick brown wallet in Hudson's hand. Realizing what had just happened, he looked around, but the girl he'd been talking to had also vanished.

"What the heck was that all about?" Anna asked as they all clustered around Hudson.

"Pickpockets," Hudson replied. "Those were Romanies. It's a terrible problem in a lot of the big cities, particularly around tourist attractions and on crowded buses and trains. Kids, mostly, working in teams. One distracts you while the others swoop in. Come on, let's all get our seats. Just watch yourselves. Some more may be working the train."

Gary stuck his wallet into the inside pocket of his coat. "Damn, they were good, the little pricks. Can't thank you enough, Hudson."

"No worries."

As they all headed toward the train, Steffi came abreast of Hudson to ask, "How did you know?"

"Their behavior, mostly," she replied. "I've done a few stories about the Romany. It's a shame that a relatively tiny percentage of them are criminals. They've made it tough on the rest. You can't blame the kids, who are often forced to do this. You just have to be real careful of them in big cities if you see them in groups, begging or trying to engage you."

"How do you manage to retain your faith in human nature?" Steffi asked. "Covering the kinds of stories you do?"

"There are enough good ones out there to tip the balance, at least most of the time," Hudson replied. "The people who step up in time of crisis. Like those who rushed to help the victims of the Boston Marathon bombing, you know?"

"I often wonder how I'd react in a situation like that," Steffi said. "You'd like to think you'd do the right thing, but I guess you never really know until you're tested, do you?"

"I think that's an accurate assessment." Hudson smiled. "Somehow, I suspect you'd do all right." They were alone on the platform now. Everyone else had boarded and the train was due to leave momentarily.

"Better get on, I guess," Steffi said. "You going to join us later?"

"Yup. I'll come find you once the conductor's gone around to check tickets." Hudson headed toward the first-class cars with a quick wave good-bye.

Steffi could see her climbing friends clustered around the windows of one of the second-class cars, beckoning to her. She boarded the steps and dropped off her bags at the luggage rack on the end, then went into the heated passenger compartment and found her seat across from Kris and Fin just as the train started to move.

As Hudson had predicted, they had the car virtually to themselves on this cold winter morning. Aside from Anna and the climbing club, the only other passengers were a middle-aged couple, a teenaged girl, and an elderly woman. Clay must have been in one of the other second-class cars.

"Boy, I have to say that getting my wallet stolen sure woke me up," Gary said. "I can't believe how slick they were."

"Probably lots of practice." Nick smoothed the sparse stubble above his lips. "Did you see those other kids take off when Hudson grabbed the one? I bet we'd have lost something else if she hadn't seen what was going on."

"What did the girl say to you?" Patti asked.

"She handed me a piece of cardboard with writing on it in English," he replied. "Something about asking for donations because she'd lost her money and needed bus fare."

Soon they were far from the city, and the voices of her friends and the subtle rhythmic cadence of the train skimming over the tracks faded to white noise as Steffi stared in wonder at the landscape ahead and around them. Living in the shadow of the Cascades, she was well familiar with impressive mountain views in winter, but this scenery was unmatched, and the extra-large windows of the observation cars allowed her nearly unobstructed views on both sides of the train.

Like the rest of Europe and much of the United States, Switzerland had seen a record snowfall this season, but she hadn't appreciated just how much had fallen until now. In the full light of day, she could see for miles, and a thick layer of white blanketed everything. The tiny hamlets and villages they passed were so deeply buried that the structures were barely discernable. Only the smoke rising from chimneys marked signs of life in the whitescape.

And the track itself was a marvel of engineering, curving and twisting through picturesque valleys as it climbed ever higher toward the heart of the Alps. There was so much to see it was hard to know where to look.

"Clay! Come sit next to me," Anna shouted from the seat behind her, where she was busily snapping photographs.

Steffi looked up to see the Kentucky farmer making his way down the aisle toward them.

"Since you've got this whole route and every bridge and tunnel memorized," Anna told him, "I expect you to give me a heads-up when we're coming to something really spectacular."

"Sure thing," Clay said happily as he joined her. "We're gonna hit a few little tunnels coming up, then the Solis Viaduct. That's the tallest one on the railway. 'Bout three hundred feet. Should be real pretty."

They came to it a short time later, a massive limestone bridge across the Albula River, with eleven tall, curved arches. Shutters went off nonstop as they crossed it, like automatic weapons' fire, punctuated by excited exclamations: "Wow, look over there," "Amazing," "Jesus, that's a long way down!"

The train shot through several short tunnels in the next section of track and over another limestone viaduct, the mountains rising ever steeper on either side as they continued south toward Italy.

"Hey, Clay, just out of curiosity…why do they call this the Bernina *Express*?" Nick asked. "We sure aren't going as fast as we were on the last train."

"Yeah, that's for sure." Clay grinned. "Normally it only goes about twenty, twenty-five miles an hour. May be less right now, with all this snow. It's called an express only 'cause it doesn't stop at a lot of the little stations."

Steffi noticed that the drifts on either side of the track came up nearly to the bottom of the windows in some places, and she wondered whether the railway had encountered problems keeping the line open during this record-breaking winter.

"Hey, guys, how's it going?" a male voice boomed out. "Everybody getting lots of good pics?" Joe Parker was heading toward them up the aisle. He had an expensive Nikon with a long zoom in his hand, and his camera bag was slung over one shoulder. Hudson was a few steps behind him.

"How do you keep from getting the glass reflecting back?" Anna asked. "These windows don't open."

"I'm having the same problem," Kris said. "Sun's too bright."

"Follow me," Joe replied. "I read online that the windows in the luggage compartments open." There was one at the front end of every car, outside the temperature-controlled passenger zone.

"You better get to gettin', if you're gonna," Clay said. "We're closing in quick on the Landwasser Viaduct, one of *the* most biggest, baddest bridges you'll ever see. Long and curving, real high, and at the end, the train shoots into a tunnel carved in the side of a cliff."

"I remember seeing a photo of that one online," Joe replied as he kept going forward toward the luggage area. Anna and Kris followed, cameras in hand.

"What's up?" Hudson paused in the aisle, looking down at Steffi with a smile. "Enjoying the ride?"

"How can you not? Want to sit?" Steffi scooted over to the window seat even before Hudson could answer. She wanted to take every opportunity she could to spend time with the reporter and get to know her better. She'd never met anyone quite like her.

"Sure. For a while." Hudson eased into the aisle seat as the train entered another short tunnel. When they emerged on the other side, they could see the stone viaduct just ahead.

After another flurry of picture-taking as they crossed the span, Steffi shut off her camera to save the battery. They surely had a lot more marvels to see in the next four hours. "I can't believe you don't have a camera," she told Hudson.

"I never bother if I'm traveling with Joe," she replied. "I know he'll get better photos than I ever could, and it leaves me free to just relax and enjoy the view."

"Hadn't thought of that. Think if I give him my e-mail address he might send me a few?"

"I'm sure he would."

Steffi was pleased to hear it, and not just because of the high-quality images she'd likely get from him to remember the trip. Having Joe's e-mail would provide her a way to keep in touch with Hudson as well. "Can you believe all this snow?" The higher the elevation, the deeper the drifts outside. "We sure lucked out getting a nice sunny day for this trip." Visibility was excellent, allowing Steffi to see mountains even in the far distance, an azure sky outlining their jagged white crests.

"Yeah. The conductor said they've had one blizzard after another for weeks. They got more than another foot up here just last night, and a new storm is supposed to come in, in a day or two."

Steffi got half out of her seat, so she could turn and talk to Clay. "What's coming up in the next section?"

"Between here and St. Moritz are some of the best tunnels of all, maybe anywhere in the world," he replied. "Four big spirals and two curved." He pulled a well-worn map from his pocket. "And...let's see, four more viaducts that go over big gorges. Gosh, I sure wish Sarah could see all this. Pictures just don't do it justice."

"You sure got that right," Hudson said.

During the next hour, Steffi and Hudson made small talk as they took in the scenery, comparing common interests and sharing stories of past vacations. Steffi also took another two hundred and fifty pictures, relying on Clay to point out the best photo ops. The train bypassed several small stations without stopping, and she noticed that two of them were shuttered and closed up for the season, the drifts of snow so high they blocked the entrances.

They didn't see Anna and Joe again until the overhead intercom announced they were pulling in to St. Moritz. Passengers on the Bernina Express were reminded they had to transfer to another platform if they were to continue on to Tirano, so everyone began collecting their gear. Joe and Hudson returned to their first-class car, and Clay went with them to help with their luggage.

"How long before the next train leaves, anybody know?" Kris asked. "Do we have time to run into the terminal for snacks?"

Nick nodded. "Clay said we have fifteen minutes or so."

Everyone dispersed once they pulled into the station. Many headed inside for drinks or extra camera batteries, Steffi, Kris, and Fin among them.

"Let's get some more lunch stuff," Steffi said when she spotted a café with sandwiches to go.

"I admit I can outeat most anyone," Kris replied. "But with what you got yesterday and this morning, don't we have plenty already?"

"It's for Clay. I don't think he brought anything along, and he doesn't strike me as having a lot of money. There's supposed to be a food cart on the train, but we sure haven't seen one yet, and you know anything on there is going to cost you double."

"Aw, that's so sweet. He's such a nice guy," Fin said.

Steffi selected a couple of sandwiches, chips, and a few assorted beverages to last Clay the whole journey. On impulse, she also grabbed a trio of different Swiss chocolate bars.

"Those for Clay or me?" Kris asked as Steffi paid for the items. "'Cause I've already got plenty."

"Neither," Steffi replied. "They're for Hudson."

"Oh? For?"

"A thanks for saving Gary's wallet."

"That all?" Kris asked. "Sure you don't have a little crush on our new reporter friend?"

"Are you on drugs?" The suggestion was ludicrous. Wasn't it? Well, maybe not *ludicrous*. Despite the amazing view out the window, she *had* found it impossible not to keep glancing over at Hudson in the seat beside her. But who could blame her? The woman was larger than life. Funny. Charming. Bright. Brave. Intoxicatingly beautiful. Okay, so maybe she did have a little crush on Hudson. But she wasn't about to admit it.

Kris laughed. "Okay, okay. Just thought maybe you'd finally decided to emerge from your self-imposed cocoon."

"May I remind you that my sabbatical from dating is a *good* thing? You, better than anyone, know how much I need this. And when I *am* ready, I'll go for someone I might have an actual chance of building a future with. Certainly not a celebrity reporter who's probably straight."

"If you say so." Kris sounded unconvinced.

"Come on, we need to find our platform."

A quick check of the departure board in the terminal led them to their next train, which looked a lot like the one they'd just gotten off. Two regular passenger cars, silver in color, followed the engine. Behind them were the red Bernina Express specialty cars: four second-class and two first-class at the very end. Just as before, many more people had opted for the cheaper cars in front than the pricier ones with panorama windows. Their car had few people in it except the climbing club.

As they pulled away from St. Moritz, Kris's innuendo continued to play out in Steffi's imagination. Hudson would certainly be a prize catch for anyone. In addition to all of her other attributes, she'd devoted her life to making a difference in the world, and Steffi respected that fact a great deal. Hudson's only downside as a potential partner appeared to be that she was on the road so much.

Stop dreaming. She's way out of your league and totally inappropriate for you. That had always been her problem: falling too fast and picking the wrong women. After all, that was why she was taking a break from involvements. When would she ever learn?

Steffi could only hope to find someone as compelling as Hudson whenever she was finally ready to start dating again. In the meantime, she had plenty to occupy her attention. This next stretch took them high above the tree line over the Bernina Pass, more than seven thousand feet above sea level. It was certain to be memorable.

CHAPTER TEN

As they headed out of St. Moritz, mountains rose sharply in all directions around them, so close Hudson could make out details with her naked eye: craggy peaks sheathed in snow, sprawling glaciers, massive rock outcroppings.

The enormous curved windows were definitely worth the price here, providing optimum views of both sides of the track, and the railway itself continued to be nearly as mind-blowing as the landscape. Another arched limestone viaduct took them over the Inn River, and then they shot through another tunnel, longer than any so far.

Twenty minutes later, the conductor came through and checked their tickets, freeing them to change seats again. Joe was impatient to resume his photographic record of the journey and immediately headed forward toward the second-class area with his camera. Hudson slung her daypack over her shoulder and followed, after she'd paused at the luggage rack to dig through her bag for the foodstuffs they'd bought at a little grocery the day before. Ordinarily, she wouldn't have minded enjoying this amazing view in solitude. But it had been a much richer experience sharing it with Steffi sitting beside her; the woman's exuberance was contagious.

She made her way slowly up the aisle, alternating her attention between the view outside and the people on the train. Both first-class cars were nearly empty, with only a handful of people spread between them.

The second-class section was only slightly more crowded and seemed to consist of an equal mix of winter sports enthusiasts—

judging from their ski parkas and other clues—and tourists here only for the view. In addition to Japanese and Italian, she heard snippets of German and Spanish as she made her way from one car to the next.

She finally spotted a familiar face in the third car she checked, but it wasn't one she expected. Or welcomed.

J.T. Steiger was an arrogant prick who shared both her interests—journalism and extreme skiing—though in her opinion he was mediocre at reporting and kept his job only because his Ken-doll good looks scored well in focus groups. They crossed paths now and then, in the field or on the slopes, and she'd long ago tired of his bullying narcissism and efforts to get under her skin. "Hudson?" He stepped out into the aisle, blocking her way. "Well, well, well. This trip just got a lot more interesting."

"I'm headed to meet friends, J.T. No time to chat."

"Don't be that way, Hudson. Join us. Relax a while." He turned toward the two guys with him. "She loves to play hard to get."

"Make that *impossible* to get…" She glanced pointedly down at his groin and smiled. "With your shortcomings, I mean."

His friends laughed, but Steiger's expression darkened. "Still a comedian. Better watch yourself the next time we meet up somewhere there's nobody else around. We'll see how funny you are then."

She took a step forward so their faces were inches apart. "You don't scare me. Your reporting does, though. I'm afraid one day you might actually get something right." The reference was to a live report he'd filed on campaign-contribution irregularities that his network had to later retract. The public embarrassment had made national headlines.

"Fucking bitch." He balled his fists.

"Hey, J.T.," one of his friends said. "Come on, man. Let it go."

"We're a long way from finished," he said in a low voice. He stayed where he was for several more seconds, glaring at her, before he turned to the side to let her pass.

Hudson went through the partition to the luggage area and found Anna taking pictures through the open window above the rack. She had her coat on, and thin driving gloves, to help ward off the chill.

"Getting some good shots?" Hudson asked.

"Amazing. I had Joe tweak the settings. Such a difference in the contrast and glare." Anna stopped what she was doing and peeked into the paper bag Hudson was cradling. "Time for lunch?"

"Getting there for me. Come on, we've got plenty."

Anna shut the window. "Lead on. I bought some stuff, too. We can have a picnic."

Clay had already joined the climbers, who were in the next car they came to. Everyone had apparently had the same idea, because they were clustered around two tables loaded with food and drinks.

"There you are," Clay said when he spotted Hudson. He had a half-eaten ham and cheese baguette in his hand. "We were gonna come lookin' for you. Your friend's up there, taking pictures." He gestured toward the luggage compartment farther forward.

"Thanks." She handed her bag of groceries to Anna. "Throw this into the mix. Be right back."

She found Joe hunched over, his telephoto lens aimed out the half-opened window. He clicked a new photo every couple of seconds, so absorbed in what he was doing he didn't notice she was there.

"Aren't you cold?" she asked.

The luggage area lacked heat vents, and Joe was wearing only his wool sweater and jeans. She could feel the cold air rushing in from several feet back, and Joe's bare hands were nearly outside the car.

"Yeah, getting there." He straightened and held out his camera. "Take this a sec." He rubbed his hands together briskly, trying to warm them. "Incredible out there, huh?"

She nodded. "Beautiful. But take a break, it's time for lunch."

They headed back to join the others. Everyone had pooled their resources, so they had a good selection to choose from: a dozen different kinds of soda, beer, wine, and water to drink, and an eclectic assortment of food: sandwiches, chips, fruit, salad, chocolate, cookies.

Hudson had hoped to sit with Steffi again, but she was currently surrounded by her climbing friends, so she grabbed a Coke, caprese sandwich, and chocolate bar and slid into the empty aisle seat beside Clay instead. He'd finished his baguette and was halfway through an apple, but his full attention was on the scenery; he glanced over at her only long enough to see who'd joined him.

"We're gonna climb now, all the way up to the pass," he said between bites. "Did'ja know this is the steepest railway in the Alps?"

"No, I didn't. But it's easy to believe."

"Keep an eye out to the left side, everybody," he told the group. "We're coming up on one of the biggest glaciers in the Alps. Supposed to be famous, but I never could find out how to pronounce it." He showed his faded map to Hudson. "Do you know?"

"Morteratsch glacier." She turned in her seat. "Did you hear that?" she asked Joe, who was across the aisle one row back.

"Yup." Joe grinned. "Can't wait."

"We're skiing it tomorrow," she told Clay.

"A glacier? You can ski on a glacier?"

"Sure. They have an actual ski run there. I'm sure it's clearly marked, and I bet it's inspected all the time."

Another sudden onslaught of camera shutters going off drew her gaze to the window. The Morteratsch glacier was a winding frozen river that bridged two high peaks. From a mile away, it was impossible to see the ski run or any people that might be on it, but the glacier's massive crevasses and building-sized ice seracs were easily visible.

The train shot past another small station without stopping and entered a wide curve, where it began to parallel the public road that ran over the pass. The road was closed for the winter, and as the train climbed steeper still, the snowpack deepened further outside their windows. They were near the edge of the tree line now, and the stunted spruces they could see were mere white cones, their trunks buried and boughs so deeply covered that nary a trace of green could be seen.

"We're almost to the pass," Clay said. "Lots of tunnels and galleries up there."

"Galleries?" Kris asked.

"Snow sheds. They help keep drifts off the track, where it comes real close to the side of a mountain," he explained.

They reached one soon, a long protected chute made of wood and steel and concrete, open on the side away from the mountain so the view from the train would not be obstructed.

Joe got up and chucked the remains of his lunch into the communal trash bag someone had started. "I'm going to take some more photos," he told Hudson. "After I go grab my coat. Need anything?"

"I'm good, thanks." Hudson was content to stay where she was, marveling at the ever-changing view. Beside her, Clay seemed equally engrossed, comparing the terrain they were traversing with the photos of his mock-up at home.

"You got it all absolutely correct," she told him. "Even down to the shape of the peaks up here."

"Snow's way off, though. Lot deeper than I guessed from looking at pictures."

"No one could anticipate this monster of a winter," she said.

As though in response to their conversation, the intercom clicked on, and a disembodied voice informed them in three languages that the next two stations—Diavolezza and Bernina Lagalb—were closed because of the record snowfall, as were the cable-car attractions both were known for.

The train rounded a steep curve and suddenly leveled off. They were finally on top of the Alps, crossing the Bernina Pass. Ahead of them lay a long, wide, twisting valley, with peaks on either side. They passed by the first closed station, a solitary shuttered building in a vast plain of white, then the second a few minutes later, as the track moved from one side of the valley to the other, skirting a frozen lake.

The climbing club had spread out around the near-empty car, so that everyone could get window seats facing the best views. Hudson and Clay were the only ones not snapping pictures.

"Hey, d'you mind if I take you up on your offer and sit in first class for a while?" Clay asked.

"Go for it. I was in 8A." She got up to let him out and dug her ticket stub out of the back pocket of her jeans. "Take this with you, just in case the conductor comes around again."

"I'll be back in a half hour or so," he said. "Once we start down the other side."

She took the window seat after he left, and almost instantly, Steffi slid into the empty one beside her, as though she'd been waiting for the opportunity.

"Are we having fun?" Steffi asked with a big grin, and once again, Hudson was struck by her infectious ebullience. "I know you've been all over the world, but come on…even *you* have to be blown away by all this. Am I right?"

Hudson smiled back. She *was* enjoying herself, especially in Steffi's company. She felt more relaxed and content than she had in ages. "I won't argue. I can't think of a more compelling train ride. Truly spectacular, and better by the minute."

"I am *so* glad I stocked up on batteries. If this nice weather holds, I'm going to fill this memory card before we get to Italy."

The farther south they traveled across the pass, the more the valley narrowed. The mountains were closing in on either side of the track, and for the first time, Hudson felt a niggling of unease as she studied the cliffs and pinnacles ahead.

The clear, temperate day might be great for photographs, but on these steep slopes, the sun's rays could also rapidly destabilize a snowpack, exploiting any weakness in its construction.

She'd seen a lot of impressive avalanches on past extreme-ski trips and had been close enough to a few not to want to repeat the experience. The resorts around St. Moritz would no doubt be using explosives and other counter-measures to trigger small, controlled snow slides, minimizing the risk to guests within their perimeter. But she and Joe were planning to do a lot of heli-skiing, off-piste, just them and an expert local guide.

Their outfitter hadn't expressed any concern about conditions when they'd checked in and gotten their tickets yesterday, and surely the company would have said something if the risk was too high. EurAdventures had an excellent safety record; they equipped all heli-skiers with an avalanche beacon, aluminum shovel, collapsible snow probe, and first-aid kit, in addition to their skis and poles. Parkas, climbing, and camping gear were all available for an extra fee, as was the latest in personal avalanche protection: airbag-like floatation devices that could be deployed with the pull of a ripcord. She and Joe had both opted not to take advantage of these because of the extra weight involved, but she was now reconsidering that decision. If the mountains they'd be skiing looked anything like these, they'd need every safety precaution possible.

Massive cornices of snow, bigger than any she'd ever seen, dangled precariously from every ridge and summit in sight. The nearest, on the mountain they were passing, was hundreds of feet long and overhung the steep slope beneath like a gigantic white tidal wave.

Her gaze followed the fall line below the cornice. When the snow balcony collapsed, it would feed into the long, wide gully beneath it, a natural avalanche chute leading right to the track. Engineers had installed a row of steel-mesh barriers along this section to protect the train, but the grills were already heavily burdened with snow from previous avalanches and didn't look capable of containing much more.

The next mile or so ahead, where the shrinking flat plain of the Bernina Pass became a deep gorge, was even more worrisome. Here, the rail line and the closed road ran side by side along a wide ledge, cut into the side of the steep mountain to their right, so the whole route seemed to be at risk of avalanche. Barriers and galleries had been erected along the route, but only in those places where the danger was greatest, and these, too, were already heavily laden.

No matter how beautiful it was, she'd be glad to be through it and on the other side.

They closed in on the gorge. The ground dropped off on the other side of the road, to her left, while the mountain to her right became an intimidating wall of white, so close to the windows she felt mildly claustrophobic.

Hudson's attention was focused on the seemingly bottomless gorge thirty or so feet from the edge of the track, when Steffi grabbed her shoulder and several excited voices spoke at once.

"Look!"

"Oh, my God!"

"Up there!"

"Holy shit!"

The cornice on the mountain to their left—across the gorge—had collapsed, triggering an impressive avalanche. The snow slide had progressed several hundred feet already and was quickly gaining momentum and size, billowing out an enormous cloud of powder as it raced downhill.

The chatter around her diminished, and the train grew eerily quiet except for the sounds of camera shutters as the avalanche advanced toward them with blinding speed. It posed no threat; the wide gorge would protect them. But the magnitude of the exploding storm of snow was awesome and terrifying nonetheless.

Hudson's heartbeat accelerated when she caught movement in her peripheral vision. The first slide hadn't even settled when the cornice of the summit beside it gave way, setting off another avalanche just as impressive as the first.

The excitement that had initially run through the train was rapidly turning to concern, judging from the renewed murmurs around her. You didn't have to be an avalanche aficionado to surmise that the danger of more slides—some potentially impacting the train—was extreme in the current conditions.

Nearly everyone in the car had drifted toward the left-hand windows and was fixated on the spectacle unfolding outside when a scream pierced the air.

Hudson half rose and turned toward the source. A teenaged girl was staring in horror up at the mountain to their right. The cliff face they were traversing was too steep for them to see the peak far above them, but in the upper curve of the glass window bloomed an explosion of white, an opaque fog that obscured the sun.

"Run!" Hudson yelled as she shoved Steffi out into the aisle amidst a growing panic of shouts and curses. "End of the car, away from the glass!"

Chapter Eleven

Steffi had barely registered they were in the direct path of an avalanche when Hudson propelled her into the aisle, half-lifting her out of her seat with a surprising strength. She didn't question the shouted directive, nor did anyone else. She fought to keep her footing as everyone rushed the aisle en route to the forward luggage compartment, the only portion of the panorama car with any measure of protection from above.

Kris and Fin reached the partition just ahead of her, and time seemed to slow as they both fumbled for the handle to open it.

Hudson bumped into her roughly from behind, and then Steffi felt more jarring jostles as others tried to shove their way through. When the door sprang open, several people fell forward into a heap on the floor of the luggage compartment, and more scrambled over them. Steffi was pinned under the weight of two or three others, though she couldn't tell who they were.

In the next instant, time slowed and the world around them became a nightmare of noise—screeching metal, the splintering of wood, a *whoosh* of wind, screams and cries, shattering glass—and the train shook so violently she chipped two teeth and split her lip when her face slammed against the floor of the car. The metallic tang of blood in her mouth registered only briefly as the bone-jarring Mixmaster of a ride continued for several more seconds.

All at once, an absolute blackness swallowed their car, giving rise to more screams and curses from all around her.

And then it was suddenly over. They weren't moving anymore, and a stunned, eerie quiet descended on the train for several seconds, punctuated only by the moans of the injured.

"Somebody got a light?" Gary's voice.

"Who's hurt?" Hudson spoke at the same time, her voice so close that Steffi realized it was her weight that was pinning her to the floorboard. When Hudson moved to sit up, she was able to roll over and breathe freely again.

Anna's cell-phone light flicked on, and then Nick's, dimly illuminating the luggage compartment, and people began to stir, shoving aside the backpacks and bags that had spilled from the racks on either side of them. Their expressions registered a gamut of emotions: shock, fear, uncertainty, and relief at being alive.

Fin groaned loudly. She was slumped against one of the luggage racks, half buried under a pair of EA duffel bags. She looked dazed, and her face was streaked with blood.

"Fin!" Kris scrambled over the chaos of luggage to kneel beside her. "Anna, get your light over here!" she said as she tossed aside the bags.

As Anna threaded her way over to them with her cell, Curt's panicked shout drew their attention toward the dark corner nearest the exit.

"Patti! Patti!" He was hunched over the still figure of his wife. "Somebody get a goddamn light over here!"

As Nick rushed over with his phone, Steffi scanned her surroundings in the dim light, searching for her backpack. When she spotted it, she dug in one of the side pockets for her mini flashlight and turned it on, then used it to find her climbing headlamp, deeper within her pack.

"Jesus, God! No!" Curt wailed in anguish, as Nick and Hudson, grim-faced, stood over the couple.

Steffi gave her headlamp to Kris, then hurried over to Curt with her flashlight. She gasped when she saw Patti's face and almost immediately felt Hudson's steadying, comforting hand on her shoulder.

Patti's neck was broken. Her lifeless eyes stared up at her husband. There was nothing anyone could do.

Curt seemed frozen in disbelief. "This can't be happening," he said, his voice breaking. "This was supposed to be our honeymoon." Tears streamed down his face as he closed her eyes, then gently enfolded her in his arms and hugged her close.

"I'm so sorry, Curt," Steffi said.

Nick crouched down and put an arm over Curt's shoulder. "Oh, Jesus, man. Can I do anything?"

"No." Curt maintained his embrace, rocking Patti's body against his. "Just…leave us. Give me time to…to…" He broke down, sobbing.

The three of them turned away to give him what little privacy was available in the small compartment.

In the space between the luggage racks, Kris had gotten out one of the EA-supplied first-aid kits and was bandaging Fin's forehead with Anna's help. From the murmured tones and everyone's frequent glances toward the corner, Steffi could tell all of them were keenly preoccupied with Patti's sudden and tragic death.

Someone, she noticed, had shoved most of the luggage back onto the racks to give them more room to work.

"Can I borrow your flashlight?" Hudson asked. "It's a lot brighter than my phone."

"Sure, okay." Steffi handed it over. "I know we've got more headlamps in these EA bags."

"I'll get some more out so we can get a look at what's what." Nick reached for the nearest gear duffel and started digging through it.

When Hudson took the flashlight and returned to the large glass sliding door that separated them from the passenger compartment, Steffi followed, anxious to see for herself how the rest of the train had fared in the avalanche. She couldn't understand why they hadn't all been swept down the mountain.

Hudson put the tip of the light against the door to minimize the glare and scanned the interior of the glass-topped car beyond. The beam of the penlight was narrow, limiting the field of view, but the powerful LED bulb cast a bright enough beam that they could see nearly the entire length of the aisle.

The passenger car was nearly intact, though one section of the glass ceiling toward the other end of the car had shattered. When

Hudson trained the light on that section, they could see a large timber and bent steel rods protruding through the place where the glass had been.

The long windows on the opposite side, facing the gorge, were intact—but beyond them Steffi could see no daylight any more, only snow, packed up tight against the glass.

"What the heck happened?" Steffi asked.

"We got incredibly lucky, that's what happened," Hudson replied. "We're in one of the snow sheds Clay told us about."

Clay. Oh God. Who else was missing? *Joe Parker.*

So much had happened, and so quickly, she hadn't registered until now that Hudson's friend and photographer wasn't with them, nor was Clay. "Where…where's Joe?"

"I'm not sure," Hudson replied. "I'm going to look for him."

"Are you certain it's safe?" The avalanche had obviously compromised the structural integrity of the shed; who was to say it couldn't collapse still further and splinter the remaining ceiling panels?

"I don't really give a rat's ass." Hudson tried to open the thick sliding-glass door to the compartment, but it seemed to be jammed. "I need something to pry this open with."

"Wait! I know…" Steffi grabbed the nearest EA duffel and pulled out an ice ax. "Will this work?"

"Yeah, thanks." Hudson inserted the blade end of the pick into the space between the door and frame and leaned on it with all her might, but it still refused to budge.

"Let me help." Steffi got next to her, and they both gripped the long handle and pulled. Together, they were able to break whatever impediment sealed the door closed, and Hudson was then able to slide the panel open far enough to squeeze through.

Hudson paused to look back at her. "I'm sorry about your friend."

"Thanks. I…I hope Joe's okay. Please be careful."

Hudson nodded and gave her an encouraging smile, but her dark eyes were worried. She set off down the aisle of the compartment, flashlight in one hand and ice ax in the other, stepping over random debris as she went: the discards from their lunch, personal possessions quickly abandoned, and the pieces of the shed that had punched through the glass. Her silhouette was outlined by the glow from her light.

Near the end of the car, Steffi saw her pause.

"There's people hurt, here!" Hudson hollered. "Bring a first-aid kit!"

"I'll go," Nick said from behind Steffi.

She turned to find him rummaging through the open EA duffel she'd wrested the ice pick from. "We both will. See if you can find more lights, too." The prospect of leaving the relative safety of the luggage compartment scared the hell out of her, but she couldn't be the only one not stepping up to do whatever was necessary.

They found Hudson hunched over an unconscious middle-aged man, her hands pressing firmly on his thigh. His pants were bloodstained, and a widening pool of crimson was spreading on the floor around him. Beside him was a woman, roughly the same age, who lay still and unmoving.

"She's dead," Hudson told them. "Nick, get out some gauze and a roll bandage or whatever you can find. We need to stop this bleeding." As he flipped open the first-aid kit and started to pull out supplies, she turned to Steffi. "Across the aisle. See what you can do for her."

Steffi pivoted, and the beam of her headlamp found a girl, probably in her early teens, slumped over in one of the seats. She had a dark, Mediterranean complexion, like the couple across the aisle from her, and Steffi wondered as she approached whether they were related.

The girl wasn't moving.

With a sick dread in the pit of her stomach, Steffi reached out and pressed two fingers to her throat. She had a pulse. Faint, but steady. "Can you hear me?" No response. "She's alive," she told the others, "but out cold. I don't know what to do. I can't see any blood or sign of injury."

"Does anybody in your group have any medical training?" Hudson asked.

There were no doctors or nurses. Had anyone ever mentioned taking first aid or CPR? "Not that I know of."

"No, I don't think so, either." Nick finished bandaging the man's leg.

"Our first priority is to get them stabilized, and warm." Hudson flashed her light beam above their heads. Though that particular curving window panel was still intact, the roof of the shed above it had been badly damaged by the weight of the snow on it; the wood was splintered and cracked in places, and a few of the steel supports were bent and pressing up against the external frame of the car. "I hate to move them, but let's get them to the other end of the car where it looks more solid and where we can keep an eye on them. Do any of you have sleeping bags?"

"No, but we have several of these." Nick pulled a small silver emergency-survival blanket out of the first-aid kit and held it up.

"Those'll help. Can you get Gary to help you move them? I'd like to keep searching for Joe."

"No prob, but don't you want somebody to go with you?" Nick asked.

"I'll let you know if I need help. But thanks."

As Nick headed off to get Gary, Hudson went to the rear door and put her light up against the window. She peered out at the walkway that led to the door of the next panorama car in line.

"What can you see?" Steffi asked.

"Not much," Hudson replied. "The next car is still there, and it's upright. Can't see much el—Wait! I see a light!" The tone of her voice changed instantly from grim to hopeful. "Someone's moving around over there." She tried the handle and slipped through the door without another word as soon as it opened.

Nick soon returned with both Gary and Kris, and as the two men bent to carry the injured man, Kris came over to help her with the girl.

"How's Fin?" Steffi asked.

"She's got a big gash on the side of her head, but I think the bleeding's stopped," Kris replied. "I'm worried she might have a skull fracture or concussion. But all things considered, she's pretty damn lucky."

Steffi knew Kris was thinking about Patti. "I feel so bad for Curt."

"Yeah. Poor guy. He's still in there, holding her. I can't imagine." Kris frowned. "We all tried to make calls out, but nobody could get a signal. Big surprise." She shone her light on Steffi's face. "Hey, what about you? Your lip is cut. And did you chip a tooth?"

"Two. But I'm fine. Forgot it happened, even."

"Good thing we have dental insurance, huh?" Kris said without humor as she bent over the unconscious girl. "I'll get her shoulders if you take her feet. We've got a space cleared out for them."

"We need to get them warm, and us, too," Steffi said as she helped hoist the girl into the aisle.

"Yeah, I'm starting to feel it. Got to be below freezing in here, and you know it's only going to get a lot colder tonight."

Steffi looked at her watch. A little after eleven a.m., still several hours of daylight left. They'd no doubt have to airlift everyone out since the road was closed and the track was probably blocked. "Don't you think we'll get rescued before then?"

"I hope so," Kris replied grimly. "I hope so." But from her expression, it was clear she didn't believe that was going to happen.

They carried the girl to the end of the car and laid her next to the unconscious man. Gary and Nick had wrapped him in a survival blanket and were unwrapping another for them. As they covered the girl with it, she moaned in pain and her eyes flickered open.

"Can you hear me?" Kris asked, kneeling over her. "Where do you hurt?"

The mumbled response was in another language.

"English?" Steffi asked. "Can you speak English?"

The girl shook her head and said something else in what sounded like Italian. She moaned and pressed her hand against her side.

"Can I see?" Kris asked, indicating she wanted to examine the girl.

The teenager nodded, and when Kris pulled her sweater up, they saw that her abdomen and right rib cage were bruised and swollen.

"Broken ribs, maybe," Kris said. "I hope she's not bleeding internally."

"Is there anything we can do for her?" Nick asked.

As they all looked at each other helplessly, the girl moaned again and seemed to come more fully awake and aware of their dire situation. She glanced about with wide eyes and, when she caught sight of the unconscious man lying beside her, shouted, "Babbo! Babbo!" and reached out to him.

"Her father, I bet," Gary said in a low voice. "How do we tell her that her mother died?"

"I say we don't, for now." Anna had come over to join their little group. She crouched over the girl and put a hand reassuringly on her shoulder. "Shhh. Rest now."

The teen seemed to understand and slumped back with a groan.

"She doesn't need more bad news," Anna said to the others. "She needs to fight to survive. Like we all do. I think it's time we got some warmer clothes on and started to make a plan."

"I'm for that," Gary replied, blowing into his hands. "I can hardly feel my fingers any more."

"Can someone loan me something?" Anna asked. "My luggage is in the next car."

"Sure," Steffi replied. "I've got plenty of stuff in my pack."

They all started rummaging through their bags for long underwear, sweaters, coats, gloves, extra socks. Steffi gave Anna one of her heavy fleece pullovers, a woolen hat, ski socks, and silk long underwear, saving her insulated ski pants and parka for herself. Kris helped Fin add another layer to what she was wearing, while Nick and Gary donned their coats and took Curt's to him and convinced him to put it on. Once he did, they stayed with him, speaking in low tones.

It felt good to be acting as a united front and actually *doing* something to improve their situation, but Steffi couldn't help but worry about Hudson. She had to be getting very cold by now herself. Had she found Joe? *Why didn't I go with her? She shouldn't have gone alone.*

What had become of the rest of the train?

Chapter Twelve

Hudson stepped carefully onto the walkway between the cars, a passageway protected from the elements by silvery, accordion-like shields that pulled out from around both doors and fastened together.

Through the window of the next panorama car, she could see a faint light—no, a pair of lights—and when she got closer, she could hear male voices.

Hudson put her light up to the window to see inside, and instantly the voices became shouts.

"Hey! Who's there?"

"Help!"

"We're trapped!"

A familiar face appeared on the other side of the glass, but it wasn't the one she'd hoped to see. J.T. Steiger stared back at her, his eyes gaunt and lacking their usual bravado. "We can't get the door open!" he yelled. "Find something!"

"Is Joe Parker there with you?" she asked.

"He's here, but his legs are all busted up. There's others injured, too."

The knowledge that Joe was alive instantly calmed a good measure of her anxious worry. "I've got this." She held up the ice ax to show him. "I'll try to pry the door. Put some muscle into it from your side."

He nodded, and she saw one of his friends step up to the door beside him.

Hudson fitted the blade of the ax into the narrow space between the door and frame as she had before and pulled on it with all her might. With all of them working together, it popped open, and she could hear relieved exclamations and a buzz of conversation from those within.

"Where's Joe?" She flashed her light around the small compartment, which was crowded with people, most of them lying on the floor or sitting with their backs against the luggage racks. She could see a mother and two children, two middle-aged Japanese couples in ski gear, an elderly woman, two young men. But not Joe, at least not right away.

She'd seen a great deal of suffering and dead bodies in her lifetime, far too much, she often thought. But like most journalists, she'd learned to disassociate from her emotions in such situations in order to do her job.

This was something else entirely, however. The occupants of this car had suffered more severely than theirs. She could see lots of traumatic injuries: broken bones, lacerations, head injuries—and there were no first responders here, or army medics, or Red Cross workers. They had no one but each other, at least for the moment. Someone—probably J.T. or one of his friends, since they were the only ones moving around and on their feet—had done a piecemeal job of trying to bandage the worst wounds with makeshift bandaging. But these people still needed considerable medical attention, and soon.

"There." J.T. pointed to a corner, at the prone figure of a man. She couldn't see his face, but she recognized Joe's worn leather boots and started toward him.

J.T. pulled her up short with a hand on her arm. "Answer some questions, first. Is help coming? What's it look like out there?"

She yanked away from him. "Our car's the same as yours. You couldn't find a way out?"

"See for yourself, if you want to. I'm getting the hell out of here." He brushed past her, followed by his friends, one of whom was limping badly. The three men all had their coats on, and hats, and gloves. They were even carrying their backpacks and EA ski bags.

Bastard. She went to Joe.

Hudson felt like she'd been punched in the gut when she saw his legs up close. They were both bent in weird angles, making him look like a damn rag doll. His jeans were stained with blood, but he didn't seem to be bleeding any more. His open wounds had been bound with what looked like shredded T-shirts. Joe's eyes were closed, and he looked more boyish and vulnerable than she'd ever seen him.

She knelt over him and put a hand on his cheek. "Can you hear me? Joe?"

His eyes flickered open. "Marco."

"Polo," she replied.

"'Bout time. Pretty damn happy to see your ugly mug."

"Same back atcha. How do you feel?"

"Like I lost a game of chicken with an eighteen-wheeler." He grimaced in pain. "How bad does it look? Pretty fucked up, huh?"

Hudson tried to keep her face impassive. She didn't want to alarm him. "You're a vision, to me. But it may be a while before we get to hit the slopes. You just hang in there, all right? We'll get you fixed up and out of here before you know it."

"Do my best. Getting pretty fucking cold, though." He'd gotten his coat and had it on, but it was open and gaping, and his jeans had been cut to treat him, exposing bare skin.

She zipped up the coat. "I'll get you warm. But I have to go find help. For you and all the rest of these people. Be right back, okay?"

"Not going anywhere."

Before she headed off to get the others, Hudson took a few moments to quickly assess the other injured and reassure them that help was on the way, not that she was certain they understood any of it. Many of those who were conscious stared up at her with blank expressions, but whether from shock or a language barrier, she couldn't know.

She also wanted a quick peek at the rest of the car. She'd hoped to make it back farther to first class to find Clay, once Joe was tended to. No matter how much she tried to tell herself that it wasn't her fault, she couldn't help but feel guilty that Clay likely had been sitting in her seat when the avalanche hit. She also wanted to get her bag, and Joe's, since they contained all their cold-weather ski gear and other essentials. But J.T. had claimed there was no exit that way.

When she opened the door into the passenger compartment and shone her light around, it became quickly obvious why there were so many casualties here. This section of the snow shed had collapsed under the weight of the avalanche, shattering all the panorama window panels and denting in the side of the car nearest the mountain. The new ceiling, a sketchy mix of bent steel beams and shattered timbers, was half the height of the old one, barely high enough to walk under, not that anyone would want to. It was a war zone, with debris and blood spatters everywhere. Halfway down the car, two legs stuck out into the aisle. They weren't moving.

Hudson couldn't see all the way to the door at the far end that led to the next car. But one thing was clear: that area bore the worst of the destruction.

J.T. was right. Doubtful anyone was getting out this way.

Not that there looked to be any easier way out of the other car.

She headed back that way to get help.

❖

"Listen!" Kris shushed them, and everyone instantly obeyed.

Steffi could hear it too, now. Male voices, speaking English. And two flashlight beams were approaching up the aisle in the passenger compartment. She met them at the entryway: three men, all in their thirties. They were warmly dressed in jackets and had their backpacks and gear bags with them. Except for their serious, determined expressions, they seemed oddly as though they'd hardly been in an avalanche at all and were heading forward to get off at the next stop. "Hey, guys!" she called out to them. "Americans?"

"Yes," the first one answered. He was tall and handsome, and he had the look of someone used to being in charge. For some reason, he also looked vaguely familiar. "What's up past this car?" he asked, looking not at her but over her shoulder.

"We haven't checked yet. We've been too busy tending to the injured," Kris replied.

"Do you know if there are any other American survivors?" Steffi asked. "A guy named Joe Parker?"

"He's got two broken legs. Who knows what else. Next car." He glanced down at Fin. "I see you've got first-aid supplies. If you have any more, there are several badly injured people back there who need help." He looked directly at Steffi for the first time. "Now, if you'll let me pass, we'll start looking for a way out of here. The other way is screwed."

Though he towered over her by several inches, she didn't budge right away. "One of our party lost his wife. We'd like a couple of minutes to move them, if you want access to the exits and the door to the next car."

He glared at her for a few seconds. "All right," he finally said. Over his shoulder, he told his friends, "Stay here. I'll go have a look while they clear the area. I'm J.T. Steiger, by the way."

"Steffi Graham."

The others had apparently caught the entire conversation, because when she turned around, she saw that Nick, Gary, and Curt were already lifting Patti's body, now encased in one of the survival blankets.

They all stepped aside to let the cortege through to the passenger compartment, where the silvery shroud was laid between two rows of seats, out of the aisle.

As soon as they'd passed by, Steffi, Kris, and Anna began searching through the EA bags, quickly compiling all their first-aid supplies. The Cascade Climbers had filled the entire luggage area of this car with their own backpacks and the gear bags issued to them by their outfitter. Since each had been given a small but well-equipped kit, they had seven in all, and they'd used only a fraction of their supplies thus far.

"Grab any flashlights or headlamps you find, as well," Kris said.

Anna chimed in. "And any personal stashes of ibuprofen, aspirin, pain pills, antibiotics."

"Warm stuff, too. I wish we had blankets or sleeping bags." Steffi fished through her backpack and took out all her cold-weather gear.

"There's a few more of the survival blankets." Kris got out her bag, and Fin's, and started to go through them.

"I can help." Fin was propped against the luggage rack. She looked much more alert than she had.

"I don't want you moving around any more than you have to," Kris said. "In fact, I'd rather you lie down. It took a long time to get the bleeding stopped."

"I can at least watch those two while the rest of you tend the others," Fin replied, glancing through the partition at the injured Italian girl and her father. "I want to help, and I'm not much good for anything else."

"You sure you're up to it?" Kris asked.

"I'll holler for help if I need to."

"I just wish one of us had at least *some* medical training," Steffi said as they all got ready to go.

"I do." Curt had finally let go of his wife and rejoined them, along with Nick and Gary. He looked haggard and bone weary, as though he'd just aged a decade. "I was an Eagle Scout and a lifeguard. Tell me what I can do."

"Come with us." Kris handed him a headlamp.

But before they could leave, another voice drew their attention.

"A couple of you should stay here and help us." J.T. Steiger motioned for his two friends to join him by the exit doors. "We'll need to clear this whole area of everything and everybody," he added, nodding toward Fin and the luggage.

"Why?" Kris asked.

"There's nothing but snow out of every door," he replied. "The avalanche completely buried us. We're going to have to dig our way out."

CHAPTER THIRTEEN

Associated Press Headquarters
New York, New York

"Everybody here?" Bob Furness, the AP's senior vice president and executive editor, glanced around the V.I.P. conference room as his secretary muted the seven large TV monitors along one wall that were tuned to the major broadcast networks, CNN, Fox News, MSNBC, and BBC America.

The daily eight a.m. editorial meeting was attended by representatives of all the major factions of the wire service. During the next ninety minutes, these twenty or so individuals would decide what major stories would be covered that day and how they would be covered—by their own staff, by stringers in the field, or through the staff of one of the fourteen hundred newspapers that belonged to the AP collective.

"Let's get started," Bob said once everyone had taken seats around the massive cherry conference table. He nodded toward the person sitting directly to his left, the head of the AP's political unit.

The political director spent the next few minutes detailing what his White House and Capitol Hill reporters would be working on. Then the next person in line did the same for their division, and so on, until all present had briefed the group.

They were almost ready to adjourn when several cell phones in the room began ringing or chiming simultaneously—a rare event that almost certainly indicated a major story had just broken.

"What is it?" the head of the entertainment unit asked no one in particular, since he was one of the few whose phone had remained silent.

"Catastrophic avalanches throughout Europe," the managing editor of the international assignment desk replied, staring down at a text on his phone. "That's our big story for today. Excuse me." He hurried out to meet with his staff.

"Let's get some domestic sidebar pieces going," Bob told the others after he'd gone. "Experts, rescuers, meteorologists, people who've survived an avalanche. You know the drill."

"The National Avalanche Foundation would be a good resource," the head of the lifestyles unit said. "They run a school in Washington state for ski patrollers, park rangers, and the like. We did a piece from there last December."

"And the American Avalanche Association," the domestic desk chief added. "We've dealt with them in the past and have contacts there."

"Sounds good. Get busy." Bob dismissed the group. Normally he'd return to his office after the morning meeting, but he didn't have any appointments so he decided to swing by the International Desk to see what kind of coverage they were putting together and to gauge the seriousness of the breaking story. Whenever a massive natural disaster happened, it usually required an enormous reallocation of their available staff, and the logistical nightmare that could entail— particularly in inclement weather—was huge. Europe had been hit even harder this winter than the East Coast had been.

The administrative offices and editorial conference room were located on the third floor of the AP's building on West Thirty-third Street and the International Desk was on the eighth, so he headed to the bank of elevators.

Like its twin, the Domestic Desk, one floor below, the International Desk was a sprawling complex of adjoined desks surrounding a raised central command post, manned by the managing editor on duty. Each cluster of desks represented a major region of the world, excluding the U.S. The staffers who manned them spent much of their time on the phone and on the Internet, gathering information and making assignments in the field. They called upon their own people when they could, supplementing them when necessary by local stringers and freelancers they'd established relationships with.

As soon as he got off the elevator, Bob knew the avalanche story was a major one. The Europe desk was buzzing with activity; they'd already diverted people from covering some of the other regions where nothing much was happening at the moment.

Their editorial staffers were consummate professionals, used to handling breaking news with calm efficiency, and today was no exception. But he could see the gravity of this particular event in their faces. Whenever a disaster was shaping up to be a particularly horrific one, with a high death toll and widespread suffering, even the most jaded veteran reporters among them couldn't help but be affected. A pall seemed to settle over the room during those occasions, and voices were unconsciously lowered, as though they'd all become part of a global wake for the dead and dying.

He'd seen it happen many times in his career. 9/11. Katrina. The Haiti earthquake. The Indian Ocean tsunami. Now the Great Global Winter of '14 had joined those ranks.

Brent Calvin, the managing editor on duty, was being briefed by two of his senior staffers. Bob went over just as they finished up.

"And get Grace to call in more people," Calvin told the pair before dismissing them. He turned to Bob, who was his boss. "This may be the biggest story of the year, if these early reports turn out to be true," he said, his face grim. "There was some kind of 'perfect storm' condition for avalanches today throughout Europe. We're getting reports from France, Italy, Switzerland, Austria, Germany, Slovenia. Entire villages buried and hundreds of miles of roads and railways affected, dozens of major ski resorts hit. Emergency and rescue services throughout the region are overwhelmed and asking for international assistance."

"Ski resorts?" *Hudson and Joe.* Bob's heartbeat accelerated slightly. "Where, exactly?"

Calvin consulted his paperwork. "Let's see…Chamonix, France. St. Anton, Austria. Alagna, Italy. Several in Switzerland, which was apparently the worst hit. St. Moritz, Andermatt, Zermatt—"

"Hang on a minute." Bob pulled out his cell and called his secretary. "Pull the file of reporter vacations and tell me what it says about Hudson and Joe's itinerary for today."

"Sure, Bob. One second." She came back on the line soon after. "They're booked at the Kulm Hotel in St. Moritz this evening."

"Thanks." He turned back to Calvin. "What do we know about St. Moritz specifically?"

"Hudson and Joe are there?"

Bob nodded.

"Damn." Calvin frowned. Hudson and Joe's penchant for extreme skiing was well known in the newsroom. "We have few details at this point. Several areas around there were hit. That's all we know. Want me to call her cell? Make sure they're okay and maybe get them in on this?"

"No. At least, not yet. I sort of half-promised Joe I'd leave them alone for once." He watched the desk staffers at work, studying their faces. Yes, this was definitely going to be a big story that would keep them busy for a long while. "I'll let you get back to work."

Bob returned to his office. He knew Hudson well enough that he was willing to bet that even if Joe balked, she'd be checking in soon herself to see what she could do, since they seemed to be so close to the worst of the devastation.

❖

Bernina Pass, Switzerland

Hudson had just started down the aisle of the passenger compartment when she spotted some of the climbers heading toward her, their headlamps blinding.

Steffi was in the lead. "How's Joe?"

"Not good. There are a lot of people really bad off back there."

"We've pooled all the first-aid supplies," Kris said. "Curt has some first-aid training."

"This way." Hudson led them all into the second car. "Marco," she called out to Joe. "We'll get you fixed up right away."

"Let me take a quick look at everybody and see who's worst off." Curt spent the next couple of minutes doing a quick triage of the injured, using pantomime to communicate with those who were alert and responsive because most seemed to know no English. Then he set the Americans to work, instructing them on the best ways to deal with the range of traumatic injuries represented: broken bones and bruised ribs, lacerations, probable concussions, possible internal injuries.

While she waited for Curt to start on Joe, Hudson opened a couple of the unlocked suitcases stacked on the rack nearby, searching for warmer clothes for the both of them. Her hands were so cold she'd lost the feeling in her fingertips.

She found several heavy sweaters and packed them around his exposed legs. Then she pulled woolen socks over his hands and tucked a small inflatable travel pillow under his head. From the same bag, she got a big hooded sweatshirt for herself, thick ski socks, and leather driving gloves that were way too big for her hands.

"We found a handful of pain pills," Curt said when he'd gotten a good look at Joe's shattered legs. "Hydrocodone. Do you have any allergies?" he asked.

"No. Bring it on," Joe replied.

They gave him one of the pills and a few sips of water from a half-filled bottle they found on the floor of the compartment. The water had already started to ice up.

"Dehydration is going to become a real danger in this cold," Curt said as he redressed Joe's wounds with antibiotic ointment and sterile gauze. "We should collect all the water and drink bottles we can find. If you come upon any, keep them tucked inside your coat so they don't freeze."

"We need to do a thorough search of every bag we can find." Anna was using dental floss and a needle from her travel sewing kit to stitch deep cuts on three of the injured. "We don't know how long we're going to be here. All these people need warmer clothes."

"Yeah, and we can cut the foam from inside the seats and lay them out on that. Be good insulation," Kris suggested.

"Once we get them all stabilized, we should move them into the other car where we can keep an eye on them," Curt said.

"Won't we risk further injuries?" Anna asked.

"None of them seem to have spinal or neck injures, as far as I can tell. Joe will be the toughest to move. He looked up at Hudson. "Find me something to use as splints. Metal, wood, plastic, anything rigid. We need two that are long enough to reach from his armpit to below his feet, and two more that go from his crotch to his feet. I'll also need something for bindings. Luggage straps. Belts. Or just rip several long strips of material. And padding of some kind."

"You got it." She shone her light around the luggage compartment. Beside the small bathroom was a tall vertical rack for storing skis. Four long EA bags, just like the ones she and Joe had been issued, were strapped in, against the wall of the car. She unzipped the nearest one. "Will these do?" she asked.

"Perfect. I'll need two skis and two poles."

She found two luggage straps and ripped strips of material from several shirts to use as bindings and padding for the splints.

"Now comes the not-fun part," he said once they had all the supplies ready. "Hudson, kneel up there by his head and put your arms under his shoulders. I want you to keep him as steady as you can while I straighten his legs and set these open fractures." As she got into position, he leaned over Joe. "How's the pain pill working?"

"Starting to kick in," he replied fuzzily. "It's a little better."

"Not going to lie to you, Joe. This is still going to hurt like hell. You ready?"

"As I'll ever be, I guess." He took a deep breath and let it out. "Go for it."

Hudson winced but held on when Joe screamed in agony. Setting the first leg was bad enough; when Curt got to the other, Joe passed out. She was almost grateful.

"Is he going to be all right?" she asked Curt as he finished up.

"Hudson, I'm no doctor," he replied quietly. "I've no idea what kind of tissue and nerve damage he might have, how his circulation is, or how close I've come to setting the bones right. Plus, we've got shock, hypothermia, infection, and dehydration to worry about as well with him, and all these others. They need to be in a hospital." He got to his feet and went to see how the rest were doing in their efforts to stabilize and treat the injured.

Steffi came over and knelt beside her as Hudson waited for Joe to wake up. "How's he doing?"

"He's going to need a lot of rehab to get back on his feet," Hudson replied. "Months, probably. And it's not going to be pretty, 'cause he's the worst patient on the planet."

"Yeah?"

"Last time he got the flu, he whined like a little girl until I got him some chicken soup from his favorite deli halfway across town."

"You mean a lot to each other."

Hudson nodded. "He's saved my life. Twice. Once in Afghanistan, when he pulled me out of a Humvee under attack by insurgents, and once in Cairo, when we got swept up in a violent street protest." She couldn't imagine her future without Joe an integral part of it, as both her dearest friend and invaluable work partner.

"We'll get him out of here soon, I'm sure," Steffi said. "Why, I bet rescue people are already out there right now, trying to dig us out."

"Dig us out? What do you mean?"

"That guy—J.T., I think his name was—he checked out the exit doors down where we were and said there's nothing on the other side but packed snow," Steffi replied. "These cars are completely buried. He and his friends, and Nick and Gary, are trying to dig out. I presume there's no way out this way, either?"

Buried? Things had happened so fast and she'd been so worried about Joe, Hudson hadn't really stopped long enough to consider the full picture. She'd just sort of assumed that there had to be more left intact than just two cars of the train, that at one end or the other they'd find a way to get out to daylight and rescue. "I don't know if J.T. went all the way down to really check. It's sketchy as hell already and could cave in farther any time."

She got up and went over to the doorway to the wrecked compartment. Steffi stood beside her with her headlamp on bright, which allowed a much better look at the full extent of the damage than Hudson had seen before. She could also now clearly see the far end; the door leading to the next car was twisted, but intact. The collapsed snow shed had caved in the ceiling of the car down there, too—it looked to be only about four-and-a-half, maybe five feet off the floor.

But there was enough room for someone to get down there, if they had reason and guts enough to do it.

"I'm going to check it out," she told Steffi. "Can I swap you the flashlight for your headlamp?"

Steffi looked horrified. "You can't be serious. That's far too dangerous."

"Nothing's shifted since the accident," Hudson said. "I'll take the chance."

"Why? I told you, the guys are already digging at the other end."

"Where they may have to dig through twenty feet of snow. Or thirty. Or forty. Who knows? Maybe there's daylight on the other side of that mess down there. Or maybe there's more injured. Clay is that way."

Steffi didn't say anything for a few seconds. "Please, Hudson. Don't go. It's not worth risking your life," she finally said.

"We won't know that for sure until I go take a look. Now, are you going to give me your headlamp, or do I have to beg someone else for theirs?"

"If you absolutely insist on doing this…" Steffi pulled it off and took the flashlight. "At least wait long enough for me to go and get my climbing helmet for you."

"All right. Deal." While she waited for Steffi's return, Hudson returned to Joe. He was still out, and that worried her, but perhaps it wasn't a horrible thing that he was spared some pain, at least briefly.

She knelt beside him. "Rest, now. Save your strength," she said quietly as she stroked his face. "Remember, it's your turn for a prank. And I expect an epic one, with all this time you're going to have to plot and plan."

When Steffi returned with her climbing helmet, Hudson strapped the headlamp to it before putting it on. She decided to take the ice ax with her as well, since it had already proved useful.

"Please be careful. I don't want anything to happen to you," Steffi said, putting a hand on Hudson's arm. "And get back here fast."

She was touched by Steffi's concern but determined to try every avenue possible to get out of here. "Not going to linger any longer than I have to, trust me." She started forward slowly down the aisle, crouching to clear the low ceiling and threading her way carefully around broken timbers, bent steel rods, and busted seats. She checked every row as she went, looking for more injured, but the only two people she came across were already dead. The legs she'd seen sticking into the aisle belonged to a paunchy, middle-aged man. His lifeless eyes stared up at nothing. Two rows farther on, she found a young man slumped down in a seat, covered with blood from the head wound that had killed him.

Scattered throughout the damage were the possessions left behind: cameras and purses, snacks and water bottles, a small CD player, day packs and children's toys. Sad reminders of the tragedy but also potentially valuable resources. She'd get them on the way back.

First, she had to satisfy her curiosity about whether the avalanche had left anything out there beyond this car. She wasn't optimistic, but she had to be certain.

CHAPTER FOURTEEN

Steffi kept her flashlight trained on Hudson as she negotiated her way carefully down the wrecked passenger compartment, her anxiety growing as the reporter edged closer and closer to the area that seemed in greatest danger of further collapse. By the time Hudson reached the far door, Steffi's heart was hammering and she found it difficult to breathe. "What do you see?"

"Hang on." Hudson's headlamp flashed up, down, left, right. "Doesn't look good. J.T. was right. Nothing but packed snow out of all the exits and windows, and it looks too iffy to be down here digging."

"Come on back, then."

"On my way." Hudson turned around and started back up the aisle. She stopped short after only a couple of rows, however, and bent to retrieve a small duffel bag. It was only half full when she grabbed it, but by the time she got back to Steffi a minute or two later, it was overflowing with potentially useful items she'd reclaimed from the debris: water and drink bottles, snacks, a ski hat, purses, a cell phone, cameras, a pair of small daypacks.

"So...the rest of the train is just...*gone*?" Steffi asked.

"Looks like it. How the avalanche left just these two cars..." Hudson shook her head in wonder. "We're damn lucky."

"I won't feel lucky until we get out of here."

"Thanks for the helmet." Hudson handed it back.

"You're welcome."

"Okay, everybody," Curt said from behind them. "Let's start moving the injured. Joe first. Hopefully we can get him situated before he wakes up again."

She and Hudson turned to look. While they'd been preoccupied, Curt had built a makeshift stretcher out of two more skis and climbing rope, the rope webbed with knots like a hammock.

"Damn clever, Curt." Hudson moved into position near Joe's head.

"Thank Boy Scout camp every summer," he replied. "Okay, Kris and Steffi, you'll be at his feet. We'll lift him enough for Anna to slip the stretcher under him, and then we'll each take a corner to transport him."

Joe never opened his eyes as they moved him into the other car and laid him beside the injured Italian girl and her father, atop a semi-insulated bed of big foam squares cut from the seats and seatbacks. They piled more foam around him before wrapping him cocoon-like in one of the silver survival blankets.

Over the next hour or so, they transported the rest of the injured and made them as comfortable as possible. They were able to match people up with their luggage and helped them find and put on their warmest clothes. They placed the few who could sit comfortably into undamaged reclining seats, while they wrapped the most critical in the remaining survival blankets with more of the thick foam around them. Joe came to after about twenty minutes and said he wasn't in quite as much pain as before, but Hudson wondered whether he was just saying that for her benefit.

As they worked, they could hear the muffled voices of the men working in the luggage compartment to dig them out. Having everyone so close together now, Steffi was able to get an overview of their situation.

All told, twenty-eight people had been in the two cars at the time of the avalanche. Four were dead, fifteen were injured, and nine had escaped with minor cuts and bruises.

Anna made it her mission to connect with each of the injured as they were treated and moved, to try to learn something about them. The language barrier made that difficult, but she persisted. All of those who were being helped seemed grateful.

The Italian girl they'd helped first was named Cinzia. Her father still hadn't regained consciousness, and Curt was at odds about what to do for him aside from making him as warm and comfortable as possible. The man's breathing was shallow and raspy, and he was so pale from the loss of blood from his leg wound that Steffi feared he wouldn't survive long without a doctor. She couldn't fathom how poor Cinzia would cope if she had to lose her father, too. Though no one had said anything to the girl about finding her mother dead, she seemed to sense the truth. She lay quietly crying much of the time, huddled against her unmoving father.

From the other car, they'd rescued two Japanese couples in their forties, all of whom had traumatic injuries: head wounds and broken bones, though none seemed life-threatening.

The two young German men they'd helped, who gave their names as Fritz and Hugo, fared better. Fritz had bruised ribs and a sprained ankle, while his friend escaped with only a dislocated shoulder—which Curt managed to slip back into place. They'd been traveling with their buddy Viktor—the young man whose body Hudson had discovered—and his death had hit them hard. Fritz was the only one of the injured who seemed to know any English, though his vocabulary was limited.

A Swiss woman who'd been traveling with her two teenage daughters kept drifting in and out of consciousness; she had both a head wound and a deep gash on her arm that required stitches. The girls, who'd escaped with sprains, cuts, and bruises, kept vigil over their mother.

The only other individual they'd found alive was an elderly woman, probably in her eighties. Like Cinzia's father, she still hadn't awakened since the avalanche, and her pulse was now so faint they could detect it only in the carotid artery in her neck. After checking on her again after they moved her, Curt said she'd probably survive only hours, at most, without professional help.

Once they'd done all they could for the injured, they moved two of the dead—Cinzia's mother and Viktor—into the other car. Curt asked them not to move Patti, at least not yet, which elicited quick agreement from the others and another round of tears and hugs.

Later, Curt went to keep watch over the injured, while Steffi and the others started piling all the suitcases and gear bags in an empty part of the car to go through them. She was pleased that Hudson chose to settle in beside her for the task, a little away from the others.

"Hanging in there okay?" Hudson asked. When she turned toward Steffi, her headlamp blinded her for a moment. "Sorry. Hey, I was so preoccupied with Joe I didn't notice you got banged up a bit yourself. Chipped a couple of teeth, looks like, and split your lip. Does it hurt?"

She was surprised to feel Hudson's hand cup her chin. Her thumb smoothed lightly over the wound, which had already stopped bleeding.

"I'd already forgotten about it," she replied. But she wouldn't forget the gentleness of Hudson's touch. "Nothing a trip to the dentist won't fix."

"You have a beautiful smile. One of the first things I noticed about you. That, and you smile a *lot*. Not many people do, in my experience."

Steffi was glad the compartment was dark, so Hudson couldn't see the blush she felt creeping up her neck. "I guess I'm generally a pretty happy person. I try to find joy in even the small things. Always counting my blessings, you know?" She wanted to add, *the first thing I noticed about you was how hot you were in that tux. Not that you're any less so in your jeans and sweatshirt.*

"If you can find any blessings in all of this, please let me know. 'Cause I'm not feeling it." Hudson called out to the others as she reached for a bag. "Let's sort as we go, huh? Food and drink in one pile, warm clothes in another, and one for everything else…like tools, lighters, rope, whatever."

"Sounds good," Kris replied.

Though she certainly appreciated the importance of the task, Steffi felt vaguely uncomfortable going through the private possessions of someone she didn't know without their consent. The first bag she opened was a woman's rolling carry-on. Inside were several conservative dresses, lingerie, two pairs of high heels, a long, warm coat, toiletries, and Swiss souvenirs: five chocolate bars, a calendar, a large cow bell, and a new Swiss Army knife with ten attachments, still in its box. From the contents, she guessed the bag belonged to the dead Italian woman, Cinzia's mother.

"Swiss Army knife with tools," she told the others, and added that, along with the coat and chocolate bars, to their growing piles of recovered resources. The woman's toiletries bag contained some small scissors and several Band-Aids, but nothing else that seemed useful.

The next bag she picked up was a long, heavy duffel with a name tag on it: Fritz Hauptmann, with an address in Munich. She carried it down the aisle and set it next to its owner.

"Fritz? Okay if I open this? We're looking for warm clothes and food." She used pantomimes as well to get across that she wanted to search his bag.

"*Ja.* All good you take." Once Curt had put his shoulder back in place, he'd given Fritz a sling and ibuprofen to make him more comfortable, and the young man seemed much happier now. He waited for her to unzip the bag before he stopped her with a hand on her arm. "Wait, please. *Zigaretten.*" Once he'd reached in and gotten out a pack of cigarettes, he smiled and nodded at her that she could take the rest.

She went through Fritz's things right there, as he lit one of the cigs and shared it with his friend. She felt better doing this in front of him, somehow, like she was reassuring him she was being respectful of his possessions, despite the situation. Ludicrous, probably. He hadn't acted liked he cared. In fact, he seemed happy if he had anything to contribute.

And he certainly had packed to their advantage. Fritz was a snowboarder and had high-quality gear. He'd already pulled out an insulated parka and ski pants for himself, and his duffel contained another set of each, as well as lots of other warm clothing.

She added his stuff to the growing stockpile. All but the parka, which she held out toward Hudson. "I bet this will fit you. It's an extra Fritz had. You're the only one without a coat."

Hudson smiled at her. "I appreciate you thinking of me," she said as she took the coat and put it on. "Fits great. Thanks, Fritz," she called out, and the young man gave her a thumbs-up.

The others were finding potentially useful things in the luggage they were going through, too. Steffi spotted lighters, jackknives, disposable hand warmers, flashlights, and several prescription-pill bottles among the "miscellaneous" pile. The food and drink pile was growing, too—lots of people besides the climbing club had brought snacks, water, soda, and candy onboard. But twenty-four people would go through it all in no time.

"This is going to be a help." Hudson examined her latest discovery. It looked like a tall draft beer, complete with foam.

"What the heck is that?" Steffi asked.

"A souvenir candle. I don't care how fugly it is, it's perfect for melting snow, and so big it'll burn for a while. All we need is something like a small pot or metal cup…" Hudson glanced around at what they'd found and picked up a soda can. "This will work. I can take the lid off an empty one with the Swiss Army knife."

"Resourceful, too, huh? Is there anything you can't do?" Steffi plucked another bag from the pile and started to go through it.

Hudson got to her feet. "Yeah. Too long a list, I'm afraid. I'm going to check on how Joe's doing." She headed off toward the injured, who were clustered in seats and on the floor near the luggage area.

"What time is it, anyway?" Anna asked from a couple of rows away. "I have no idea how long we've been here."

Kris replied. "Almost four thirty."

"Already? That's not possible." Though Anna spoke, the realization so much time had passed hit all of them. Steffi could tell by the sudden, absolute silence that followed. They'd been so busy since the avalanche hit, the time had flown; the knowledge that no one had come to rescue them in all that time was sobering. After several seconds, they all resumed searching the bags, and Anna spoke again. "When does the sun go down?"

"That shouldn't matter too much," Steffi replied. "I'm sure they search at night, too. Helicopters these days have all this high-tech gear. Big searchlights. Infrared. Things like that. Don't they?"

❖

Hudson knelt next to Joe, tilting her headlamp so it didn't shine directly in his face. His eyes were closed, but his pained expression suggested he wasn't asleep. They'd wrapped him up so thoroughly to keep him warm that only his face was visible, his head covered by a wool hat. She hated seeing him like this, especially since she was powerless to do anything about getting him help.

When Steffi had asked what she *couldn't* do, the first thing that had sprung to mind was, *sustain any kind of meaningful relationship.* But that wasn't entirely true. She might have never had much luck with women, but she did have Bruce, and her brothers, and Joe.

She laid her palm on his forehead to gauge his temperature and he opened his eyes.

"Hey there, tough guy. How you feeling?"

"Rough. Can I have another pain pill?"

"I'll ask Curt."

He was sitting a couple of rows away, where he could keep an eye on the two unconscious survivors.

"Yes, you can give him another," Curt said. He reached into his pocket for the pills. "Here. You take them. Instructions are on the label. We found some other pain meds that aren't as strong, when these run out."

"I can't tell you how much I appreciate all you've done and all you're doing for him, Curt." She laid a hand on his shoulder. "I'm very sorry about your wife. I know this has to be so hard for you."

"Having something to occupy my mind is…welcome. And if I can help somebody else stay alive…well, Patti would have liked that. She was always doing kind things for people." He put his head down and started to sob. "I just can't believe it, yet."

"Let me know if there's anything I can do, okay?"

"I will. Thanks, Hudson."

She returned to Joe and gave him a pill. She had one of the water bottles in her jacket, and after she helped him drink from it, she took a couple of sips herself. They had all agreed to try to ration their intake for the time being until they had a better handle on when they might get out of here.

"Can I ask you a favor?" Joe asked.

"Anything, you know that."

"Find my camera, if you can. Even if it's busted, I want the memory card. I know it sounds crazy right now, but I got the shot. *The* shot. The avalanche coming down on us. I know I did. Not to mention all the hundreds of others on there I want to save. This is a story, Hudson. I know it doesn't feel like one now, but when we all get out of here, we've got a hell of a tale to tell. From what I've overheard, we're *it*, right?"

"Yeah, looks like that's the case."

"And the cars are fully buried?"

"Yup."

"That sucks."

"Where were you when it hit?" she asked.

"Taking pictures out the luggage-compartment window. I was getting the avalanches across the gorge, so I was shooting like five frames a second, you know?" His voice took on the excitement of the moment. "All of a sudden this fine mist of white rained down, covering the train just before it went into the snow shed. I never stopped shooting, the whole time. Not until we really got hit a couple seconds later and I went flying."

"Who patched you up?"

"Bud."

"Bud?"

"One of J.T.'s friends. They were all in the luggage compartment with me when it happened. J.T. was giving me grief about you, actually. Asked how I could bear to put up with your shit all these years."

"And you said?"

"I told him I gave as good as I got, and that I'd never want to work with anyone else."

"Inseparable," she said.

"Got that right."

"I'll go look for your camera." She found his Nikon among the pile of loose items they'd recovered from the other car. "Still works, I think," she told him. "But this lens is toast."

"And the last few pics?" he asked.

"How do you play them back?" She held the camera in front of his face and put her light on it.

"Upper left, the little triangle."

She called up the last several photos. Joe had captured a series that well represented the horror of the disaster. The avalanches they'd seen across the gorge, the veil of white that signaled their impending doom, then several frames of chaos as Joe went down and his finger finally disconnected from the shutter-release button.

"Did I tell you?"

"Yes, you did. They're incredible." She shut off the camera. "I'm going to tuck this next to you so you can keep an eye on it, okay?" His camera was his most precious possession.

"I want you to keep the memory card for me," he said. "Just so it doesn't get lost."

"You sure?"

"Yeah. Please."

"Whatever you say." She took it out of the camera and tucked it into the inside pocket of her borrowed parka. "I'm going to see how the digging's going. That pill kicking in?"

"Yeah, better. Tired, though."

"Rest. I'll check on you in a bit. Tell Curt to come get me if you need me." She headed into the luggage compartment, which was rapidly filling up with snow.

J.T. and his friends were taking turns digging out of the exit, while Nick and Gary moved the snow away from the area where they were working. They were packing it everywhere they could away from the exit, though they'd left the little bathroom accessible.

"How's it going?" she asked Nick.

"Hard work. The snow is so compacted it's more like ice. Make that concrete. On the upside, at least we've got tools to work with, thanks to EurAdventures. Our ice axes are helping them chip through it, and EA issued these to the skiers." He held up the avalanche shovel he was working with. Made of sturdy aluminum, with a telescopic handle, it was too small to move much volume at one time, but it was holding up well against the hard-packed snow.

"How far have they dug?"

"Probably fifteen feet. Still no sign of daylight."

CHAPTER FIFTEEN

Rega Operations Center
Zurich Airport, Switzerland

The Rega Operations Center, where all Swiss air-rescue operations began and ended, was in the midst of a multi-million-dollar technology upgrade when it faced the greatest challenge of its sixty-four-year existence. Though its highly trained staff of pilots, physicians, dispatchers, and support staff had handled fourteen thousand missions the previous year, it was finally overwhelmed to the breaking point by a record number of distress calls posted within a matter of just four hours.

The director of the center, Eckhart Glaus, got his first inkling of the day to come when he reported for work at eight a.m. The Institute for Snow and Avalanche Research had just issued a warning of treacherous conditions throughout the Alps, particularly on north-facing slopes. In the high altitudes, two feet of wet, heavy snow had fallen in the last forty-eight hours on top of a weak, older snowpack, and the forecast for warming temperatures that day would make for a highly unstable environment.

The first calls started coming in less than three hours later. Eckhart immediately summoned all personnel to work, even those on the overnight shift who were home in bed. Not long after, he called in additional help from Rega's usual partners: the Swiss Air Force, Touring Club Suisse—a roadside assistance organization similar to AAA—and the Swiss Alpine Club, the largest mountaineering organization in the country, with one hundred and ten thousand members.

But three hours into the crisis, even those resources were stretched, and an appeal went out for international assistance, especially for high-altitude rescue helicopters and trained avalanche search-and-recovery teams. Their Alpine neighbors could offer nothing. Rescue services in France, Germany, Italy, Austria, and Slovenia were all operating at full capacity.

The situation was so dire that the outlook for many of those affected by the onslaught of avalanches was bleak. By the time outside aid arrived, most would be beyond help. At last report, more than two hundred avalanches had been recorded across the region in a matter of hours, and calls were still coming in about more.

Under normal circumstances, a single helicopter or air ambulance answered each plea for help. But not today. None of these calls were single-casualty affairs that could be resolved quickly. Most involved widespread devastation, with dozens or even hundreds of people missing, stranded, or feared dead.

The first calls came from St. Moritz. Though the surrounding resorts had minimized the risk to their in-boundary slopes with explosives, six massive slides had hit the backcountry areas popular with extreme skiers and snowboarders. Several large parties were missing.

Ten minutes later, the switchboard lit up again, this time with three calls at once. Verbier, a high-altitude village in the canton of Valais, had been wiped out. Another slide had taken out the cable-car system that was the only way to reach Bettermeralp, a car-free ski village near the Italian border. And an adventure group of ten hikers had been stranded by deep snow at the Margherita Hut, the highest building in Europe, and was out of provisions.

The center had all of its own field resources already assigned by the time the transportation sector began phoning for assistance. Several sections of roadway throughout the Alps had been obliterated under thirty or more feet of snow, burying an unknown number of cars. The worst hit was a busy ten-mile stretch between Leuk and Gampel.

Federal Railway and Rhaetian Railway officials, meanwhile, reported they'd lost contact with three trains: one near Andermatt, another a few miles from Zermatt, and a third somewhere in the Bernina Pass.

While two of his aides began making calls seeking manpower to deal with the blocked roads, Eckhart himself asked the Swiss Air Force for assistance in locating the trains. Though the major in charge did have three utility choppers still available, their fleet of Eurocopter AS332 Super Pumas, equipped with forward-looking infrared, was already committed to other tasks.

"We'll have the choppers airborne within the next fifteen minutes," the air-force major told Eckhart. "They'll radio you directly for the coordinates and keep you apprised of what they find."

"Thank you, Major." He'd barely hung up the phone when one of his senior dispatchers handed him a printout with still more bad news.

Another massive storm system with high winds and heavy snow was headed their way and would arrive sometime overnight, suspending all rescue operations.

❖

New York, New York

Two hours after his initial visit, Bob Furness headed back down to the International Desk to get an update on the situation in Europe. He'd cancelled the rest of his appointments for the morning once he realized his mind was never far from Hudson and Joe. "Well?" he asked Calvin without preamble.

"It gets worse by the hour," his managing editor replied. "The media over there are comparing this to the so-called Winter of Terror, 1950 to 1951, when nearly six hundred and fifty avalanches occurred over a three-month period, causing widespread destruction and loss of life. Total casualties from this event are still unknown but expected to number in the hundreds, if not thousands."

"And St. Moritz?"

"They've got a small army of search-and-rescue people probing through five major slides in the backcountry," Calvin said. "One person—a German national—has been rescued alive. Sixteen bodies have also been recovered, but they're not releasing names until next of kin are notified."

"So, I take it we haven't heard from Hudson and Joe?"

"No. Want me to call them?"

"Yes. Just to check in," Bob replied. "Unless Hudson volunteers, don't assign them anything. They've earned this vacation."

"You got it." Calvin got Hudson's private cell number from his computer and made the call. Seconds passed as he listened. "Hudson, it's Brent Calvin. Please call the desk when you get this message. We just want to touch base and make sure you're both okay." He hung up the phone and tried Joe's number next. It, too, went to voice mail, and Calvin left essentially the same message for him.

"Call every hour or two," Bob said once he'd hung up. "And if you don't reach them, leave a note for whoever replaces you to keep trying."

"Yes, sir."

Bob headed back to the third floor and asked his secretary to call the hotel where Hudson and Joe were booked. He knew he was overreacting, but he had a real soft spot for both of them and wasn't going to get much done until he knew they were safe.

But she reported back that neither had yet checked in.

"Let me see the itinerary they left," he said.

The printout listed only their flights and hotel reservations, but the letterhead told him they'd booked their vacation through an online agency called EurAdventures. "Try calling this agency," he told his secretary. "See if they have any information we don't about where they are. Maybe they booked some ski guides for them, or a driver or something."

"Right away."

"I'll be in my office. Let me know what you find."

Fifteen minutes passed before she knocked on his door.

"Well?"

"It took some convincing, but they finally agreed to fax me what they had." She set the printout in front of him. "Hudson and Joe were supposed to be on an Alpine sightseeing train today—the Bernina Express—if they're using the tickets they booked through the agency. But the woman I talked to said half the rail system is pretty much shut down right now. When the avalanches started, they had all mountain trains pull into the next depot and stop until further notice. She had no other information."

"Could be why they're not answering their cells. If they're stranded up where they can't get a signal."

"I'm sure that's it," she replied. "Want me to keep trying the hotel?"

"Yes. Every hour."

Once she'd gone, he loosened his tie and went to the window. A light, fluffy snow was falling, and he wondered how something so delicate and beautiful could claim so many lives.

❖

Over the Bernina Pass, Switzerland

Swiss Airman Jurgen Dorflur, pilot of the Eurocopter EC635, fought a grueling headwind as he steered the chopper higher toward the Bernina Pass, following the rail line. So far, he'd passed over six regular passenger trains parked at high-altitude stations. The dispatcher at Rega had told him he was to locate the Bernina Express, a mix of silver cars and red ones, which was believed stranded somewhere on the long plain of the Bernina Pass, or just beyond on the early descent section.

His mission was to assess the status of the train and report its precise location to Rega. In the event he came upon injured and felt it safe to attempt a rescue, two other airmen were along to operate the winch and load the lift basket. In addition to the three crew members, they had room for two seated passengers and a litter.

He studied the mountains around him for further risk of avalanches as he gave each wide berth. Scores of enormous cornices remained over the nearby peaks, and he was afraid the noise of his rotors might trigger more slides if he got too close.

Jurgen loved being airborne, and he never tired of the magnificent views that were a part of nearly every mission. But he also had learned to respect the dangers of Alpine flying and the sudden and unpredictable weather that could cause widespread destruction in an instant. He was especially vigilant today. Before he'd left the air base, he'd been watching the news on television; this was a black day for Switzerland.

He reached the flat expanse of the pass and leveled off. For a few seconds, their forward momentum slowed as he gaped at the scenery ahead.

The crewman sitting beside him gasped aloud.

The mountains on either side of the helicopter rose like sentinels, still draped in massive, gravity-defying white cowls, the likes of which he'd never seen before. The snow was so deep on the flat plain, he couldn't tell where the road once was, save for the rare sign pole in the sea of white.

The railway here was easily visible, but a slide a half mile ahead had covered a section of track. New avalanches had also recently dumped tons of snow on several slopes to their left, testifying to the ideal conditions that day for widespread slides.

Jurgen hovered near the section of rail that had been buried. The avalanche here had dumped most of its load before it ever reached the track, some distance away. The snow looked to be only four or five feet deep, at most. A chore to clear, but the slide wasn't big enough to completely hide a train beneath.

He continued on, seeing evidence of more avalanches on both sides of the pass. The numerous barriers that had been set up to contain them along the rail route all were laden to capacity from the season's record snowfalls.

Halfway across the pass, they reached another section of track that had been buried. The devastation was much worse here. A half mile or more of the rail had been buried, beneath probably forty or fifty feet of snow. If the train was there, underneath that glistening chaos of white, there was no way of knowing.

With a sickening dread spreading in the pit of his stomach, he pushed the copter forward and soon lost count of the number of avalanche fields they were passing.

The third section of track that had been hit was the worst. At the far end of the pass, where the railway hugged the mountain to begin its descent to Italy, a mile of track was gone, along with the road beside it. It was hard to gauge the depth, but it had to be considerable. The track just seemed to suddenly disappear into a steep white slope.

Studying the contours of the peaks above the devastated area, he could see that this massive slide had been the result of not one, but two avalanches, on neighboring peaks, which accounted for the mind-numbing volume of snow.

As they got closer, they could see into the deep gorge below the avalanche field.

"Dear God," the crewman beside him said, as he made the sign of the cross.

Jurgen saw it, too—the end of a smashed red car sticking up out of the vast snow load that had been dumped into the gorge. Nearby, a long piece of twisted metal from one of the silver local cars reflected sunlight back up at them like a signal mirror from one of the lost souls.

They made several passes over the site to make absolutely certain there were no survivors, though it had been clear to them from the outset. The shattered wreckage of the Bernina Express was mostly buried at the bottom of the gorge.

Such a profound loss of life. One of many this dark day. Jurgen radioed the Rega Control Center. "I regret to report that the Bernina Express train was swept into a deep gorge by a massive avalanche. There are no survivors. The entire length of the Bernina Pass has been made impassable by ground. Probably for weeks. Avalanches have covered several areas of the railway. Estimated depth, forty to fifty feet. Over."

"Roger that, Alpnach 9. Thank you for your help, gentlemen. We'd like a full debriefing on the situation, but we have another mission for you, first. Stand by for new coordinates."

CHAPTER SIXTEEN

S hut the fuck up and stop moving around!" J.T. shouted, and everybody in the luggage compartment froze. "What did you say, Bud?"

J.T.'s friend Bud was the current tunnel rat, a task so hazardous that he was roped to the luggage rack so they could reach him quicker if the snow shifted and enveloped him. It was also the most grueling job, requiring the rat to chip away at compacted snow until his forearms ached. The men had dug a squarish-shaped tunnel at a slight upward angle away from the train. It was too small to turn around in unless you were a circus contortionist, but wide and high enough that a large man with a backpack could crawl through without feeling too claustrophobic.

Nick had been right. Bud was about fifteen feet from the exit door now, maybe a bit more. Hudson gave them props for rigging a very efficient system to remove snow from the tunnel.

They'd attached a rope to two ends of a large duffel bag. Bud had one end of the rope, and J.T., positioned at the doorway of the train, held the other. Bud would fill the bag, and J.T. would pull it through the tunnel and empty it on the floor at his feet. Two men would then shovel the snow from the pile into another area farther away, while Bud pulled the bag back to fill it again. The five men had been at it for hours, so at this point, one was always resting, and they rotated the jobs every thirty minutes.

When the luggage compartment fell silent, Hudson could hear only the low buzz of indistinguishable conversation from those in the passenger area.

"What's that?" J.T. asked.

Bud shouted something. Hudson couldn't make it out, but J.T.'s expression brightened instantly.

"What'd he say?" Gary asked.

"He hears a plane or helicopter out there!" J.T. told them.

Hudson went to the door of the passenger compartment to relay the news. "There's an aircraft outside! We may be close to rescue!"

A hum of excitement reverberated through the car as everyone still mobile gathered in and around the luggage compartment, their faces expectant and hopeful. Steffi materialized beside her and slipped her gloved hand into Hudson's, as though it was the most natural thing in the world.

Bud chipped away at the remaining barrier of snow with renewed intensity. The rapid *thwack thwack thwack* of the ice ax echoing in the tunnel kept time with Hudson's racing heart.

"Joe's going to be just fine. Help is coming," Steffi said as though reading her mind, and squeezed Hudson's hand reassuringly.

J.T. had moved into hyper-drive as well, extracting the duffel of snow from the tunnel as quickly as Bud could fill it. While the rest stayed out of their way, people began inching forward, clustering around the exit to try to see how much farther Bud still had to go to break through.

Ten minutes later, Bud let out a shout of victory as a shaft of sunlight illuminated the tunnel.

"What do you see?" J.T. shouted.

"Nothing yet. Hang on," Bud hollered back, and the sounds of the ice ax resumed with a fury. The shaft of light got brighter, flooding the area around the exit door.

Then silence filled the tunnel.

Hudson held her breath, awaiting the official notice from Bud that they'd been found.

But no shout of discovery came. After a minute or two, Bud scooted backward down the tunnel, and when he turned to face them, his face was ashen.

"There was a helicopter," he said. "I punched through just in time to see it heading away, back the way we'd come. But they were too far away to see me."

The disappointment hit her hard. Hudson let go of Steffi's hand and dropped into the nearest seat.

"That's all right," Steffi said, though her tone of voice lacked its usual buoyant optimism. "They know where we are. They'll be back."

"But probably not today," Bud said. "The sun's setting fast. It'll be dark soon." He set down his ice ax. "Nothing to do now but wait."

"What's it look like out there?" J.T. asked.

Bud shook his head and frowned. "Nothing but snow. No sign of the rest of the train, and no safe way for us to get anywhere. I just hope to hell we don't have any more slides."

"We should mark the outside opening of the tunnel," Curt said. "So they can see where we are and that there are survivors when they do come back. Something big and colorful that will draw their attention."

"Anybody got any ideas?" J.T. asked. "You guys have been going through the luggage, haven't you?"

"We have a lot of bright-colored clothes nobody's using," Kris replied. "We could tie them together, string them out of the tunnel like a big clothesline."

"Do it," J.T. said, as though appointing himself in charge.

Kris and Anna immediately headed back toward the large pile of clothing they'd gathered to put something together.

"We also found some avalanche beacons in the EA ski bags," Gary said. "Won't those help them find us if we turn them on?"

"No, those are short-range, only. They reach maybe two or three hundred feet at most. They're meant for ground searches." Elliot, the third member of J.T.'s crew, was a short but wiry man. He was favoring his left leg, and his jeans at the calf were stained with dried blood.

"Did you get that taken care of?" Hudson asked him, nodding toward his leg.

"I'm all right."

"Come on and sit down. Let me take a look." Curt beckoned him toward the passenger car and Elliot followed.

"So, if we're here overnight, let's try to make the best of it," Hudson said. "Everyone should have something to eat and drink, and we need to melt some of this snow."

They were all subdued, even Steffi. They did what needed to be done, but with little conversation. Curt stitched up a four-inch cut on Elliot's leg while Anna and Kris finished the distress banner of clothing. By the time they hung it out of the tunnel, darkness had enveloped the pass.

An hour later, they all gathered in seats near the injured. Kris and Anna rationed out some of the foodstuffs they'd amassed. No one got enough to really quell their hunger, but enough to quiet their rumbling stomachs. They agreed by a group vote to save the bulk of their supplies for their uncertain future.

Dehydration was more of a concern in this dry, cold climate, especially for the men who'd been doing hard labor digging the tunnel. They and the injured each received a full bottle of water, juice, or soda, while the rest made do with half that.

Hudson knew that in these cold, arid temperatures, they should all be drinking more than usual, not less. So once she'd helped Joe eat and finished her own portion—they each got half a small cheese sandwich—she began melting snow for water.

When she went back to their piles of supplies to get the candle and Swiss Army knife, she spotted the small pile of hand warmers and made a quick count of how many they had. She grabbed one and went to find Curt, who was checking on the injured.

"How's Joe's condition, do you think?" she asked.

"His pulse is strong and he seems to be warm enough. I'd hate to think what he'd feel like if we didn't have pain pills."

"And the others?"

"I don't think that elderly woman will make it through the night. Cinzia's father worries me, as well. He took a bad blow to the head. Fin bears close watching, too. She seems pretty lethargic. The others, I think, are stable, and we don't have any with hypothermia or frostbite yet."

"We have twenty-six of these." She held up the hand warmer. "Do the injured need them? Or, I guess I mean to say, might these become a matter of life and death to them? Because I'd like to use some to heat snow."

He seemed to consider the question carefully. She respected Curt's opinion, even after knowing him such a short time. He'd really stepped up in every way, though facing probably the worst day of his life. Hudson wasn't certain how Joe would be doing if it weren't for him, since the rest of them seemed pretty clueless about first aid.

"You know, if we had to get stranded in this kind of harsh environment, we could have done worse, I suppose. At least this protects us from the elements," he said, looking around the car. "Anyway, to answer your question, I'd like to have a few of those on hand just in case. But with all the warm clothes we've got, I don't anticipate we'll need them. Leave me, say, half? And use the other half for getting water? That *is* a much more immediate concern."

"Great." She scooped up the supply and gave Curt thirteen of them, then whistled for attention. "Hey, everybody. We're planning to split our stock of these between the injured and melting snow. Everybody good with that?"

Since no one objected, she went on. "These are good for up to ten hours. I suggest we take one of the wide-mouth drink bottles—we've got several empties—fill it with snow, stick it in an insulated jacket pocket with the warmer, and keep adding snow as it melts. Maybe activate four of these, for now, and see how much water we can generate. I'll try to melt some snow with this candle I found."

"I'll babysit a couple of the bottles." Curt held out a hand. "I'm not going to sleep any time soon."

"Me, either. Count me in for the other two," Bud said.

Hudson tossed them each a couple of the hand warmers, and they got up to fill bottles from the cache of snow in the luggage compartment while she rigged her own water-making device. She set the candle on a flat spot next to a wall of the car, directly beneath a small trash bin. Then she cut the top off a soda can with the Swiss Army knife and poked two holes in opposite sides near the rim so she could give the can a shoelace handle to drape over the bin. It suspended the can directly over the flame.

She fed it with snow scooped into a climbing helmet and had been tending it for a few minutes when Curt came down the aisle. "Not bad, Hudson. Sure you weren't a Girl Scout?"

"Seems to be doing the job," she replied with a smile.

"Would work even better if you could get some kind of metal shield around the whole thing, concentrate the heat even more. Like aluminum foil, or…hey, I know! Put the shovels around it."

She took his advice, and the snow began melting much faster. Within an hour, she'd filled two water bottles and was working on a third.

"How's it going?" Steffi asked as she slipped into the seat beside Hudson's and switched off her headlamp.

Hudson had noticed that most of them had done the same, to conserve batteries, and the whole car had darkened significantly. "So far, so good. I was afraid this was one of those cheap candles that burn down in no time, but God bless the Swiss for their quality souvenirs."

"How's Joe doing?"

"Okay, I guess. Sleeping a lot, which is probably a good thing. I really hope we get out of here in the morning."

"I bet we will," Steffi said. "I mean, surely they'll send the helicopter back at first light, and they can't miss our distress signal."

Ever the optimist. At least outwardly. And thank God for that. Even from their first meeting, Hudson had been drawn to Steffi's cheery demeanor, and in their current situation, it could be one of their most valuable assets. She provided a voice of hope that kept everyone else motivated and hanging on. Steffi was obviously putting on a brave front right now, trying to keep her from worrying about Joe, even though one of her own friends was also in rough shape. "How's Fin?" she asked.

"Kris gave her some ibuprofen, but she still has a wicked headache. And she's not herself at all. Really subdued. Hasn't said much since the avalanche hit. She's strong, though, and a fighter. I'm sure she'll be okay."

"They been together long?" Hudson asked.

Steffi looked a little surprised that she'd clued in to the fact that they were a couple, since they hadn't been particularly demonstrative with each other. "Five years or so, I guess. How'd you know?"

"Takes one to know one," Hudson replied. "And, in times of crisis, people tend to be more unguarded. Kris is pretty easy to read."

"I'd never have guessed you were lesbian, too," Steffi looked inexplicably pleased by Hudson's revelation, and she wondered why. "No?"

Steffi shrugged. "I'm pretty clueless in that regard. I can rarely tell by looking. Well, unless maybe she's got a crew cut and a rainbow-flag tattoo."

Hudson laughed. "Well, it's often tough for me to tell. You, for example. No clue."

"Are you asking whether I'm gay?" Steffi smiled. "Aren't I as easy to read under crisis as the others?"

"When the worst happens, it's relatively simple to see connections between people," Hudson replied. "Your climbing club, for example. You pulled together when all this happened; a testament to your friendships and trust in each other. I can tell you have a particular closeness to Kris. Very understandable, since you work and climb together. And the way you are around them tells me you're supportive of them as a couple. But that certainly doesn't mean you're lesbian."

"True." Steffi seemed amused and a little impressed by her observations, but in no hurry to confirm or deny.

The next thing that came out of Hudson's mouth was completely spontaneous, and she immediately regretted it. "Maybe it's just wishful thinking." *What did I just say?*

"Wishful thinking?" Steffi repeated, with an expectant expression.

Damage control. Major *damage control. Are you really flirting with her? Right here and right now? Have you lost your mind?* "Uh... yeah. I mean, it's just very affirming to see confident, capable, young women these days who are out and proud, even in small communities, and acting as great role models. Not so many when I was in my twenties and just out of college. I can easily see Kris helping gay kids who come into your library, for example." Brilliant follow-up, she tried to tell herself. Not at all a transparent backpedal for an admission that had come from *nowhere.* Completely inappropriate. And at the absolutely worst time possible, no less. Not to mention it made her sound ancient.

"You're absolutely right about that," Steffi replied, letting her off the hook about the come-on while still avoiding the real question. She looked disappointed, though, by Hudson's explanation. Was it possible she also felt an attraction building between them, and welcomed it, despite the circumstances?

"Kris has helped at least a half dozen kids that I know of," Steffi continued. You know, finding them help if they're being bullied or have problems at home. Things like that. Doesn't happen much, fortunately. The climate in and around Sultan is very open and accepting, for the most part."

Though she was more curious than ever about whether Steffi was indeed lesbian, that topic was apparently a minefield for Hudson's subconscious mind at the moment. Better to focus on something more neutral and pertinent, like the fact that their lives were in danger.

She worried sometimes about her seemingly innate ability to disconnect at times from the full horrific reality of what was happening all around her but considered it necessary for her job in the field. With all the things she witnessed, to be too emotionally involved could drive her mad with frustration, anger, and sadness.

But she was alarmed that she could be thinking anything so distractingly personal right now, when her whole focus should be on getting Joe the help he needed. "Do you mind tending this for a few minutes while I go check on how Joe's doing?" she asked.

"No. Of course not." Steffi got up to let her out into the aisle. "By the way," she added when Hudson rose and faced her, "the answer's yes. I'm gay all the way."

Hudson bit her tongue and just smiled.

Chapter Seventeen

Steffi replayed the exchange with Hudson several times in her mind as she fed more snow into the soda can. Hudson's "wishful thinking" comment had seemed an uncharacteristically personal remark, a departure from her usual reticence to go beyond the usual safe topics—job, hobbies, interests. Although her elaboration of the sentiment was perfectly believable—yet another example of Hudson's uncanny ability to read people—Steffi had heard the unmistakable undertone of flirtation in there initially, hadn't she? *You're being ridiculous. Now who's doing the wishful thinking?*

"I've got Fin settled in to sleep and I'm going to join her," Kris said from the aisle. "Want to come cuddle with us? Keep you warmer."

"Sure. I'll be there in a while, okay?" The massive adrenaline rush that had energized her throughout the initial part of their ordeal had long since worn off, and she was starting to feel fatigued. But she wanted to babysit the candle until Hudson returned.

"I'll leave a spot for you. We've got some padding laid out for us."

"Thanks, Kris." She glanced down the aisle. The whole car had gotten darker and quieter. Most people, it seemed, had the same idea and were making themselves comfortable in the seats or on the floor. Curt was still rotating among the injured, taking their vital signs and looking for complications. And J.T. and his friends were huddled off by themselves near the luggage area, conversing in low tones.

Hudson rejoined her just as she finished filling one water bottle and started on another. "Thanks for spelling me."

"Sure." She got up and let Hudson take over but didn't feel like napping just yet, so she sat in the aisle seat. "How's Joe?"

"Same. Sleeping. I feel so powerless."

"Yeah, I wish I could do more to help Fin. And I hate what Curt is going through. What do you say to someone who just lost his wife so terribly and suddenly?"

"Not much you can say or do, except be there for them if they need a hug or want to talk." Hudson fed more snow into the can. "You haven't witnessed much death, I take it? Don't get me wrong. You've really stepped up in all this. You and all your friends have been great. But you're trying very hard to hide how much this has affected you, no?"

"What makes you say so?" Steffi asked. It was true enough, though she thought she'd been acting pretty responsibly and normally, under the circumstances.

"I don't know, call it a hunch."

"Well, you're right. Seeing Patti like that…it's still kind of surreal. I'd only seen one other dead body. My grandmother in her coffin, when I was six. I was too young to remember much."

"You're lucky you haven't lost more people close to you," Hudson replied. "Makes sense this is especially difficult for you. Not that it's ever easy, but if you've dealt with a lot of loss—particularly of friends and peers—or seen mass casualties up close…I've just been to too many funerals, I guess. I don't mean to sound insensitive."

"You don't. Not at all," Steffi said quietly. "I *have* been lucky. This all has reinforced *how* lucky I am, believe me." She looked toward the section where they'd laid Patti's body. "Life is so fragile. You think you're invulnerable and there's always plenty of time."

"Yeah. Until someone too young is suddenly taken, and it hits you personally."

"Exactly." Steffi flashed back to that afternoon, when they were all laughing and getting to know each other, none of them suspecting that, in a few hours, so many lives would be cut short. "I can't help but think of Clay as well. How his family is going to be so devastated when they realize he's not coming home."

"I've been thinking about him a lot, too. And I don't mean to sound callous, but maybe his death was a blessing in disguise."

She couldn't believe what she was hearing. "Excuse me?"

"Clay was terminally ill with a brain tumor. His whole town chipped in to send him on this trip." Hudson fed more snow into the can. "I think everyone who knew and loved him had their chance to tell Clay how much he's meant to them. Had time to process and accept that he wouldn't be around much longer. Most of us never get that opportunity."

"He was dying?" Clay had appeared to be such a healthy, gentle giant.

"I think about how happy and excited he was, being here on this train. Better to die doing what you love. And the end was probably pretty quick." Hudson leaned back in her seat. "I doubt that Clay wanted his wife and kids to have to see him get progressively weaker and more incapacitated. A shell of the robust man he once was. Who wants their loved ones to remember them like that?"

"I guess you have a point. But I still feel awful for them. Somebody should contact them when we get out of here. Let them know what happened," Steffi said. "That he didn't suffer."

"I think they'd also like to know he made a lot of friends and was really excited to share his whole passion for this train with us."

"Did you get his last name?"

"No, he never said," Hudson replied. "But he used my phone to call home, so I have their number. I'll call them when I can get a signal again."

"That's very thoughtful. I'm sure he'd appreciate that." Steffi got to her feet. The more she got to know Hudson, the more impressed she was. How she'd gotten Clay to open up so quickly, how her kindness to him had enabled him to reach out to his family in what would be his final hours. And now she'd used her insights about him to reassure Steffi that perhaps his tragic, sudden death had a positive aspect. But as much as she wanted to spend more time with Hudson, she suddenly felt the fatigue of the long day. "It's getting late. I'm going to try to sleep." She put a hand on Hudson's shoulder. "You should rest, too. You've got a lot of water stockpiled. Take a break."

Hudson smiled up at her. "I will. Soon. Sleep well. And Steffi?"

"Yes?"

"If I had to be stuck in a situation like this with anyone, I'm glad it's you."

"Me? You're the one who's been our leader, taking chances, getting us all *doing* something to help better our situation. Heck, if you hadn't shouted that the avalanche was coming, many more of us would probably be dead right now."

"Maybe. But you're the one who's keeping us all thinking positive. And we need that, more than anything, right now."

"I'm glad you think I'm helping. Sweet dreams, Hudson."

"You, too, Steffi."

Steffi detoured to the pile of extra clothes, looking for something to use as a blanket, but too many others had been there first with the same intention so pickings were slim. One of her heavy fleece pullovers was unclaimed, so she put it on as another layer under her parka and added a pair of silk liners under the thick wool socks she had on. When she pulled her hood up over her knit ski hat and fastened the front of it, only the top of her face was exposed and she felt pretty comfortable.

She found Kris spooning Fin protectively, in a wide space of flooring near the end of the car, and for a brief moment, she felt envious of their intimacy. Room had been left for her behind Kris on big, seat-sized foam pieces laid end to end. The foam actually wasn't too bad as a bed, at least that was her first reaction when she lay down. Whether it did its job and kept her from getting chilled was another matter. Kris and Fin had the long woman's coat she'd found draped over them like a blanket. Fin was also cocooned within a survival blanket, like Joe.

Everyone seemed warm enough now, minimizing the risk of hypothermia. And they'd been able to produce water pretty well. Those who'd escaped serious injury could survive like this quite a while, even with their limited food supply, though she hoped they wouldn't need to.

They were lying between the bench-table seating where they'd eaten lunch, she realized. Steffi was jarred by how long ago that seemed already, so much had happened. Her well-ordered, meticulously planned life had been taken out of her hands. She just hadn't had much time to really think about it until now.

She hated losing all say in where and how she would spend tomorrow. And the next day. And the day after that, if help didn't find them right away. She'd try to stay positive, if Hudson thought it beneficial. But the uncertainty of it all and the loss of control scared and unsettled her.

Most of all, Steffi tried not to think about what would happen if another avalanche rained down on them. Would it rip them off the mountain and into the gorge? Perhaps even as they slept? No matter how hard she tried, it was impossible to put it completely out of her mind for very long.

Sleep was elusive.

❖

Rega Control Center
Zurich Airport, Switzerland

"Airman Jurgen Dorflur is here to see you," Eckhart Glaus's secretary said from the open doorway of his office.

"Show him in." Eckhart got up and greeted the airman halfway with an extended hand. "Thank you for coming," he told the pilot, then turned to introduce the other two men present, already seated in chairs pulled up before his desk. "These gentlemen are officials from the railway and roadway commissions. Will you tell us specifically what you saw up on the Bernina Pass?"

"Of course, sir."

Eckhart beckoned the man toward the empty chair beside the others before he went around to take his own behind the desk. Spread out before them all was a detailed map of the entire rail line in that area, with topographic detailing of all the peaks and gorges.

"Huge snow cornices still remain on all the peaks along here," Dorflur said, as he smoothed his hand over the peaks at the northern entrance to the pass, "though there have been many avalanches on both sides of the valley."

The helicopter pilot put his finger on the rail line about a half mile from where it flattened out on the northern end of the pass. "The first section that is covered by snow is along here. The slide is several hundred feet long and maybe four or five feet deep at best."

"Our machines can handle that, though it will take time," the railway official said. The Swiss rail line employed a pair of heavy rail-clearing machines that worked in tandem in the high elevations. The first carved a path several feet wider than the train and funneled the snow between the rails. Then the second machine, a powerful rotary blower, picked up the snow and shot it up and away from the train, handling tons of the white stuff every hour.

"There have been more avalanches all along here, on both sides of the pass." Dorflur continued moving his finger southward over the line on the map. "The railway is still visible, but all the snow barriers that protect it are full or overflowing."

When he got to the halfway point of the pass, the pilot paused and looked up at the railway official. "This portion was the next that was buried, and it was much worse. A half mile of the track is beneath a huge avalanche field, maybe forty or more feet deep."

The railway man blanched. "Are you certain?"

"Yes, sir."

"Go on," Eckhart said.

"This area…" Dorflur skipped the next section and put his finger directly on the track where it left the pass and began its descent to Italy. "Is where the train was hit. Where the rail and road run along a ledge cut into the mountain?" He looked at the railway man, who nodded that he was familiar with the area in question.

"A mile or more of the track here is gone. It's just a…a big white slope, now. Two avalanches, from neighboring peaks, dumped into this same stretch." He pointed to the gorge, indicated by darker contour lines, very close together. "The train ended up in this gorge. You can see parts of two cars sticking up in the avalanche debris—one red and one silver—but most everything is completely buried."

"Do you think it merits a closer look by ground teams?" Eckhart asked. "Or infrared from the air, when we can get access to that?"

"Sir, I don't think it's possible for anyone to be alive up there. And you're not going to get ground access to the area until there's significant melting. The snow is just too deep."

"We can't just shut down the railway up there indefinitely," the train official said. "We've never closed the pass."

"We've never had a situation like this before," the road commissioner said. "I recommend we suspend all rescue operations at the pass for the time being, since there seems to be no viable chance to recover survivors and too many other situations need our limited resources."

❖

New York, New York

"Nothing yet from Hudson or Joe?" Bob asked the overnight man who'd replaced Brent Calvin as managing editor of the International Desk.

"No. We've left several voice mails for them and have also called the hotel every hour, as you asked. They still haven't checked in."

"Damn it. Something's got to be wrong. It's four a.m. there. Have we gotten any update from the Swiss about that train they were supposed to be on?"

"No. Not yet."

"How many do we have working the story there?" Bob asked.

The editor consulted his assignment sheet for the day. "We've got two of our own people on the headline stories coming out of St. Moritz, and a local we've used before doing sidebars."

"Get the stringer looking into the train," Bob said. "We need somebody on site getting some real answers."

"Right away."

He should go home. He'd already missed dinner again with his family and tucking his kids into bed. But Bob couldn't sleep, or concentrate on anything else, until he knew Joe and Hudson were safe.

He decided to rest a while on the sofa in his office and hope the news was better when he checked in again. First light in Switzerland was only a couple more hours away.

❖

Bernina Pass, Switzerland

"Still awake?" Curt slid into the seat beside Hudson.

She'd been melting water by rote, her mind so far away she hadn't heard him approach. Though she should be working on ways to improve their situation, all she could think about at the moment was Steffi. For some reason, her company and upbeat attitude helped soothe Hudson's anxieties about Joe and their predicament. When she'd left to get some rest, Hudson had felt her absence keenly. "Can't sleep. You?"

He shook his head. "I just checked on the old woman. She's gone."

"Shit."

"Do you think we should move her away from the others?" he asked. "I mean, I don't want to disturb anybody right now, but I also don't want any of the injured kids to have to wake up to a dead body beside them first thing in the morning. They have enough to deal with as it is."

"Good point. I'll help you."

Working as quietly as possible, they carried the woman's body down the aisle and into the next car. There they laid her beside Viktor and Cinzia's mother.

Once they'd reclaimed their seats by the candle-stove, Curt said, "You've been around the world a lot more than the rest of us. Seen a lot of life-and-death situations."

She couldn't imagine what he was getting at. "Yeah. So?"

"I know this may be a crazy question," he replied. "But, do you think, when they come to get us…" He looked at her with sad, worried eyes. "Will they let me take Patti home? I can't bear to leave her here. I'm so afraid they won't have the time, or the resources, or whatever, to recover all the dead. What do they do in situations like this, do you know?"

"I wish I could reassure you, Curt. But I'm not sure. It varies. In most places, recovery of the dead after a mass disaster is usually a high priority. But this is still a very dangerous, high-risk situation for rescuers. There are a lot of survivors and injured to focus on getting out of here. They may decide it's too unsafe to risk removing the dead as well."

"That's what I'm afraid of. I can't bear the thought of her ending up here forever. Entombed alone, on a frozen mountain, halfway across the world." He wiped at his eyes. "What am I going to say to her parents? She was an only child. I was supposed to take care of her."

"You'll find the right words when the time comes." Hudson put a hand on his shoulder, wanting to reassure him. "And we'll all talk to whoever comes to get us out of here," she told him. "We'll make them understand how important it is that Patti goes home with you."

"I hope we can." He picked up the bottles she and Steffi had filled. "I'll add these to our stash. We've got them all wrapped up so they don't refreeze. There's plenty for a while, by the way, so why don't you get some sleep?"

"I will if you will."

"All right. And thanks for the talk, Hudson."

"Any time, Curt."

As he left to find a place to nap, she blew out the candle and drank the water that had accumulated in the can. The half cup or so of tepid liquid wasn't enough to fully quench her worsening thirst, but she hoped it would help get her mind off it for a while.

After a brief detour to the little bathroom in the luggage compartment—which was going to get pretty nasty in no time, with no power to flush it—she curled up beside Joe. She didn't expect she'd actually fall asleep, but the long day and the sound of his rhythmic, soft snoring lulled her quickly into dreamland.

CHAPTER EIGHTEEN

Next morning

"Marco."

Hudson tried to ignore the voice. She rolled over, clutching tight to her dream. She was on a boat in the Aegean Sea. The sun was warm, the drinks were cold, the views incredible. Blue sky, azure water, white sand beaches, and Steffi was there, too, in a sheer red bikini, smiling at her provocatively, and—

"Marco, God damn it!" Louder, more insistent.

She came fully awake in an instant, the reality of where she was and who she was with shattering the blissful, though unexpected images and pushing aside the temporary reprieve of sleep. "Hey, Joe. I'm here. I'm up." She fumbled around in the dark for the headlamp and turned it on. "What's the matter? You hurting?"

"Yeah. Bad. Got any more of those pills?"

"Right here. Hang on." Hudson fished the prescription bottle from her pocket and reclaimed a bottle of water from Curt's stash. "Let me help you." She held his head up while he drank, then tucked him into the survival blanket again. "You warm enough?"

"Yeah, I guess. What time is it?"

She checked her watch. "A little before six."

"Anybody else awake?"

Hudson glanced down the aisle. She didn't see any other lights on. "Doesn't look like it. Not yet."

"Do you think they'll come for us soon?"

"Sure. The helicopter was right here, right outside. Bud saw it. They'll be back after first light, and they'll see the banner we put out. No worries."

"And if they don't? Is there a plan?"

"They will. I told you, don't worry. I'm going to make sure you get help. Whatever it takes."

Her reassurances seemed to calm him, or else the pill was doing its job, because Joe drifted off again after a few minutes.

But his questions had only heightened her own fears. What *would* they do if help didn't arrive today? She hadn't allowed herself to think too much about the worst-case scenario—that rescuers wouldn't be able to locate them or that their tenuous location would prove impossible to reach.

Screams of pain and distress suddenly shattered the silence in the car. Female.

Steffi? Hudson bolted to her feet and followed the sound, as several others stirred awake and lights flicked on throughout the car.

It wasn't Steffi, though. It was Cinzia, the Italian girl, clutching at her father's chest. She must have awakened to find him dead and sounded inconsolable.

"Damn," Curt said from beside Hudson. He reached down and checked for a pulse on the man's neck to make sure, but it wasn't necessary. He'd been dead for a while. His skin already had a bluish cast.

Anna joined them. "I'll take care of her." She knelt beside Cinzia and put her arms around the girl, enfolding her in a soothing embrace. She smoothed her hair and rocked her while murmuring words of reassurance and comfort.

Despite the language barrier, Cinzio seemed to welcome the contact, and her wails soon diminished to quiet sobbing.

"Give her some time before you move his body," Anna said. "I'll tell you when."

"What's going on?" Steffi appeared by Hudson's side, her face etched with worry.

Without thinking, Hudson put one arm protectively around her shoulder and turned her away from the dead man's body. "Cinzia's father died during the night. You really don't need to see this."

J.T. appeared behind them, with his friend Elliot, also drawn by Cinzia's screams. "Lost another, huh? Pity." But Hudson saw no trace of sincere concern in J.T.'s voice as he consulted his watch. "It'll be light in an hour or so. We should be out of here before we lose anyone else." He turned to Elliot. "As soon as the sun comes up, we should start posting someone on watch at the end of the tunnel to make sure they see us. You want to take the first shift?"

"Yeah, okay," Elliot replied. "Can I have something to eat, first? I'm starving."

"You can have one of my PowerBars. Side pocket of my pack," J.T. told him.

"You've got food you didn't contribute?" Anna asked pointedly. "I thought we all agreed to pool what we had. You ate some of our food last night."

"We earned it," J.T. said. "We burned a lot of calories digging and shoveling. You'll benefit, so I wouldn't bitch about it."

"Hey, man, don't talk to her like that," Curt said. "We're all trying to be fair, that's all. The common-good concept, you know? Doing the right thing?"

"I like the survival-of-the-fittest concept better, myself." J.T. got in Curt's face and towered over him. "Don't make a big deal of it. Not worth it. Believe me." He stood there a moment, waiting to see whether Curt would do anything. When he didn't react, J.T. smirked, and he and his buddy headed off toward their gear.

"Asshole," Curt said after he'd gone.

"Got that right." Hudson had wanted more than anything to just punch the bastard once and for all, even if she got the worst of it back. But now wasn't the time or place. She had to focus on Joe. "Don't let it bother you. He's always been a dick. That won't change him."

"You *know* that jerk?" Anna asked.

"We've crossed paths. He's a reporter, too. For Fox News."

"That explains it," Anna said wryly, and Hudson had to stifle a laugh in deference to poor Cinzia.

"Her screams sure woke up the train," Curt said, glancing down the aisle. "Do we have enough food left that we can give everybody a little something?"

"Yes, but don't you dare give any more to that fuckwad and his friends," Anna replied. "They're on their own."

"I don't plan to." Curt headed off toward the cache of supplies, and Hudson and Steffi followed him to help distribute what they had. Everyone but J.T. and his crew got another meager meal, but breakfast put a serious dent in their remaining food stores. The only items left were chocolate bars and a half dozen bags of chips and pretzels.

J.T. and his buddies made no issue of getting passed over, but the conflict over the food only increased the already chilly friction between that group and the others. The three men didn't speak to anyone when they headed toward the luggage compartment a short while later to watch for the helicopter's return.

Nevertheless, Hudson, Steffi, and Nick headed that way as well, anxious to see whether rescue was imminent.

Elliot took one of the ice axes with him as he entered the tunnel. He called out when he was halfway through. "Lots of snow in here and the exit's blocked again."

"Another avalanche?" Bud asked.

"Don't know yet. Hang on," was the shouted response.

Several tense minutes passed with no further update from Elliot, though they could hear muted chopping sounds from the tunnel as he cleared the exit hole.

"Duffel's full," he shouted finally, and J.T. reeled in the snow-and-ice-laden bag and dumped the contents at his feet.

The bag went back up the tunnel and returned twice more with a full load before Elliot followed it back and rejoined them, brushing snow from around his face and hood.

"Well?" J.T. asked.

"The blockage was from new snow overnight," he told them. "Heavy and wet, but not packed solid like it would have been from another avalanche. The clothes we put out there were all covered, but I managed to get the line shaken out and back in place."

"I take it you didn't see anybody?" Bud asked.

"No. And no one's coming any time soon. A blizzard's raging. Visibility is crap."

No one spoke for several seconds.

"I know this may be a stupid question, but has anybody tried to get a cell signal out there?" Nick asked.

"I did, yesterday," Bud said. "Nothing. Not even one bar."

Hudson and Joe both had top-of-the-line phones with exceptional global coverage. The AP made sure their international staff was able to stay in touch as much as possible, even in remote locations. Though she had no expectations they'd have any better reception up here in the mountains, it was worth a try. "Mind if I see if mine works?"

"Well, of course yours will," J.T. replied with a smug expression. "Go on. Let's see you save the day and work a miracle. We'll start calling you Saint Hudson, like all the other misguided, liberal fucks who think you hung the moon."

Hudson ignored him and turned on her phone to check how much battery she had left; less than a quarter charge remained. She stuck it back in her pocket as Elliot stepped aside to give her access to the tunnel.

"Be careful," Steffi called after her.

Hudson nodded in acknowledgement as she tilted up her headlamp and got on her knees to crawl through the entrance and up the chute of hard-packed snow.

Though the tunnel didn't have much of an angle, it had enough of a slope that Hudson kept slipping backward, because the bottom was smooth and iced over from having the duffel slide repeatedly back and forth along its length.

Mild claustrophobia was also a brief concern. She hated such tight, enclosed places, but the far end drew her forward, beckoning with a muted light and a blast of fresh air.

When she reached the opening, she pulled herself forward until half her body was outside the tunnel, exposed to the elements. Snow was coming down hard, and a stiff wind was blowing it around, reducing visibility to a quarter mile or less. She couldn't even see the mountain on the other side of the gorge clearly. No way would a helicopter risk coming back here until the storm subsided, and that wasn't going to happen soon. The sky was overcast as far as she could see in all directions.

Bud had been right when he'd reported that no trace of the rest of the train was visible from the exit. All she could see were big expanses of white—above, below, and on either side. The slope they were on was so steep, there appeared, at first glance, anyway, to be no safe way out of there except through an airlift rescue.

Hudson pulled out her phone and checked the display. No bars, not even when she held it up in all directions. If hers didn't work, none of the others likely would, either. It had been a long shot, but she was still disappointed. Reluctantly, she retreated back down the tunnel to the others.

"So?" J.T. asked as soon as Hudson reappeared.

"Nothing," she replied, for the benefit of the others who were watching her expectantly.

"Big surprise."

"What now?" Nick asked.

"I wish we knew what the weather's supposed to do," Bud said. "Did anybody look at a long-range forecast before all this happened?"

No one spoke.

"I wish we had a radio that worked," Elliot said. "We'd get the weather and maybe even an update on the search for us. You'd think a missing train would be big news."

"We found a CD boom box with an AM/FM radio," Steffi replied. "Did anybody try that?"

"It won't work up here if the phones don't." J.T.'s tone was, as usual, condescending and dismissive.

"Not necessarily," Hudson said. She wished she could remember more about radio waves and how they traveled, but she did recall that AM waves were better at transcending physical barriers like mountains than FM, and definitely had a longer reach. "We should try the AM band. Especially after sunset. AM waves bounce off the ionosphere at night and can travel hundreds of miles."

"How the heck do you know that?" Steffi asked.

"A prerequisite course for a journalism degree," she replied.

"I'll go get it." Nick went to find the boom box.

"You're just a wealth of knowledge, aren't you?" J.T. said to Hudson.

"That's something you should know, too, I would think," she replied. "Oh, that's right. You got your degree at a clown college, didn't you?"

"Shut the fuck up. I'm so over you." He turned to his buddies. "Let's go play some cards. There's nothing for us to do but wait."

The three men returned to their seats as Nick reappeared with the boom box.

Hudson and Steffi huddled beside him as he hunched down near the exit tunnel and turned on the radio. He slowly dialed through the whole AM bandwidth and back again, stopping whenever he heard the briefest trace of a voice or music, but nothing was clear enough to get any information from. He tried the FM band, too, but all he got there was static.

"Sorry," Nick said. "Do you think it would help to try it at the other end of the tunnel? Would that make a difference?" he asked Hudson.

"Let's wait until later," she suggested. "Save the batteries." The depressing series of disappointments had crushed her hope of getting Joe out of this quickly, with minimal long-term effects.

As usual, Steffi was quick to offer positive encouragement. "I'm sure you're right about it being better at night. The blizzard will probably be over, then, too. It's just a few hours, and I bet we'll hear there's a big effort underway to find us."

"Hold that thought," Hudson replied. "I'm going to go check on Joe."

He was still sleeping soundly. Curt was checking his pulse.

"How is he?" she asked in a low voice.

Curt shrugged. "His pulse is strong. His color's okay. And he doesn't seem to have a fever, which is all good. I just don't know beyond that, Hudson. I'm sorry."

"Nothing else we can do for him?"

"Just keep him hydrated and warm." Curt glanced around and apparently noticed that no one was keeping watch in the luggage area. "What's it look like out there? Why did everybody come back inside?"

"A big blizzard," she told him. "No one's coming to get us any time soon."

"Damn."

"We tried to get a signal on an AM radio we found," she said. "No luck right now, but reception should be better at night. We're hoping to hear the weather forecast and status of the search for us."

"Where is it?" he asked. "The radio."

"Nick has it. Why?"

"Go get it, would you?" Curt took his flashlight and started scanning the interior of the car, particularly along the ceiling, where a wide strip of metal framing separated the windows curving up from either side. "And the Swiss Army knife."

"Okay, sure." She had no idea what he had in mind, but she'd been impressed so far with his MacGyver-like Boy Scout ingenuity, so she played along.

When she got back to him, he was training the light directly over his head, at one of the round plastic covers that concealed the train's intercom speakers.

"Mind if I ask what you're up to?"

"We'll have a better chance of getting a signal if we boost the antennae," he replied as he took the knife from her and set the radio on a seat. "But there's nothing to stand on to get up there."

"Put somebody on your shoulders. Steffi, maybe?" Hudson suggested. She seemed to be the lightest of all of them, except for the kids.

"That should work. Steffi!" He called down the aisle and she headed toward them.

"What's up?"

"We need your help. See the speaker up there? That plastic circle with the holes in it?" He showed her with his flashlight.

"Yeah, so?"

"I want you to take this…" He handed her the Swiss Army knife. "And get up on my shoulders. Pry the cover off, pull out the speaker, and cut all the wires to it."

"All right. I can do that." She climbed up on his shoulders, and, with Hudson helping to steady her, did the job in only a minute or two. "Done. Now what?"

"Hold on. I want you to do the same with the next one." Curt steadied her with his arms around her legs and moved slowly down the aisle about twenty-five feet to the next speaker.

They passed by the injured, who seemed fascinated.

Once she'd finished with the second speaker, Steffi said, "Okay. That's done."

"One of the wires you just clipped should lead back to that other speaker," he replied. "That's the one we want—just yank on each wire until you get the one that's not attached any more, and pull the whole thing out."

"Got it." Steffi pulled and tugged, arm over arm, and a long string of wire came out of the speaker hole.

Curt let her down and trained his flashlight beam on the wire to examine it more closely. It looked like the same kind Hudson had at home on her stereo—coppery-colored braided wire, encased in a clear plastic sheath. "Copper. Perfect. If we attach one end to the radio and trail the other end out of the tunnel, I bet we get much better reception. We used to do this with our transistor radios at camp, and at night we could get stations four states away, on the other side of the Cascades. Want to try it now?"

"Absolutely," Hudson said.

Steffi grabbed the radio as Curt gathered up the twenty-five feet of wire, and the three of them headed toward the tunnel. Their acrobatics in the aisle had not gone unnoticed, however, and several others trailed after them, curious. J.T. and his boys, Kris, Nick, Gary, Anna—everyone who was mobile and healthy gathered around as Curt attached the wire to the rigid antennae of the boom box.

"Give me the other end." Hudson knelt at the entrance to the tunnel and Curt handed her the wire. She wrapped it twice around her right glove, so she wouldn't lose it crawling through the slippery tunnel, and set off to lay it in place.

The blizzard had lessened slightly in intensity, but visibility was still poor. She stuck her upper body outside only long enough to get a good look around and to trail the end of the wire as far as it would reach.

She crawled backward toward the others. Nick was waiting for her return, and so was everyone else. Even Fritz and Hugo had joined the crowd in the luggage compartment.

"Okay, give it a go. Let's see if it works."

Chapter Nineteen

Nick flipped on the radio and turned the volume up full. No one moved and everyone was quiet. He started at the beginning of the AM band, and almost immediately they picked up a faint voice and heard a few words in German, then static again.

Never before had Steffi wished so much she'd have taken another language in school when she'd had the opportunity.

"Go back," Bud said.

"I'm trying," Nick tweaked the dial back and forth across the area where they'd heard it, but the voice seemed to be gone.

"You realize if you get something, it's probably going to be in German, or maybe Italian," J.T. said.

"Fritz can help translate." Steffi beckoned to the young man and urged him forward. "You understand, right? Can you tell us what they say on the radio?"

"Ja. Sure. I try." He was using a ski pole as a cane for his sprained ankle. Everyone cleared a space for him to limp through, and he went to stand by Nick, leaning against the wall of the car for support.

Everyone fell silent again as Nick continued trying to locate a clear signal. Suddenly, a male voice, speaking German, filled the car, and all around Steffi people erupted into spontaneous cheers and cries of triumph.

But the enthusiasm dampened at once when the voice gave way to a pop tune, also in German.

"I know this station," Fritz said, and shook his head. "All music." He indicated to Nick that he should keep searching.

The next signal they got that was clear enough to make out, farther down the bandwidth, sounded more like a newscast. A deep male voice spoke in a clipped, regular cadence as though he was reading from prepared material, with an undertone of urgency.

"What's he saying?" J.T. asked.

Fritz didn't answer right away. He waved at J.T. to be quiet and continued to listen intently. Finally, he began to translate, speaking haltingly as he searched for the right words, and pausing now and then to listen some more. "Big storm now bring more snow to Alps. Many avalanches has been already. In ski places, villages, roads... very bad. Many dead. Weather today stops planes and...and, how you say...*hubschrauber*?" He made a whirling motion with his finger.

"Helicopter?" Bud asked.

"Ja, helicopter." Fritz nodded and listened some more. "Uhmm... Switzerland ask to have help, very fast. Also Germany, Italy."

The next part of the newscast made him frown, and Steffi made out the words *Bernina Pass* and, later, *Bernina Express*. Most everyone else, apparently, had also caught the references, because several of them inched forward, their faces tense and strained.

"He say..." Fritz looked around at the others once the radio newscast switched to music. His expression told Steffi he really did not want to be the one to pass along whatever he'd heard. "He say Bernina Pass closed...long time closed, maybe one month. No trains, no cars, because many avalanches."

"What did they say about the search for us?" Hudson asked.

"He say, Bernina Express train...*abstürzen*?" Fritz looked to Hugo, but Hugo just shook his head, so he resorted to pantomime. His hand became the train, moving smoothly forward, then suddenly toppling over, and down, down, down...thrown off the mountain. A pretty graphically accurate representation of what had happened, except for their two cars. "*Abstürzen*?" Fritz looked at their faces to make sure they understood.

"Crashing, smashing, falling. We get it," J.T. said impatiently. "What about the search?"

Fritz looked down forlornly. "No search. He say, train found, in...*klamm*." Frustrated that he couldn't find the right word in English, he pantomimed again, this time drawing two big mountain peaks in the air, with a deep depression in between. He said the word *klamm* again when he made the dip for the valley.

"The train went into the gorge," Hudson said, and Fritz nodded. "No search," he repeated. "All die. No search."

"That helicopter yesterday must have seen the wreckage of the other cars and thought the whole train was toast," J.T. said.

"Which means what, exactly?" Steffi asked.

"Sounds like they've called off the search for us and aren't coming back because they're convinced we're all dead," Hudson replied. "They've got other emergencies to deal with. If the pass has been closed, we have no chance of being rescued unless a plane passing overhead sees us. Which is highly unlikely. Probably impossible."

"So, what do we do now?" Anna asked.

"Figure out a way to save ourselves," J.T. replied. "Who's got a good map?"

"We found several of the railway in purses and luggage," Steffi replied. "They don't show much other than the stops, though."

"Map?" Fritz repeated. "Viktor has map."

"Who's Viktor?" J.T. asked.

"I'll go." Hudson threaded through the others and headed away down the aisle toward the other passenger car.

"Be careful," Steffi called after her. "Viktor was their friend," she added, for J.T.'s benefit. "He died, in the other car."

"I thought you guys said that there's no safe way out of here by ground," Nick said.

"Safe? No," J.T. replied. "But if it's down to a choice between taking a risk and maybe getting off this mountain, or waiting here to die, I know which one I'm taking. I just need a route and a destination."

"Do you suppose we can ski out of here?" Bud asked.

"That's what I'm thinking. Fastest way, and the two of us can handle pretty steep slopes," J.T. replied. "We've just got to be able to traverse away from the gorge safely."

"Two of you?" Elliot asked. "I'm coming with you."

"Not with that leg, you're not," J.T. said. "That's jacked up, man. You'll never go the distance."

"I can make it. It feels a lot better today."

"No way. You're staying here."

Elliot didn't look happy, but he didn't argue further and seemed to accept J.T.'s pronouncement.

On the one hand, Steffi was relieved to hear that someone was going to try to get help, since it sounded like the rest of the world had given up on them. But she wished it were anyone but this J.T. character, who seemed to have nothing but his own best interests in mind. Could they rely on him to do whatever it took to get rescuers here as soon as possible? Did they have any choice?

"Do we trust this guy?" Anna asked her in a low voice.

"I was just thinking the exact same thing," she replied. "He's a creep. And all about himself. He doesn't give a damn about anybody else."

"*But*, if he's a narcissist *and* a TV reporter, won't he want to play hero and get all that good publicity and airtime?" Anna asked. "That's a powerful incentive, I would think, for him to get people here in time to save us, if he can."

"I hope you're right."

Hudson reappeared. "Found the map. Let's take it to one of the tables." There were two bench-table setups in each passenger car, capable of seating four.

Hudson took one of the seats and spread out the laminated guide. Made for Alpine hikers, it was a very detailed representation of the whole region around the Bernina Pass, showing topographic contours of the peaks and valleys, as well as all populated areas, glaciers, roads, railways, remote buildings, and major hiking trails.

J.T. and Bud took the two seats across from Hudson, and the remaining one stayed vacant for several seconds as everyone else gathered around, looking at each other. Finally, Elliot slipped into it.

Steffi wondered whether he was still hoping to convince J.T. to let him come along.

With four headlamps trained on the map, every detail was clearly illuminated.

"Where are we, exactly?" J.T. asked. "Anybody know?"

"Around here," Hudson replied, putting her finger on the map. "This is the gorge, right next to the rail line where it starts descending."

"So, what's the closest civilization?" Bud asked.

All four heads bent closer to the map to examine every small dot and line. Some had captions, like *Alp Grüm* or *Galleria Lunga*, but many were unmarked.

"I say we backtrack to this last rail station," J.T. said. We can follow the track, get back down in the valley, call from there."

"That station and the one before it were closed," Steffi reminded him.

"Doesn't really matter. Somebody probably lives there, even if it's closed right now. Or, worst-case scenario, we break in to use the phone."

"If you go that way, you're going to have to cross a lot of avalanche fields," Hudson said. "This whole section," she pointed to the map, "had tons of cornices, and all the snow barriers were already overflowing. You'd be better off going south."

"That's a lot farther to go to get to anything," J.T. said. "And we'd have to get up and over the mountain we're on. You're crazy." He turned to Bud. "Let's pack up. It's still early. We can probably make it there before nightfall if we get going."

"Whatever you say. Only take me a few minutes." Bud started off toward their gear.

"Visibility is shit out there," Hudson said. "You wouldn't even see a slide coming at you. Not to mention the wind you're going to have to battle. Going now is suicidal."

"We'll be in the valley so fast visibility won't matter. And we have the right clothes for the wind. We *will* need water. At least a couple of bottles each." J.T. got to his feet and started to take the map, but Hudson stopped him.

"You'll get your water, and you can take the map," she said, "when you go. I want to copy down the major landmarks and things first, in case we need it later."

He laughed. "You so sure I'm not going to make it?"

"I really hope you do," she said. "I'd love to see you prove me wrong about you if it gets Joe to a hospital. But I like to hedge my bets."

"Just make sure you spell my name right," he replied before heading off.

"Need something to make your map with?" Steffi asked.

"That I have, thanks." Hudson got up and retrieved her daypack from a few rows farther on. "A reporter is never without pen and paper, you know, even on vacation." Hudson sat down and ripped a couple of pages from her spiral notebook. "Though I'd trade everything in here right now for a satellite phone, or a big roast turkey, or pizza for everybody—"

"Please stop. You're making me hungry."

"Sorry, my bad. My stomach is growling. I'm surprised you can't hear it." Hudson started tracing over the map, copying the track line, railway stations, topography of nearby peaks, and any buildings in the proximity. She was focusing, Steffi saw, on the features south of them—the alternate way out she'd been advocating.

J.T. and Bud came stomping up the aisle in their ski boots not long afterward. They were carrying their skis and poles, and had packed their essential gear into two of the smaller backpacks they'd recovered. Strapped to each pack was an avalanche shovel and collapsible snow probe, and J.T. had also claimed one of the coils of climbing rope. Steffi recognized both packs: J.T. had Viktor's expensive North Face bag, and Bud's bright-red one belonged to one of the Japanese women.

J.T. took the map from Hudson, folded it up neatly, and tucked it into an inside jacket pocket.

"Here's your water." Curt had retrieved four bottles from their cache.

"Thanks." J.T. stuck two in the side pockets of his pack and gave the others to Bud. "Well, time to go."

"Are you carrying avalanche beacons?" Hudson asked.

The question clearly took J.T. by surprise. "No. Why?"

"So that if you get into trouble, in the first stretch anyway, we might be able to save your undeserving ass."

"I'll get 'em," Bud said at once, before J.T. had a chance to respond, and he headed back to retrieve the devices from the stuff they'd left behind.

"You'd really go out there and save me." J.T. was unconvinced.

"That's the difference between us," Hudson said. "You'll never understand anyone going out of their way for someone else."

"Yeah, you're such a sterling example of pure selfless love for all mankind. Excuse me, Saint Hudson, while I go hurl."

Bud returned with one of the beacons already clipped to his jacket. He had two more in his hands, and he gave one each to J.T. and Hudson.

J.T. and Bud turned theirs on and set them up to transmit, while Hudson put hers into receive mode.

"Don't make us have to use this," she told the men. "I think you're stupid for going right now. And I have no warm-and-fuzzy feelings for you, asshole," she added, to J.T. "But I really hope you make it. For everyone's sake."

He gave her a half smile. "Touching, I'm sure. Let's go, Bud."

Hudson turned to Steffi. "I'll go out and keep an eye on them. Will you get me a probe and shovel while I put on some better boots and pants?"

"Sure," Steffi said. "You should put on a harness, too, so we can have a rope on you if you have to go out."

"Good idea."

"And I'll back you up," Nick volunteered. "I took an avalanche search-and-rescue class."

"Count me in," Gary said. "So did I."

Chapter Twenty

New York, New York

"Boss?" The expression on his managing editor's face hit Bob Furness like a sucker punch. The news was bad. So bad, he was hesitant to share it. He stood just inside the doorway, biting his lip.

Bob had been down to the International Desk several times during the day seeking updates on Joe and Hudson, but they hadn't been able to track down the pair. The rash of avalanches throughout Europe continued to be a monster of a story, demanding extra staffing and freelancers, but he still demanded that they assign one person solely to the task of finding out the fate of the sightseeing train they'd been on. And he wasn't going to leave the office until he got some answers. "Tell me."

"They've called off the search for the Bernina Express—the train they were supposed to be on. A helicopter flyover confirmed it was derailed by an avalanche and plunged into a deep gorge. There were no survivors." The man coughed nervously and went on. "Their hotels still haven't heard from them, nor have they called in to us. Their voice mails are both full."

Bob let the reality sink in. He'd been in the business long enough to know other journalists who'd been killed too young, mostly on the job. It was never easy. But Hudson and Joe had been almost like his own kids. He felt sick to his stomach. "Do we have any information on recovery of the bodies? I want the company to help expedite everything, if it can." Tears sprang to his eyes.

"The media there are reporting that the whole area where it happened—a high mountain pass—is closed indefinitely because of all the snow and danger of more slides. They're not going to attempt a recovery at this time."

"Damn," he muttered under his breath. "All right. Thanks. You can get back to work."

"I'm sorry, Bob. They were both…well, both just exceptional people. Do you want me to tell the rest of the staff?"

"No. I'll take care of that." He wasn't happy with the resolution of the search for Hudson and Joe. Even if they were dead, it seemed… disloyal, somehow, and coldly uncaring, to simply accept the news and move on. To leave the two of them up there without a proper burial, where their bodies would be exposed in the spring thaw like some litterbug's discarded refuse.

He wanted to bring them home. He had to. Somehow, he had to find a way to make that possible. He personally, and the company he represented, owed it to Hudson and Joe.

Bob rang his secretary. "Get me on the first flight to Zurich that leaves after…" He checked his watch. It was almost seven p.m. now, and he'd need at least ninety minutes to get home, pack a bag, and get to the airport. "Let's say, anything after ten. I'm leaving now. I'll pick up the tickets at JFK."

"Do you want me to also book your return?" she asked.

"No. Just the flight over. Thanks." He disconnected and looked up the emergency-notification contact numbers that Joe and Hudson had provided on their personnel records.

Hudson had listed Joe first, and Joe had listed Hudson. It didn't surprise him too much.

Bob went on to their second choices. Joe had named his mother and Hudson her brother. He added their numbers to his phone but didn't dial them. No reason to awaken anyone with such tragic news. He'd make the calls when he had some information on when they could hold the funerals.

❖

Bernina Pass, Switzerland

Hudson stepped carefully out of the tunnel, into the deep depression in the snow the men had made while putting on their skis.

The blizzard had lessened and visibility was noticeably better, though she still couldn't see the peak of the mountain that towered over them because of the low cloud cover. The slope they were on was steep, scarily so, and difficult to navigate—the once-smooth surface, as far as she could see, had been carved out and churned up into the chaos typical of avalanche fields.

She was glad Steffi had suggested the harnesses and ropes for safety. Nick and Gary were waiting inside, already roped up as well, with twenty feet of line separating them from each other. In the event they had to go after J.T. and Bud, Kris and Steffi were also standing by to help. Kris would belay them, using the massive built-in luggage rack as an anchor, while Steffi fed her information about what was happening from the outer exit.

Fortunately, all three of the would-be rescuers had transceivers, probes, and shovels, courtesy of the injured Japanese. She was hoping to hell they didn't have to use them, but she had a very bad feeling about the whole situation.

J.T. had been deluded when he'd thought they'd get out of the danger zone quickly. He and Bud were heading uphill, to put a safer distance between themselves and the gorge, and at the rate they were progressing, they'd be traversing the wide avalanche field for the next couple of hours at least, at risk of another snow slide all the while, and they'd gotten several more inches of heavy snow last night.

Hudson kept an eye on the men as they negotiated their way carefully through the avalanche debris, but she also used the opportunity to get a better look in all directions. She was warm enough, thanks primarily to Fritz's borrowed snowboarding jacket and pants, but though the winter boots she'd found were much better suited for the conditions than her own, they were a bit too large to be really comfortable, even with two pairs of heavy wool socks.

She studied the landscape to the south. The snowfield in that direction was pristine after only a couple of hundred feet of slide debris, which meant they were nearly at the outer edge of the avalanche field. Gazing up, she spotted a long, winding ridge running up toward the peak, so steep the snow couldn't cling to the charcoal rocks, which stood out in vivid contrast to the white that surrounded it. The ridge had acted like one side of a funnel when the avalanche hit, directing the river of snow from above right onto the passing train.

And it would do it again, if more avalanches rained down from the same peaks.

But the terrain did confirm that a southern route out was a better one, though longer and more demanding. From what she could see, it looked as though once you got beyond the ridge, you were relatively safe from avalanches. At least a lot safer than J.T. and Bud were at the moment.

Hudson hugged herself and kept moving around enough to keep herself warm. Though she hit places now and then where she'd sink to her waist, she was a little surprised to find that most of the time the snow seemed only knee-deep—the depth of what had fallen overnight. Below that lay the deep layer of hard-packed avalanche snow, compressed to concrete-like consistency.

"Can you still see them?" Nick shouted up the tunnel.

"Easily," she yelled back. "Though I lose them now and then when they go behind a big pile of snow. They're picking their way along. Very slow going on skis. They've probably only gone three or four hundred feet."

"I'm coming out." Nick crawled up the tunnel and joined her. "Unbelievable," he said, once he'd taken a good look around. "This slide was massive. As far as you can see."

"I've witnessed others. Never anything like this," she said.

"Can't believe how lucky we were."

"Yeah. You can see why they called off the search. Freakishly small chance of surviving an avalanche that size."

Nick turned to watch J.T. and Bud. "They hardly look like they're moving. Think they'll make the rail station by nightfall?"

"Doubtful. Those skis aren't helping them at the moment. They're hindering them. I'm surprised they haven't taken them off."

"Maybe they're afraid they'll sink too much without them," Nick said.

"It's not that bad in most places. The avalanche really compacted it."

"Yeah. Sure took a long time for them to dig through it."

"Room for one more?" Gary called up through the tunnel.

"Come on up," Nick shouted back.

Gary emerged and did the same "survey the surroundings with a stunned expression" that they'd both just experienced. "Holy shit."

"Yeah. Makes you feel small, doesn't it?" Hudson asked.

"And damn fortunate."

"Mind if I ask you a question, Hudson?" Nick asked.

"Shoot."

"What's with you and him?" He nodded toward J.T.'s receding figure. "You two obviously have a history."

"Is it that obvious I loathe the man?" she asked.

"Not hard to see why. We're all just concerned that he's the one we're all banking our lives on, and you seem to know him."

"We've crossed paths more times than I can count," she said. "Mostly at natural disasters: tsunamis, floods, tornados, that kind of thing. The type of event that brings out the best and worst in people."

"And?" Gary asked.

"J.T. is the only reporter I know of in those situations who'll fly in, tape his half-ass recap as quickly as possible, and fly right back out again," Hudson replied. "He's so fucking self-absorbed it doesn't even cross his mind to stay to help. I mean, when every other journalist, tourist, or passer-by around you is pitching in, desperately trying to find people in earthquake debris or in the aftermath of Katrina, how can you just get back in your taxi and go home?"

"Unbelievable," Nick said.

"He shouldn't be in this profession," Hudson said. "He's in it for the rush he gets being on the air and being recognizable, not because he wants to make a difference. So I give him grief at every available opportunity."

"Do you think he'll—" Gary stopped short and froze.

Hudson felt it, too. A slight vibration under their feet.

The three of them turned in unison to stare up in horror at the mountain. The peak was still obscured, but the blossoming mist of white that was racing toward them was undeniable. And unbelievably fast.

"Avalanche!" Hudson shouted.

They all scrambled to get back into the tunnel. Nick dove headfirst into the icy passage, with Gary tumbling in almost on top of him. Hudson stumbled slightly in her oversized boots and reached it last, but made it into the relative safety of the chute just before the wall of snow reached her. Her momentum carried her down the slick tunnel on her ass, feet-first, and she landed hard on top of the two men, who were piled up at the exit door of the train.

"Fuck!" Gary shouted, and clutched at his arm.

Nick screamed, almost simultaneously, from the bottom of the heap of bodies. "Off! Get off! I'm hurt!"

Kris and Steffi helped extricate and untangle them; the climbing rope that had connected the trio was now looped around legs and bodies.

"I think I broke my wrist," Gary said as he got up, gingerly cradling his left arm. "And my glasses, too, damn it," he added when he saw the broken frames.

"Shit!" Kris was the first to see the worst of it.

One of the thin, metal avalanche probes had impaled Nick's left calf.

"Fuck, that looks bad. Curt! Curt!" Hudson hollered as she tried to unclip herself from the climbing rope.

He came running up the aisle. "What's wrong? What is it?"

"Son of a bitch, it hurts!" Nick groaned and rolled onto his side.

"Get the first-aid stuff. You've got two more patients," Hudson told Curt. As he raced off to get the bag of supplies, she turned to Kris and Steffi. "Get this rope off them and untangle it. I'm going back to try to find Bud and J.T., if I can still get out." She grabbed an ice ax and crawled back up the tunnel.

It was blocked again, as she expected it would be, so she chipped away at the barrier of quickly seizing snow with furious blows, praying it wasn't too thick. She broke through after only a few minutes and carved out a hole just big enough to slip through, then slid back down the tunnel.

Curt had removed the probe from Nick's calf and was bandaging his leg. Gary was still clutching his arm, waiting for his turn.

Steffi and Kris, meanwhile, had done as she'd asked. The climbing rope was neatly coiled near the tunnel entrance, and Kris was ready again on belay.

"You're going out there alone?" Steffi asked as she handed Hudson the end of the rope.

Hudson clipped it to her harness. "I'm not optimistic I'll find them. They'd gotten a good distance from us, and the slide may have swept them into the gorge. But I have to try. Will you keep watch from the tunnel if I need you to haul me back?"

"Of course." Steffi stopped her with a hand on her arm and looked intently into her eyes. Her usual optimism had been replaced by dread. "Hudson, please be careful. I...I can't bear the thought of anything happening to you."

The tender, raw emotion in Steffi's expression melted something inside Hudson: an icy wall of distance and detachment she'd kept in place for far too long. She laid her hand on Steffi's reassuringly. "Nothing's going to happen to me. I'll be back before you know it."

Hudson scrambled back up the ice chute and emerged once more onto the steep slope. The slide was over, the mountain quiet again, though errant airborne puffs of powder still drifted down on her from above. This avalanche hadn't been nearly as big as the first, but it was enough to deposit at least another few feet of snow onto the lower slope where they were stranded.

She saw no sign of the two men, no trace of color or movement at all in the debris field. Hudson checked her transceiver. Two signals were visible. Using the directional arrows on her device, she headed toward the nearest one, moving as fast as possible while stumbling over the uneven surface. She had to skirt snow piles the size of small houses, and now and then she'd sink in to her thighs. The tone emitted by the transceiver became louder the closer she got to the first beacon buried beneath the snow.

She was acutely aware of how much time was passing. The survival rate for victims of an avalanche was very high—more than ninety percent—if they were found within a fifteen-minute window. Well, that was if they weren't killed during the impact. After a half hour, it dropped to just thirty percent.

The avalanche had pulled the men downslope, but their signals indicated they hadn't been swept into the gorge. She was forty feet or less from the edge when the booming tone and arrows told her she'd reached either J.T. or Bud. She used her probe and hit something solid a few feet to her left, about five or six feet down.

She scooped away debris with the shovel like a madwoman, stopping to use her hands when she reached a big chunk of ice or compacted snow. After three minutes of digging, she saw her first hint of color—part of a burgundy jacket. Thirty seconds later, she'd unearthed a good-sized air pocket and Bud's face.

"Thank God," he said after sucking in several lungfuls of air.

"You hurt?" she asked.

"Shit, yeah." He winced in pain. "Leg's fucking killing me. I think it's broken."

"Hang tight. I have to find J.T." She stood and trained her receiver on the other signal. It led her to her left and even closer to the edge of the gorge.

Probing again, she hit something only three or four feet beneath the surface, and her shovel quickly found J.T.

He wasn't breathing.

Hudson dug furiously until she could pull him up and out of his snowy tomb. She felt for a pulse and, finding none, began CPR. Or what she hoped was a pretty good facsimile of CPR, learned from TV and watching others, alternating mouth-to-mouth breathing with chest compressions.

"Don't do this, J.T.!" she screamed at him as she tried to restart his heart.

CHAPTER TWENTY-ONE

L et me try," Curt said from behind Hudson.
   She whirled around, so surprised by his sudden appearance she nearly pissed herself. "Jesus, Curt. Give me some warning next time."

He had his makeshift stretcher balanced over one shoulder and the first-aid bag strapped to his back. As he got to his knees and took over for her, counting the compressions aloud, Hudson noticed that he'd come out on a separate rope from hers.

"Come *on*," Curt said as he worked on J.T. "Breathe!"

Hudson had given up hope, but Curt continued CPR until, a couple of minutes later, J.T. sucked in a deep breath.

Curt put a finger on his throat. "Got a pulse!"

J.T. wasn't opening his eyes, but he was breathing again, and she felt an unexpected wave of relief.

"We'll never be able to get them back with just the two of us," Curt said. "The snow's too uneven to drag them over it, and they'll get damn heavy in the stretcher over that long a distance."

"Who all do we have left who's not injured?" Hudson tried to remember everybody.

"Kris is on belay with me, Steffi with you. Anna's lookout. Elliot's pretty mobile, but I don't think his leg is up to this. I think that's it," Curt said.

"Who are the two strongest of the women, do you think?" Hudson asked.

"Kris and Steffi. They're both very good climbers."

"Let's get them out here, then, and put Anna and Elliot on belay. "
"Good plan," Curt said. "You go. I'll get Bud dug out."
"He thinks his leg is broken."
"Bring back something for splints, then, too."

Hudson hustled back toward the tunnel, using the winding, carved path she and Curt had already dug through the snow, which saved time and energy. She was getting used to the boots, so she was able to move fast enough to be winded by the time she neared Steffi at the entrance.

"They're both alive," she said, and saw Steffi smile in relief. "But J.T.'s unconscious and Bud has a broken leg. We have to stretcher them out. We'll need you and Kris to help haul them, with Anna and Elliot on belay."

"Got it. We'll get harnessed up, give them a quick belay lesson, and be right there," Steffi replied. Hudson could see the hesitation in her eyes; she clearly didn't want to go out on the avalanche field, but she was pushing her fears aside.

"I'm going in, too. I need to find something to splint Bud's leg with," Hudson said as Steffi got ready to enter the tunnel. "Are there any more skis and poles?"

"The Japanese had a bunch, but I'm not sure where they are," Steffi replied, then called out to the others, "Gangway, I'm coming down."

Hudson gave her a few seconds to clear the way before following.

❖

"You okay?" Kris looked intently at Steffi.

"Yeah, sure. I'm good." Steffi knew Kris could read how scared and nervous she was. This was way outside her comfort zone. But it had to be done, and talking about it only reinforced those feelings. "Ready to go?"

"Whenever you are."

Hudson breezed past them with skis, poles, and binding material, and headed toward the luggage compartment. "See you out there," she said over her shoulder.

"Right behind you," Steffi replied. She was last up the tunnel. By the time she clipped onto the rope, Hudson was already a good distance away on the avalanche field.

Kris had waited for her. "You want me to lead or follow?"

"Lead, of course."

Kris clipped on and headed quickly down the path that Hudson and Curt had cut through the snow. Steffi followed about ten feet behind, trying to keep pace, but Kris began to pull away from her about halfway there because of her longer legs. She had to be completely focused on where she stepped to keep from falling.

She heard Bud scream as she neared. Hudson and Curt were setting his broken leg.

"Stop!" Bud yelled. "Wait a—" He screamed again.

"Worst is over," Curt said. "I'm sorry, but we need to do this fast and get you out of here. We're all vulnerable on this slope." He started splinting the leg. Bud's pants had been sliced open so Curt could bandage the wound beneath, and there was quite a lot of blood on the snow around them. "We've got some pain pills left. I'll give you one when we get back."

Curt looked up at Steffi and Kris. "He still had one ski on, so his leg got really busted up. And it was hell digging him out of there."

Steffi glanced over at J.T., who was laid out on the skis-and-webbing stretcher awaiting transport. He was so still that, had she not been told otherwise, she'd have thought he was dead.

Curt did a quick but thorough job on the splint, then bound Bud's broken leg to his good one to stabilize it as much as possible. "Okay. Done here. Let's get J.T. transported so we can come back for him."

"You're not leaving me here alone?" Bud asked. "Fuck that. Take me first. J.T. got us both into this."

"No, Bud," Curt said. "I'm sorry, but he's the more critically injured." He motioned for her and the others to go stand by the stretcher. "We'll be back to get you as fast as we can."

"Come on," Bud said. "Don't leave me."

"Let's go. Hudson, you want to get at his head, Kris and Steffi at his feet." Curt grabbed the other corner, by J.T.'s left shoulder. "Ready? Lift."

Even though J.T. wasn't a small man, with the four of them dividing his weight, it was doable. The hardest part was watching where they stepped and keeping the skis from digging into their hands. Halfway back, they set down the stretcher and switched sides to give their hands a break.

They were nearly to the tunnel when J.T. opened his eyes.

He looked disoriented for a moment, until he spotted Hudson. "Oh, fuck. I'll never hear the end of this."

Hudson laughed, the first laughter anyone had heard since the wreck. They couldn't help but join in, though the situation was anything but funny. They'd accomplished something, getting J.T. here safely, and the laughter felt really good, like it somehow released some of the stress they were all carrying.

"How do you feel?" Curt asked. "Are you hurting anywhere?"

"More like everywhere. Like I just went ten rounds and got my ass kicked." J.T. gritted his teeth and grimaced in pain. "Fucking headache's the worst of it."

"We'll get you inside and comfortable," Curt said as they set the stretcher down near the entrance to the tunnel. "I'll go down first, you lower him after me," he told them. "Once we get him settled, we'll go back for Bud."

They carried J.T. to where the other injured were clustered, then went back out to repeat the same hairy round trip to transport Bud. Steffi noticed how they slowed down considerably on the final leg of the journey. By the time they were all back safely to the tunnel, the rest looked as exhausted as she felt.

The hard labor of hauling and the failure of J.T.'s rescue trek so soon after it started left them all quiet, as did the knowledge that four more of the once-healthy among them had joined the injured list.

❖

Dinner that night, or what passed for it, was a subdued affair with meager portions for all.

Knowing they had no foreseeable rescue coming, as a group they voted to limit everyone to a small square of chocolate and a cup of water each. The injured got served first, then those still mobile—

Hudson, Kris, Steffi, Curt, and Anna—clustered together around one of the bench seats to have theirs. Elliot stayed with J.T. and Bud, trying to make them more comfortable.

"This is the end of the water," Anna said as she poured for Curt. "I'll start melting more snow when we're done."

Curt pulled a handful of the pocket warmers from his jacket. "Here. Try to make them last."

Hudson had given Joe another pain pill from the bottle Curt had handed her, which left only three more. "Didn't you say we had more pain meds, too? I'm about out."

"We've got some Tylenol with codeine. I gave one to Bud," he replied. "But there's not many. Both of them are going to be really hurting in another day or two."

They all went silent for a long while, no one daring to bring up the elephant in the room, until Anna finally broke the tension.

"So, what happens now? We just…wait?" She looked at each of them in turn.

"I don't think we have much choice," Kris replied.

"I know one thing we might do to improve our chances," Curt offered. "We need to build a signal fire of some kind outside the exit. Get everything we can that will burn, pile it onto a piece of metal or something, so we can light it if we see a plane go overhead. Has to be something that will create a lot of smoke, though. The blacker, the better, for visibility."

"How do you get black smoke?" Anna asked.

"Petroleum products, rubber, some plastics," he replied. "Things like tennis shoes, rubber bands, water bottles."

Hudson had been mulling over their options as well during the whole operation to save J.T. and Bud. "I'm going to leave in the morning, if the weather clears up a little," she told the others. "And try to get out of here by going south."

"By yourself? That's crazy." Steffi appeared shocked. "You can't!"

"Look," she said, "realistically, it sounds like we have a snowball's chance in hell of somebody finding us before more people die. No offense to your fire idea, Curt."

"None taken," he replied. "I know it's a real long shot."

"So, I figure we either all sit around here and watch each other get weaker and weaker, or I roll the dice and hope I catch a break. It's worth the risk."

"How can you go south?" Kris asked. "The mountain's in the way. You'll never skirt it. The slope is way too steep."

"You're right," Hudson replied. "I've got to go up and over. I think I can, via that rocky ridge that's right above us. Of course, I'd stand a much better chance if I had someone along with climbing experience. I know it's a lot to ask."

"That leaves me out," Anna said.

Hudson told Curt, "And you're needed here, to look out for the injured."

Steffi and Kris looked at each other.

"I don't want to be a shit," Kris said, "but I can't leave Fin."

That left only Steffi, who was apparently so terrified by the mere prospect of going that Hudson saw her hands start to shake, though she moved them quickly into her lap to keep the others from noticing. "I don't know…I—"

"Just think about it, Steffi," Hudson said. "You can give me your answer in the morning."

She got to her feet. "I'm going to get the map from J.T. and plan a route, then try to get some sleep so I can leave at first light."

❖

New York, New York

Bruce Fowler let himself into Hudson's apartment and put her mail on the table beside the front door. When he saw she had seven messages blinking on her answering machine, he frowned. Unless she was completely off the grid on the job, it was very unlike her not to check her landline messages at least every other day.

It didn't surprise him too much, though, since she hadn't answered any of his texts or cell voice mails, either, which was a major red flag that something was wrong. Particularly since she'd even asked him to feel free to call if he felt blue about his breakup with Andy.

He'd heard on the news this morning that there had been a bunch of avalanches in the Alps, with hundreds missing and feared dead. There couldn't possibly be a connection, he tried to tell himself. What were the chances? Still, he wanted a closer look at the EurAdventures itinerary she'd stuck on the fridge. He studied what she and Joe had planned for this week. Skiing in St. Moritz. He remembered that was one of the areas affected.

She'd left the name and number of the hotel where they'd be staying, so he dialed the front desk. "Hello, may I have Hudson Mead's room, please?"

"I'm sorry, sir. Miss Mead never checked in. We're still holding her room, however."

Bruce felt a chill at the back of his neck. "How about Joe Parker?"

"He hasn't checked in either, sir."

"All right, thank you." He hung up and started pacing. If she wasn't answering her cell or her home phone, and she hadn't checked in to her hotel, something had happened to Hudson. If she was in a region that had been hit hard by avalanches, he hoped she was just busy doing what she always did when in a situation like that: helping out.

He couldn't bear to think of the alternative.

CHAPTER TWENTY-TWO

Have you decided what you're going to do?" Kris asked in a low voice as Steffi settled in beside her. Fin was already asleep, and the rest of the car was dark and quiet though it was only ten p.m.

The day had been long and tiring, but though her body was aching and ready to rest, Steffi was still worrying about whether to accompany Hudson in the morning. "I change my mind every ten minutes. She can't go alone, but the whole idea scares the living crap out of me. I don't know that I can do it."

"I'm not going to talk you into it or out of it," Kris replied. "It's your decision. I've reconsidered, myself. But with Fin…well, I just can't bear to leave her."

"I don't blame you. If only there was someone else to go besides me."

"I know you probably don't want to hear this. And I'm not advocating that you go. Like I said, it's got to be your decision," Kris said. "But you have a tendency to underestimate your abilities. And if that's what's holding you back—that you're not sure you're up to it—I think you're more than capable."

"Gee, thanks. That's a big help. I need more reasons *not* to say yes. I don't need you adding to my conscience, which is already nagging me to go."

"You'll make the right choice, I know." Kris rolled over on her side. "Get some rest."

But Steffi stayed awake long after she heard Kris's breathing change to the soft, rhythmic cadence of sleep. She wrestled with her fears, imagined the risks, and tried to calculate their chance of success if she joined Hudson in her crazy idea.

Finally, she drifted off, still not making any decision.

She woke up hours later to the sound of muted voices at the other end of the car. Kris and Fin were both still asleep, so she eased quietly away from them and kept her light off until she was a few feet down the aisle.

She found Hudson, Curt, and Anna in the luggage compartment. They had amassed all the climbing and ski gear into a big pile.

"You're definitely going to want crampons," Curt told Hudson. "And ski poles."

Hudson looked up when she realized Steffi had joined them, and it was the expression on her face that finally convinced Steffi she couldn't stay behind and let her do this alone.

Until right this very instant, Hudson had seemed imperturbable. The first to sound the alarm when the avalanche was upon them. The first to venture into the damaged cars to search for victims. The first to venture onto the avalanche field to search for J.T. and Bud. She'd handled all that had happened with courage, calmness, and unflappable resolve. But the unguarded fear in her dark eyes this morning compelled Steffi to ignore her own numerous reservations. Hudson needed her. And that was reason enough. "I'm going with you."

Relief washed over Hudson's face. "I'm glad. We'll make a good team."

"When do we leave?"

"As soon as we're packed. I've already checked outside. It's not snowing any more, and the sun is just peeking up over the mountains."

"How long do you think we'll have to travel before we get somewhere?"

"I'm not sure," Hudson replied. "At least two days, I'm guessing. Maybe three."

"You'll probably have to dig a snow cave tonight, so you need to take shovels along," Curt said. "I can go over the basics of that with you. And if you take the candle, it'll keep you warmer than you think in a small space like that, as well as let you melt water."

"Appreciate that," Hudson said. "And any other tips you might want to pass on."

They spent the next half hour packing two backpacks with gear and getting tips from Curt. Each of them would be equipped with a harness, crampons, two ice axes, a one-hundred-eighty-foot length of climbing rope, helmet, snow probe, avalanche beacon, shovel, two ski poles, and hardware—ice screws, pitons, cams, carabineers, and belay, ascending, and rappelling devices. They also got some of the first-aid supplies, a lighter, two survival blankets, a chocolate bar, PowerBar, and two bottles of water each, some foam pieces to lie on, Hudson's candle and soda-can melting pot, and the Swiss Army knife. Hudson tried on several pairs of the insulated ice-climbing gloves available and took Fin's because they fit best.

"In case you see any aircraft," Curt said, "you'll want to have these to try to signal them with." He handed them a couple of small mirrors they'd retrieved from the luggage they'd gone through. "And this, too. Nice and bright, won't take up much room. A good ground cloth for the snow cave, and it'll help you be seen from the air if you spread it out." He unfolded a cheap plastic tablecloth, bright red in color, that had been found in one of the suitcases.

"Great. Thanks, Curt," Hudson said.

"Do you both have sunglasses?" Curt asked. "You might have a problem with snow blindness if the sun ever comes out."

"Yeah, I do," Steffi replied. "Thanks for the reminder."

"I've got mine in my daypack," Hudson said. "I'll go get them. And I need to talk to Joe before we go."

"Are we forgetting anything you might need?" Anna asked.

"Who knows until we need it?" Steffi replied. "I can't think of anything. I'm going to get my gloves and maybe another layer. And I need to say good-bye to Kris and Fin."

She got what she needed from her bag and moved quietly down the aisle to where she'd left her friends. They were still sleeping, so she hunched over Kris and gently shook her shoulder.

"Yeah, okay, okay. 'Sup?" Kris yawned and put her hand up to shield her eyes from the glare of Steffi's headlamp.

"We're leaving. I'm going with Hudson."

"You are?" That got Kris fully awake in a hurry. She sat up and fumbled for her light. "So, you're really going, huh?"

"Yup. Wish us luck."

"You got it. We're all counting on you."

They both got up, and Kris followed her back to the luggage compartment. They bypassed Hudson, who was kneeling over Joe. Steffi couldn't hear their conversation, but it sounded like they were arguing.

"Everything all right?" she asked Hudson once she'd joined them.

"He's not happy I'm going," Hudson replied. "You'll keep an eye on him, right?" she asked Curt. "Even if he gives you grief?"

"You know I'll do whatever I can for him. Don't worry about Joe. Just concentrate on getting somewhere safely."

As Steffi double-checked her gear one last time, Anna handed her a tube of ChapStick. "Might want this. Wish I had more to contribute."

"Thanks." She stuck it in her pocket and hugged Anna, then Curt. Finally, she turned to Kris. "Hold down the fort, and take care of Fin until we get back, okay?"

"I'll go up and watch you leave," Kris said.

"No. Say good-bye here. No need for you to get cold. Or color, anyway."

Kris enfolded Steffi in a bear hug and held her close for several seconds. "You be careful. I don't want anything to happen to you," she whispered, close to Steffi's ear. "I love you, you know?"

"I love you, too. Say a prayer or two for us. Couldn't hurt, right?"

Kris let her go. "You got it."

"Ready?" Hudson asked.

"Let's do this. After you."

Hudson got into the tunnel, dragging her laden backpack behind her, and Steffi followed close behind.

"Stay safe! Watch out for each other!" Curt called after them.

❖

Rega Control Center
Zurich Airport, Switzerland

Eckhart Glaus perused the latest dispatches as he sipped his first coffee of the morning. He'd been up until three a.m. dealing with the latest slew of distress calls, as avalanches continued to rain down from Alpine peaks.

During the four hours he'd been sleeping in his office, the control center had gotten another eight requests for emergency assistance. Most were relatively minor affairs, involving single-crew rescues of hikers, skiers, and motorists hit or stranded by snow slides. But one of the calls had been another major disaster, requiring numerous search-and-rescue resources: a small, remote village of two hundred plus in the canton of Ticino had been entirely buried in the middle of the night.

Eckhart went to his window and stared out at the overcast sky and the Alps, far in the distance. Never in his thirty years with Rega had he witnessed such weather as this. If global warming was at fault, which seemed likely, did they have more cruel winters ahead of them?

A knock on the door got his attention. "Yes?"

The door opened. "Sir, a gentleman from America is here to see you," his secretary said. "He apologizes for not making an appointment, but it's about some employees of his who were on the Bernina Express."

Glaus didn't ordinarily deal with the public, the PR office did, and he wouldn't have a minute to spare today if it was anything like the last two. "Tell him I'm sorry, but I'm much too busy to—"

"I'm sorry," a male voice interrupted in English, and a well-dressed older gentleman appeared behind Glaus's secretary. "Director Glaus, my name is Bob Furness. I'm senior vice president and executive editor of the Associated Press. You know of it?"

"Of course, Mister Furness. We utilize your news service here, especially weather-related and breaking stories." He nodded at his secretary. "It's fine. Thank you."

She stepped aside to let his guest in and shut the door behind her as she left.

"Won't you sit down?" Eckhart motioned toward the couch he'd just napped on. "Would you like some coffee?"

"Yes, please. Black."

He poured another cup and handed it to Furness before joining him on the couch with his own mug. "I apologize in advance that I haven't much time. How may I help you?"

"I'm fairly certain that two of my employees, reporter Hudson Mead and photographer Joe Parker, were on the Bernina Express train that was hit by an avalanche." Furness paused and cleared his throat. Eckhart heard a slight catch in his voice, an emotional quiver that told him that Furness had a deep and personal connection with the people he was talking about.

Eckhart understood that. He felt the same about the people at Rega, especially those who were the risk-takers: the pilots who flew in inclement weather, the paramedics and search teams who put their own lives on the line while searching for avalanche victims.

"I understand that you don't intend to search any more in that area," Furness said.

"No, sir, not at this time. The helicopter that found the debris reported no survivors. I'm afraid the train was swept into a gorge."

"With no disrespect, sir, " Furness said, "but in my line of work, I've heard of a great number of, what some might call 'miraculous' survival stories. Without a ground search, or at least an infrared search by air—which I'm told was not done—how can you be absolutely certain everyone's dead?"

"Mister Furness, I wish we had the resources to go over that area again, but the sad reality is, we do not." Eckhart took a sip of coffee. "We're still operating beyond capacity, with every bit of our resources working overtime—and relying on international help—just to keep pace with the new calls that keep coming in. Of course efforts will be made to recover the bodies, but only after this current crisis is past and there is some probability of success. It's a dangerous place to be right now."

Furness frowned and drummed his fingers on his knee. "What about…what about if I hire a private company to search? Would they have to get any special permits or permissions or anything?"

"If it's a Swiss company, no. It's not restricted air space. But if that's a decision you do make, I'd like you to keep us abreast of when you go and what you find." Eckhart pulled one of his business cards out of the breast pocket of his suit and gave it to the AP executive.

"I'll do that." Furness got to his feet. "I've taken up enough of your time. Thank you for seeing me."

They shook hands.

"I'm sorry I couldn't be of more help," Eckhart said. "If... if you're not able to find them, perhaps you'd like to give me your number. I'll telephone you when we're able again to get up to that area to search. I assure you, a high priority will be placed on recovery of the bodies, as soon as it's safe."

"I'd very much appreciate that." Furness handed him a business card. He started to leave but paused halfway to the door. "You don't, by chance, know of a pilot you can recommend?"

"I'm sorry, no. Every freelancer in our contact list is already out in the field, working for us."

"All right. Thanks, anyway."

As soon as he'd departed, Eckhart's secretary reappeared. "They're waiting for you at the morning briefing, sir."

"Yes, I know. On my way." He said a silent prayer for some relief today from more avalanches.

Chapter Twenty-three

Bernina Pass, Switzerland

"Think we should put our crampons on?" Hudson asked as they stared up at the mountain. Why did it look so much higher and bigger than it had the day before?

"Definitely. The slope gets steeper the higher we go." Steffi dug in her pack and pulled hers out. "I take it you have a route planned?"

"Yes. I've been studying the map. If we can get up this…" She pointed to the long, jagged charcoal ridge that towered over them. "We'll be able to avoid the avalanche fields. Up and over the top, down the other side, where we pick up the railway and follow it until we see something. That's the southern face of the Alps, which should be getting less snow."

"How far to civilization?"

"No telling, really. The rail line does a bunch of long loops down that eat up a lot of miles. If we can find a more direct route, we can cut a ton of distance. And there are a few little squares on the map before the next railway station that might be something. It's hard to tell what they are—they aren't marked." Hudson got out her crampons as well and strapped them on.

"Not quite the climbing adventure I expected to have, by the way."

Hudson had to smile. "Thank you for doing this. I wasn't at all sure you would."

"You know, I didn't really decide to," Steffi replied, "until a millisecond before I told you I would."

"Really?" Hudson looked at her. "What made you say yes?"

Steffi looked down and color came to her cheeks. "Well, you're kind of a...kind of a larger-than-life individual, you know?"

Hudson had never been called that before and didn't quite know what to make of it. Was it a compliment or a criticism? "How do you mean?"

Steffi shrugged. "You just...step up and take charge. Do what's necessary, quietly and efficiently. Fearless. No thought to your own safety, always putting others first."

Now that definitely sounded like a compliment. "Okay. And?"

"I'd kind of gotten used to seeing you as sort of...invincible. Nothing's really seemed to rattle you. Or at least, not for long," Steffi said. "But this morning, I could see a...well, I guess a vulnerability in your eyes that I didn't expect. And it apparently brought out a protective streak in me that's stronger than my fears."

"I'm not invincible, Steffi. Plenty rattles me. I guess I've just sort of learned to roll with the punches and seek solutions to problems," Hudson said. "Whatever your reasons, I'm very glad you're along. And not just because you're fabulous company," she added, which brought a smile to Steffi's face. "It'll greatly increase our chances having two of us, especially with your expertise. All advice is welcome. You sure know more about this than I do."

"I don't think we should rope up going across this avalanche field," Steffi said. "We won't have any anchor points. If one of us falls, we'd just take the other into the gorge with us."

"How about we think positive, huh?" Hudson asked.

"I'm just saying, we need to think about the safest way to handle every part of our journey," Steffi replied. "Do you know how to do a self-arrest with an ice ax?"

"No. I mean, I know what it is. I've seen videos of it but never tried it or taken a class or anything."

"Well, now's not the time to teach you," Steffi said. "So...just don't fall, okay? Slow and steady."

"Got it. I'll do my best. How about I take the lead getting out of the avalanche field, and we switch off when we get up by the ridge?"

"Okay. I'm right behind you."

Hudson started off across the uneven terrain at a slow pace, getting used to the feel of walking with crampons. The spikes in the strap-on metal plates would make walking on ice a lot safer, but her feet were still slipping around some in her borrowed boots. She picked up the pace a little when she looked up and saw a gust of wind trail a long spindrift of powder off the peak. She'd relax a little when they were off the avalanche slope and protected by the ridge.

Most of the time, she sank only up to her calves at most. The snow that had been swept downhill to this dump zone had been packed so solid she'd never guess the railway was twenty or more feet beneath them.

She was conscious of the fact that though Steffi was obviously very fit, she was also a few inches shorter and had a much smaller stride. Every now and then, Hudson would half turn her head to see how much distance was between them, and if Steffi seemed to be lagging at all, she'd slow a little until she caught up.

After traversing for forty minutes, they came to the edge of the debris field. Two steps beyond it, in the pristine, untouched slope of smooth, even powder, Hudson sank to her waist. "Oh, this isn't good," she muttered under her breath.

After she took a few steps, however, it wasn't as bad as she'd feared. The top half was mostly loose powder. Hudson plowed forward, carving a trail with her body and using ski poles to help keep her balance. She was still mindful of every step, because the slope was getting steeper, and she worried that an unstable underlayer of snow might give way beneath her feet.

As she trudged on, ever upward, she listened intently for errant sounds—any possible hint of the snowpack on the mountain changing, shifting, moving. But it was eerily quiet, the only sounds the occasional *whoosh* of wind and her own labored breathing.

They'd nearly reached the bottom of the ridge when Steffi called out, "Hudson? Can we take five?"

She turned to find Steffi half bent over and breathing hard, some twenty feet behind her. "Sure. Of course."

Steffi caught up before she took off her pack and got out one of her water bottles. After taking only a couple of small sips, she put it back. "I can already feel the burn in my legs."

"From trying to keep up to me. Sorry, I kind of got in a zone there and just kept pushing." Hudson took a sip of water, too, and stared up at the long, rocky ridge that was their next obstacle.

"No, it's fine. Just need a short breather."

"So…what do you think?" Hudson asked, nodding up at the ridge. "What's the best way to get up there?"

"You want me to decide?"

"You're the rock hound."

"But I never lead. Kris does."

"Kris isn't here," Hudson said. "And like I said, I know squat about this."

Steffi got a slightly panicky look on her face at first, but after she took a couple of deep breaths and looked up intently at the ridge for a couple of minutes, studying its surface, her expression relaxed. "Actually, I think I see a pretty good way." She turned to Hudson. "Have you ever done any climbing at all? Even a rock wall at a gym?"

"Yeah, a couple times."

"That's something. How about rope work? Rappelling?" Steffi asked.

"No. I'm afraid not."

"At least tell me you're a fast learner."

"Now *that* I can give a wholehearted yes to. And I'm pretty athletic."

"Yeah, I noticed," Steffi said. "You're leaving me in the dust so far, and I thought I was in great condition."

"You are. This is very hard work. So, you ready to do this?"

Steffi took another look up at the ridge. "Yes. But first, we need to get our helmets and harnesses on and rope up. Once we get to the base of the ridge, I'll go over some fundamentals."

Hudson watched a change come over Steffi after she accepted the challenge of leading the next, much more difficult stretch of their trek. So far, she'd stayed in her comfort zone of willing and eager soldier, putting aside her personal needs and fears in order to step up to help out others, but never really taking the initiative.

But now, her timidity and hesitation vanished, replaced by a steely determination that made Hudson proud. When they got to the rock face, Steffi spent half an hour patiently and efficiently explaining knots, belaying, ascending, safety issues, and everything else she thought would help get them up the ridge. She explained all the hardware and what it was used for as she rigged what they'd use. Then they spent another several minutes going over how to climb through the glazed-over sections with crampons and ice axes.

Hudson hated relinquishing control, and she especially detested putting her life in the hands of others, but Steffi's methodical and detail-oriented nature and obvious knowledge of climbing reassured her. Her crash course covered all the basics and then some.

Steffi insisted they not proceed until Hudson could demonstrate adequate knot-tying skills and confidence with belaying, which took another ten or fifteen minutes. By the time she was satisfied, Hudson was anxious to get started.

"See that crack in the rock?" Steffi pointed to a thin fissure in the gray rock of the cliff face that ran at a diagonal most of the way to up the top of the ridge.

"Yes."

"That's our boulevard up. And where it meets that ledge…" Steffi pointed to a small protrusion about one hundred fifty feet up that was covered with snow, "is where I'll stop and belay you." She turned to look at Hudson. "Watch where I'm finding holds. And please, keep the rope really taut."

"Every moment, I promise. Don't worry. We have to trust each other on this."

"Yes, we do." Steffi's expression was hard to read. "Okay, here goes nothing. Climbing." She worked her way up the rock face, searching for the safest and most secure holds. She paused now and then to insert a piton, cam, or nut into the crack to anchor the rope, or an ice screw where a thick layer of ice obscured the rock.

Hudson was impressed with the progress she was making. Though obviously very cautious in her approach, Steffi was a strong and capable climber. She reached the ledge and called down, "Okay, I'm on belay. Take your time, and be careful!"

"Climbing!" Hudson hollered back. She reached up and grasped the first handhold. Fin's ice-climbing gloves had been keeping her hands warm and dry and were now providing her with an excellent grip and dexterity. The crampons were another story. They worked well in gaining purchase in the glazed-over areas but were difficult at times to balance with on the sheer, rocky surfaces. Steffi had warned her to maintain three strong points of contact at all times—she'd drummed that into her, as a matter of fact—and Hudson took the advice to heart.

Thirty feet from the narrow ledge Hudson was aiming for, Steffi called down, "You'll need your axes for this last bit. Clip your harness to the next piton to secure yourself before you try to get them out."

"Got it," she yelled back.

When she reached the anchor in the rock, Hudson clipped on, grateful for any momentary pause to catch her breath. She reached around and unclipped the ice axes from her pack, then threaded her hands through the wrist straps. "Climbing!" she yelled when she was ready to proceed, and Steffi pulled the belay rope taut.

She unclipped from the anchor and back onto the rope, then dug into the ice with her right ice pick and crampon, making sure that both contact points were secure and solid. Her left hand, jammed into the crack of the rock, formed the third contact point, though she had to stretch to reach it.

She thought she was fine to take her left foot off the small protrusion of rock where it was precariously balanced. But as she kicked back to plant the other crampon firmly in the ice, her hand slipped out of the crack. *No!*

She fumbled for a new handhold, but it was no use. She was already too off-balanced because of her pack. The ice ax popped out. Then the crampon. *Fuck!* Hudson fell backward, arms pinwheeling helplessly as she plummeted toward the ground eighty feet below.

CHAPTER TWENTY-FOUR

"Curt, please don't think I'm insensitive, and if what I'm about to ask is too difficult, I'll absolutely understand." Anna had waited until he was done checking on the injured and had moved off by himself. He was seated beside his wife's body, which made what she was going to say even more difficult.

He looked warily at her. "Go ahead."

"Well, as you know, we're kind of crammed in here like sardines, now…" She paused, hoping she didn't have to spell it out, because she could imagine how he was feeling. As much as she joked about her husband, she'd be lost without him.

The passenger car seemed more crowded now that additional injured were taking up precious floor space in the undamaged section. To get up the aisle, you had to really watch where you walked, and Nick and Bud had been laid uncomfortably close to the section where the glass ceiling had caved in.

When Curt didn't take the hint, Anna continued. "I'd like you to help move Cinzia's father into the other car, so we've got more room. I've prepared her as best as I can. She's had time to say good-bye."

Tears welled in his eyes. "And you want us to move Patti, too."

"If we can. If not, like I said, it's totally cool."

He got up. "It's all right. I can still visit with her if we move her."

She'd already enlisted Kris to help carry the Italian's body as well, since he was a big man, and to move him, they'd have to step over several of the injured. Hugo, Fritz, and Elliot had promised to keep Cinzia distracted. They'd taken her into the luggage compartment to try to get an update on the radio.

No one spoke while they transported the bodies, except for brief instructions from one or another to slow down or to be watchful of what they were stepping over or edging through.

When it was done, Curt remained behind with Patti's body in the second car while the rest of them returned to what would be their home for the indefinite future.

"I'm going up to see if they're still in sight," Kris said. She'd been monitoring Hudson and Steffi's progress up the mountain every now and then, and reporting it back to everyone else. They were all clustered together now, injured and uninjured, with little to do but wait. Whenever Kris re-emerged from one of her forays outside, the rest gathered around for the latest update.

Anna was on her way to see how Cinzia was doing when J.T. hailed her as she stepped over him.

"Hey! You! Blondie! Where's Curt?"

"Blondie? What are you, a caveman as well as an asshole?" Anna replied. "My name is Anna."

"Just answer my question."

She shone her headlamp directly into his eyes.

"Fuck! Stop it!" He put up a hand to shield his face and groaned with the effort.

After examining J.T. thoroughly, Curt had told Anna that he was battered but would recover. He had a couple of broken ribs, a possible concussion, fractured ankle, and hideous bruises over his entire body.

She had no sympathy for him whatsoever. She'd always hated guys like him, so self-absorbed and arrogant they thought everyone else was there to serve them. She felt sorry for his wife. "Curt's busy. Probably will be, for a while."

"Elliot, then. Where's Elliot?"

"He's in the luggage compartment with Fritz, Hugo, and Cinzia. They're trying to get a signal on the radio."

"Tell him I need him."

"What do you need?" she asked.

J.T. didn't answer right away. He just stared up at her with a frustrated expression.

"Suit yourself," she said, and started away.

"Wait!"

She pointed her light into his face again. "Don't try my patience."

"You're a real piece of work, you are," he said. "Look, bitch, I just want something to eat."

She leaned over him and gave J.T. the voice she used for her misbehaving sons. "You'd better watch that mouth of yours if you want any food to put in it."

"I don't need your fucking little squares of chocolate. I've got my own stuff. Just bring me my damn bag."

"Oh? Didn't I mention that?" She loved being the one to tell him. "We confiscated all the edibles from your bag, and Bud's. Cost of saving your asses. Elliot was happy to contribute his. He sees the value of cooperating." She smiled. "Nice haul, by the way. Welcome to the group collective, whether you like it or not. As a matter of fact, we're all splitting some of your PowerBars. But not until this evening."

He looked as though he was about to pop a vein. "You can't take my fucking food!"

J.T. grabbed the nearest seat and tried to use it to sit up. But he cried out in pain halfway there and sank back again onto the foam they'd laid him on.

His distress was sweet payback, as welcome to her ears as the laughter of her children. "We can, and we did. And you're done now. Done complaining, done demanding, done being a sonofabitch." She got closer to his face, until he had to shut his eyes to keep from going blind from the light. "You're going to be nice from now on, understand? Just remember, you don't know me. You don't know what I'm capable of. A little hint? Ever see the movie *Misery?* You're James Caan and I'm Kathy Bates."

She walked away before he had a chance to respond. His expression, though, was priceless. A little like their Chihuahua had looked after they'd had him neutered.

"We got another newscast," Elliot said when Anna joined the group in the luggage compartment. They'd shut the radio off again to save the batteries. "Fritz says they didn't mention us or the Bernina Pass at all. There have been lots of other avalanches all around the country, though. One last night buried a whole village."

"Did they say anything about the weather forecast?" Anna hoped that Hudson and Steffi would at least not have to worry about any more blizzards before they reached civilization.

"Yes. The next three days are supposed to be overcast and cloudy, with a storm front moving in overnight tonight. But not a big accumulation, and no snow in the forecast after that for at least forty-eight hours."

"Was that the weather forecast?" Kris asked from the tunnel entrance as she rejoined them.

"Yes," Anna replied. "Should be all right for Hudson and Steffi, if they can get an ice cave built tonight. Can you still see them?"

"Barely. They're little specks. They've made it to the ridge and are partway up," she informed them. "Once they reach the top of it, I think we'll lose sight of them pretty quickly from this angle."

"Do you think they'll make it?" Elliot asked.

"We *know* they'll make it," Anna replied. "Good karma and all that, right?"

❖

Hudson's breath was knocked out of her when she jerked to a sudden stop, her fall arrested after thirty feet when the rope she was tied to reached the next anchor point. Then she slammed sideways into the cliff face, and a burst of pain radiated along her shoulder and hip. As she fought to breathe, she bounced off and hit again, this time with her left knee taking the worst of it.

"Are you all right?" Steffi hollered from above.

She couldn't answer until the pain subsided and her lungs began working again. "Yeah. Still here."

"Can you get your weight off the rope?" Steffi shouted. "I can't hold you much longer! You're going to pull me off this ledge!"

Hudson snapped to and started grappling at the rock face, searching with her hands, eyes, and feet for a secure contact point as her heart hammered wildly. With her left hand she found a crack in the rock, then with her right crampon located a hint of ledge, three inches wide. She dug the tip of the ice ax dangling from her right wrist into a block of ice that hugged the cliff face and had three points of contact she could rest her weight on. At least for now. How much longer, with legs shaking like saplings in the wind, she didn't know. "I got a tentative hold, not a good one," she yelled, and the pressure on the rope lessened.

She tried to take deep breaths to quell her panic as she blindly sought a fourth contact point with her left foot.

"Stay calm." Steffi called out as though she could read her mind, though they couldn't see each other. "Is there someplace you can jam a cam?"

"Don't have a free hand."

After flailing wildly about for seconds that seemed like minutes, Hudson finally caught something to stick her left crampon to, but the contact point didn't feel secure enough for her to let go with either hand. Her whole body still trembled from the massive adrenaline dump of the fall.

"What's happening?" Steffi asked.

"Give me a sec." Hudson searched the cliff face for a place to set an anchor and spotted a pocket in the rock near her left hip that she might be able to wedge a cam into. Steffi had given her a half dozen of the spring-loaded devices, and they were hanging from her harness.

At the moment, they felt so unreachable, they could have just as easily been hanging on the moon.

"I need you to support my weight for a few seconds while I get the cam in," she shouted.

"Okay. Make it fast. On belay!"

Hudson took a deep breath and gathered her courage as the rope grew taut again. With quick efficiency of movement, she took her left hand out of the crack, grabbed the cam, stuck it into the pocket, and released the trigger so it expanded to grip the rock. She pulled on the loop attached to the device, and it seemed secure, so she clipped her harness to it. But before she called back up to Steffi, she tentatively put her full weight on the cam to see if it would hold her.

It did, though she immediately reclaimed her hand- and footholds as well. "Okay, I'm anchored! Now what?" she asked.

"Off belay," Steffi called down. "I'm putting in another anchor up here. If I tie you off, can you come up with your ascender?"

Ascender. Hudson glanced down at the hardware on her harness, more grateful than ever for Steffi's thorough briefing. "Yeah. I hope so, anyway." She'd need a lot of upper body strength to reach the ledge, but Steffi had taught her how to make a sling for one foot so she could stand between each upward push, using the rest of her body to help.

She unclipped the ascender and attached it to a sling on her harness, then locked it to the rope. Once she got the foot sling ready, she called out, "Let me know when you're done up there."

"You're anchored. Good to go."

"Almost ready." With some trepidation, she put her foot on the sling, unhooked herself from the cam, and let her full weight rest on the rope. Then she removed the cam and clipped it back onto her harness, and took the ice axes off her wrists and strapped them to her pack. "Okay, here I come!'

She gripped the ascender firmly and slid it up the rope. It moved freely upward, but when any downward pressure was applied, it locked into place, allowing her to pull herself up a couple of feet at a time. Though her nerves had calmed somewhat since the fall, she still had enough adrenaline pumping through her to assist her in the initial phase of her climb up the rope.

Every foot gained, however, was more difficult than the last. Halfway to the ledge, her arms were burning, and her calves were, too.

"You're doing great!" Steffi called out.

Hudson was too focused on the rock face in front of her to risk looking up to see how close she was to the ledge. She was also playing a mental game with herself. If it was still farther than she imagined, facing that discouraging reality might sap her remaining reserves of strength. So she concentrated solely on advancing one foot higher, then the next, then the one after that.

Finally, she heard Steffi's voice say the magic words, from just above her. "You got it, Hudson. Reach up. You're here."

She looked up to find Steffi extending her hand, about a foot or two above her head.

Hudson pulled herself up the rope one more time, then grabbed Steffi's hand and the edge of the ledge and hoisted herself up and onto the narrow platform of rock. As soon as she did, Steffi clipped Hudson's harness to the same ice-screw anchor that she was secured to and then enfolded her in a bear hug. Neither spoke, or moved, for a long while. They just held each other until Hudson caught her breath.

"Well, that was exciting, wasn't it?" she finally said, once her racing heart had quieted. "Thanks for saving my life, by the way."

Steffi pulled back and looked at her like she was crazy. "You scared the shit out of me. And nearly killed us both."

"Yeah, there was that," Hudson said as she reluctantly let go. They sat side by side on the ledge, their legs dangling over the edge. "Rather hope not to have that happen again." Every part of her body ached, particularly her arms and left side, where she'd slammed against the rock. But despite her brush with death, she couldn't help but be impressed by their view. She could see much more of the Bernina Pass than before and the tops of the surrounding peaks, and in every direction she looked, the vista was stunning in its cold, brutal beauty. But she didn't spot any sign of civilization.

"This whole idea was insane." Steffi got out her water bottle and took a sip.

"Probably. But no one offered a better one." Hudson shifted her weight so she could look up at how much of a climb they had left to reach the top of the ridge.

"Don't tell me you're actually thinking about continuing?" Steffi asked, incredulous.

"No choice. I'm not going to let Joe die." Hudson looked at her. "And it's obvious that I need you, to have any chance of succeeding. Are you with me?"

Steffi looked aghast. She'd evidently already decided they had no reasonable choice but to turn back. That shot of determined resolve that had gotten her this far had evaporated under the stress of Hudson's fall. She didn't speak for a long while. "I don't know. I'm just not the person for this."

"What do you mean, person for this? There's no one else, Steffi. No one *plans* to have to risk their life to save others. And no one knows what they're really capable of until they're put to the test." Hudson pulled out her water bottle. It was starting to ice up badly, but it held enough liquid to quench her thirst. "I'd never have imagined I could do what I just did."

"Yeah, but you can just…push on, even when shit's happening. I don't have that same level of fearlessness. Not nearly."

"You have a lot of courage. More than you think, to be up here right now," Hudson said. "And going on isn't about fear, or lack of it. Of course I'm afraid. I have no idea what we might face, how difficult it might be. All I try to think about is Joe. I keep his face in my head, and it pushes me on."

"That easy, huh? I just think about Kris and Fin, and everybody else waiting back there for us to get help?"

"If that doesn't work, I can try to come up with other reasons to convince you. But that'll take up precious time we could spend climbing up this ridge."

Steffi exhaled a long breath of surrender. "You rest a while longer, while I take a better look at how to get us the rest of the way to the top."

CHAPTER TWENTY-FIVE

Steffi wasn't certain whether they were being nobly heroic or just naively suicidal in deciding to go on. She just knew she had to stay with Hudson, whatever the cost.

When Hudson fell, it had forced Steffi to go beyond what she thought were the limits of her strength and endurance, and she still hadn't recovered from the terror of feeling they were both about to die.

Surely—she'd thought all the while that Hudson was ascending— *surely this will convince Hudson we were foolish to try this.*

But no. Apparently, nothing short of her own death or disabling injury was going to deter her.

Steffi had come to admire and respect Hudson very much as she'd gotten to know her better and watched her in action during this crisis. She took charge without hesitation and exuded an air of confidence that was reassuring.

But had those qualities, and her growing attraction, which she could no longer deny, blinded her to Hudson's flaws? She was brave, sure, but she often just dove into things without considering or caring about the implications or repercussions. Like when she'd gone out onto the avalanche field or into the damaged car. Steffi preferred a much more measured, cautious approach: always thought before action.

Hudson's slip off the rock was certainly understandable. After all, she'd never really climbed before, and this was far from an easy situation. The last section had been a tough pitch, with lots of patches of ice, and they had the added emotional burden of all the people counting on them.

Even so, Hudson's misstep had increased Steffi's anxiety about this venture a hundredfold. It was hard enough to deal with the uncertainty of what lay ahead and the responsibility she'd accepted when she'd agreed to lead. Now she also had to worry about whether Hudson's sometimes-impulsive nature might get them both killed.

She looked up at the rest of the rock face between them and the top of the ridge. Scaling it would require two more pitches, or lengths of their rope. The first would be mostly rock climbing, and the second, all ice. If their strength held up, the route appeared to be difficult but manageable, except for a thirty-foot-wide section of rock that looked too smooth to be negotiable.

Steffi pondered their options. She didn't see another way up, at least not from where they were. And they'd waste too much time and energy going down to scout a different route. But the only way across the problem area was using a pendulum technique she'd never tried.

One that required Hudson to be able to support her weight.

Steffi's own arms and legs were still not completely recovered from having to keep the both of them from falling, and she'd come to Switzerland in great shape, from outings with Kris and Fin and trips to the gym.

Hudson seemed fit, sure. From what Steffi could see, she had a great physique. But she'd plowed through the deep snow getting up here, taken a beating in the fall, and endured a grueling climb up the rope that would have sapped even seasoned climbers. How much was left in her?

Steffi wasn't anxious to have to rely on Hudson to belay her right now, but she couldn't be anchored to the rock face and still have the flexibility she'd need to reach the ledge.

Though it was apparently the only alternative, Steffi was far from ready to embrace it.

Hudson pressed the issue, as though she knew from Steffi's body language that she'd worked out how to proceed. "So?" she asked. "See a way up from here?"

Steffi shook herself from her reverie of doubt and glanced down at Hudson, still sitting on the ledge. "Yes. Not going to be a cakewalk, though. Are you rested enough to belay me?"

"If that's a polite way of asking, 'Are you absolutely certain you're capable of holding my weight if I slip, so I don't plunge to my death?' I would say, absolutely yes. Or I wouldn't attempt to resume our trek."

"I don't think this is anything to joke about."

"Sorry." Hudson looked Steffi in the eyes. "Look, I know you're scared. Petrified, in fact, though you're fighting it admirably. I also realize you don't have a lot of faith in me right now, and I don't blame you. But I know my limitations and capabilities very well, and I'm acutely aware I have your life in my hands. I take that as my priority. Not going on, not saving Joe and the others. Right now, all I'm thinking about is my responsibility to you, if that helps."

The unexpected remark didn't entirely assuage her anxiety, but Steffi did relax a little. "Actually, it does. You know, I can see why you're so successful as a reporter. Not only do you read people well, but you're very persuasive in getting them to do what you want." She sighed and looked up at the next section. "Two more pitches to reach the top. We can follow the crack for the next one most of the way. See that little ledge just above where it ends? That's where I'll stop to belay you."

❖

Hudson got to her feet and looked where Steffi was pointing. The so-called ledge she was referring to was only a slight protrusion in the rock, probably not more than a few inches wide at most, and four or five feet long. And the space between it and the end of the crack was thirty feet or more. Thirty feet of what looked like, from here, smooth, unmarred rock, with no visible handholds at all. "I see it. Looks tiny. And how are you going to get from the crack over to it?"

"I spotted some handholds above the end of the crack," Steffi said. "If I can get up on a diagonal and set an anchor halfway across, I can get us there."

"How?" Hudson asked.

"You'll see," Steffi replied. "Okay, let's get set up for the belay."

Hudson wasn't surprised that, before they continued, Steffi triple-checked every knot and piece of equipment and the whole length of the rope they were using. Under normal circumstances, she might find such OCD behavior annoying, but on this occasion she felt more reassured by it than anything.

When Steffi started climbing, Hudson paid even closer attention than before to her technique and to where she was finding handholds and footholds, while also being fully attentive to her belay duties.

She makes it look so easy. She'd gained a healthy dose of respect for Steffi's abilities in the last couple of hours. *How* did *she support my weight? I have to have twenty pounds on her, at least.*

Once Steffi had worked her way to the end of the crack, setting two anchors along the way, she climbed straight up for several feet, then over on an upward diagonal until she was right over the problematic smooth zone they had to cross. She set a cam there and clipped to it. "I'm anchored. You can relax a minute," she called down.

Hudson gave her arms a welcome rest. She hoped they wouldn't have to do much of this tomorrow, because she wasn't sure she'd be able to. Sometimes when she and Joe skied all day, she could hardly move the next morning. *Joe.*

When she'd gone to tell him her plans, he'd tried to talk her out of it. In a cajoling way at first, because he probably didn't really believe she was leaving. When convinced she was serious, he'd begun to plead with her, then argue. It hadn't ended well.

"What do I have to say to convince you this is suicide? You're not going!"

"I am going," she replied calmly, not for the first time.

"You're so fucking stubborn and always fucking right," Joe said. "Well, you're not right this time, Hudson. There has to be another way."

"There isn't, Joe. This is our only shot to get rescued."

"I don't believe that. You're just going off half-cocked again, without looking at all the options. We need you here. I need you here."

"Curt and Anna are going to take good care of you. One of them will always be in earshot if you need anything."

"That's not what I mean, damn it!"

Hudson couldn't remember when she'd last seen him this angry. Maybe never.

"Just because I can't get up right now and kick your ass," he ranted on, "doesn't mean I'm going to let you do this."

"I'm sorry, Joe. You can't stop me. I have to do this."

"God damn it, Hudson!" He'd broken down then; she'd shattered the last of his emotional reserves, and he started to cry.

She leaned down and kissed his cheek. "See you soon, Marco. That's a promise." She'd hoped he'd answer, but Joe had remained stubbornly silent as she got up and headed toward the tunnel.

Had he forgiven her yet?

"Okay, I've caught my breath. Ready?" Steffi called out.

"Whenever you are."

"I'm going to come back down to the end of the crack. Keep the rope taut."

"You got it. On belay." Hudson got into position.

"Climbing!" Steffi shouted, and started a slow retreat the way she'd come.

Hudson noticed she'd threaded the rope through the high anchor she'd placed.

When she got back to the end of the crack, Steffi looked over at Hudson. "You're going to have to support my weight for several seconds. Maybe a minute or two, even. Can you?"

Hudson glanced down and visually inspected her gear to make sure everything was in order. She had a firm grip on the rope. She was anchored, herself, to the ice screw. "Yes. No problem."

"I'm going to swing over there," Steffi said. "Be ready to give me a little slack really quick when I tell you, if I can't reach on the first try."

"I understand. Whenever you're ready. I've got you."

"Here I go," Steffi shouted, though she hesitated a few seconds more before she pushed off, and Hudson took her weight on the rope.

Steffi swung wide to the right, like the pendulum of a clock, but not far enough to reach the tiny ledge. As she swung back to the left, struggling not to spin around as she did, she yelled, "Slack!"

Hudson gave her several inches more rope, her biceps burning with the effort, and when Steffi kicked off and swung back toward the ledge a second time, she got closer to her goal but still fell short.

"A little more!" Steffi hollered as she careened back left.

Hudson let the rope out another few inches, hoping it was enough. She wasn't sure how many more tries she could endure.

Steffi pushed off again, and this time when she swung right, she was able to grab a handhold with her right hand, arresting her momentum and enabling her to get her feet on the narrow ledge. Hudson watched her quickly and efficiently jam a cam into a pocket near her waist with her left hand and clip her harness to it. "Okay! I'm secure."

Hudson gave the rope a little slack to give her arms a rest. "Impressive!"

"You're next," Steffi shouted back. "Be careful. When you get to the end of the crack, kick off squarely, with both feet, or you'll spin around."

"I hear you."

They readied for the change in belay, and once Steffi signaled she was set to go, Hudson gave the "Climbing!" response and advanced forward along the crack, edging toward the pendulum point.

The last thing in the world she wanted to ever experience again was dangling from a rope with nothing but air beneath her, her whole body weight in the hands of a petite woman she'd known only a few days. But she knew they both had to suspend their misgivings and fears if they were to have any chance of success, and Steffi had earned a good measure of trust when she'd caught her fall.

"All good?" Steffi yelled when she saw that Hudson had reached the kickoff point but was hesitating to go farther.

"Yeah. You ready?" Hudson replied, gathering her nerve.

"I've got you."

She took a deep breath and kicked off with both feet.

As Hudson careened right, she fought to stay oriented with her face toward the rock, but she was so focused on the ledge she started to spin to the right as she neared Steffi. In her mind's eye, she wasn't going to make it—she was going to smash into the rock again, out of control, landing on the same side of her body that had already taken a battering.

How Steffi managed to grab her harness *and* keep the rope taut was a mystery. But before Hudson knew it, she'd stopped swinging and Steffi was screaming at her to clip herself onto the anchor.

She grappled for her carabineer and got it secured to the loop of a second cam Steffi had put into the rock, next to the one she was anchored to. Once she got her feet planted on the ledge, she started to breathe again. "Well, that was gnarly." She looked over at Steffi. "You're pretty amazing, you know. Figuring out that maneuver to get us over here. And I don't have a clue how you managed to catch me."

"Took a lot out of me, though," Steffi replied as she looked over their next, final pitch. "And we've still got a wall of ice to climb."

"I could use a rest myself, and some more water. My mouth is so dry…" She started to reach for her bottle.

"Look!" Steffi pointed to the top of a neighboring peak.

They caught sight of another slide in progress. It wasn't a massive slab avalanche this time like the one that had buried the train, but just a sluff—a loose, powdery snowslide without much volume or weight. Yet it was still a chilling reminder of the dangers that surrounded them.

"Oh, great." Steffi held up her water bottle. She had very little liquid left; the rest was a block of ice, and their other three bottles were the same. After drinking what remained during a ten-minute rest, they prepared themselves for the final push to the top of the ridge. Hudson got ready on belay, and Steffi retrieved her ice axes and looped them over her wrists.

"Looks like good, solid ice," Steffi remarked. "I'll find out soon enough if I'm right." She readied the axes, gripping both firmly, with the toothed pick ends ready to dig into the thick glaze on the rock face. "All set?"

"On belay," Hudson replied.

"Climbing." Steffi edged over and kicked her right foot into the ice once, then again, until she was satisfied the crampon was secure. Her right hand followed with the ax. The sharp pick bit into the hard ice and sent shards flying. She repeated the process with her left crampon and ax and began to work her way up toward the top of the ridge, moving slowly and making sure every point of contact was a good one before she trusted it with her weight and continued to the next. Every thirty feet or so, she'd pause to set an ice screw and clip to it for a minute or two to rest before pushing on.

They'd used nearly the entire length of their hundred-and-eighty-foot rope by the time Steffi reached the top of the ridge, pulled herself over, and disappeared from view. "I'm here! Wait before you start!" she called down.

"Okay!" Hudson got her ice axes out and at the ready. *You can do this.* If she had anything to say about it, no way in hell was she going to put herself into a situation where Steffi had to save her ass a third time. Her ego couldn't stand it, and Steffi had to be close to the limit of her endurance, strength, and willingness to proceed.

"On belay!" Steffi replied a minute or two later.

"Climbing!" Hudson shouted back. She mustered her strength and moved onto the ice the same way Steffi had, first with her right crampon and then her right ax. In fact, she tried to mirror everything Steffi had done, making sure each hold was secure before she moved on to the next. She could see the pick marks and chipped-out footholds Steffi had made during her ascent, and she utilized the same ones whenever she could.

As before, she never looked up to see how far she still had to go. She concentrated solely on the ice in front of her face and with maintaining at least three good contact points with the wall at all times.

Her wrists, forearms, and left knee were screaming from the exertion by the time she reached the top, but she got herself up and over without further incident and collapsed on her back beside Steffi, out of breath.

Steffi let go of the rope and sat, looking as spent as Hudson felt. "We made it," Hudson said once her heart had calmed.

"I wouldn't celebrate quite yet," Steffi replied. "You haven't taken a look at what's coming up next."

CHAPTER TWENTY-SIX

"Can you still see them?" Anna spoke as soon as she spotted Kris coming back down the tunnel. She'd been gone a long time on this most recent foray outside to check on Steffi and Hudson's progress.

"Where are they now?" Curt asked at the same time.

He was melting snow for water with a few more of the hand warmers while Anna carefully cut some of J.T.'s crumbly PowerBars into quarters until she had enough for the remaining twenty survivors. It wouldn't be much to call dinner, but they figured they'd all be here at least another couple of days, probably longer, and they wanted to stretch their supplies as far as possible. Their confiscation of edibles from J.T.'s crew had been a boon: the three men had been carrying a total of fifteen PowerBars, three chocolate bars, and half a dozen energy drinks.

"I sure wish I had binoculars," Kris said as she exited the tunnel and brushed snow off her clothes. "I lost sight of them a little while ago. The good news is, they made it up to the top of the ridge."

"And the bad?" Anna asked. Kris's tone, and her worried look, told her there was more.

"The storm front that the radio talked about is moving in. It's started to snow."

"That's not good," Curt said. "That'll really cut their visibility, just as they're getting up to the peak."

"I know. Not only will it make their hike up there more dangerous, with all those cornices, but they won't be able to scout a route down."

"How much daylight do they have left?" Anna asked.

Curt consulted his watch. "Sunset's about six, I think. So, another three and a half hours or thereabout."

"It's taking them longer than I thought it would," Kris said. "Really hard to gauge the distance and conditions from here, though."

They all quieted and turned toward the passenger compartment when they heard loud, excited voices in the distance. Young girls.

Before any of them could move, Anna spotted a flashlight heading their way in a hurry up the aisle.

It belonged to one of the daughters of the Swiss woman who'd been mostly unconscious ever since the avalanche. Though the mother had seemed on a few occasions to be minimally responsive—moaning when her daughters tried to give her some water, or when Anna helped them change her soiled clothing—she'd never fully regained consciousness.

The girl ran right to Curt, her face flush with excitement. "Mama! Mama!" She tugged at the sleeve of his coat, pulling at him urgently to follow her.

"Go," he told her, and followed as she returned to the corner of the car where she and her older sister had been watching over their mother.

Kris and Anna trailed at his heels, and the addition of their headlamps illuminated the area well.

The older girl was helping her mother sip some water from a bottle. The teenagers had placed some clothes beneath the woman's head and back to raise her up to a half-sit. When she finished drinking, she looked up at them all with a shocked and confused expression, fully awake now.

"Hello, I'm Curt." He knelt on one side of her. "Do you speak English? Can you understand me?"

"Understand, yes," she replied. "Speak, not good."

"Okay." Curt took off his headlamp and set it down, positioning it so she could see him better. "Do you know where you are? Do you remember what happened?"

Her brows furrowed. "I...we," she glanced at her daughters before looking beyond them, at the railway seats and windows illuminated by all their headlamps. "The train!" Her cloud of confusion began to clear, but not entirely. "What happened?" she asked, when she could apparently make no sense of what she was seeing.

"There was an avalanche," Curt told her. "This car is buried under snow."

She had a panicky expression; she obviously understood every word.

He immediately tried to reassure her with a hand lightly on her shoulder. "We've dug a way out, and two people have gone for help. Rescue will come."

She tried to say something and motioned for more water when she had trouble getting out what she needed to. The older girl opened the water bottle again and helped her mother take a few more small sips. "Are you doctor?" she asked.

"No," he said. "I know first aid. I'm all we have. You have a head injury, which is probably why you've had a very long sleep since the accident. And you had a bad cut on your arm. Do they hurt much?"

"Head, yes. Arm, not so much."

"Your daughters have been taking very good care of you," he said. "Changing your dressing, keeping you warm, trying to give you water."

The woman looked anxiously at her daughters and spoke to them in German. They answered in a reassuring tone, but their mother evidently wasn't willing to take their word for it, because she asked Curt, "They were not hurt?"

"No, just a few cuts and bruises. This one has a sprained ankle, too," he said, nodding toward the elder girl, "but she's staying off it like I told her to. They'll be fine."

"When help is coming?" the woman asked.

"We don't know," he replied. "Two days at least, probably."

She looked distressed at the news.

Anna knelt on her other side. "Don't worry, honey. We've already been here for a couple of days. We only have to wait a few more. Just remember, you're very lucky. Both your girls are fine, and we're going to make sure you will be, too. Are you hungry?"

That seemed to calm her a little, or else the mention of food had sparked other priorities. "Yes, please. I'm very hungry. And for my girls?"

"We've been sharing with them," Anna assured her. "Everyone gets the same. I'll get the food." She got to her feet and started toward the luggage area.

"I'll help you pass it out," Kris said, trailing after her down the aisle.

"Think it's okay if we give her an extra portion?" Anna asked. "She's missed all our other feedings."

Kris laughed. "Sure. But you make it sound like we're zookeepers."

"I'm a mother of twin boys. I *am* a zookeeper."

They scooped up the PowerBar portions and water, dividing the cache between them.

"Say, do you mind if I claim sole responsibility for taking care of J.T.?" she asked Kris.

"Be my guest. Certainly not something I look forward to. Mind if I ask why?"

"Not much to do but sit around and wait," Anna replied. "He might provide me some amusement, seeing as he's as dependent as a little baby and Elliot's not going to do anything for him."

"I thought they were friends," Kris said.

"Nah, he's J.T.'s brother-in-law, and I don't think he even likes him very much. He came along on the trip only because he's really into skiing. Besides, Elliot's still pissed at him for leaving him behind when they went off on their little rescue mission. He's lucky he didn't go, if you ask me."

"How do you know all this?"

"People tell me things," Anna replied. "Also, I'm a notorious gossip."

❖

Hudson sat up and looked at the next part of their route. Hiking along the top of the ridge was going to be yet another test of nerves. Right where they were, they had plenty of room to walk between the sheer cliffs dropping away on either side. They'd pulled themselves up onto a flat plateau about fifteen feet wide.

But the closer they moved toward the peak, the narrower and sharper the ridge crest became, until the whole thing looked like a giant, steep-pitched roof. "Peachy. Isn't any of this going to be easy?"

"And I don't suppose you noticed that," Steffi said from beside her.

Hudson followed her gaze. She'd been so intent on getting up the rock face she hadn't noticed the storm moving in from the northwest. A wide bank of low, dark clouds was streaming right toward them at a rapid clip. "Looks like there's no time to waste. Ready to get moving?"

"I don't want to be stuck here, that's for sure." Steffi got to her feet and started coiling the rope.

"Ever dealt with anything like this ridge before?" Hudson asked. "Any advice on how to get across?"

"No. And yes. Very, very slowly and carefully. One slip, and you're dead."

"That's helpful." Hudson put away her ice axes and unclipped the ski poles from her pack. Though she wasn't anxious to test the viability of navigating the narrow ridge, she knew that Steffi had probably had her fill of going first, at least for a while. "Want me to take over the lead this next stretch?"

"I won't object."

"Okay. Here we go." Hudson set off, with Steffi following not far behind. The first hundred feet were a breeze, relatively speaking. Beyond that, the footing got dicey real fast.

She picked her way along, testing each step before she committed to it, using the ski poles to keep her balance. The going was torturously slow.

Halfway up, where the ridge narrowed to a near-knife's edge, Hudson stepped on a small patch of loose, gravelly rock and began to slip. She went to her hands and knees and caught herself after sliding only a few inches, but the misstep put her dangerously close to the edge and made her heart pound like a jackhammer.

"You all right?" Steffi asked.

"Yeah." Hudson gingerly got to her feet and began moving forward again, even slower than before. The new burst of adrenaline left her feeling shaky; she moved on rubbery legs and doubted every step as she took it.

By the time they finally reached the upper end of the ridge, it was snowing heavily and the wind had started to pick up. Once they found a way down, they'd still have a stretch of steep, white slope to climb to reach the peak of the mountain.

"We need to get off here before we're blown off," Steffi said as she took off her pack.

They had barely enough room to stand together on the ridge top. On either side and ahead of them were long, treacherous drops to the slope far below.

"How?" Hudson asked.

"Rappel." Steffi got out the gear they'd need. "It's not that hard. I'll show you how. I just hope our rope is long enough to reach, or that I can find a ledge if it's not."

Hudson watched her hammer in a piton to anchor them. Despite their many close calls and her numerous reservations about what they were doing, Steffi was keeping it together admirably, maintaining her focus and attention to detail. Once again, she did a quick check of the rope and their gear for damage, and when it came time to brief Hudson on rappelling, her instructions were clear and succinct.

Though she'd had a lot of reservations about Steffi when they'd started out, primarily because of her diminutive stature and timid nature, Hudson had been increasingly impressed by her at every step. Not only was she a strong, resourceful climber, but she'd faced down her fears and done an admirable job with the leadership role that had been forced upon her.

"I'll go first, and I'll get down there pretty quick," Steffi said as she rigged her figure-eight descender to the rope. "You probably won't be able to see me at the bottom, so listen close for my yell. Might be hard to hear, with the distance and this wind."

"Got it."

Steffi got into position and backed up until her feet were poised at the edge. She looked at Hudson with a determined, all-business expression. "See you at the bottom. No more unnecessary excitement, huh?"

"Do my best. Good luck."

Steffi backed up slowly and disappeared over the edge.

Hudson lay down on her stomach to peer over, but the angle was such that she couldn't see shit beyond the first few feet of rope. She had no idea what was happening or how Steffi was faring. When minutes passed with no shout from below, she began to worry.

Then she saw the line go suddenly slack.

"You all right?" Hudson hollered as loud as she could. She listened intently for an answer but heard only the rising wind. *Please let her be all right.* Her heart clenched at the thought that Steffi might have fallen. That she might be seriously injured, or…"Steffi? Can you hear me?"

Silence.

Hudson waited another minute or two, her anxiety increasing. *Fuck it.* She readied her descender and backed up to the edge of the cliff.

Chapter Twenty-seven

Zurich, Switzerland

Bob Furness slammed the phone down in frustration and got up to look out the window. The snow was coming down hard, and traffic on the street below his hotel had slowed to a crawl.

He'd gone from the Rega Control Center into the Zurich Airport terminal, where he'd made the rounds seeking a helicopter or small plane he could hire. When that proved futile, he'd started making calls from his hotel room, methodically working his way down the phone listings of charter aircraft companies in Zurich, Bern, Geneva, and Sion.

As Rega's director had forewarned, Bob had no luck finding a private pilot and aircraft not already committed to the massive national search-and-rescue effort. He turned next to helicopter tour companies, with the same result. Even if he'd found one, an immediate search was apparently impossible. The last company he'd spoken to who flew the Alps told him that low visibility and an approaching storm front had grounded all small aircraft indefinitely.

Bob was almost out of options, though he was still determined to stay in Switzerland until he had conclusive word on Hudson and Joe's fate.

He had only one thing left to try, and though reluctant to call in that favor, he had little choice. Bob checked his watch. Five p.m., which meant it was eleven in the morning at the Pentagon. His former college roommate should be reachable in his office.

"Deputy Secretary Macklemore, please," he told the switchboard operator. "It's Bob Furness calling."

Five minutes passed before his old friend came on the line. "Bob! Hey, long time. How's it going, man?"

"Mac, good to hear your voice. Hope I'm not taking you away from something crucial to our national security."

Macklemore laughed. "Actually, I was in the head, taking a dump."

Bob laughed, too. It had been a running joke during their frat years that no one dared venture into any bathroom that had been recently visited by Big Mac. "Jeez, Mac, tell me you have a private john. That stuff that comes out of you is toxic."

"Enough shit about me." Macklemore laughed again. "What's up? You never call unless you need a favor."

"Guilty. I promise I'll make it up to you the next time I'm in D.C."

"Dinner at Charlie Palmer's and eighteen holes at Whiskey Creek?"

"Deal. Here's the situation, Mac. I'm calling about two of my people—I think you know Hudson Mead and Joe Parker?"

"Yeah, sure. I met them both in Afghanistan. So?"

Bob briefed him on the situation and his failed efforts to find a private charter for a more thorough search of the Bernina Pass. "Nothing's flying right now," he said, "but the weather's supposed to clear in a day or two. I know this is a long shot, but since it involves U.S. citizens, I was wondering if we can get U.S. military aircraft involved."

"We've already loaned some crews and aircraft to the Swiss," Mac replied. "Might be possible. Hang on a minute. First, let me see what we have available in the area." He was gone for several minutes. "We use Pave Hawks a lot for humanitarian search-and-rescue, and we've got a couple at Ramstein," he said, referencing the U.S. air base in Germany. "Let me make a few calls and get back to you. Where are you?"

"Zurich." He gave Macklemore both the hotel and room numbers, and his direct cell. "I'll wait to hear from you. Thanks, Mac."

He hung up and ordered a steak and double bourbon from room service. Nothing to do now but wait. God, how he hated waiting.

❖

Bernina Pass, Switzerland

The pain was so awful that Steffi screamed, but the wind had been knocked out of her by the fall so none of her agony was audible. She doubled up on her right side into a fetal position, clutching her left arm, as her lungs fought for air.

Her battle through that initial burst of intense, excruciating hell lasted a couple of minutes, about as long as it took for her breathing to become normal. When the pain subsided finally enough for her to open her eyes and begin to think about anything else, all she saw was snow.

She let go of her arm to sweep the snow away from her face. Her right glove came away stained with blood, and the sight of it sent her into a mild panic. What the hell had gone wrong?

When she'd reached the end of the rope, she was still ten feet or so above the ground. The slope beneath her had been nearly level in the spot where she'd land; there was a natural depression in the rock there, and the snow looked deep enough to cushion her fall.

Steffi had taken off her pack and tossed it down first, and when she'd released from the rope, she'd tried her hardest to protect herself from injury: bending her knees, trying to land upright or to the side, with her arms up, cradling her head and face.

The snow had done its job well in breaking her fall. She didn't have any broken bones as far as she could tell. But somehow she'd hurt her arm, and it was bleeding like a sonofabitch. She clamped down on her injury again.

"Steffi! Steffi! Are you hurt?" Hudson's panicked voice sounded so distant, Steffi might have imagined it. "Answer me! Steffi!"

She rolled onto her back and looked up. Hudson was descending the rope, and fast. She was more than halfway down already and quickly closing the distance between them.

"Slow down! Watch out!" Steffi yelled.

Hudson immediately applied the brakes, still several yards from the end of the rope but close enough where they could hear each other well. "You all right? What happened?"

Steffi got to her knees, then shakily to her feet, still clutching her arm. "Get down here and I'll tell you, but be careful. The rope ends just beneath you. You'll have to drop from there."

Hudson slowly lowered herself farther.

"The snow's deep enough to cushion your fall, but pitch your bag first," Steffi said. "Try to land on your feet, knees bent, and roll to the side."

Hudson got to the end of the rope, took off her pack and tossed it, then followed it down. She didn't seem to hesitate in the slightest, though it'd taken Steffi a while to work up the nerve to let go.

"What happened?" Hudson hurried over and knelt beside her. She spotted the blood and frowned. "Oh, shit. You hurt yourself."

"Yeah, must have landed on something. Will you take a look and tell me how bad it is?"

"Of course. Does it hurt a lot?" Hudson fished in her pack for the first-aid supplies.

"Like hell at first, but a little better now. Still bleeding a lot, though."

Hudson got out several large gauze pads, a roll bandage, and antiseptic ointment. "Can you take your arm out of your coat?"

As Steffi slipped her arm out of the parka, she noticed a large hole in the upper sleeve right over where she'd been injured, and corresponding holes in all the layers of clothes beneath: fleece pullover, turtleneck, silk long underwear. All were saturated with a growing circle of red.

Hudson cut the holes wider with the Swiss Army knife, so she could peel away the material and inspect the wound.

Steffi didn't dare look. "And?"

"I would guess…" Hudson paused her examination to fish around in the snow for Steffi's pack. She picked up one of the ice axes strapped to it and held it aloft. "That you hit this." The tip of the serrated pick was bloody. "Went right through the fleshy part of your arm and came out the other side."

"Can you stop the bleeding?"

"I'll put a couple of butterfly bandages on it before I wrap it. That should work." Hudson doctored her wounds with gentle efficiency and, once Steffi got her parka zipped up again, handed her a couple of ibuprofen. "If you can make it, I think we should try to get over the peak before nightfall. The southern slope has a gentler grade and is protected from this wind. We can dig a snow cave and talk about what's next."

Steffi looked up at the peak. "I can make it. Will you lead?"

"I planned to. Do you need me to take your pack?" Hudson asked.

"No. I can handle it, if you help me put it on." As they got ready to set off again, Steffi glanced up at the rope dangling overhead. "Hate to leave that, but it can't be helped."

They still had a ways to travel before they could rest, but Steffi was glad to give her arm a reprieve from rock climbing, at least for the rest of today. She didn't want to think yet about what her injury meant for the future of the rescue mission. She was just ready to get to wherever they were going to stop for the night.

"Okay, here we go." Hudson set off slogging through the deep snow.

Steffi followed, grateful not to have to break trail. Going second was still exhausting, but at least the conditions helped her maintain solid footing as the slope got steeper. And their route had kept them protected from the threat of avalanches.

The snow was increasing in intensity and dusk wasn't far off by the time they finally reached the mountaintop, crossed over, and got a look at their new view, such as it was. Visibility was limited to a quarter mile or less, allowing them to see the terrain of the slope around them, and a bit beyond, but nothing in the far distance.

"We need to head that way, and fast. We're running out of daylight." Hudson pointed to the left, at a somewhat precipitous slope barely visible through the haze of blowing snow.

"Can't see shit," Steffi replied. She pointed to a more moderate slope off to the right. "But that looks a lot less steep."

"Got to trust me on this," Hudson said. "We don't have time to debate."

"Trust me is not a phrase that's working really well for me," Steffi replied. She was so tired she just wanted to get out of this wind as quickly as possible.

"Then how about…I know how to read a topographic map?"

"Let me see it. I can, too." She called them up all the time online, to scout out new places to climb.

"Oh, for Christ's sake." Hudson unzipped her jacket and reached into an inner pocket for the laminated map. Careful not to lose it in the wind, she folded it to expose the area where they were. "Here, see this?" She pointed to a trio of lonely concentric circles next to the peak, just off to the southwest, a small natural depression near one of the ridges leading down. It had to be very close.

"Okay. Fine. Go!" Steffi said.

Hudson tucked the map away and immediately headed off left, using her ski poles for support on the steeper portion at the top. Steffi followed, barely using her left pole to spare her arm. Though the wound ached and burned, the pain had subsided a lot from that initial agony.

They'd hiked only a few short minutes when they reached the depression on the map, and it was good they did, because there was barely enough light left to see anything. The base of the area was flat and protected from the howling wind by a rock wall that towered over it, but the winter had dumped an enormous snowdrift there deep enough to build a snow cave.

She had to give Hudson some credit. It looked like an ideal place to stop for the night.

"Sit." Hudson got out her headlamp and turned it on. "This is going to take a while. Try to keep warm, and rest your arm." She started scooping snow with her avalanche shovel, carving out a tunnel just big enough to crawl through and packing the sides smooth as she went. At least the snow here seemed to be of a good consistency for the purpose: heavy and condensed enough to pack well instead of the concrete-and-powder mix of the avalanche field.

Once she'd tunneled into the drift a few feet, Hudson started carving out a domed-ceiling interior with a raised sleeping platform big enough to fit the two of them and high enough for them to sit up comfortably.

While she waited, Steffi emptied her bladder and then hunkered down, her parka hood closed up tight to keep the wind and snow off her face. She was so exhausted she almost dozed during the hour it took Hudson to finish the snow cave enough to move in.

"Still have to pack and smooth the sides," Hudson said after Steffi joined her inside. She'd finished the sleeping platform and laid the plastic tablecloth out as a ground cover, but the domed ceiling was still pretty roughly hewn.

"I can help with that, at least one-handed." Steffi took care of the ceiling and walls around her, while Hudson smoothed and packed the snow on her side. "You did a really nice job on this, Hudson."

"Thanks."

When they finished, Hudson got out her avalanche probe and punched a hole through the ceiling on her side, near the wall. She let the bottom of the pole rest on the floor, with the top sticking out of the hole she'd made. "Do the same on your side. We need to make sure we keep these vent holes about two inches wide at least, so wiggle yours now and then to make sure it stays open. It'll keep carbon dioxide from building up."

While Steffi got her probe out of her pack and punched her own vent hole, Hudson used the shovels to block the entryway.

"Curt said the candle could raise the temperature twenty degrees or so in here." Hudson got her beer candle and jury-rigged soda can and set them up. "Not that I need that right now. In fact, I should get out of my base layer. I really worked up a sweat digging this cave and need to dry off." She took off her parka and pulled the other layers she had on beneath it—sweater, turtleneck, and long underwear—over her head in one swoop, leaving her wearing only her black bra.

Steffi had stretched out her survival blanket and foam pads with Hudson to her right, so she wouldn't inadvertently bump her injured arm. So when Hudson stripped down, she had a perfect, close-up view of Hudson's battered left side. Ugly bruises covered her shoulder, arm, and side, no doubt from when she'd bounced off the rock wall.

"Looks like you got beat up pretty good," she said. "Those hurt?"

Hudson glanced at the bruises. "Not too bad. But I can tell I put my body through the wringer today." She peeled the damp long underwear away from the other clothes and put the turtleneck and sweater back on. "My knee's the worst," she said, rolling up her left pant leg to get a better look.

Steffi saw that it, too, was purple and swollen. It must have hurt a lot for Hudson to be kneeling on it while digging out the snow cave, yet she'd never complained.

"We make quite a pair," Steffi said. "I'll be surprised if either one of us can move tomorrow."

"You could be right, but I hope not. Here." Hudson offered her the first soda can of melted snow.

"Thanks." Never had warm water tasted this good. Steffi was so dehydrated she downed the whole thing in seconds and handed the can back.

Hudson refilled it with snow and set it back over the flame. "We should drink as much as we can tonight."

"Yeah, and be more careful with our bottles tomorrow. I thought they'd be okay in our packs, but we need to keep them closer to our bodies so they won't freeze."

Hudson looked at her. "So…does that mean you think you can go on?"

"I'll reserve final judgment until morning. See how I feel. But if my arm isn't killing me, and it doesn't look like we have to scale some massive wall to get out of here, I'm willing to try."

"How's it feeling now?" Hudson asked.

"I'll take another couple of ibuprofen if you have some." Her arm had begun to throb a bit, and she knew she'd rest easier with another dose.

Hudson pulled the pill bottle from her jacket and took a couple of the tablets out for herself before handing the rest to Steffi. "Here, why don't you hang on to this and take them as you need them."

"Thanks." She took two, and they split the little water that had accumulated to wash them down.

As Hudson refilled the can with snow, Steffi dug in her pack for sustenance.

"Well, we have two PowerBars and two chocolate bars to last us. Want to split a PowerBar tonight? Maybe have a couple squares of chocolate for dessert?"

"Sounds good," Hudson replied. "Though I could eat an entire turkey by myself right now."

"Yeah, I'm with you there." She was ravenous, too, from all the calories they'd burned getting here. She used the Swiss Army knife to divide the PowerBar, and they ate their portions slowly, savoring every bite. "You know, this chocolate bar was supposed to be yours," she commented as they each broke off a chunk.

"That so?"

"Yeah, I bought three of these for you at the last train stop, to thank you for saving Gary's wallet. Just never got the chance to give them to you."

"Well, it was a nice gesture," Hudson replied. "And certainly welcome right now."

"Call it a peace offering. I'm sorry if I got a little...you know, testy...during the hike up here." She was thinking specifically of the grief she'd given Hudson about which direction to take once they'd reached the peak, especially now that she'd witnessed her working so hard on the snow cave when she'd obviously been hurting.

"It's all right. This has all been a very tough and scary ordeal, and I know it's hard to put your trust...and your life...in the hands of someone you don't know well. I kind of have some trust issues, myself."

"Yeah?" Steffi relaxed back onto her foam-piece bed. "Well, we've got nothing but time at the moment. Care to elaborate?" She didn't really expect Hudson to take her up on the challenge. So far, she'd been pretty tight-lipped about volunteering anything very personal.

But Hudson was full of surprises, and tonight proved no exception.

CHAPTER TWENTY-EIGHT

Hudson was in a reflective mood, a frequent occurrence since the avalanche had hit the train. She'd always viewed disasters from the outside before, been a mere witness to the aftermath and not a victim. Though what she saw often touched her emotionally, nothing on the job had ever prompted the kind of life self-critique she'd been experiencing the past few days.

But Joe's injuries and the death of Clay and so many others had driven the fragility of life home. And her own mortality as well, especially today, after so many close calls herself.

During the hours spent slogging through the snow, she'd had ample time to think about her life and the choices she'd made. Though proud of what she'd accomplished, she had regrets, too, mostly concerning decisions she'd made long ago about her personal life.

She didn't know why she found Steffi so easy to open up to. Certainly she could no longer deny the fact she was seriously attracted to her, but it was more than that. Perhaps it was because of what they'd been through together. Maybe it was also partly the timing—after today's trials and tribulations, who knew whether they'd live through tomorrow? Whatever it was, they were in this together, dependent on each other, and Hudson felt an unusual closeness to her, in a way she hadn't felt with anyone in a very long time..

"I don't trust many people," she told Steffi. "Never have. Joe and my neighbor Bruce, both of whom I've known forever. And my two brothers. But that's about it."

"Your parents?"

"I haven't seen them or talked to them, in…" She had to do a quick calculation in her head. "Nearly twenty-five years."

Steffi stared at her incredulously. "Oh, God. I can't imagine. I'm so close to mine. Something major must have happened, I would guess?"

"Yeah, they found out I was gay."

"That…that's all?"

"I take it you had a good coming-out experience with yours?"

Steffi nodded. "They're pretty cool people, and they have a lot of gay and lesbian friends. I don't think they were very surprised."

"How old were you when you told them?"

"Sixteen. When I realized I had a crush on a new girl in school. You?"

"My parents found out when they visited me one weekend, my third year of college. They hadn't told me they were coming." Hudson rarely revisited the memories of that time. Though long scarred over, they were still painful. "Anyway, I answered the door in a bathrobe—I was living in a dorm—and they just sort of barged right in. It was pretty easy to ascertain what I'd just been doing with the naked woman lounging on my bed."

"Oh, no."

"They were both conservative Catholics. I mean, as in, go-to-church-three-times-a-week-or-more Catholics. As soon as they realized what was up, they left, my mom in tears."

"And?"

"They wouldn't answer the phone the rest of the day. Dad called the next morning and basically said that either I would repent my sinful ways and agree to go to counseling with a priest or they'd disown me and stop paying my tuition."

"Oh, my God. I can't believe that."

"They were true to their word. He didn't want to listen to anything I had to say. When he kept pushing for an answer, I told him I couldn't be something I wasn't. He hung up, and I never spoke to either of them again. Oh, my brothers have tried to patch things up, but I haven't been interested in reconnecting with them."

"And they really just cut you off and out of their life? Just like that?"

"Just like that. I only made it through college because my oldest brother was already married and had a good job as an architect. He supported me until I could graduate, and I paid him back much later."

"Wow. I've heard a few bad coming-out stories, but nothing like that."

"Attitudes are a lot different these days, at least among most people," Hudson said. "Not so much, then. There weren't a lot of role models around. On the plus side, the experience made me very self-sufficient."

"I know I'm very lucky to have a close family. I can't imagine growing up without the sense of security and comfort that provides," Steffi replied. "The Christmases and special occasions together, sharing good news and accomplishments. Having them there to support me during the bad times."

"I've always claimed…even to myself…that I rose above it all and did just fine without them. But I've begun to realize how much it took out of me. In terms of my ability to get close to people, I mean."

"This may be too personal," Steffi said. "But are you saying you've never…you know, had a serious romantic relationship?"

"One. Many years ago. It took forever for her to get me to trust her. Once I did, though, I was all in. Totally committed. If there had been gay marriage then, I'd have proposed."

"How long were you together?"

"Almost seven years." Six years, eleven months, and two days, to be precise. The fact that she could remember that, after all these years, bothered her. "We got together when I was just starting out at AP. She was a journalist, too—we met in college—and she'd scored a job at a local TV station. We got an apartment together, and everything was great for a very long while."

"What happened?"

"I got promoted and started going overseas," Hudson replied. "A few weeks a year at first, then more. I was ambitious and loved my job, so I was always up for anything, no matter how tough or long the assignment might be. It got so I was hardly home any more, and sometimes when I was in remote areas I'd be completely out of touch for days, even weeks, at a time."

"And she got tired of that?" Steffi asked gently.

"She tried to tell me that she was unhappy. That she couldn't keep playing second fiddle to my career forever. One day, after a month on the road, I got home to find she'd packed up and left. Took most everything we owned with her, too, except for my clothes and a few personal items."

"Oh, my God."

"Even so, I tracked her down. Tried to make it right, promised her I'd be home more, though I wasn't sure I really could. I was—and am—a workaholic, for sure. But it didn't matter, anyway. That ship had sailed. We kind of kept in polite touch for a while, but not for many years now."

Steffi exhaled loudly. "Well, it's no wonder you have trust issues."

"Ya think?" Hudson laughed without humor. "Since then, I haven't really allowed myself to get close to another woman. Oh, I've dated some, though not for a long while. And even then, it's only on a no-strings-attached basis. Mostly, I've just focused on work."

"No disrespect, Hudson. I know your work has helped a lot of people, but that sounds like a lonely way to live. And I can't imagine doing it as long as you have," Steffi said. "It's only been ten months since I dropped out of the dating pool, and it's driving me crazy, sometimes. I really miss being with someone. The physical intimacy, laughing together, having someone to curl up with at night."

"Yeah. I miss that, too." *I miss that a lot, as a matter of fact.* Hudson drank from the soda can and refilled it with more snow. She was curious about why someone with so much going for her had given up on going out. "What did you mean, 'dropped out of the dating pool'? That sounds like a story, and I think it's your turn to dig up old dirt for a while."

"All right. Fair's fair," Steffi replied. "Well, I decided to take a year off from dating. I kept going from one relationship right to another, making the same mistakes, and I needed some time on my own to figure out why."

"And have you?"

"I think so. I've worked most of it out, anyway, I think."

"What kind of mistakes?"

"I tend to mistake instant lust for something more, for one thing. I get lost in this glorious haze of hormones instead of getting to know her well first, and I jump in with both feet."

"Ah, the U-haul effect."

"Exactly. Move right in before the reality shatters the bliss that you're not at all right for each other. Problem was, each time, I convinced myself it was love until I got some distance from it and saw it for what it really was. Still didn't stop me from doing the same thing over and over, though. Until the last time, when it wasn't just my heart that got broken, but my trust in people, as well."

"What happened?"

"A woman I'd lived with for fourteen months and, again… *thought* I loved," Steffi replied, "moved out while I was away on a weekend club climbing trip. No note, no forwarding address. Out of the blue, when everything had been great and normal the night before I left."

"Pretty harsh." Hudson offered Steffi more water, and Steffi drank it right down.

"That's not the half of it. I didn't realize it right away, but within a couple days, when I went to fill an online order, I realized she'd taken a bunch of my most valuable first editions. Not only were they worth a fortune, but some were from my private collection."

"It's really tough to recover from someone who gains your trust for some ulterior motive, especially if they end up using it against you."

"Yeah. It hit me pretty hard. I couldn't believe that someone so close to me—someone I thought I knew well—could betray me and use me like that. I felt terribly naive. But I'd always wanted to believe the best in people. I'd trust anyone and everyone unless or until they gave me a reason to think otherwise. That was especially true of the women I was with."

"Sounds like you've gained a lot of insights during this break from dating. I'm sure that when you decide to dive back in, you'll find somebody more right for you," Hudson said. "They'll probably be lining up, as a matter of fact." It wasn't difficult to come up with a million reasons why Steffi was a great catch. "You're bright, brave, vivacious, with a refreshing zest for life. A natural beauty with a ready smile that lights up a room. You shouldn't let a few disappointments deter you from going after what you want."

"Gosh, Hudson, I don't know what to say. That's very sweet." A rosy blush colored her cheeks. "And you know, I'd say the same of you. You should allow yourself another chance of finding someone special. You've got so much to offer. I've never met anyone like you. Whoever wins your heart is incredibly fortunate."

"I'll admit this whole experience has made me re-evaluate the balance I've chosen between work and a personal life, as well as the distance I keep between myself and others. I don't want to find myself looking back with regrets." She glanced over at Steffi. "Sort of comes down to what's more important to leave behind: your name on a plaque somewhere and a byline on old news stories? Or the people you loved, who will think about you, and miss you, and never forget you?"

"Well, you'll have a couple of train cars full of people who'll never forget you, if we reach civilization."

"Forget *us*," Hudson said.

"Us, then." Steffi nodded. "But mostly you. I'd never have the courage to do half the things you've done. I don't know whether to call it brave, or foolhardy—how you jump into action in a crisis. Risking your life to search for Joe, and searching the wrecked car. Going into the avalanche field after J.T. and Bud. How do you do it?"

"Conditioning, I suppose. Ever heard of the bystander effect?" Hudson asked.

"No, I don't think so."

"It's a proven psychological phenomenon. When most people witness an accident or emergency and others are around, it diffuses their sense of responsibility to help. So everyone sits around doing nothing. The more people there are, the greater the chances no one will step up. I did a story on it a few years ago after a two-year-old girl was hit by a truck in China. She lay in the street for seven minutes before anyone helped, and she died as a result. It stuck with me. So I guess I'm just more aware that if someone acts quickly in a bad situation, it can make a real difference."

"Lucky for us."

"We could use some luck tomorrow, that's for sure." Hudson was pleasantly surprised at how much the candle was warming the interior of the snow cave. The temperature had risen several degrees while they talked, allowing her to take off her gloves. "And you know, a lot of the credit for so many people making it is due to Curt, not me. Bless those Boy Scout skills."

"Yeah, I can't believe how cozy it's gotten in here." Steffi took off her boots and removed her parka to use as a makeshift blanket. "I tell you, after today, I think I'm going to sleep really well, regardless of where we are."

"Pretty beat, myself." Hudson checked the soda can. All the snow had melted. "Here, drink this. I need to make a pit stop before I turn in." She put her headlamp back on before she crawled out through the tunnel and quickly relieved herself. The snowfall had slowed to a few flurries, but the wind was still going strong.

Steffi had repacked the soda can and set it back over the candle by the time she returned and sealed the entrance again. Fortunately, the design of the cave had allowed little of the warm air to escape during Hudson's brief trip outside.

She took off her boots in favor of a second pair of thick wool socks and glanced over at Steffi as she lay back on her foam pads with her survival blanket.

Steffi was wrapped up snug in her silver cocoon, eyes closed. Maybe already asleep. Her parka-blanket had slipped to one side, so Hudson reached over and pulled it up and over her again.

"Thanks." Steffi yawned but didn't open her eyes. "Night, Hudson."

"Good night, Steffi. Sweet dreams." Hudson was exhausted to the bone, but sleep was elusive.

The last thing she remembered thinking before finally drifting off was how nice Steffi's hair smelled.

Chapter Twenty-nine

Next morning

Steffi became aware of several things at once when she woke up to darkness the next morning. She remembered immediately where she was because she'd rolled onto her left side and her injured arm was throbbing. She needed to pee. And her feet were freezing, but the rest of her was pretty warm.

Probably because Hudson was spooning her.

Her arm cradled Steffi's waist protectively, and she was hugging her so close that Steffi could feel Hudson's soft, regular exhalations on the back of her neck.

Despite the discomfort to her arm and the urgings of her bladder, she didn't move or speak.

She was enjoying this, much to her surprise. A lot, in fact. Despite her sometimes-impulsive nature, Hudson made her feel safe. And Steffi felt a lot closer to her after their conversation last night. She'd been surprised that Hudson had divulged so much about her past. It explained a lot about why she'd previously avoided personal questions, especially about her family.

Steffi had been surprised as well by her own admissions. But Hudson had made it easy. She was never judgmental, always encouraging, with a wise and mature outlook, gleaned from years traveling the world and really listening to all types of people.

She was a find, that's for sure. Steffi hoped they'd remain in touch long after this ended. She was somehow more encouraged this morning that they *would* make it. Their conversation had increased the trust between them, and that couldn't help but improve their odds.

Had that been Hudson's intention, at least in part, when she'd turned last night's conversation into one of sharing secrets?

Finally her injured arm couldn't stand any more. Reluctantly, she put it over the one Hudson had wrapped around her and stroked it gently as she said, "Hudson? Hey, you awake? I need to get up."

"Mmm?" Hudson's arm went from totally relaxed to rigid in a heartbeat. "Oh. Sorry." She pulled away, and as Steffi rolled over onto her back, a headlamp flicked on.

"Don't be sorry. I'm not. You kept me warm, and it was frankly kind of nice to wake up to," Steffi said as she reached for her boots. It was more than nice, actually. It was pretty damn fantastic, despite the circumstances. But she wouldn't allow herself to even daydream about the possibility of them ever being together, of waking up in Hudson's arms every morning. Not after Hudson's explanation of why she avoided romantic entanglements. "I didn't want to wake you, but I really have to pee, and my arm needs more ibuprofen."

"I'm blaming it on the cold and the fact you reminded me how much I miss cuddling up with someone," Hudson replied with a smile. She relit the candle. "Must have gotten dripped on. Still have half of it left."

"Be right back." Steffi put her parka, headlamp, and gloves on and went out the tunnel, brushing aside the powder that had gathered around the exit. The first rays of dawn were just peeking over the mountain. The snow had stopped and visibility looked to be much better, though the sky was still overcast.

She did her business and went back inside, sealing the exit again. "Looks pretty good out there. Weather's cleared up and it should be light, soon."

"Here's some water to take your pills with." Hudson handed her the soda can, which had begun to ice up again. "We need to stay here at least long enough to melt some more snow for the trip."

"How are you feeling this morning?" Steffi asked.

"Knee's complaining a bit, but otherwise okay. Just sore."

"Here. We have plenty." Steffi handed over two of the ibuprofen.

"Don't mind if I do. Then I need to make a trip outside, too."

Once she'd finished that bit of business, Hudson got the map out and they sat side by side on the sleeping platform, with the laminated paper spread out on their laps.

"This is the route I was looking at." Hudson traced her finger from their current position down a ridge, to a place where the topographic lines indicated a steep drop in elevation to the rail tracks below. "We follow the rail line from there. But it depends on us being able to rappel that cliff. Think your arm is up to it? And do we have enough rope?"

"My arm, yes. The rope is another matter. Hard to tell from this how far a drop it is, but it's probably more than our hundred and eighty feet. We'd have to be able to do it in stages, with ledges. Won't know until we get a good look at it." Steffi looked at her. "Do you have a plan B?"

"How about...we'll work on a plan B together if and when we need one?"

"All right. Sounds reasonable."

Hudson put the map away and went to check on the water situation.

Steffi took off her boots to massage her feet, trying to warm them. When Hudson turned back around with the can in her hand, she had a big smile on her face. "Curt slipped me a little something special when we were packing. He found it in the pocket of a coat he got out of the pile." As she offered it to Steffi, she added, "and there was only one packet, so I get half, please."

Steffi caught the intoxicating aroma of coffee as she brought the can to her lips and took a sip. It was even pretty warm. "Heavenly." She took another sip and offered it back to Hudson.

Hudson drank and sighed contentedly. "Yup. Liquid gold." They passed the can back and forth, taking little sips to make it last as long as possible.

They ate another couple of squares of chocolate for breakfast and packed their gear while Hudson melted more snow so they'd have water to take with them.

By the time they left the cave and were ready to start off again, the sun was trying hard to peek through the thick layer of cloud cover, and visibility had improved dramatically, allowing them to see the surrounding peaks and the valley far below.

"I'll break trail to start," Hudson said as they got out their ski poles and put their crampons on.

"Ready when you are," Steffi replied. As they set off through the thigh-deep snow, she kept reassuring herself they would find help in a matter of hours. By tonight, the injured would be in a hospital, and she and Hudson would be celebrating over a nice meal somewhere warm, this long nightmare finally over.

❖

"How much does that leave us?" Kris asked, as Anna finished portioning out PowerBar pieces for all of them.

"Lean pickings for tomorrow, if we're still here," Anna replied. "Potato chips and chocolate. My boys would be loving this."

"We're running out of hand warmers, too," Kris replied. "We may have enough to get water through the rest of the day, but that's about it."

"If the wind has died down, I might be able to get a fire going outside to melt more," Curt said. "We haven't got much to burn—a couple paperbacks, notebooks, a few other odds and ends. And I'd have to find something to build it on, like a big piece of metal." He gazed around at the rest of the luggage compartment. "I'll go hunt for something."

"Every little bit helps," Anna said. "We should try the radio again, too. See if we can get a weather report."

Curt reached for his portion of breakfast. "I'll do that while you guys feed everybody."

Kris took half the supplies, Anna took the rest, and they headed into the passenger compartment.

"Still torturing J.T.?" Kris asked.

"Girls just wanna have fun," Anna replied. "He's gotten *so* much more polite in just twenty-four hours."

Kris chuckled. "I pity your boys, sometimes." She started with the Japanese couples while Anna gave her first rations to Fritz and

Hugo. They moved on down the car, distributing the food and what water they had, which amounted to about a cup per person.

Finally, Anna came to J.T.

"Good morning, asswipe," she said, shining her headlamp directly into his face. "Are we ready to play nice with others today?"

"Good morning, *Anna*," he replied through gritted teeth, making her name sound more like a curse than a greeting.

"Not bad. But let's put some joy and enthusiasm into it next time, huh? You don't sound very convincing, and you might need some help with that bedpan again before long." They'd had to resort to using climbing helmets as bedpans for Joe, J.T., Bud, and the two Japanese men because of their injuries, and none of them were happy about it. Curt and Elliot teamed up for the unpleasant and noxious duty, but they were almost out of toilet paper, and the two bathrooms they were using as a dumping ground were both rapidly approaching the point of unbearable.

"Whatever you say," J.T. replied, though the expression on his face gave new meaning to the cliché "if looks could kill."

She gave him his piece of chocolate and allotment of water, helping him to sit up enough to drink it. "Good boy. That's a good boy," she said, in the tone she used for Bella, their Chihuahua.

He waited until both the chocolate and water were finished before replying. "Bite me, bitch. I swear to God, you better hope we *don't* get rescued if you keep this up."

"Awww. Mister Cranky Pants is back, I see. There goes your chance of getting a gold star today. Shame, too, 'cause I was going to offer you these for dessert." She held up two ibuprofen, then put them back in her pocket.

"You can't—"

"Oh, yes, I can. Just watch me." She got up and headed back toward the luggage compartment.

"God damn it! Come back here!" J.T. shouted after her.

"I warned you about that potty mouth," she hollered back. She decided to make him stew for a few minutes before he got his pills. Serve him right.

Her momentary pleasure at J.T.'s frustration didn't last long. As soon as she caught sight of Curt and Kris's worried faces, she knew something was up. They were standing by the entrance to the exit tunnel, talking in low voices.

"What's the matter?" she asked.

"The radio wasn't picking up much, so I went to check the antenna," Curt replied. "We must have had another avalanche last night, because the exit is blocked again."

"How bad is it?"

"Pretty bad. I can't see any light, and it's set up like concrete again. We're going to have to work in shifts to dig it out. Elliot should be able to help, too."

"I'll get that duffel bag they were using before to move the snow," Kris said. "Seemed to work pretty well."

"And I'll start digging." Curt grabbed an ice ax and shovel. "One of you can relieve me when I get tired.

❖

Zurich, Switzerland

Bob caught the phone on the second ring. He'd fallen asleep in his clothes on top of the bedspread and was surprised to see it was already full light out. "Yes?"

"Bob, it's Mac. I've got some good news for you."

"Knew you'd come through, buddy."

"I've got a helicopter pilot and two man rescue crew at your disposal for the next twenty-four hours," Mac said. "A Sikorsky HH-60 Pave Hawk, out of Ramstein. Got a pen?"

Bob grabbed the hotel pen and notepad off the nightstand. "Shoot."

Macklemore gave him the pilot's name and the time and place they were to rendezvous at the Zurich airport. "I gave him your cell number. If they're delayed in getting there for any reason he'll contact you directly."

"You're the man, Mac. Thanks, again."

"I'll wait to hear about a tee-off time. Good luck. Hope you find them."

Bob hung up and checked his watch. He had about an hour before he was to meet the rescue team. Just enough time to shower, grab a bite to eat, and get to the airport.

The U.S. Air Force pilot was leaning against a column outside the main entrance to the Rega Control Center when Bob first spotted him, but as soon as he got out of the cab and started toward the lieutenant, the man straightened, arms at his sides. He was in his military flight suit. "Mister Furness?" He extended his hand. "Lieutenant Tommy Douglas. At your service, sir."

"Very grateful for the help, Lieutenant. Please, call me Bob."

"As you wish, sir. The director is expecting us. Shall we go in?"

"After you."

Director Glaus's secretary led them into his office as soon as they got there.

"Mister Furness." The director greeted him with a handshake. "And Lieutenant Douglas, I presume?"

"Good to meet you, sir." They shook hands.

"Thank you for seeing us on such short notice," Bob said as Glaus beckoned them to sit in the chairs in front of his desk.

"Not at all," Glaus replied. "I'm very happy to hear you were able to find help to search for your people." Bob saw that he'd spread out a map of the pass on his desk. "The crew that flew over the pass three days ago reported several avalanches along this section of track," he told the lieutenant. "They found the train debris below a massive avalanche field here." He indicated an area at the end of the pass, where the track had a mountain on one side and a gorge on the other. "They could see parts of two cars sticking up out of the snow in the gorge."

"May I take this map?" Lieutenant Douglas asked.

"Of course." Director Glaus wrote down a number and handed it to the airman. "Keep in touch with us at this frequency. I'll have a dispatcher working with you if you find anything and need additional resources. We'd also like an update on the overall conditions up there. The first helicopter reported that the avalanches had made the line impassable for weeks."

"Yes, sir. I'll make contact when we reach the top of the pass."

A waiting go-cart shuttle took them to the olive-green Pave Hawk helicopter, parked far away from the commercial runways and terminal at the edge of the airfield.

"You'll be more comfortable in a flight suit, sir," Lieutenant Douglas told Bob when they reached the chopper. "We have one that should fit you, though it might be a little big. What you're wearing probably won't be warm enough at altitude."

"Whatever you say." After he donned the suit, the lieutenant introduced Bob to his crewmen—a flight engineer and rescue paramedic—and they all buckled in, Bob in the second-row seat next to the window. The chopper's roomy interior held seats for eight passengers in addition to the crew, and floor space for several litters and other cargo.

Bob pulled on his headset just as Lieutenant Douglas was receiving flight clearance from the control tower.

Five minutes later, they were headed toward the Alps.

CHAPTER THIRTY

Hudson stopped when she reached the beginning of the ridge, and Steffi was glad she did, because even though she wasn't the one breaking trail, she could hardly keep up. She was really winded and almost relieved to see that Hudson was, too.

"Holding up?" Hudson asked.

"You're setting a pretty wicked pace and I don't know how you're doing it." Steffi smiled. "But once I catch my breath, I'm good. My arm's not hurting too bad."

"This looks iffy. We've got to be real careful through this stretch. Big cornices there on the northern slope." Hudson pointed to the ridge they were about to follow. At least this wasn't a knife-edged sharp-peaked one like the last, more a wide shoulder of snow leading down. Ample room to walk, but Steffi could see they'd have to keep to the far-right, southernmost part. To the left, they'd be walking on top of cornices that could collapse at any moment, carrying them down the mountain to their death.

Knowing that Hudson had to be terribly fatigued, Steffi volunteered to lead the next stretch.

"You sure?" Hudson asked. "I can go awhile longer."

"My turn." She looked at Hudson. "Only fair we share, right?"

Hudson smiled. "You know, you keep surprising me.

"Do I? In a good way, I hope."

"Absolutely. The more challenges we face, the stronger you get. Yesterday, you were hesitant about taking the lead and ready to turn back. Look at you now."

Steffi thought about that. It was true that she was more relaxed and confident today, despite her injury and the uncertainties ahead. Why was that? Perhaps because she'd surprised herself with what she'd been capable of yesterday. It felt good to stare down her fears and triumph over them. And Hudson's calm bravery and resolve throughout their whole ordeal had also made a profound impact on her. She was truly an inspiration. "Maybe it's because you set a good example, Hudson. Come on, let's go."

She set off down the ridge, probing the snow with her ski poles, trying to hug the right edge of the ridge to avoid the cornices. The snow on the exposed ridgeline was thigh-deep, so it was tough going plowing through it, and after an hour she'd begun to sweat under all her layers of clothing.

When she paused for some water and to catch her breath, she unzipped her parka to vent and cool off a bit. Hudson, who'd been trailing twenty feet or so behind, seemed grateful for the break.

"Sun's really trying to come out," Hudson remarked after a few sips of water.

Steffi had been so focused on the terrain she hadn't noticed. But indeed, the sky was beginning to clear off to the north; she could see vague patches of blue in the dirty-yellow sky. "Good for visibility. Once we get over this big hump on the ridge we should be able to see where we're going pretty well."

"Still okay to lead, or you want me to take over?"

"I'm good for a while. Just needed to catch my breath and vent a little. I was getting overheated."

"Easy to do. This is a hell of a workout."

"No lie. I will feel absolutely no guilt whatsoever about eating my way through the first patisserie we come to, once we get rescued."

Hudson laughed. "Don't be mean. Now I'm going to be thinking about pastries all day."

"Call it motivation. Ready to go?" She took one more sip of water before putting the bottle away.

"Lead on."

They pushed forward over the broad, high rise in the ridge they were following, and when they reached the crest were able to see for the first time where the rail line continued on south, past where the train had derailed. After it skirted the mountain they were on, the track began a long, looping descent to the Italian border far below. Steffi still couldn't detect any sign of civilization: no houses or buildings, or even smoke rising from a distant chimney. The vast vista contained only mountains, snow, and more snow, as far as she could see.

Refusing to be deterred, she kept on, ignoring the increasing pain in her arm. Finally, around mid-morning, they reached the end of the ridge and the sheer cliff down that Hudson had spotted on the map.

Steffi took off her pack and was sorting through her climbing gear when Hudson caught up.

"How's it seem?"

"I'm going to set an anchor so I can clip on and get a closer look. Not able to tell much from here, but it's for sure a longer rappel than we have rope for." Steffi hammered a piton into the rock near the edge of the cliff. "Get your stuff out and gear up," she told Hudson as she got out her harness and rope.

Ten minutes later, they were both rigged to descend. Steffi backed up to the edge of the cliff, rope in hand. "Once I'm over the side and down a ways, I should be able to see whether we can do this in stages. If I see ledges or places to stop, I'll yell *rappelling* and keep going. When you feel the rope go slack, clip on and start down to me."

"Got it."

"If, on the other hand, all I see is a smooth rock face like yesterday," she said, "I'll holler *pull me up!* I'm not sure I can get back up here with my arm, so I'll need your help. Then we come up with a plan B."

"I'll be ready," Hudson replied. "I'll get you back up here if it comes to that. You don't have to worry, okay?"

"I'm not. I know you have my back." Steffi gave her a smile before carefully stepping over the edge and out of view. The response had come easily. She was a little surprised by how much she'd come to trust Hudson, but she did. Their conversation last night had soothed many of her misgivings about her. She felt sure now that Hudson would do anything and everything possible to keep them both safe.

She kicked off and allowed herself to drop several feet before bouncing back to the cliff face. Then she kicked off again and descended several feet more before she paused to study the features of the rock below.

The rappel would be difficult but possible. She spotted two small ledges they could use, the first several feet right of her current position and about a hundred feet below. "Rappelling!" she called as loud as she could and heard an answering whistle at once from Hudson.

Steffi used the descender to drop farther toward the ledge until she was almost even with it. Then she kicked off, pendulum-swung toward it, and found a handhold with her right hand that steadied her enough to jam a cam in with her left and quickly clip her harness to it.

Once she was secured to the rock, she unclipped from the rope and tried to calm her racing heart while she waited for Hudson. So far, her left arm was holding up, but she'd be grateful to be on solid footing again.

Hudson came over the lip of the ridge and started down, reaching Steffi not long afterward through the same kind of swinging motion she'd used herself. Fortunately, the distance was so short she didn't get twisted around like yesterday and made it to the ledge without incident.

"So far so good," Steffi said once Hudson had clipped in to the anchor. "We should be able to make the bottom in two more pitches." She retrieved the rope and set a second anchor for the next leg of their descent.

"Can we have a break for more drugs, first?" Hudson asked.

Steffi laughed. "I'm all for that." She got out the pill bottle and each of them took a couple more tablets.

The final two legs of their descent could hardly have gone smoother. Steffi found the handholds she needed to get them to the second ledge, and her arm was able to withstand the grueling effort. Hudson, meanwhile, seemed to be getting almost too comfortable with rappelling—she came down even faster than Steffi did during the final push down the rope, like she was on vacation and this was all part of a planned adrenaline adventure.

When they finally reached the bottom, they were only a quick, half-hour hike away from the rail line. Seeing this man-made path heading downward to civilization so near felt like a huge accomplishment, and

Steffi was more encouraged than ever that they'd make it all the way to find help.

"I can't believe how much less snow there is on this side of the pass," Hudson said as they re-bagged their climbing gear and coiled the rope. "With all the snow that's fallen this winter, you'd think it'd be equally bad everywhere."

"It's like this in the Cascades, too," Steffi replied. "It's all about the way the weather blows in. Mountains block so much."

The difference in the snow depth was noticeable, but there was still enough of the heavy, wet stuff that it was a chore to reach the track. Once they did, though, the going was much easier. The snow was only calf-deep at best over the rails because it had been regularly plowed until a few days before, and they were able to walk side by side for the first time. To their left was the deep gorge that had claimed the rest of the train. It was wider here, and shallower, than where it began at the end of the pass, but still a grim reminder of what had happened.

"How you holding up?" Hudson asked.

"Other than starving, thirsty, and every muscle aching? Oh, not too bad. You?"

"Ditto, ditto, and ditto." Hudson smiled. "I'm making a list for when we reach help. After everyone's rescued, of course. My priorities *were* big meal, long, hot bath, and a warm, comfy bed. But I'm definitely going to have to add a massage in there, somewhere."

"Count me in."

"What will you do, really?" Hudson asked. "I mean, in terms of your vacation. Will you head home right away?"

"You know, I hadn't thought that far ahead at all. I guess it depends a lot on what the others do. Some of them will probably have to be in the hospital a while. Nick. Fin. Gary. And Curt will have to arrange for Patti's body to be transported back to the States. I may hang around a few days, if I can be of help."

"Yeah, I think Joe will have to be treated here, too. I'll stay until he's ready to go home."

"Look at us," Steffi said. "You'd think we're absolutely convinced we're going to make it."

"Aren't we?" Hudson feigned shock, and Steffi laughed.

"Course we are. We're an unbeatable team."

"That we are," Hudson said, looking over at her with a grin. "That we are."

Steffi broke into Queen's *We Are The Champions* at the top of her lungs, and Hudson joined in. They segued from that into any and every other upbeat, victorious pop tune they could think of, gasping for air between each one because of the altitude. Before they knew it, they'd covered another mile of track.

"Wait a minute." Hudson pulled them up short after they rounded a bend and got a look at the next section of rail. Their elevated perspective gave them a great vantage point. "Look there." She pointed to where the track began a big, wide loop to avoid a glacier spilling down from the neighboring peak. "There's one of the potential shortcuts I told you about. If we can traverse the glacier instead of following the track, we can cut off at least four or five miles, looks like."

"That's so dangerous, though," Steffi said. "Even with rope. If one of us falls into a crevasse, we're screwed."

"Might make the difference whether we reach someplace today or have to build another snow cave. Would it ease your mind any if I said I'd lead?"

"Probably not much. I'm not any more anxious to see you get hurt than I am myself." Steffi stared down at the glacier. Though they were covered with new powder, she could still make out the faint color variations that indicated an abundance of deep crevasses marring the deceptively smooth surface. "But I won't be the one to hold us back. If you think we should, I'll be right behind you."

CHAPTER THIRTY-ONE

M y arms can't take any more," Elliot said as he emerged
from the tunnel. "It's like digging through rocks. Breaking
into a vault would be easier."

"I'm up next." Anna hadn't yet taken a turn, so she pulled on her
gloves and took the ice ax and shovel from him. They hadn't told the
injured they were buried again. No sense in giving them any more to
worry about.

They'd been initially confident they'd break through in short
order, but after four hours of chipping away at the stubborn blockage
they could still see no indication they were getting close to the surface.

Anna crawled into the ice chute. As much as she was trying to
remain optimistic, this latest development had dampened even her
hope of rescue, and she'd begun to think about the effect her not
coming back would have on her husband and the boys. As much as
she joked and complained about their antics, they were a devoted,
close-knit family, and her death would have a devastating impact on
them all. Had she been selfish, pressing for this annual alone time?

The thought of maybe never seeing them again was unbearable.
She took out her frustration on the hard-packed snow, chopping away
furiously with the ice ax until her hands blistered.

Don't you dare let me die in here. Thwack, thwack, thwack.
They need me. Thwack, thwack, thwack. *Leaving her husband alone
to handle those two terrors by himself was not an option.* Thwack,
thwack, thwack. *They'll probably tell him they want to be NASCAR
drivers, and he'll be all for it.* Thwack, thwack, thwack. *They'll all*

live on pizza and soda until they're big as houses. Thwack, thwack, thwack. Tears rolled down her face when she imagined them gathered around her casket at the funeral.

An hour later, she dried her tears and crawled back down the chute, her anxiety, energy, and frustration spent, but still without any indication they might be close to breaking through.

"Sorry. I've had it." She dropped the ax and shovel by the entrance and went to sit by Curt while Kris wordlessly took up the digging. Elliot had returned to the passenger car.

"No closer?" he asked.

"Not that I can tell."

"Where do you imagine Hudson and Steffi are? Think they're close to getting somewhere?"

"Probably hasn't been long enough, yet," she replied. "But maybe by tonight. Tomorrow, for sure."

"I hope you're right," Curt replied. "We're using the last of the hand warmers now. In a few hours, we won't be able to make water and people will start going downhill pretty fast."

"How's everybody doing?" she asked.

"Surviving. That's about all I can say. We ran out of pain meds this morning and are down to aspirin and ibuprofen, which don't do much against these kind of traumatic injuries. In another few hours, we're going to have some very miserable people. Not like they aren't already, but the meds have at least been making them more comfortable and allowing them to rest."

"We're going to run out of food tonight, too," Anna said. "All we have left are some chips, and they're so full of salt they'll just make everyone more thirsty."

"Think it's worth going through the luggage and the cars again, see if we missed anything?"

"Sure, worth a shot. What else do we have to do?"

They enlisted Elliot to help clear snow for Kris while they searched.

"Our best bet for finding anything is in the next car. Hardly anybody's been back there, except to use the can," Curt said.

They passed by the dead, laid out side by side in the luggage compartment just inside the entrance of the second car. Curt paused a moment to kneel beside the body of his wife. Then they continued into the badly wrecked second panorama car. Curt got on his hands and knees, methodically searching between and under every single row of seats, while Anna crouched near him with her headlamp, trying to help him see.

"Half a sandwich!" he announced, as he pulled a smashed ham-and-cheese from where it was wedged between seats. Someone had obviously been in the middle of eating it when the avalanche hit—it had a bite gone, and it wasn't in a wrapper. But it was still food, and Anna was happy to see it.

"Did all of these get checked, do you know?" She indicated the little pocket behind each seat, similar to the type found on airplanes. They seemed too small to hold much, but she'd noticed Curt had looked right past them. Perhaps Hudson had as well when she'd initially searched the car for resources.

"Oh, right," Curt replied. "How did I not see them? I'll take this side of the aisle, if you'll check the ones over there."

She found a KitKat and a half bottle of frozen water in the fourth one she checked. "Bingo! Candy bar!"

"Got another two over here," he replied. "I'm beginning to feel like I'm on a treasure hunt. Hudson obviously didn't check these."

"We weren't as desperate, then." She continued up the aisle and found a bag of peanuts and another candy bar. Curt scored a gigantic but half-eaten chocolate-chip cookie and a frozen can of soda.

"Not much, but more than we had," he said as they gathered up their loot.

A second check of the luggage was far less productive; apparently they'd all been very thorough in the first pass and had missed only two sticks of gum and a few breath mints.

By the time they returned to the luggage compartment, Kris was through with her stint in the tunnel and Elliot had taken over again.

Kris looked ready to collapse. They all did, yet they all kept working.

She couldn't imagine what state they'd all be in right now if the train had been full of cowards, or bullies, or narcissists, like J.T. She'd been damn lucky to get stranded with the people fate had thrown her way.

❖

"We're doing this on one condition." Steffi stared out at the glacier.

They'd already roped up, twenty-five feet apart, and had their avalanche probes out. Hudson was about to set off, so the last-second catch came as a surprise. "Oh?"

"You promise to go half as fast as you want to."

"Are you all right? Really tired?" Hudson was suddenly worried; they were both fatigued and low on energy, that was a given, but walking on the railway had been the easiest part so far, and Steffi had seemed all right during their impromptu duet.

Steffi looked at her and smiled. "No, I'm okay. But you tend to get in a zone when you lead, and you can start to speed along. Definitely not a good approach for this."

"Got it. Just tell me if I start doing it again." She wanted to be sensitive to the fact that Steffi's shorter stature meant she'd taken a lot more steps getting here and it was aerobically more difficult to keep up, though her younger years and fitness level probably mitigated that disadvantage somewhat. She also didn't want to put either of them at more risk than necessary or dampen Steffi's resolve to continue.

So when she advanced onto the glacier, it was with extraordinary caution, an approach she usually reserved for places like minefields and blind dates. Hudson had her avalanche probe in her right hand, ski pole in her left. Before every step, she sank the probe deep into the snow in front of her, looking for instabilities in the under layer.

Usually she hit hard ice after a foot or two of snow, but not always. Sometimes the probe pierced only snow for several feet, which told her she might be at a fragile snow bridge over a crevasse. On these occasions, she'd veer left, or right, probing for a more solid under layer.

Their progress across the glacier was painstakingly slow, and Hudson began to wonder whether they were really gaining that much time over the rail route.

Three-fourths of the way across, the under layer became much more unpredictable than it had been thus far. Instead of hard ice, the probe was hitting crusty snow, which made it much tougher to determine whether she was really on solid ground.

She edged forward, foot by foot.

When she thrust the probe into the next section ahead of her, the thin metal rod far too easily pierced soft snow for several feet, raising the hairs on the back of her neck. She froze in place and tried the probe to her left, then right, with the same result. She half turned toward Steffi, trailing far behind. "Stay there. This whole area is really—"

Suddenly, the snow beneath her feet gave way and she was falling, flailing with her arms to try to grab something to stop herself. Panic overwhelmed her as she plunged into the crevasse.

She fell ten feet or so before the rope pulled her up short and knocked the wind out of her. As she fought for air, Hudson kicked desperately at the icy sidewall of the crevasse, trying to gain purchase with the tips of her crampons. She had just gotten her right foot planted into the ice when the rope went slack.

She dropped again, another couple of feet, falling sideways and wrenching her right knee in the process before her crampon disengaged from the wall. She cried out in pain as the rope caught her again, arresting her fall.

Fuck. Her heart was hammering and her whole body trembled uncontrollably. The pain in her knee was excruciating, and it kept her from immediately doing anything to better her situation.

"Hudson!" she heard Steffi scream. "Are you all right?"

"No," she called back as she awkwardly grappled for the ice axes hanging from her pack. She fixed her left crampon in the ice, and then the ice axes. Three points of contact made her feel a bit more secure. Gritting her teeth, she kicked at the wall with her right foot. The crampon bit into the ice, not very securely, and as it did, another burst of pain shot through her damaged knee.

"Can you get yourself up?" Steffi hollered.

"Don't know." Hudson was doing all she could just to keep from slipping farther into the crevasse. Her body was so full of adrenaline she had trouble keeping a firm grip on the ice axes, her arms trembling badly. "You got me?"

"Yes!" Steffi yelled back. "Can you make it? Should I try to pull you up?"

Hudson took deep breaths, willing herself to calm. *You can do this.* "I'm climbing. Help me if you can!"

"You got it!"

She started up, dislodging her right ice ax first to plant it higher. Her useless right leg prevented her from maintaining the three-solid-points-of-contact rule, so she had to put her weight on the rope and trust that Steffi could hold her.

Hudson inched her way up the ice wall, assisted by steady, firm pulls on the rope, until finally she was able to pull herself up and over the lip of the crevasse. She collapsed onto the snow, gasping for air. "Don't come any closer. It's too dangerous!" she shouted when she saw Steffi start toward her with a panicky look on her face.

Steffi stopped where she was, several feet away. Hudson could see she'd somehow managed to set an ice screw into the glacier and threaded the rope through it. "All right, I won't. Where are you hurt?"

"My knee. Twisted it bad. Don't think I can put any weight on it."

Steffi frowned. "Shit. We can't stay here." She looked over the remaining stretch they had to cross to get back to the rail line. "If I help you, think you can make it at least off this glacier? It's not that much farther."

"Then we'll both be at risk of falling through."

"It's a risk we'll have to take. We'll just have to go very slow. We can talk about what to do next once we get somewhere safer."

"Stay there. I'll come to you." Hudson had started hitting crusty snow several feet before she fell through, so she wasn't confident at all about the integrity of the under layer beneath her. She crawled toward Steffi on her hands and left knee, trailing the other leg behind her. Steffi kept the rope taut in case she fell through again.

Steffi dropped to her knees and they simultaneously reached for each other and embraced in relief, once Hudson reached her. Hudson was still trembling, and Steffi was, too, both so badly shaken by the latest near-catastrophe.

Neither spoke. They just hugged each other for a long while.

"I was so afraid," Steffi said finally. "When I saw you break through...I...I tried to hold you, but—"

"You did, Steffi. You saved my life."

"But the rope slipped, and—"

"And you got it again. You did great." Hudson held her close, trying to ignore the throbbing in her knee.

"I can't stand the thought of anything happening to you," Steffi said quietly. "I've gotten pretty fond of you, you know."

"Oh, yeah? That so?" Hudson's heartbeat kicked up a notch, and not because of their dire situation this time.

"Yeah. I think you're amazing, as a matter of fact."

"Hmmm. That's interesting. 'Cause I think you're pretty amazing, too." She pulled back and looked into Steffi's eyes. "Can't say much for our timing, though."

"What are we going to do now, Hudson?" Steffi asked. "If you can't walk, what are we going to do?"

"One step at a time. First, we get off this glacier. Help me up?"

"Let me stow the gear first." Steffi packed the rope, ice axes, and her ski poles. Hudson had lost her avalanche probe and one ski pole into the crevasse, but she still had one pole to lean on.

Steffi pulled her up and put her left arm around Hudson's waist as Hudson put her right arm over Steffi's shoulder. Steffi held her avalanche probe in her right hand, extended to its full ten-foot length. "Ready to do this?"

"Whenever you are."

Steffi probed the snow in front of them, and when the end of the metal rod hit satisfying, solid ice, they took an awkward step forward. Another probing, another step.

Hudson tried to keep her weight distributed, leaning equally on Steffi and the ski pole whenever she lurched forward on her crippled leg. She'd hoped to discover that the injury to her knee wasn't as bad as it seemed. Maybe she could keep going, with Steffi supporting her.

But not only couldn't she put any weight at all on her right leg without intense pain, using only her left was rapidly creating its own set of issues. Her left knee was still sore and bruised from when she'd bounced off the cliff face the day before, and it couldn't handle the added stress. By the time they reached the edge of the glacier, she was in so much pain from the waist down she couldn't keep from groaning aloud with every step. "Set me down," she told Steffi as soon as they were out of danger.

Steffi helped her sit, legs outstretched, and then sat down beside her, both of them breathing heavily. She dug in her coat for the ibuprofen and gave Hudson three of the pills. "Feeling pretty rotten, huh?"

Hudson took them with a long drink of water. "Understatement. This is as far as I go."

Steffi looked at her, stunned, and with tangible fear in her eyes. "You sure? I mean, we made it this far. If you just keep leaning on me, I—"

"No, Steffi." As much as she didn't want to believe it herself, Hudson knew she wasn't capable of walking any more, with or without help. "Both my knees are whacked. I almost passed out from the pain during those last few yards."

Steffi bit at her lip as she looked around. "My turn to dig a snow cave, then. Over there, maybe?" She pointed to a big drift a little way up the slope they were on.

"You're not getting me." Hudson waited for Steffi to look directly at her. "It's up to you, now, Steffi. You have to go on without me, and you need to get going right now if you're going to stand a chance of finding anything before nightfall. Too many lives depend on you. I'll dig my own cave, once I've rested a while. Don't worry about me."

"Not happening. I'm not leaving you. We're in this together."

Chapter Thirty-two

"We're coming up on the pass now," Lieutenant Douglas told Bob over his headset as the helicopter gained still more altitude. "We should be at the wreck site shortly."

Bob gaped at the scenery outside his window. Despite the solemn purpose of this journey, he couldn't help but wonder at the magnificent vista of the Alps in winter and the mind-boggling amount of snow that had been deposited at this high elevation. Though he spotted signs of recent avalanches on nearly every steep slope they passed, the peaks were still heavily laden.

They reached the first place where snow had covered the track, then another avalanche field farther on, even wider and deeper than the previous one.

"U.S. Pave Hawk Four to Rega Control Center," the pilot said, and almost immediately, a dispatcher answered. Bob could hear the whole conversation in his headset.

"This is Rega Control. Go ahead, Pave Hawk Four."

"We're about midway over the Bernina Pass. So far we've seen two avalanches covering the track." The helicopter hovered over the second big avalanche field. "One is very deep. Maybe forty feet at least, and a half mile long. I concur with the initial assessment that the road and rail up here are both impassable for some time to come."

"Roger that, Pave Hawk Four. Have you spotted the debris from the train?"

"Not yet. We'll keep you apprised. Pave Hawk Four, out."

The sun came out of the clouds as the helicopter continued forward. The three crewmembers and Bob all scoured the landscape below for a sign of the train or survivors. But all he could see was white. Endless white and a cruel, unforgiving environment. What little hope he'd held that they might find someone still alive was fading with every mile.

After another few minutes, near the end of the pass, they came upon another massive snow slide, even bigger than the last one. A mile of the track was buried here, right where it hugged a mountain and paralleled a deep gorge. "This should be the place," the pilot said, and slowed the chopper to hover over the area.

Bob peered out the window, using his hand to shield his eyes from the glare off the snow. The devastation to the track was sobering; it was buried under more than twenty or thirty feet of avalanche debris. If the train had indeed been there when the slide gave way, he doubted anyone had survived.

But he needed confirmation, and he refused to leave without it. "Do you see the wreckage?" he asked the pilot.

"Nothing yet," Douglas replied. He urged the helicopter forward until it was directly over the gorge. "Supposed to be down there somewhere, but I'm not seeing anything. Anybody?"

The other two crewmembers were just as mystified.

"Maybe it's farther on," Bob said. "Could it be another section of track? This gorge goes on for miles."

"Don't think so," the pilot said. "We're at the end of the pass. This is right where the director indicated, and it looks just like he described, except for the wreckage."

"Still, can we go a little farther?" Bob asked. "Just follow the track for another few miles? Maybe they were mistaken."

"Whatever you like, sir," Douglas replied. "Certainly worth a look." He took them higher, to skirt around the mountain to their right, and soon they were on their way again.

❖

"This isn't getting us anywhere." Steffi fought to keep her temper. She crossed her arms over her chest and glared down at Hudson. "I tell you, there's no use arguing about it any more. I'm not going, and that's final."

"You *are*. You can't put me ahead of everyone else. One life versus twenty. It's a no-brainer."

"You can say that all you like, but we're not breaking up this team. This was your idea, not mine. Besides, I can't do it without you." The last part wasn't entirely true; Steffi probably did have the stamina to go the distance to civilization now that the hardest part of their journey was over, but she couldn't fathom leaving Hudson behind.

"Of course you can. Look at all you've accomplished. You've been the real leader of this little expedition the whole time. It's just a matter of distance from now on, anyway. Shouldn't be any more climbing. Following the track should lead you to something, probably by nightfall."

"Can we rig a sled or something, maybe, so I could pull you?"

"Jesus, you're pig-headed." Hudson blew out a loud, exasperated breath.

"So I've been told. A trait we have in common, it seems. So, a sled?"

"With what? Rope and a survival blanket?" Hudson shook her head. "We've got nothing to build one with. And I doubt you could pull me very far with that arm of yours, anyway. You've got to face facts and get going."

Steffi didn't answer right away. *Face facts, huh? Okay, let's see how you like these facts.* She didn't want to have this conversation, at least not right here and right now, because she didn't really have a handle on it all herself, yet. The emotions were too raw, too new. But the moment that Hudson had disappeared into the crevasse, it was as though someone had put her heart in a vise, like there was no air left in the world. In that horrific split second, she'd realized the depth of her feelings for this brave, incredible woman.

It was time to admit to her still-raw epiphany, regardless of how Hudson might view her declaration. For it was really the only way Steffi could explain why she couldn't go on alone.

She sat next to Hudson. "Face facts, you said. Okay." Though she could feel heat rise to her cheeks, she forced herself to look directly into Hudson's eyes. "The fact is, I…I just can't leave you. You've become too important to me. I know it's incredibly selfish, and it probably sounds absolutely crazy…considering all this, and how long we've known each other…but I'm pretty certain I'm falling in love with you."

Hudson's dark eyes gave nothing away of what she felt about Steffi's admission, and she didn't respond for a full, torturous minute or two. When she finally did, it was with an uncharacteristically quiet, subdued voice. "I'm pretty certain the feeling is mutual, which is precisely why you have to go."

Steffi had a moment of blissful elation—Hudson loved her, too?—before the rest of it registered. "I…I don't understand you."

"Look, whatever this is…or might become, providing we *do* get out of here…" Hudson cleared her throat. "It doesn't have a chance if we haven't tried all we can to do the right thing. Whatever the cost. You know that. So you have to try. Go." Tears sprang to her eyes. "I'll be waiting right here when you get back."

Steffi knew they had no other choice, had really known it all along, she supposed. She couldn't possibly forget about Kris, Fin, Curt, and the others. But she hadn't been able to leave without telling Hudson how she felt. "You'd better be. I'll never forgive you if you're not." She opened her pack and pulled out the rest of their food: a PowerBar and half a bar of chocolate. She gave it all to Hudson, along with the rest of the ibuprofen.

Hudson started to object but must have seen her look of determination and decided to let her have that, at least.

"And you keep this." She handed Hudson the red plastic tablecloth Curt had given them. "Put it outside your cave so we can spot you."

"All right. Probably won't even have time to get it built before you get back, though."

"Keep thinking that." She was packed and ready, with no further excuse to delay. Well, maybe one. She knelt beside Hudson, cradled her face in her hands, and kissed her like it wasn't good-bye, kissed her like a promise. With passion, and heat, and more to come.

Hudson's arms enfolded her and drew her closer, and she returned the kiss with the same intensity of feeling.

Finally, they parted. Steffi got up and started away before her teary eyes spilled over. "See you soon," she called to Hudson over her shoulder. She couldn't look back.

As soon as she reached the railway, she took off her crampons. The snow wasn't that deep, and the footing was good. She started off south along the tracks, moving as fast as possible, even breaking into a jog now and then in areas where the wind had blown the track clear.

Steffi wasn't tired any more. In fact, she felt invigorated. She *was* going to make it. She needed more of those kisses.

❖

Hudson didn't start the cave until Steffi was just a speck in the distance. She was really moving fast, especially once she reached the railway. That made her even more optimistic that Steffi would make it, which meant Joe and the others would make it, too.

Her own future was more uncertain, especially if Steffi didn't reach help by nightfall.

The snowdrift Steffi had pointed to as a site for the cave did look promising, and it wasn't too far. She crawled there in a matter of minutes and started to dig. She didn't intend to reproduce what they'd had the night before, because she wasn't in any shape for it. She couldn't stand or comfortably kneel, so she did most of her work sitting up or lying down.

No tunnel this time, she decided, just a small entrance she could block off with her pack. And a cave just big enough for her to lie in, with her gear and the candle.

It took her forty minutes, and by the time she was done, she was soaked with sweat. *Really not good.* Before she went inside, she spread the red plastic over the top of the cave, pinning the edges down with snow.

Dinner was half a PowerBar, with more ibuprofen for dessert. She drank all her water, but it didn't quench her thirst, so she started making more with the candle, drinking it as it accumulated.

Nothing now to do but wait. Wait for rescue or death. Which would it be?

She'd accomplished everything she'd set out to do in the way of her career, and then some. Hudson was proud of that. She'd made a difference in people's lives.

But she regretted that she'd given up a personal life in the process. Her past relationship was ancient history, and so were the scars. Why had she let them keep her from moving forward and finding love?

Maybe because it wasn't time to meet her, yet. You had to wait a few years for Steffi.

One thing was for certain. Steffi had given her a taste—quite literally—of how much she was missing. *My God, that woman can kiss. Crazy-good kisses.*

A distant roaring, indistinct, disturbed her reverie. She immediately tensed. *Avalanche!* The slope she was on had looked benign, under no threat from above, but her heartbeat accelerated anyway as the noise increased. *Wait. That's not...*

A helicopter. Definitely. She knew the sound very well, from her time in Afghanistan and elsewhere. And it was getting closer.

She scrambled half out of the cave, barely registering the pain in her knees, before she remembered the signal mirror Curt had given her. She went back for it.

The big military helicopter was just rounding the mountain, headed in her direction, as she crawled outside with her pack.

And the sun was out, thank God. Hudson tried to signal the chopper with the mirror.

"Down here! Please, see me!" She shouted at the top of her lungs, though no way in hell would they ever hear her.

The chopper seemed to veer off. It hadn't seen her; it was following the railway. Desperately, she kept signaling with the mirror. "For God's sake! Look down here!"

It was almost past her, traveling over the gorge, when it stopped its forward momentum suddenly, then changed direction.

They'd seen her! *Thank you, God.* She wept tears of joy and relief as it neared. *They'd made it. They were all going to make it.*

The helicopter hovered directly overhead, its rotors blowing a maelstrom of powder around her cave. She spotted a uniformed airman exiting the open side cargo door and descending on a cable. As he got closer, she was stunned to see the American Air Force insignia on his flight suit.

"Ma'am? You all right? What are your injuries?" the young man said as soon as he'd unclipped from the cable and sent it back for the litter.

"Can't really walk," she replied. "Banged up both my knees, especially the right one."

"Is anyone with you? Are you alone?"

"There are twenty-one other survivors, all from the Bernina Express. One woman is walking south right now along the railway, trying to find help. The others are in two cars, buried under an avalanche on the other side of this mountain."

"Twenty-one more alive? Buried?" he asked incredulously as the stretcher-basket reached them.

"Yes. Many with traumatic injuries. Broken legs and arms, head injuries."

He helped her into the basket and strapped her in, along with her gear. As she started up toward the helicopter, she heard him relaying what he'd learned to the pilot over his radio.

Hudson couldn't stop smiling. She could hardly believe it. *We made it!* She wouldn't relax completely, of course, until Steffi and Joe and everyone else were safe. But it was only a matter of time, now.

The litter had started a slow spin on the way to the helicopter, so the airman at the cargo door of the chopper had a brief struggle getting her straightened out and inside. She was so focused on him, she never saw the familiar face in the chopper until he unbuckled from his seat and came back to crouch over her.

She had to blink twice to make sure she was seeing right. Could this be any more surreal?

Not only was it her boss, Bob Furness, but he was openly weeping, worse even than Bruce did every Christmas during *It's a Wonderful Life.*

"Holy Christ, Hudson. You shortened my life at least a decade."

"Pretty damn good to see you, too, Bob." She started crying, too, from relief, from happiness, and just so touched that he'd come all this way to find her.

He leaned down and kissed her forehead, then looked into her eyes. "Joe?" he asked.

"He's alive, Bob. Needs a hospital badly, though. Both his legs are broken."

"We'll get to him, soon. He'll get the best care possible, I promise. What about you?"

"Banged up. My knees are the worst."

"Anything I can I do for you right now?"

"Got any water?"

"You bet." He grabbed a bottle from a cooler in the back and gave it to her.

The second airman had returned to the helicopter, so they closed the cargo doors and prepared to set off again. Bob buckled in next to Hudson's litter.

"You said a woman is following the railway south?" the pilot called back.

"Yes. She should be easy to spot, and not too far. She left here a couple of hours ago." She told them what Steffi had been wearing, and while they headed south over the track to find her, Hudson filled in the crew about the other people on the train and their injuries.

"I asked Rega to send another helicopter, but they didn't have one big enough," the pilot informed them. "So we've got another Hawk coming from Ramstein. We can get only about half your people aboard, and it'll be dark soon. I didn't want the rest to have to wait until tomorrow."

"Help me out of this so we free up some floor space," Hudson told Bob. "I can't really walk, but I can sit okay."

"You sure?"

"Yeah, help me undo these straps, would you?"

He got her out of the litter and helped her slide into the window seat beside him.

"Hungry?" Furness reached into his flight suit, and only then did she realize how big it was on him, and that he was wearing his usual starched white shirt and tie beneath. He pulled out a half a bagel and cream cheese. "Didn't finish my breakfast."

She grabbed it out of his hand and devoured it, to much laughter. "What the hell are you doing here, anyway?"

"They said you were dead. I couldn't believe it." He shrugged.

"So you brought the cavalry? How'd you manage this?"

"Called in a favor."

"Oh, that's right. You have friends in high places. Thank them for me, will you?"

"You bet I will."

"Oh, and by the way." She reached into her pocket and pulled out Joe's memory card. "Joe got pictures of the avalanche as it hit the train."

His eyes lit up. "No shit?"

He started to reach for it, but she held it up away from him. "I promised Joe I'd keep it safe for him. You'll get it soon enough."

Furness smiled. "I understand."

"There she is!" one of the crewman shouted, and Hudson looked out the window. She didn't have the vantage point to see Steffi yet, but when the helicopter slowed and turned slightly, she spotted her on the tracks below, jumping up and down and waving her arms.

CHAPTER THIRTY-THREE

Steffi stared up at the helicopter, at the blessed sight of the crewman descending toward her on a cable. It was over. They'd been found. Not only would those on the train finally get the help they needed, but Hudson would be okay, too. Her worst fears in the hours since they'd separated had centered on whether she'd reach civilization in time to save Hudson, more dangerously exposed to the elements than the rest of them.

As the crewman unclipped from the wire, she noticed to her puzzlement that he was wearing a U.S. military flight suit.

"Hi there," he said. "Are you all right? Are you injured anywhere?"

"Nothing that can't wait. Boy, am I happy to see you," she replied. "There's a whole bunch of injured people trapped in a train, buried by snow, on the other side of this mountain."

"We know." He reached up for the litter that was coming toward them on the cable. "Get in. We're headed there to get them, as soon as we get you aboard."

Steffi lay in the wire basket and he strapped her in. "You know?" How was that possible?

"Yes, and we're trying to get a second helicopter up here, so we can get everyone out today." He gave a thumbs-up to his crewmates and she started upward, closing her eyes against the blowing snow churned up by the chopper's powerful rotors.

She spotted Hudson's beautiful, smiling face as the winch man in the helicopter pulled the litter aboard.

He couldn't get the straps off her fast enough.

She flew into Hudson's arms, and Hudson squeezed her so tight she almost couldn't breathe.

"I was so worried—"

"Thank God, I thought that—" Hudson said at the same time.

They both laughed, giggling like girls at a pajama party, Steffi's own relief and joy mirrored in Hudson's warm, dark eyes.

"Something tells me you two might like to sit together," the man beside Hudson said, as he unbuckled from his seat and stood, smiling.

"Steffi, I'd like you to meet my boss, Bob Furness. Bob, this is Steffi Graham, the woman who saved my life more than once the last couple of days."

"Then I'm very, very pleased to meet you, Steffi," Furness said, offering his hand. "And I'm forever in your debt."

"Your boss?" Steffi looked at Hudson. "Your boss came all the way here to find you?"

"Unbelievable, huh? And he even managed to get us this wicked cool ride."

Steffi ignored Furness's outstretched hand and pulled him into a hug, instead. "I don't know how I can ever thank you."

"I'd say we're even," he replied. "Hudson is very precious to me."

"To me, too," she replied.

"Everyone get seated, please," the pilot told them all as the ground crewman returned on the cable and they readied to head for the train.

Steffi buckled in next to Hudson, and Bob took a seat nearby.

As the helicopter turned around, Hudson took her hand, and it felt like the most natural thing in the world. Just...*right.*

❖

Anna tried all of the hand warmers, but every one had gone stone cold. "That's it, then," she told the others. "We're out of water, too." They'd distributed the last of their foodstuffs an hour before.

"I can still build a fire and melt more snow, if we can ever get out of here," Curt replied.

"Without food and water, I'm not sure how much longer we can dig," Kris said. "I can tell I'm getting so much weaker by the day. That last hour took everything out of me."

"You're not alone." Elliot looked over at the tunnel. "Within five minutes, I'm exhausted."

"Anybody have any ideas?" Anna asked. No one spoke. "Should we fill the others in?"

"I don't want Fin to know," Kris said. "Maybe that's selfish, but I'm already struggling to keep her positive. And there's still a chance Hudson and Steffi will make it."

"So, we hold off, for now." Anna got to her feet. "I guess it's my turn. Who's going to move the snow for me?"

"I will," Kris said.

She picked up the ax and shovel and crawled into the snow chute. They'd been in and out of the tunnel so many times that the bottom and sides were slick and slippery, and she used a lot of energy just getting up the slight incline to the blocked exit.

Anna situated herself so she had room to wield the ax, but just as she swung back to take her first big chunk out of the blockage, a muted noise, close by, made her freeze mid-swing.

She held her breath, listening intently, and heard it again. The sound was certainly man-made because it had a rhythm to it.

Someone was outside, digging.

Her heart went into her throat. "We're here!" she shouted. "We're in here! We're alive!"

"What's happening? What is it?" Kris yelled up the tunnel.

Anna turned to look. Kris, Curt, and Elliot were all clustered at the entrance, looking up at her with expectant expressions. "Someone's outside! They've found us!"

"Come on out," Curt said. "Let me dig!"

Anna slid down the chute like a slide, and they quickly got out of her way. Curt grabbed the ice ax out of her hand and scrambled up the tunnel. In no time, they heard the solid, rapid blows of his desperate effort to bridge the remaining barrier to their rescuers.

"Keep digging, we're alive in here!" they heard him shout between blows. "You're almost to us!"

Anna hugged Kris in her excitement. Elliot joined in, and they jumped up and down excitedly in a huddle of relief and camaraderie. They'd made it, because they'd all pulled together.

Fifteen excruciatingly long minutes later, a shout of triumph from Curt told them their long wait was over. They were going home.

Curt slid back down the tunnel, and, a moment later, a young, clean-cut man in a U.S. Air Force flight suit followed. He looked shocked to see them and their surroundings—the luggage compartment was barely discernable for what it was, because it was so packed with snow from their digging.

"I know you're all anxious to get out of here," he said. "And we have two women up there in the chopper who can't wait to see you."

"They made it!" Kris shouted, and hugged Anna again.

"We can take probably half of you," the airman told them. "Starting with the most seriously injured. We've radioed for another helicopter for the rest. It should be here shortly. I'll need some help getting people up through this tunnel, though. The litter wouldn't fit."

Elliot volunteered. "I'll help."

"We all can," Anna said. "Just tell us what we need to do."

"The injured are right this way," Curt told the airman. "I can point out who needs to go first."

"Great. Lead on."

The sight of a stranger coming up the aisle elicited a chorus of cheers and cries of joy from the cluster of battered survivors in the passenger car. One of the Japanese women got to her feet and hugged the startled airman, and so did the two Swiss girls.

Even with all the healthy ones pitching in to help transport the injured, it took almost an hour to fill the chopper with the most seriously in need of help: Joe, Nick, J.T., Bud, Fin, and both Japanese couples.

Anna and Kris went outside to watch it leave. Before he'd gone, the airman had told them the second U.S. helicopter should be arriving in an hour or so.

"I suppose things will be crazy from here on," Anna said. "We'll get split up, and who knows if I'll see you and your friends again. I sure don't want to lose touch after this, not after all we've been through together."

"No way will that happen," Kris said. "Come on, let's get ready to go. We can trade phone numbers on the chopper."

"We should bring all the wallets, purses, phones, cameras, and passports we can find," Anna said. "I'm not sure any of the injured had theirs on them, and they'll be glad if we don't leave them behind."

"Great idea," Kris replied. They gathered up everyone's important personal items and were outside a few minutes before their ride arrived.

Getting all of them aboard should have gone quicker than loading the first chopper, because most of the remaining survivors were ambulatory. But Curt refused to leave without his wife's body, and Cinzia began crying uncontrollably when she realized they were leaving her dead parents behind. The pilot initially balked at the request because of the delay, until Kris and Anna, who were already in the chopper, told him about all Curt had done to keep them alive.

And so he gave his okay, and the three silvery shrouds were brought aboard in the litter.

The rest of them packed in almost on top of each other, and they pulled away from the site just as the sun was beginning to disappear behind the mountains.

All the survivors were taken first to Zurich airport, where a fleet of ambulances waited to transport them to University Hospital. Anna rode with Hugo and Fritz, and when they pulled up outside the Emergency doors, she was startled to see a number of reporters and photographers clustered around the entrance. Shutters started going off like crazy as soon as the rear doors were opened, and microphones were shoved into their faces as they got out and were escorted inside by the paramedics.

"Were you on the Bernina Express?" one of the reporters yelled, as others jostled for position with similar questions, some in English and some in German.

"How many of you survived?"

"What was it like?"

"We heard the train was buried by an avalanche, can you confirm that?"

"How did you get rescued?"

Fritz and Hugo barreled past the reporters without saying anything, but Anna paused. "Yes. We were buried by an avalanche.

Twenty-two people survived, thanks to the heroic efforts of two women: Hudson Mead and Steffi Graham."

She didn't wait for the follow-up questions. She went inside but brushed off the doctor who wanted to immediately escort her to an examination room. "In a minute. First, I need you to direct me to the nearest pay phone." Her cell was dead.

"Reverse the charges, please," she told the operator once she'd given her the number. "Tell them it's Anna calling." As she waited impatiently for the connection to go through, she imagined the state her family must be in after not hearing anything from her for days.

The phone rang only once before her husband picked up. "Hello?" He sounded weary, and tentative, not at all like himself.

The operator cut in and gave her name, and he immediately consented to accept the call.

"Honey? I'm all right. I know you had to have been worried—"

"Anna? It's really you? Boys! Come quick!" He started bawling like a baby, and pretty soon, she was crying, too.

❖

Steffi was irritated that they'd separated her from Hudson when they reached the airport, transporting them in separate ambulances. Hudson hadn't seemed thrilled about it, either, but had told her to come find her in the hospital once she'd had her arm seen to.

So as soon as the doctor had cleaned and stitched up her cuts, Steffi went to the ER nurse's station. "Do you know where Hudson Mead is being treated?"

Before the woman could answer, a well-dressed man waiting farther down the counter approached and spoke to her. "Were you on the train, miss?"

"Yes. Are you a reporter?" They'd all been barraged with questions as they got out of the ambulances, and she wasn't anxious to be further delayed from seeing Hudson.

"No, I'm from the railway. I'm here to extend our sincere regret for all you've suffered and to tell you we've arranged for hotel rooms for all of you and will cover the costs of your treatment and return home. We're also happy to assist in any other way we can, if you need money, clothes, help with passports, and so on." He offered her his card. "We have representatives waiting at the hotel to make arrangements for whatever you need. When you're ready to go, just look for the Park Hyatt van outside the main entrance."

"I'll do that. Thanks." She took the card. This was a welcome development. At least they'd all be put up in the same hotel, so she'd be able to spend time with Hudson later. Provided she got released tonight, that is, and didn't want to hang around to be with Joe.

Steffi turned back toward the nurse. "Hudson Mead? Can you tell me where she's being treated?"

The woman consulted her computer. "The doctor's in with her now. Are you a family member?"

"Yes," Steffi lied. "She's my sister."

"Room 212. Fourth one on your left," the nurse said, pointing down the hallway.

"Thank you." As she neared the room, she spotted the doctor heading out. He'd left the door cracked, so she went right in.

"Miss me?"

Hudson looked up and grinned at her. "Of course. What a silly question." She was in a faded white patient gown, bedcovers pulled up. Steffi had caught her in the midst of devouring a tray full of hospital food. "Want some?"

"Hey, they didn't offer to feed me," she replied as she pulled a chair up to the side of the bed.

"They didn't offer to feed me, either. Gotta speak up." Hudson handed her a small plastic spoon. "Pudding or mixed fruit?"

"Pudding." She held out her hand.

"It'll cost you." Hudson held it up out of her reach.

"Oh? Name your price."

"One kiss."

She laughed. "Here?"

"Here, there, and everywhere."

"You're feeling no pain, are you?"

"Nope. The Swiss have very good drugs. Almost as good as their chocolate. Come on." She put a finger to her lips. "Right here. You know you want to."

"I sure won't argue that." Steffi got up and sat on the edge of the bed. Hudson met her halfway, and this kiss was every bit as memorable as the first, though a gentler, sweeter version. They took their time exploring each other's mouths with their tongues, until the doctor returned and broke up their moment of bliss with a nervous cough.

"Sorry, ladies." He came over to Hudson's bedside as Steffi returned to the chair. "I've just checked on your friend. He's still in surgery, but everything looks good. They should be through in an hour or so."

"Thanks, Doc."

"Not at all. I'll be back in a while to check on you." He left and shut the door behind him.

"Joe?" Steffi asked.

Hudson nodded. "Bob's waiting for him in recovery."

"What about you? What did the doctor say about your knees?" Steffi asked.

"The left's just badly bruised, but I tore the ACL in my right one. It'll probably need surgery."

Steffi frowned. "When? I was kind of hoping you might get released tonight. The railway's arranged for hotel rooms for everyone."

"Yeah, their guy came to see me, too." Hudson took Steffi's hand. "I'm not getting the surgery here, but I'm also not going to get released. Bob's trying to arrange for us to get flown to New York tomorrow on a private medical charter, if Joe's stable enough to travel."

Steffi's heart sank. "Tomorrow?"

"Yeah. And I want you to come with us. Spend the rest of your vacation with me, and fly home from there. It'll give us some time to figure things out."

"Figure things out?"

"By things, I mean how we're going to make this living-on-opposite-coasts situation work. That's presuming, of course, that you meant what you said. About falling in love with me, I mean."

"Well, I wasn't due to end my no-dating sabbatical for another couple of months," Steffi replied with a grin. "But I guess I can make an exception for you. Count me in."

CHAPTER THIRTY-FOUR

New York City, New York
One month later

"So, tonight's the night, huh?" Bruce asked.

"Yup. *Finally*. I appreciate you doing this, you know." Hudson leaned on her crutch so she could use both hands to unwrap the new sheets.

"Hey, I'm looking forward to playing host. Joe's a great guy. And I can't wait to see his reaction to these." Bruce chuckled at the linens she'd bought for his guest room: Tinker Bell sheets and a SpongeBob SquarePants comforter.

"I hope they give him nightmares. He talked Steffi into putting a fake snake under my pillow last night. As many times as he's done it, you'd think I'd learn."

"Where did he get it?"

"Oh, he sent her out with a shopping list yesterday—magazines and snacks, supposedly. But that was probably the real reason." Joe had been staying with Hudson since his release from the hospital two weeks earlier. He had lots of physical therapy ahead before he could walk again, but he was doing well, though complaining about how much his skin itched under the twin casts that extended from his toes to his pelvis.

Steffi had been sleeping on the daybed in her study since they got back from Europe. When her vacation ran out, she'd asked for another month leave of absence from her job, both to extend her time with Hudson and to help with the cooking and other chores while

Hudson and Joe recovered. Though Kris had also asked for extended time off to be with Fin, their boss at the library had readily agreed after all they'd been through; she'd use their numerous volunteers to fill the gap.

Hudson and Steffi had used their month together to get to know each other better, and they found they had a great deal in common. Their bond grew with every passing day, as did their devotion to each other. But though they'd engaged in numerous long make-out sessions on the couch, they'd agreed to avoid having sex. Hudson wanted time to recover, and Steffi wanted to be certain she wasn't making the same mistakes of the past—jumping into a relationship with blinders on, mostly because of a powerful physical attraction, only to find out they weren't really suited to be together long term.

It had become more difficult as time went on for both of them to honor their decision to have one month of abstinence. They'd nearly slipped up on more than one occasion, but lots of cold showers and having a third person in the apartment helped them stick to their promise not to consummate their passion until the one-month anniversary of their rescue.

Steffi had made it unbearably difficult the night before, however, to wait even one more day.

"Time has never passed more slowly, I swear to God." Steffi cuddled closer and nuzzled Hudson's neck. They were on the couch, ostensibly watching a movie on TV, but Hudson was unaware of anything but how incredible Steffi smelled, how enticing her lips were, and how much she wanted to peel off her clothes and take her right then and there.

"You can't keep doing that," Hudson replied. "You know our chaperone has gone to bed, and my willpower is pretty nonexistent at the moment."

But Steffi only increased her kisses along Hudson's jawline.

"I can see it was a big mistake to let you know I'm particularly sensitive there," Hudson added, but made no effort to pull away.

"Tell me again why we have to wait? You're in fine, and I do mean fine, shape," Steffi said as she ran a hand very lightly over Hudson's left breast. "Nearly all better."

"Cruel. You're a cruel woman," she replied, which made Steffi laugh. "It's not just about me. You said—and I'm quoting here—that you wanted one whole month to make absolutely certain that I'm the woman you want to spend the rest of your life with."

Steffi stopped her nuzzles and pulled back to look at her seriously. "Honey, I don't need more time for that. I think I knew when we were still on the mountain. This last month has only solidified those feelings. I've never been more certain of anything than that I love you with all my heart. Now and forever. I think we're perfect for each other."

"You know I feel the same. I'm so head-over-heels for you that it hurts—physically hurts—not to be able to make love to you. I have no doubts whatsoever about us."

"So? Why not tonight? Why do we have to wait two more days?"

The longing and love in Steffi's eyes nearly undid her. She hated having to refuse her anything. But Hudson was determined to make their first time as special as possible. "Trust me. It'll be worth the wait."

Steffi frowned. "Not fair. Using the word trust, I mean. I do trust you, Hudson. More than anyone. More than I ever thought possible."

Technically, their one month wasn't up until tomorrow. But tomorrow was also the day they'd agreed to appear on a TV morning show with other survivors from the train, so it was likely to be a long, tiring day, and Hudson was still recovering. Since she wanted to be in the best possible shape for Steffi, she planned to move up their first time to tonight.

Bruce had agreed to take care of Joe to give them some privacy, and Hudson had arranged for a special dinner for the two of them.

Now, they just had to spring the surprise on Steffi and Joe, who were back in her apartment watching TV.

They took the elevator and found the pair in the midst of a heated discussion.

"Of course he died," Joe was insisting. "The guy in the Members Only jacket shot him. It was a reference back to the episode called Members Only, the only other time Tony got shot in the whole series."

"No way," Steffi replied. "That's what they *wanted* the audience to believe initially, when they showed him looking suspicious and watching Tony, but then they reassured us he'd be okay when they had the guy walk past him toward the bathroom. Sort of a nod to how they've caused the whole audience to be as paranoid as Tony himself."

"What the heck are you two talking about?" Bruce asked.

Steffi, Joe, and Hudson all looked at him incredulously.

"The finale for *The Sopranos*? Greatest series ever on television?" Joe replied.

Bruce shrugged. "Never watched it. I'm a *Project Runway* fan, myself." He looked at Hudson and winked. "But I'll let you watch whatever you want tonight, Joe."

Joe looked up at him in confusion from his wheelchair. "Tonight?"

"You're bunking with me to give these two ladies some alone time."

Now Steffi was the puzzled one. "Oh?"

"Remember last night when I said 'trust me? It'll be worth the wait?' Well, the waiting's over," Hudson said.

Steffi's face lit up. "I'm all for that!"

"Come on, Joe," Bruce said as he got behind the wheelchair. "Let's get you packed."

❖

Hudson buzzed in the two men from the Four Seasons while Steffi was in the shower. She'd gone way overboard, she knew, to make their first time special, but it had been so long since she'd done anything even vaguely romantic she was enjoying every part of this, and Steffi deserved only the best.

The two delivery guys had brought a portable, stainless-steel food-warming cabinet for their multi-course dinner, and the restaurant's best china and silver. While they set up and poured the wine, Hudson lit candles and put on some music. She'd had flowers delivered as well, and they were scattered about the apartment in vases large and small, their fragrance a reminder that spring would soon chase away the last of their long, memorable winter.

She tipped the men and showed them out, then peeked at the food before she went to get Steffi. They were having Maine lobster dumplings and a butter-lettuce salad with blue cheese and cashews to start, followed by filet mignon, grilled snapper, and an assortment of dessert choices.

Everything looked and smelled incredible, but Hudson's ordinarily ravenous appetite was playing second fiddle to her libido. If it were up to her, they'd have dinner *afterward*; she could hardly contain herself any more from touching Steffi everywhere. But she wanted Steffi to have an absolutely perfect night, one to remember for the rest of their lives.

She went to the door of the study and knocked. "Steffi? You about ready? Dinner's here."

"Yes, Hudson, I'm ready," came the sultry reply from within. "Come on in."

She opened the door, and her breath caught in her throat when she saw what Steffi was wearing or, rather, *almost* wearing.

She'd changed from her usual jeans and sweatshirt into a short, cream-colored negligee with spaghetti straps. The sheer fabric left nothing to the imagination. Hudson could see her full breasts and erect nipples, the soft curve of her waist, the tantalizing temptation at the juncture of her thighs.

"You like?" Steffi asked. "I bought it yesterday, just for you."

Hudson only nodded, still too stunned to speak.

"You going to just stand there?" Steffi smiled.

Breathe. Air in, air out. "God, you're so beautiful." Still, she didn't move. She'd often imagined what Steffi looked like naked. In fact, she hadn't been able to think of much else the last couple of weeks, but none of the pictures in her head came close to the real thing. Steffi's climbing exploits had sculpted her body into something worthy of adoration. "But if I come over there, there's no way we're going to be eating the fabulous meal I ordered any time soon."

"Fine with me," Steffi said. "There's only one thing I'm hungry for right now."

That was all the permission Hudson needed. She closed the distance between them and pulled Steffi close for a long, passionate kiss, conveying with her mouth how much she wanted and needed this amazing woman. "My bedroom?" she asked when their lips finally parted.

"Yes, please. I need to feel you. You have far too many clothes on." Steffi led her there, one arm around her waist, Hudson slowed by the one crutch she still needed to keep the weight off her knee.

"Oh, my," Steffi remarked with delight when she opened the door and spotted the candles, the sheets turned neatly back, and the red rose petals strewn on the bedspread. She looked up at Hudson. "All this for me?"

"For us," Hudson replied. "Is it okay?"

"Perfect. But all I really want and need is you." Steffi led her to the bed and had Hudson sit on the edge. "Do you have any idea how much I want this?"

"Show me."

"Oh, I intend to." Steffi took the crutch and propped it against the dresser, then returned to kneel in front of Hudson just as she was starting to unbutton her shirt. "Oh, no, you don't. That's my job."

Hudson gladly let her take over.

Steffi stripped off her clothes so slowly and so provocatively that Hudson's whole body was aching with need long before she was fully naked. She started with Hudson's shirt, kissing the skin beneath as she exposed it, one button at a time, working her way down between Hudson's breasts to the flat expanse of her stomach. As she pulled off the garment, Steffi lavished more teasing kisses and licks on Hudson's throat, behind her ear, along her jaw, everywhere but her mouth, fueling Hudson's passion ever higher.

"Let me kiss you." Hudson was struggling to keep from pinning Steffi to the bed and just taking her. She wasn't used to giving up control, but she also had to admit she'd never been more turned on than right now.

"Not yet. Soon." Steffi next unhooked Hudson's bra, but the kisses she followed with this time to the skin beneath were frustratingly light, a mere brush of Steffi's wonderful lips over her breasts, driving her mad with desire.

"I don't know how much longer I can endure this," she said. An involuntary moan escaped her lips when Steffi responded with a quick brush of her tongue over one of Hudson's sensitive nipples. "Oh, that's just mean."

Steffi laughed and playfully pushed her to lie flat on the bed so she could slip her black sweatpants off. Hudson had been living in sweats and pajamas since the surgery on her ACL; none of her regular pants or jeans would fit over the bandaging on her knee.

Steffi raised her eyebrows when she saw that Hudson was wearing a thong beneath. "Oooo. Very sexy. You have such an amazing body." She climbed up on the bed and straddled Hudson without taking the thong off. Her eyes were full of longing and want.

Hudson could stand no more of her teasing prelude. She pulled Steffi down on top of her so that the lengths of their bodies were pressed together and kissed her soundly, thoroughly, with all the pent-up passion that had been building during their weeks together. They clung to each other, tongues dueling for dominance, locked in such a tight embrace she could scarcely breathe.

She'd somehow imagined their first time making love would be slow and tender. Hudson had intended to draw it out as long as possible, make the most of her first time being able to kiss and explore every inch of Steffi's incredible physique.

But they'd been tempted and denied for too long, and so their first time was frenzied and heated: the coupling of two people who couldn't get close enough to each other to be satisfied. Steffi's new negligee and Hudson's thong became rags on the floor, ripped off in their delirium of passion.

And then they put their mouths on each other: Steffi on top, a sexy sixty-nine of pleasure that took them to the height of ecstasy together and left them spent and gasping for air, cuddling close together beneath the sheets.

"Wow," Hudson said once her heart slowed.

"I second that." Steffi hugged her close. She was curled up on Hudson's left side, her face on Hudson's shoulder. "Definitely worth waiting for."

"Quite a mouth you have there."

Steffi laughed. "I was about to say the same." She nuzzled Hudson's neck. "I could kiss you forever."

"I accept. Just give me a minute to catch my breath. I'm not quite a hundred percent yet."

Steffi's big smile faded slightly. "Hudson? What *are* we going to do? I have to go back in another week."

"Well, I've given that a lot of thought, as a matter of fact."

"You have?" Steffi half sat up so she could look her in the eyes. She looked so beautiful, yet so vulnerable, her eyes beseeching Hudson to tell her she'd somehow found a way for them to be together.

"Yeah, I called Bob this morning. You know that Joe won't be able to go back to work for at least six months, right?"

"He told me. So?"

"Well, even though the doctor said *I* should be good to go in another month—for limited duty, anyway—I asked Bob for a six-month leave. I don't want to work with anyone but Joe, and that'll enable me to make sure he does his physical therapy. Bob agreed."

"That's great," Steffi replied, without much enthusiasm. "But how does that help us?"

Hudson pulled a brochure out of her nightstand and handed it to Steffi.

She'd done a lot of online research before settling on the right place; the information had arrived the week before.

"Core Physical Therapy," Steffi read aloud. Then she noticed where it was. "Seattle?"

"Yup. We'll get an apartment in Sultan, and I'll drive him to his appointments."

Steffi looked shocked but excited. "You're coming to Sultan?"

"That's the plan, if it's okay with you. I've already talked to Joe. Now, it'll be up to you where I stay. I can bunk with him or get him a nurse until he's—"

"I'll take the *or*, please!" Steffi hugged her tight. "I've got plenty of room! I can't believe you're coming to stay with me!"

"I can't let you go. You're far too precious." Hudson kissed her on the top of her head. "That gives us another six months to work on a long-term solution. But I'm not worried. The nice thing about being an international reporter is that you can be based just about anywhere. Especially if your boss likes you."

EPILOGUE

Next morning

The limousine from *The CBS Morning News* came to collect them at six a.m. sharp. The driver helped Joe from his wheelchair into the back, after Hudson and Steffi got in. Since their return from Switzerland, they'd been bombarded with requests for interviews from around the world, but they'd turned them all down.

Hudson and Steffi were particularly pursued after Anna's quote, crediting them with the rescue, appeared in numerous publications. But they'd wanted their privacy during their developing romance and had felt that the story had already been told sufficiently: Hudson had written it up for the Associated Press, accompanied by Joe's pictures.

However, a week ago, they'd gotten a request that none of them could pass up. *The CBS Morning News* was flying in as many of the survivors of the train as could attend, for a mini-reunion in their studio, and they all wanted to see how the others were faring. Steffi had been keeping in touch with Kris by phone, so she knew that everyone from the climbing club planned to go.

"Do you think J.T. will be there?" Steffi asked.

"If he's healthy enough, he will be," Hudson replied. "He won't pass up a chance for national exposure on a rival network."

"I'm glad Curt's coming," Joe said. "Bob got us out of there so fast I never got the chance to really thank him."

"I'm sorry I didn't get to Patti's funeral," Steffi said. "Kris said it was really well-attended, though. She had a lot of friends."

The limo pulled up in front of the CBS Broadcast Center on West Fifty-seventh, where a cordon had been set up to keep bystanders and paparazzi at bay as the avalanche survivors arrived. Two aides were waiting to escort them to the Morning News studio.

"Ladies, if you'll follow me," one of the aides said, "I'll take you to hair and makeup." The other got behind Joe's wheelchair. "And you're with me, Mister Parker."

"What do you think they'll ask us?" Steffi asked as they sat side by side in front of a long mirror, getting their makeup applied. "I've never been on TV before. I'm really nervous."

"Probably just want us all to recall what we can," Hudson replied. "If a lot of us show up, I bet we each only get a question or two, at most. It'll be over fast."

After hair and makeup, they were taken to the green room to wait. Hudson had done interviews before, so she was a bit surprised to see the television in the room was turned off. Ordinarily, guests were able to tune into the show as it was happening. She was also mystified about why they were the only two people in there, since the show had already started. Where was Joe? Where were all the others?

Fifteen minutes later, a woman wearing a headset came to get them. They walked down a long hallway and through a set of double doors onto the set, where they waited behind big stage curtains to be introduced. They still couldn't see anything: not the audience, or the hosts, or any other guests.

Hudson could tell they were currently in a commercial break, from the audio playing on a monitor somewhere, but that was about all.

The deodorant-ad soundtrack was soon replaced by a woman's voice. "Welcome back to *The CBS Morning News*. I'm Nora O'Donnell. We're continuing with our special program today, a reunion of the survivors from that incredible train accident in the Swiss Alps. You've heard their stories, so now it's time to finally meet the two women being hailed as heroes. Please give it up for Hudson Mead and Steffi Graham!"

"What did she just say?" Steffi asked with a shocked expression.

"That's you, ladies! Go!" The aide gave them a gentle push forward, through the curtain.

The moment they appeared, a roar of applause filled the studio. The audience was on their feet, and so were all three hosts. Pictures of Hudson and Steffi, much larger than life-sized, filled the big projection screen behind the anchors.

Perhaps the biggest surprise, though, was that every single person from the train was cheering them, too, some of them from wheelchairs and with canes and crutches, but not a single one was absent. Joe, of course. The whole climbing club, and all the Europeans, too. Cinzia was with an elderly woman, probably her grandmother. Anna had brought her husband and the twins. Fritz and Hugo were fist-pumping into the air. J.T was even there, clapping along with the rest. It took her a second to recognize the unfamiliar woman and three kids who were standing with them all. The light dawned when she saw what they'd brought with them: a small part of Clay's model Bernina Express display. She and Steffi had called his family once they got back, but she had no idea they'd be here, as well.

Steffi looked happy to see everyone but terrified of all the attention.

Hudson took her hand and squeezed. "And you said you didn't have a story. Want me to lead this pitch?"

That got a laugh. "You lead now. I'll take the lead tonight?"

"Deal."

About the Author

Kim Baldwin, a former network news executive, has made her living as a writer for more than three decades. *Taken by Storm* is her eighth romantic adventure novel published by Bold Strokes Books, and she is also co-author of the Elite Operatives Series, written in collaboration with Xenia Alexiou: *Lethal Affairs, Thief of Always, Missing Lynx, Dying to Live, Demons are Forever*, and *The Gemini Deception*. The final book in the seven book series, *One Last Thing*, is forthcoming January 2015.

In addition to her full-length work, Kim has contributed short stories to six BSB anthologies, and has narrated audiobook versions of her own novel *Breaking the Ice* and the Rose Beecham mystery *Grave Silence*. A 2012 Lambda Literary Award winner and 2011 Lambda finalist, she is also the recipient of a 2011 Rainbow Award For Excellence, a 2010 Independent Publisher Book Award, three Golden Crown Literary Society Awards, eight Lesbian Fiction Readers' Choice Awards, and an Alice B. Readers Appreciation Award for her body of work.

Kim lives in the north woods of Michigan, but takes to the road with her laptop and camera whenever possible. Her website is www.kimbaldwin.com and she can be reached at baldwinkim@gmail.com.

Books Available from Bold Strokes Books

Edge of Awareness by C.A. Popovich. When Maria, a woman in the middle of her third divorce, meets Dana, an out lesbian, awareness of her feelings bring up reservations about the teachings of her church. (978-1-62639-188-8)

Taken by Storm by Kim Baldwin. Lives depend on two women when a train derails high in the remote Alps, but an unforgiving mountain, avalanches, crevasses, and other perils stand between them and safety. (978-1-62639-189-5)

The Common Thread by Jaime Maddox. Dr. Nicole Coussart's life is falling apart, but fortunately, DEA Attorney Rae Rhodes is there to pick up the pieces and help Nic put them back together. (978-1-62639-190-1)

Jolt by Kris Bryant. Mystery writer Bethany Lange wasn't prepared for the twisting emotions that left her breathless the moment she laid eyes on folk singer sensation Ali Hart. (978-1-62639-191-8)

Searching For Forever by Emily Smith. Dr. Natalie Jenner's life has always been about saving others, until young paramedic Charlie Thompson comes along and shows her maybe she's the one who needs saving. (978-1-62639-186-4)

A Queer Sort of Justice: Prison Tales Across Time by Rebecca S. Buck. When liberty is only a memory, and all seems lost, what freedoms and hopes can be found within us? (978-1-62639-195-6E)

Blue Water Dreams by Dena Hankins. Lania Marchiol keeps her wary sailor's gaze trained on the horizon until Oly Rassmussen, a wickedly handsome trans man, sends her trusty compass spinning off course. (978-1-62639-192-5)

Rest Home Runaways by Clifford Henderson. Baby boomer Morgan Ronzio's troubled marriage is the least of her worries when she gets the call that her addled, eighty-six-year-old, half-blind dad has escaped the rest home. (978-1-62639-169-7)

Charm City by Mason Dixon. Raq Overstreet's loyalty to her drug kingpin boss is put to the test when she begins to fall for Bathsheba Morris, the undercover cop assigned to bring him down. (978-1-62639-198-7)

Let the Lover Be by Sheree Greer. Kiana Lewis, a functional alcoholic on the verge of destruction, finally faces the demons of her past while finding love and earning redemption in New Orleans. (978-1-62639-077-5)

Blindsided by Karis Walsh. Blindsided by love, guide dog trainer Lenae McIntyre and media personality Cara Bradley learn to trust what they see with their hearts. (978-1-62639-078-2)

About Face by VK Powell. Forensic artist Macy Sheridan and Detective Leigh Monroe work on a case that has troubled them both for years, but they're hampered by the past and their unlikely yet undeniable attraction. (978-1-62639-079-9)

Blackstone by Shea Godfrey. For Darry and Jessa, their chance at a life of freedom is stolen by the arrival of war and an ancient prophecy that just might destroy their love. (978-1-62639-080-5)

Out of This World by Maggie Morton. Iris decided to cross an ocean to get over her ex. But instead, she ends up traveling much farther, all the way to another world. Once there, only a mysterious, sexy, and magical woman can help her return home. (978-1-62639-083-6)

Kiss The Girl by Melissa Brayden. Sleeping with the enemy has never been so complicated. Brooklyn Campbell and Jessica Lennox face off in love and advertising in fast-paced New York City. (978-1-62639-071-3)

Taking Fire: A First Responders Novel by Radclyffe. Hunted by extremists and under siege by nature's most virulent weapons, Navy medic Max de Milles and Red Cross worker Rachel Winslow join forces to survive and discover something far more lasting. (978-1-62639-072-0)

First Tango in Paris by Shelley Thrasher. When French law student Eva Laroche meets American call girl Brigitte Green in 1970s Paris, they have no idea how their pasts and futures will intersect. (978-1-62639-073-7)

The War Within by Yolanda Wallace. Army nurse Meredith Moser went to Vietnam in 1967 looking to help those in need; she didn't expect to meet the love of her life along the way. (978-1-62639-074-4)

Escapades by MJ Williamz. Two women, afraid to love again, must overcome their fears to find the happiness that awaits them. (978-1-62639-182-6)

Desire at Dawn by Fiona Zedde. For Kylie, love had always come armed with sharp teeth and claws. But with the human, Olivia, she bares her vampire heart for the very first time, sharing passion, lust, and a tenderness she'd never dared dream of before. (978-1-62639-064-5)

Visions by Larkin Rose. Sometimes the mysteries of love reveal themselves when you least expect it. Other times they hide behind a black satin mask. Can Paige unveil her masked stranger this time? (978-1-62639-065-2)

All In by Nell Stark. Internet poker champion Annie Navarro loses everything when the Feds shut down online gambling, and she turns to experienced casino host Vesper Blake for advice—but can Nova convince Vesper to take a gamble on romance? (978-1-62639-066-9)

Vermilion Justice by Sheri Lewis Wohl. What's a vampire to do when Dracula is no longer just a character in a novel? (978-1-62639-067-6)

Switchblade by Carsen Taite. Lines were meant to be crossed. Third in the Luca Bennett Bounty Hunter Series. (978-1-62639-058-4)

Nightingale by Andrea Bramhall. Culture, faith, and duty conspire to tear two young lovers apart, yet fate seems to have different plans for them both. (978-1-62639-059-1)

No Boundaries by Donna K. Ford. A chance meeting and a nightmare from the past threaten more than Andi Massey's solitude as she and Gwen Palmer struggle to understand the complexity of love without boundaries. (978-1-62639-060-7)

Timeless by Rachel Spangler. When Stevie Geller returns to her hometown, will she do things differently the second time around or will she be in such a hurry to leave her past that she misses out on a better future? (978-1-62639-050-8)

Second to None by L.T. Marie. Can a physical therapist and a custom motorcycle designer conquer their pasts and build a future with one another? (978-1-62639-051-5)

Seneca Falls by Jesse Thoma. Together, two women discover love truly can conquer all evil. (978-1-62639-052-2)

A Kingdom Lost by Barbara Ann Wright. Without knowing each other's fates, Princess Katya and her consort Starbride seek to reclaim their kingdom from the magic-wielding madman who seized the throne and is murdering their people. (978-1-62639-053-9)

Season of the Wolf by Robin Summers. Two women running from their pasts are thrust together by an unimaginable evil. Can they overcome the horrors that haunt them in time to save each other? (978-1-62639-043-0)

The Heat of Angels by Lisa Girolami. Fires burn in more than one place in Los Angeles. (978-1-62639-042-3)

Desperate Measures by P. J. Trebelhorn. Homicide detective Kay Griffith and contractor Brenda Jansen meet amidst turmoil neither of them is aware of until murder suspect Tommy Rayne makes his move to exact revenge on Kay. (978-1-62639-044-7)

The Magic Hunt by L.L. Raand. With her Pack being hunted by human extremists and beset by enemies masquerading as friends, can Sylvan protect them and her mate, or will she succumb to the feral rage that threatens to turn her rogue, destroying them all? A Midnight Hunters novel. (978-1-62639-045-4)

Wingspan by Karis Walsh. Wildlife biologist Bailey Chase is content to live at the wild bird sanctuary she has created on Washington's Olympic Peninsula until she is lured beyond the safety of isolation by architect Kendall Pearson. (978-1-60282-983-1)

Windigo Thrall by Cate Culpepper. Six women trapped in a mountain cabin by a blizzard, stalked by an ancient cannibal demon bent on stealing their sanity—and their lives. (978-1-60282-950-3)

The Blush Factor by Gun Brooke. Ice-cold business tycoon Eleanor Ashcroft only cares about the three Ps—Power, Profit, and Prosperity—until young Addison Garr makes her doubt both that and the state of her frostbitten heart. (978-1-60282-985-5)

Slash and Burn by Valerie Bronwen. The murder of a roundly despised author at an LGBT writers' conference in New Orleans turns Winter Lovelace's relaxing weekend hobnobbing with her peers into a nightmare of suspense—especially when her ex turns up. (978-1-60282-986-2)

The Quickening: A Sisters of Spirits Novel by Yvonne Heidt. Ghosts, visions, and demons are all in a day's work for Tiffany. But when Kat asks for help on a serial killer case, life takes on another dimension altogether. (978-1-60282-975-6)

Smoke and Fire by Julie Cannon. Oil and water, passion and desire, a combustible combination. Can two women fight the fire that draws them together and threatens to keep them apart? (978-1-60282-977-0)